The Best Friend

By

Leanne Davis

Sister Series, Book Three

Contact Information: dvsleanne@aol.com
Publishing History First Edition, 2015 Print
Print ISBN: 978-1-941522-11-0
Sister Series, Book Three
Edited by Teri at The Editing Fairy
(teri@editingfairy.com)
Cover Design by Steven Novak
(novakillustration@gmail.com)
10 9 8 7 6 5 4 3 2 1

Dedication

To the one person in the world who is forever my best
friend…
My sister, Marianne Miller.

Acknowledgement:
To Teri for your amazing work editing my novels.
I could not imagine publishing without your expertise
and polish.
Thank you so much!

Chapter One

GRETCHEN HENDRICKS BROWSED THE produce aisle of the grocery store, seeking some organic fruit that didn't look totally unappetizing or rotten. She sorted through the pears, trying to find ones that were not too bruised or misshapen. Placing a few in her basket, she prepared to go down the next aisle to search out some hair gel. Turning the corner, she stopped dead in her tracks.

Tony? Tony Lindstrom? Her mouth dropped open in shock. Surprise. No, in complete and utter horror. When did he get back? And when did *that* happen? She swallowed the instant lump that lodged in her throat. Will, her ex-husband and Tony's best friend, didn't tell her anything about it. How could he not? The tears pricking her eyes were immediate and real. She quickly backed up and hid behind the soda pop display, scolding herself for her cowardice. *She could not hide from him*, but she also could not, in good conscience, turn and ignore him after seeing him. That would be an inconsiderate, mean, and heartless thing to do. That would make her the worst person ever. But… what the hell could she say to him? *Hey, Tony. How are you? How did you lose your arm?* Of course, she already knew how Tony lost his arm: from fighting in the war.

She didn't know the particulars yet, but obviously, he got hurt and lost his left arm.

Oh, God! Not Tony. It wasn't fair. It was horrible. He was a good, decent man. Or at least, he had been. She hadn't seen much of him in more than five years; but had known him since they were in middle school together. He often stayed at her house after he and Will went out drinking, or just to hang out. She was married to his best friend and he was the best man at their wedding. He came over and got drunk with her after her divorce from Will was finalized, when he was at home briefly, visiting his parents on leave.

She knew soldiers went to war, and some soldiers didn't return. Or they returned irrevocably changed. But Tony? No. It should not, and could not, have happened to Tony. But... it did.

She straightened her shoulders and lifted her chin up. If he could fight for the country and sacrifice his arm, she could muster up the courage to face him. She wasn't an insensitive person. She should have been able to face an old friend, no matter what happened to him.

But the churning of her stomach soon had bile climbing up her throat. Her hands trembled. Could she do this? Could she face him? And finally, how could she not?

She started down the aisle, but hesitated a few feet back from him. He stood behind his cart, staring at spaghetti sauce brands. His right hand, the one that was uninjured, came up as he chose a jar and set it into his cart. She inhaled a sharp breath when she saw his shirtsleeve pinned against his chest.

"Tony?"

He whipped around. She probably should have been louder and not crept up from behind him. It had to be a common thing for any soldier not to appreciate someone sneaking up from behind. She remembered how jumpy Will often was after he returned from special missions. She hated being married to a soldier. He was gone all the time, out being heroic. And she was stuck at home, complaining and hating his deployment; and acting the complete opposite of heroic.

She steeled her nerves and clenched her teeth to keep a polite smile of greeting and her eyes directly fastened on his. She refused to look down or avert her eyes. She would not act as if she and Tony didn't share twenty years of history between them. Losing his arm didn't change that.

He was almost unrecognizable. His hair was long and pulled back into a rubber band. He used to be clean-cut, sometimes even shaving his head for cleanliness. He had a full beard now that changed his looks completely. It made him look older, harsher, and more sinister. His hair and beard were light brown and his brown eyes had a small scar over his right eyebrow. She remembered how he and Will were playing in the woods near their houses when he fell and cut himself on a wayward piece of barbed wire left over from an old fence. She knew a lot of personal things about Tony. Just not how he lost his arm.

He looked much older now. Harder. More uncompromising. Wearing a flannel shirt over a t-shirt and gray sweats, she recalled how meticulously dapper and well put together he always was in the past, so unlike now. His expression didn't change although his eyes widened barely a millimeter in reaction to seeing her. Did he not recognize her? She hadn't changed all that much. She used to have long hair and now it was short.

"Hi," she said directly to him. *Brilliant.* She was handling this with total class and dignity.

He didn't answer her. Did something else happen to him? Were his mental faculties still intact? Did he suffer from a traumatic brain injury or something?

Finally, he nodded and said, "Hello Gretchen." His tone was deep and low. She recalled that about him. His voice reminded her of an announcer on nighttime radio. Kind of hypnotic, almost sexy.

Her relief was swift. Okay, he could still speak and he remembered her name.

"Uh, hi. It's been a long time. I didn't know you were back home."

His piercing, brown eyes drilled into her. "Yeah."

Oh God, her eyes kept wanting to dart down. *To look.* It was excruciating to resist. It was like having a fully-grown elephant sitting between them. The absence of his arm was so obvious, but how could she mention it politely? She had no clue. She bit her lip and smiled. "Will didn't mention you were… back."

He raised one eyebrow. Gretchen was never able to do that, raise one eyebrow, but not the other. She felt like she was losing her mind, grasping at straws, or anything else to *not* stare, to *not* let her gaze fall down to his amputated arm. She could not do that without being a complete and utter heel, as well as every other awful cliché out there. It was just really hard for her not to steal a glimpse. But that was as gauche as asking someone at a funeral if he or she was feeling better.

"Will doesn't know. I haven't spoken to him in several years."

"What? Since when? Why? Why haven't you stayed in touch? You two were the best of friends. Brothers in arms, soldiers…" Gretchen stopped mid-sentence, wishing she hadn't mentioned "arms."

He shrugged, turning his body so his right arm was toward her. "Things change."

What could have changed? How could Will ever turn his back on Tony? It was *Tony,* for God's sake. Will and he were best friends since... forever. Long before Gretchen entered the picture, as well as after she exited.

"Holy crap, is that Gretchen Moore?"

Gretchen turned, surprised. There, walking towards her, was Donny Lindstrom, Tony's younger brother. She smiled and allowed Donny to lean down and kiss her cheek while hugging her. Wasn't that how Tony should've greeted her? He used to. He used to smile and crack jokes with her, teasing her mercilessly. He used to be fun and charming. But that was all before he lost his arm. "I can't believe it's you. It's been years. Way too long, in fact."

Donny was three years younger than Tony and she. He was always the smiling prankster in high school, evoking laughs from all, but never unkind or malicious. He was probably the nicest person Gretchen ever knew.

Still smiling, she stepped back from Donny's enthusiastic embrace. "It's Hendricks now."

"Ahh, shit. That's right. You went and married the bastard. He was the crazy SOB who let you go, huh? Why'd you keep his name?"

Tony shifted uncomfortably, and Gretchen saw him in her peripheral vision. She felt odd discussing Will in front of him, which was ironic. Tony was the one with whom she used to regularly discuss Will. He gave a heart-wrenching speech at their wedding reception. He was the one they first called to announce their engagement. And the first to take them out for a beer and toast their upcoming nuptials.

Now, he scowled at merely seeing Gretchen's warm, affectionate greeting toward his fun, harmless, little brother?

"I kept his name because it's legally my name now. He and I have long since buried the hatchet."

Donny nodded. "That's because you're the nicest person alive, and the only one I know who would want to remain friends with an ex."

Maintaining a friendship with her ex was the least of it. She also helped treat Will's second wife, Jessie, for sexual abuse, and his sister-in-law, Lindsey, for domestic abuse. Lindsey even lived with Gretchen briefly while fleeing her husband. So it was in Gretchen's nature to be nice. But no, that was so not true. Look how hard she found it to just look Tony in the eye and say: *What happened? Are you okay? I'm so sorry that you lost your arm.*

Instead, she said nothing, but chatted as if they'd just bumped into each other at the grocery store after a minimally short separation, and nothing for him had changed.

Donny grinned as his eyes ran the length of her. "You look as good as always. What the hell are you up to?"

She shook her head, smiling at him. "You're still incorrigible. I'm a child psychologist. I work mostly with kids who have learning or behavioral disorders."

Donny sighed. "That sounds… rather impressive. Like years of schooling and such shit. What are you now? A doctor or something?"

"Well, yes, I am."

He rolled his eyes. "Sure, a doctor and you look like this. Sure. Uh-huh. Never one to waste your time, were you?"

She rolled her eyes right back at him, grinning at his teasing tone. "What are you up to?"

"Believe it or not, I'm an IT guy now." That he could sit still long enough to type on a computer actually surprised her.

"Donny, we need to get going."

They both turned towards Tony, who stood there glaring at them. Donny jumped as if Tony's reminder just electrocuted him. "Oh, right. Sure. We've got to get you to the doctor."

Not the best reply. Tony's lips curled up and his eyes narrowed in disgust at his little brother. "Shut the fuck up, Donny."

Donny didn't notice or didn't care. Heat filled Gretchen's face as just witnessing Tony's impatience and anger became too much for her. Quickly, she said, "I'm sorry I kept you. It was nice to see you, Tony, Donny."

Donny rolled his eyes and waved a hand towards Tony. "Ignore his sour-ass. He blames his lack of manners, couth, and courtesy... among other things, on losing his left arm."

The ensuing silence felt stifling. What could she add to that without making the moment even worse? Leave it to Donny to come right out and say it. She cleared her throat and fiddled with her basket handle, adamantly refusing to lift her gaze from the red, plastic handle she gripped way too tightly.

Tony spun on his heel and walked off, leaving the cart half filled with food. Donny watched him go and sighed.

"He isn't doing too well."

"What happened?"

"His team got hit. A suicide bomber took out a small section of his base in Afghanistan, where he was stationed. He was knocked over and had shrapnel embedded into his left arm. He lost three good friends

7

that day too. Of course, he came home, but he hasn't been right since. As you can probably imagine."

"Maybe you should be a little kinder about it and give him more time."

Donny shrugged. "Shit, we tried that. We've tried everything. We pussyfooted around him at first. We were all kindness and sympathy. We wept and told him how glad we were he was still alive. We did it all, but nothing penetrates the shield he's got up now. He's a dick. All the time. It never stops. It never wavers. It would be easier if he were shell-shocked or emotionally impaired. Hell, it would be nice to know if he had any emotions left inside him. It's like his heart was ripped out along with his arm."

She gasped. Donny was too much. Too forward. "It's got to be excruciating. He lost a limb. The pain. The shock. The helplessness for anyone would be too much deal with. Let alone, a soldier like Tony. He and Will lived primarily to be soldiers. They lived for their next mission. And for each other, far more than they felt obligated to anything or anyone at home. He's got to have some PTSD."

Donny nodded. "Sure, sure. We're not new to this, Gretchen. We, my parents and I, have been through all of this with him. It's been two years now. And nothing has improved. He's been to the VA for support, as well as counseling. He's also been in therapy, both mental and physical. None of it makes any difference to him. He's like a complete stranger. And a shitload of too much to live with."

"I'm sorry. For him and for you. It must be frustrating to witness on a daily basis."

He shrugged. "He's pretty much lived with my folks since it happened. He was discharged, of course, since lack of one's arm pretty much ends your career as a soldier. He hasn't worked since. He fuckin' sits around, doin' nothing and bein' nothing. It's hard to watch, but even harder to tolerate his shitty attitude. We all try. Honestly, we do. I come by and hang with him almost daily and drive him to his doctors and various therapies. As do my parents. But we're all about as appreciated as dogshit under his shoes for how he treats us or acknowledges our efforts. It was okay at first. Even understandable. He was thrown a cruel, awful curve ball. No doubt. And we all saluted him for that. But... there's only so much you can say to people, and yourself, before it becomes *too much*. And people are only understanding up to a point."

She shook her head as tears filled her eyes and clogged her throat. "What about Will? Two years ago? How could Will not tell me anything about it?"

"Shit, he hasn't talked to Will in even longer than that. He won't talk to anyone. He pretty much cut all ties with friends. And if anyone from his unit or soldiering days even attempts to contact him, he shuts it down instantly."

"I'm sorry, Donny."

"Yeah. Hey, why don't you come over for dinner?"

Dinner? Just Donny and her? It was too weird. She couldn't even imagine how awkward a dating situation could be for the boy who used to take pleasure in how often he could burp her name, or moon her. So... no. She couldn't imagine dating Donny.

His eyes widened and he threw back his head in a laugh. He must have read the surprise and displeasure on her face. "No. Not a date! Just come over to my parents' house. They'd love to see you. And honestly, I wonder if perhaps you couldn't at least try to get Tony to talk. He always had the hots for you. Maybe that would cut through something that's still alive in him.

Maybe lose some of the apathy. Make him a little less of an asshole."

A blush crept into her cheeks. Tony had the hots for her? *When? As if.* No. No, there was no way Donny could be correct about that statement. They never had such a relationship. There was never even one moment of awkwardness between Tony and her. So no, there was never a time he *liked* her. Not like that, at least. Not like having a crush. It was always Will and she. She started mooning over Will Hendricks in the seventh grade. And Tony knew that. He could never have felt anything romantic towards her. She was always Will's. And Tony was the kind of guy who lived by staunch rules, like never coveting your best friend's girl.

"You're mistaken on that front."

Donny grinned. "What? About Tony having a crush on you? No. I'm not. He liked you, always. From seventh grade on. But you were always hung up on Will, so he had to settle for just being your friend."

"He told you that?"

"Yeah, right. No. It's just a fact. I knew it. My parents knew it. Will knew it."

"Will did not."

"Will was not dumb or blind. He sure as shit knew; he just ignored it so he could still be Tony's best friend. Just as Tony ignored it so he could still be Will's. And yours."

Her brain felt like it would explode in her head. In five minutes, Donny managed to rewrite her entire teens and early twenties. Those were not her truths and experiences. There was just no way.

"Well, he sure doesn't want to see me now."

"He doesn't want to see anyone. Don't take it personally. In fact, try to be different than everyone else. Don't let him pull that shit with you. It's all shit, designed to protect his injured, fragile ego because he lost his arm. The thing is: he lost his arm, not his life, but he's living as if he did, and seems prepared to keep living the rest of his life that way."

She pressed her lips together, her heart twisting at the tragic circumstances of Tony and his former personality. He used to grin all the time. He liked to drink beer and throw darts. He liked to dance. He liked to play golf. He liked to shoot his guns at the shooting range. He liked to do a million things.

"I'll come. If you can convince him to let me, and clear it beforehand with your mom. Here's my number. Call me if you really think I could help."

Donny turned towards his cart with a shrug. "Well, you sure as shit can't hurt. Nothing could get worse for him."

****

Stupid fucking brother. What was he doing? Why was he taking so long? Just finish eye-fucking Gretchen and come already. He wanted to leave. He was tired of being there. He was tired of being stared at. He was tired of watching his brother's cheerful, happy flirting. He would, no doubt, get her damn number. Well, sure. *Fine. Great.* She was probably a great lay. Good for Donny. He just wanted to go… *and now.*

Donny finally rounded the corner of the aisle, pushing the cart and coming to a stop where Tony stood waiting by a cash register.

"Took you long enough. What did you do? Get her number?" Tony snarled. He turned his face so his brother couldn't see the disgust. As if he cared. Why should he care whom Gretchen went out with? Or fucked? Or screwed? He'd already tolerated her doing his best friend for years. He even discussed it with Will. And often heard them, for Christ's sake, any number of times he stayed overnight in their then, very small and thin-walled, apartment.

Will Hendricks. The name tasted like ashes in his mouth. Will and he had been best friends their entire lives. Even after Gretchen Moore entered their sphere. They were young, hormone-filled boys and both of them liked her. They got into a fistfight over her in eighth grade. But… Gretchen simply chose Will, and they started dating their freshman year, and never broke up. That was that. Tony drove them to dances and double dates with women he never could remember the names of. He toasted their engagement and spoke at their wedding.

When Will joined the Army, so did Tony. He followed Will because he and Will were inseparable and both wanted to serve their country. It seemed the only thing to do beyond high school and Will always talked about it. That was all there was for Will: being a soldier. And Tony had no other prospects, so why not become a soldier? His grades sucked; there was no college in store for him. He thought about entering a trade school, and becoming a plumber like his old man, but it never resonated with him. Going to war to kill the enemy seemed a lot more interesting to him at the age of nineteen.

His mother wept when he came home and told her he joined up. It went on for days, and every time he returned after a furlough. She worried about him year after year. She never got used to it. She was proud, but nonetheless terrified for him.

He didn't understand her. Nothing could happen to him. No way. Surprisingly, especially to him, he became a damn fine soldier. Not a Will Hendricks perhaps, but a solid, trustworthy, hardworking soldier. Will went on to join Special Forces; and Tony served proudly as an infantry soldier with the 82nd Airborne. He became a sergeant and was proud of it. He wasn't like Will, who was a heroic, accomplished soldier with plenty of ambition to climb as far up the Army command chain as he could. Tony had no such designs or desires; he just wanted to be a good soldier.

He loved Will. As if he were his own brother.

But then... Will quit. He fucking quit the Army. The day Will announced it, Tony turned and walked away without another word. *How could Will just quit?* He was the reason they chose to do it. He was the one who loved it. He was destined to become a great, high-ranking leader in the Army. He was that good at it. But he just up and quit.

After that, he moved to butt fuck nowhere, and now had a wife and kid. He worked a nine-to-five job as a civilian. Will became a hard-working family man that Tony never imagined he'd ever be. Will never even attempted to be that way for Gretchen, but only for his second wife.

Tony had no opinion of her. Jessie Bains was merely the name of the woman his best friend married before he checked out of life, and the Army. He never really heard or understood the entire story. There had to be more to it than Will told him. Maybe he just didn't want to know. What mattered was that she made Will quit the service, abandoning the only life and calling he ever knew. And now, it was the lifestyle and career that Tony also wanted. But Will left it behind, and Tony ceased any further correspondence with Will since that day.

He sure as fuck didn't try to explain to Will how it felt to have your arm blown off while tossing a football back and forth with half your platoon. One moment, he was laughing, watching the ball twirling towards him, his arms outstretched to catch it, the sun frying his eyeballs, and the next… everything was black.

He woke up in a hospital bed with his left arm gone.

What does one say after discovering that? Nothing.

He sometimes wished it had happened in a nobler way. Maybe if he'd had a gun in his hand, instead of a football, or he was fighting at the time, it might've felt different. Maybe even a little better.

He scoffed, *yeah, right*. As if the circumstances could make the sensation of your flesh melting off your bones feel any better.

Still, returning home, and trying to live amongst civilians again wasn't going very well. People ran around, worried about their Halloween costumes, what to buy for dinner, whether to go organic or not, or what color to paint their overpriced houses. It was all so stupid to him. He couldn't get over how mundane they seemed. His own parents and his brother too were worried about mortgages on houses they didn't need. They worried about traffic, or if it might rain tomorrow. *What shit!* It was nothing real and nothing that mattered. Nothing about his existence here mattered.

Donny shoved the cart into the line for the cashier. He rarely scowled, glared, or even ceased smiling, except with Tony. "I invited her to dinner. With Mom. I thought Mom would like to see her. Don't worry your sorry ass, since you most likely already scared her away."

He flinched. *Gretchen*. He really never wanted to see her again. Not with his empty sleeve hole, and his lopsided shirt. *Fuck no.*

Still… "What did she say?"

Donny started assembling groceries onto the conveyor belt, only stopping to glower at Tony. "She said yes. Yes, if it was okay with your sensitive, little-girl ass. So is it, Tony? Is it okay? Do you think you could let an old friend come over without letting the usual crass bullshit spew freely from your mouth?"

Tony spun on his heel and stormed out of the grocery store. Let Donny bag his own stupid groceries. That was beside the point; most of the groceries were for him; and his mother was paying the bill.

Chapter Two

"YOU WON'T BELIEVE WHAT happened to me."

Gretchen sighed deeply, stepping back as her younger sister burst through her front door as she was opening it. Trailing behind her was Tracy, her other sister.

"Hi Tracy. And hello to you too, Vickie," Gretchen muttered to Vickie's back. She was already pacing Gretchen's living room in agitation as her blond curls, similar to Gretchen's own, bounced around her shoulders. Vickie stopped and waved her hand in the air. "Don't be so prudish. We're sisters. We don't have to be polite to each other. Anyway, do you want to know what happened or not?"

She rolled her eyes and shut the front door. "I don't know? Do I want to know, Tracy?

Vickie glared while Gretchen and Tracy exchanged a weary glance. Tracy stifled a smile.

Something was usually happening to their youngest sister. "Well, you'll tell me either way. So what is it?"

Vickie was back to pacing. "They cut up my credit card! Right there. In the store. In front of *everyone*."

Gretchen winced. Not at the news her careless sister, once again, wasn't paying her bills, but that she should feel sorry for her. "Where?"

Tracy rolled her eyes. "It wasn't everyone. It was one other person. She was at The Clothes Closet, downtown."

"It was more than one person. How dare they?"

"Have you paid your bill?"

Vickie stopped pacing and glared at Gretchen. "It's a credit card. What good is it if you can't use it for credit? You're supposed to get some time to pay."

Gretchen shut her eyes. Lord, the economics of paying for one's purchases totally escaped Vickie, in addition to her inability to keep any job, ever. Vickie never saw it as her fault, however.

"We've talked about this. Why were you even at The Clothes Closet? That place is way beyond your budget."

Gretchen, Tracy, and their parents spent years taking turns and trying to get Vickie's lethal spending habits under control, while encouraging her to keep a job. She got them easily enough, she could just never hold onto them. She never worried about them or how she'd pay her bills. Somehow, some way, Vickie usually landed on her feet.

Vickie stiffened and cast a dirty look at Gretchen. "*You* shop there."

Tracy saved Gretchen from having to point out the obvious. "Gretchen works full time at a high paying profession. You don't even have a job."

Vickie nearly screeched. "Well, how am I supposed to get a decent job without decent clothes? It's an investment in me, and how I project myself."

Gretchen coughed to cover her laugh. As if Vickie ever got an interview at any kind of place that would care how she "projected" herself.

"Tell her the rest of it."

Vickie frowned at Tracy. "Why do you sound so sarcastic? Well, I just used another credit card."

"You still bought the stuff? Even after one credit card was declined?"

Vickie rolled her eyes. "Of course. I told you, it's an investment in me. I deserve it after all I've suffered from Parker."

Gretchen wearily turned and started for her kitchen. There was no arguing or reasoning with Vickie. Her twenty-eight-year-old sister never learned, never matured, and never got a clue. She had a four-page resume of past employment listings. She managed to work in every conceivable retail job, from beauty consultant to fast food. There was nothing Vickie hadn't done. She had also been married three times, so far, with three divorces under her belt. The first was at age twenty, and lasted less than a year. The second was at age twenty-four, and lasted a year-and-a-half. Her most recent nuptials lasted less than nine months. For each wedding, she had all the trimmings, and loudly claimed that "this was it," so didn't their love deserve the grandest of celebrations? After all, it was the last wedding she'd ever have. Each of her poor, unsuspecting grooms was never married before, so for all of them, it was their first wedding. That was how Vickie justified it; didn't her grooms deserve to experience a first big wedding? Gretchen's parents quit footing the bill after the second one. The last groom, Parker, paid for it. Parker's family was overjoyed at the news Vickie was joining their family and marrying their son. She was a charming, delightful, and beautiful girl. Everyone liked Vickie. Most however, didn't realize, until it was far too late, that she invariably bled them dry of their money, their love and their patience.

The worst part was: she didn't even know she did it. She didn't *mean* to be so materialistic, flighty, manipulative, careless, or lazy. She just was.

Gretchen didn't feel like arguing the same old battle again. Vickie left Parker, claiming he was too boring and set in his ways. She needed more color and excitement. He was currently paying alimony for her boredom. "You guys want some coffee?"

"Sure." Tracy set her ginormous handbag down on the couch and wandered closer to the breakfast bar. Tracy was thirty years old with two kids, ages nine and eight, and a loving husband of ten years. She could not have been any more different from Vickie than if they were born to different mothers. Then again, neither could Gretchen.

Vickie was a preemie baby and almost died due to lung complications. She stayed in the hospital for five weeks. From the time she came home, their parents never once treated her like the other two older girls. Vickie was fragile, vulnerable, and therefore, special. Unfortunately, that label never changed, not in her twenty-eight years.

Gretchen loved Vickie. Both sisters also babied and protected her. Not until she was divorcing her third husband did they begin to really see the narcissistic, needy, forever unhappy, always seeking what she didn't have, monster they all helped to create. But hating her was like hating a young child. No matter how mad they got, or how much she screwed up, and how fed up they got with her theatrics, it never stopped them from trying to help her. They couldn't turn their backs on their sweet, kind-hearted, almost stupidly naïve, and selfish, little sister.

Vickie rummaged around her fridge. "Got any diet pop?"

Gretchen poured the coffee. "There's some in the back."

"So, what's new with you?" Tracy asked, sipping the coffee and watching Gretchen over the rim of her cup.

Gretchen walked over to the bank of windows that flooded her condo with natural, bright sunlight. The big squares looked like warm puddles over the light carpet. Looking through the windows, she stared down at the grass, trees, and specks of people now enjoying the green city park below her.

"I had an interesting day at the market, too."

Tracy swiveled on her stool. "Oh, yeah? What happened?"

"I ran into Tony Lindstrom."

"Oh my, that's a name from the past. Will's best friend? How is he?"

Gretchen nodded. "Yes, actually, he was both Will's and my best friend," she said blowing out a deep, weary breath before she continued. "The thing is, he… he lost his left arm. And I was so shocked by it, I froze up and acted like an immature jerk. I pretended it didn't happen. I never even asked him about it."

Tracy's jaw dropped open in disbelief. Vickie stopped pouring her can of pop into a cup and blinked in stunned shock, asking, "Gone? What do you mean gone?"

"Like he lost it in the war. Like it was amputated. What else could I mean?"

Vickie stuck her tongue out. "You don't have to get so bitchy. I just wasn't sure you meant that. Wow. Holy shit."

"That's so tragic," Tracy said, much more appropriately.

Gretchen stared down at her hands. "He isn't well. I mean, he is nothing like the Tony you remember."

Vickie wandered out and sat on the loveseat, pulling her legs up underneath her. "He was so hot and so sweet. Remember? He always tagged along with you and Will. He was always the first to help you with anything. That's so awful."

He was? Gretchen frowned and tried to envision her past. She couldn't get a mental picture of Tony doing such things for her. Did he? Had she really never noticed before? He had always been there for her... for years and years. He and Will came over together to hang out with her; to do anything from going to dinner, to the movies, to simply hanging out and doing nothing. The three of them used to spend all their time together. Will was never one to ditch his friends just because he had a girlfriend. Gretchen and he used to fight about that, even after they were married. She needed more one-on-one time with him, although he didn't with her.

"Not well? How?"

Gretchen shook her head and sat down across from her sisters. "His whole attitude, I guess. I mean, he's fine mentally. He just seemed... so angry. The rage fairly dripped off him. His disdain in talking to me was as obvious as his arm being gone. He made it pretty clear he did not want to see me."

"That's weird. Vickie's right. He was always so solicitous of you."

He was? Where was this all coming from? And if Vickie even noticed it, how did she fail to see it?

"His brother, Donny, was there too. He was exactly as you remember."

Vickie suddenly sat up. "Donny Lindstrom? I haven't seen him in years. Oh, he was to-die-for-hot. Remember?"

21

Gretchen rolled her eyes. Vickie thought every man who breathed was to-die-for-hot. "Donny? Yeah, he's cute still. Funny. Nice too. He invited me to dinner."

Vickie frowned. "You? What? No! You can't date Donny Lindstrom."

Gretchen glanced at her sister. "Well, I'm not. But if I were, why would you object so?"

"Because you're like old and responsible, and shit. Donny is fun and the life of the party material. He can't be interested in your type, no offense."

"Oh, no offense taken. Besides, he doesn't appear that way anymore. Donny is all grown up. He was nice, normal, and sounded much more responsible."

"Vickie! You can't talk like that to Gretchen," Tracy admonished her sister.

Vickie looked around, her eyes big. "What? I didn't mean anything negative by it. Just that Donny was *the* guy to date. I never even stood a chance with him. And yet, you do?"

Gretchen didn't know whether to throttle her little sister or laugh at how oblivious she was when insulting someone. "No, don't worry, he doesn't want to date me. It was an invitation to come over to his mother's house, where Tony apparently now lives. I don't think Tony sees too many people. Donny wanted me to try and... well, I don't know what he wanted me to do, actually."

"Are you going to?"

Gretchen cradled her coffee cup, pulling a foot under her. "I don't know. It was so awkward for the five minutes we talked. He is really angry. And so different. How would an entire dinner go? Yet, he was such a dear friend of mine for so many years. I had no idea this even happened to him. Now that I know, how can I not try and reconnect to him?"

"Well, you *are* a therapist."

"A child therapist. Big difference."

Tracy shrugged. "Same principles. You're a sensitive, caring person. You should do this, Gretchen."

"That's the other thing. What is wrong with Will? How could he not tell me about it? And get this: Will and Tony aren't even talking anymore. I never dreamed Will could be so cruel."

Vickie snorted and nearly spit out Will's name. "*Will Hendricks.* Why are you so delusional about him? He recruited you to save his second wife. That's not only weird, but so selfish. To ask you to deal with his new wife. You think I'm narcissistic, but I would never do that to you."

One reason Gretchen found it easy to forgive Vickie's considerable carelessness sometimes was because of her unending loyalty. She hated Will Hendricks for how he treated Gretchen, although Gretchen had long forgiven him for breaking her heart. Vickie, however, did not.

"Vickie, it was so much deeper than that. Which is beside the point. Why did Will turn his back on Tony? First off, I need to talk to him, I guess."

Tracy nodded. "I think you should pursue this. He was a good friend for a long time. He and Will practically lived with us when we were all young. So if you can help him, you definitely should."

Vickie's expression suddenly brightened. "Hey, can I come? To the dinner? Ask if I can come along. They all know me. And I'd love to see Donny. Is he married?"

Gretchen could not restrain her eye roll. Everything comes right back to Vickie. "I have no idea. He wasn't wearing any ring. Vick, you're not going to try and date Donny Lindstrom? I'm simply trying to rekindle an old friendship with someone who became the victim of a horrific injury."

Vickie waved her hand around. "Oh, you should do that, Gretchen. You should try to save Tony. You should be his friend. Meanwhile, I'm going to enjoy some nice eye candy in Donny Lindstrom. Please? I'll be a great icebreaker."

Gretchen's lips tugged into a reluctant smile. Yeah, Vickie could be counted on as a great icebreaker.

"I'll think about it and let you know."

Vickie got up to use the bathroom and Tracy quickly sat next to Gretchen. "Anything new on Olivia?"

"Nothing new. Helen's getting very weak. She had to quit work, finally."

Tracy grabbed her hand. "What you're going to do… it's wonderful; you know that, right? You're the perfect person to do that."

Gretchen stared at their linked hands and the doubts weighed heavily on her chest. Only Tracy, Lindsey, her parents, and Helen knew of the impending adoption. Helen Carver, Olivia's paternal grandmother, suffered from stage four breast cancer. She had recently asked Gretchen to become Olivia's adoptive guardian when she died. Gretchen tried to argue, and reassured Helen she would beat the cancer, but quickly stopped when Helen begged her to simply "get real." She needed to know that Olivia would be okay, and the only way that could occur was if Gretchen promised to take her permanently. Gretchen was stunned. But how could she refuse the bald, skinny, pasty and feeble Helen, now begging for a little peace in the knowledge that her granddaughter, whom she raised since infancy, would not end up in foster care?

Gretchen consulted first with her parents and then with Tracy for their advice. All of them knew Olivia, and all unconditionally encouraged her to do it.

Olivia first came on Gretchen's radar when she was only a toddler. Helen brought her to Gretchen because her father had died recently, and she thought the counseling might help Olivia accept it more easily. And it did; while in the process, she and Helen became friendly. After Olivia was coping much better, they stayed in contact simply because they grew closer and Olivia soon became more of a friend than just a former patient. When Helen first noticed the lump in her breast two years previous, no one ever considered it might kill her. Gretchen remained there for Helen, first by babysitting Olivia, and later began accompanying Helen to her appointments while Tracy looked after Olivia.

But Gretchen *never* considered becoming Olivia's adoptive mother. At first, the thought paralyzed her. But now, the appeal began to outweigh the fear, as well as the life changes and burdens. She'd had the knowledge for about two months, but it wasn't long enough for her to go from thinking of herself as a single adult to accepting the care of a grief-stricken, young girl, which would, in only a matter of months, be solely in her hands.

However, due to the sensitivity of the issue, Helen and Gretchen had yet to include Vickie in on the plan. They didn't trust her not to say something to Olivia. She might have known her grandmother was sick, and could be dying, but she couldn't quite conceive all the gruesome details of it.

They stopped talking when Vickie stepped back into the living room, describing her latest attempt to get a job. Finishing their drinks, they soon left and Gretchen wandered out onto her patio to gaze out over the park as the sun dropped from sight. Calliston is a small town in California that spreads out well into the horizon, and is bordered by distant mountains and somewhat obscured by the countless treetops. It is a quiet, small town on the edge of the Oregon/California border. Gretchen was born and raised there. As were Tony and Will. Those two were best friends since kindergarten. And now… they weren't. How could that happen? Why did it happen?

She turned and headed back inside. The August sun lingered forever at this time of year. It was Sunday night and she had to work tomorrow. Did she want to tackle that subject now? Yeah, she did. Will had no right to treat Tony like that.

****

"How could you not tell me?"

When Will answered the phone, Gretchen spoke with no preamble.

"Gretchen?"

"Yes, it's Gretchen," she said rudely. "Why didn't you tell me about Tony?"

She could hear Will shuffling around and he paused when she said "Tony."

"Tony? What are you talking about? Jesus, I haven't talked to him in years."

"I know that now. But why? Why haven't you talked to him? And how could you not, at least, tell me he lost his arm? You owed me that much, Will Hendricks."

"He what? What did you just say?" Will's tone rose sharply.

She instantly regretted blurting the news out to Will and leaned her head into her hands. Finally, she whispered with audible regret, "You didn't know?"

"No. Obviously. What the fuck, Gretchen? What? What happened?" Will's tone became almost panicked.

She let out a long breath. It made her feel slightly better to know that Will wasn't so heartless that he didn't care about what happened to Tony or just forgot to tell her. There was more shuffling while Will obviously had his hand over the receiver, speaking in murmurs, and no doubt, updating his wife, Jessie. Gretchen waited until he came back. She had no problem with Jessie. Jessie showed up long after she and Will had already split and divorced. Who she did have a problem with was Will Hendricks. But no one really knew that. Not anymore, that is.

Will Hendricks stole her heart when she was only a girl. Thirteen years old, to be exact. She loved him from age thirteen until she was nearly thirty years old. They married when they were both twenty-three; and divorced when they were twenty-six. However, she still loved him for years after. Only recently had she totally, finally, and forever, gotten over him. She adored and cherished him, which ultimately resulted in her being crushed by him. All the while, Will never *really* knew what he'd done to her. Just as no one else really knew how very long she loved him. Seventeen years was quite a long time to love one person.

He first asked her out in their freshman year of high school, in the hallway of the science building. Will soon became her boyfriend throughout her high school years. They shared friends, dates, dances, footballs games, and summers. He owned her entire youth, and there were few things he hadn't been involved in. Will had no family to speak of, and consequently, spent most of his teenage years being a part of her household, or Tony's. Her parents easily accepted him. He came home with her almost every single day after school, and was there most weekends. He also was invited to every family vacation they took. Her parents loved Will, and almost considered him the son they never had. They trusted him being with Gretchen far more than what most parents would.

Will and Gretchen started sleeping together in their junior year of high school. Until she divorced, Will was the one and only for her. And he was so good at it. She learned since the divorce that not all men were as satisfying or generous in their lovemaking as Will Hendricks.

Will and she were very different kinds of kids. He was physical and played at any and all sports he could find. He lifted weights every day, and was in an ideal shape that most high school boys envied. She, on the other hand, was quiet, scholastic, and shy even. She studied hard for all the honor and college-bound classes. She had every ambition to go onto college and beyond. And Will? He decided to enter the Army. He told her that when they were in seventh grade. The thing is: he never once waffled on it; even after they graduated and she begged him not to.

At nineteen, Will Hendricks and his best friend, Tony Lindstrom, joined the U.S. Army together. They enlisted barely a year after graduation, and didn't tell anyone they were doing it. Not Tony's family. Not their mutual friends. And certainly, not Gretchen.

She cried the night Will came over and admitted that he enlisted. When he left for basic training, she stayed in bed for days. She was terrified that Will might die. At only age nineteen, she didn't know much about war, or life's conflicts, or politics, or even what the hell one did in the Army. She only knew that he left her. He was physically gone, and could not return unless the Army allowed him to. And he could die. It was never something she chose to live with. She wished in vain for years that Will would simply come to college with her, or get a job around their hometown, and continue dating her. But no, he was destined for far more than just that.

After nearly four years, she managed to convince Will to marry her. She was finished with college and due to start her graduate work. At the time she'd needed to know which state to do it in. In order to move across the country to be near Will, she required Will's full commitment to her. Perhaps she pressured him too much, but he did marry her, and throughout their brief union, Will was popping in and out of her life. She went with him to North Carolina and did her graduate work there. But by the time she started her doctorate, they were heading for a divorce and she moved home to California to finish it.

The baby was what finally broke them up. She was pregnant. It was unexpected, but okay, all the same. She soon become excited and cherished the idea of having Will's baby. Unfortunately, she eventually miscarried. Will was gone on a mission when it happened. He tried to show more care and was ultra sensitive and kind to her, but to no avail. That was what did it for her: seeing how little the loss of the baby meant *to him*. He couldn't even remotely understand or feel the emotional trauma of what she endured. Their baby was no more than an abstract concept to him because he was gone for the entire pregnancy. As he was gone for most of their married life. She never rated higher than his missions or training as far as his priorities were concerned. He was always, first and foremost, a soldier. And Gretchen never came first.

Although she filed for the divorce, it was her heart, and not Will's, that broke into a million pieces, taking years to put back together. He just never knew that.

"Gretchen?"

She shook her head and zoned back into Will's anxious tone. "I ran into him at the grocery store today. His arm is gone. His left arm was completely amputated. It's been two years. Donny was with him. He spoke to me, but Tony barely did. He's… different. You can't even imagine how different. I thought… I thought you didn't tell me on purpose."

Will was silent. Then he said softly, "I would have told you, Gretchen. You have to know that. I would have told you if I'd known. I know how much he meant to you. To both of us."

Us. Sometimes, once in a great while, Will spoke to her as if he remembered all the years he spent as her husband. And lover. And best friend. And the love of her life. Sometimes, he acted like it really did happen between them. They had a shared history that nothing could obliterate, not even his new life and wife.

She let out a breath and shut her eyes as tears filled them. "Oh Will, he was *not* Tony. He was not *our* Tony. He was angry. And so rude. He was… awful, actually. Donny and he nearly came to blows. Whatever happened totally changed him. And what happened between you two? How could so much time pass without you knowing that about him? He was your best friend. How could you not know?"

Sighing heavily into her ear, when he finally spoke, she could tell he was muffling his voice so no one else could hear him. Most likely, Jessie. "To be honest? Jessie happened. I got so entrenched with her, I inadvertently let things go with Tony. He didn't know most of what I was up against with her. And didn't understand what I was doing. When I quit the Army, he lost his fucking mind with his resentment toward me. I don't quite know why he got so mad. Honestly, I just kind of let it go then and didn't pursue him. He was so pissed off at me, I didn't even try to argue him out of it. Time just passed. And suddenly, years went by. I had no idea he'd even gotten hurt, let alone, so catastrophically."

She slid down and sat on her bed, feeling despondent. "I'm sorry I attacked you. I was just so furious and thought you deliberately didn't tell me."

"I know. I get it. I do. Look, it'll take me a few days to get things squared away here, but I'll be there as soon as I can."

She jerked to attention. "You're coming? Here?"

He chuckled. "Well, not to your condo. But yeah, to Calliston. It's way overdue that I saw him. Way too long overdue."

She exhaled. It was nice to know not all of Will's life was so easily replaced with his new one. "That's good. That's really good."

"I'll be there as soon as I can. Thank you for calling, Gretchen." His tone returned to normal. The brief moment of a shared past was over.

"Yeah, sure. See you soon then."

She hung up and threw the phone across the bed, then stared at it in frustrated silence. Her entire condo was silent. She sighed wearily. *Tony. Will. Her.* Things did not turn out for any of them like she foresaw. She shook her head and got up to seek a distraction. How could she feel sorry for herself? It wasn't like *she'd* lost a limb.

Chapter Three

TONY SHOOK THE SHIRT around his shoulder and flipped the collar up before quickly buttoning the front row of buttons with deft, expert, one-handed ease. He had become pretty proficient at doing almost everything without needing another hand. It was just so fucking irritating, he sometimes pretended he couldn't in front of others. He quickly pinned the empty sleeve to his chest. He hated seeing the fucker hanging down and flopping all around. It got caught on things, and dipped into food or got stuck in car doors. So he pinned it.

He messed around for a while with prosthetics the first few months at home. He even used a body-powered one, but hated how conspicuous it made him feel and how uncomfortable wearing the harness over his trunk felt. He also tried a cosmetic one, but decided it wasn't even remotely worth wearing. It did nothing, except give the appearance of being "normal." It didn't take more than a minute before most people realized it was a fake arm. It wasn't worth the trouble. None of them were. After several skin infections, and numerous uncomfortable fittings, he decided to screw the whole thing. No prosthetics for him. The amount of his arm that was missing went almost to his shoulder, which didn't leave much to attach the prosthetics to.

Throwing the towel he used into the laundry, which his mother continued to do for him, he ran his hand through his long hair. Hot beads of water flew off around him. Running his hand over his chin, he felt the beard pricking his palm. Deftly grabbing a rubber band, he swiftly tied it around his hair. That wasn't as easy as buttoning a shirt. Frustratingly, the hair didn't usually stay when he pulled the band around and looped it twice. That's why it always looked like crap. Half of the strands stuck out, or got caught in a ratty mess around the band. Good thing he didn't care.

The doorbell pealed through the house. He paused and waited a moment, listening for some sounds. Nothing. No footsteps overhead. His parents might not have been home. He sighed. *Damn.* Who would show up at two o'clock on a Wednesday? Most people were at work.

Where was his mother? He should have listened harder when she hollered downstairs earlier while he was playing X-box. Double points should have been given to him no matter what he played, as he did it one-handedly. Again, no easy feat.

He now occupied the basement of his parents' two-story house. It was equipped with a small kitchen, half-sized fridge/stove/sink, and maybe a three-foot counter space. His bed was five feet from the couch that was front and center from his TV. It was just enough space. It had the original nineteen-eighties carpet and could have used a major updating. But it was cheap and easy. Besides, his mother did most of the cooking and laundry anyway.

He took the stairs two at a time. They opened up into the kitchen and living room, which all flowed together in a large space. The doorbell pealed again.

"Yeah. Yeah, I'm coming," he yelled as he reached for the doorknob and twisted it.

Will Hendricks stood on his doorstep.

They stared at each other for a full thirty seconds until Tony shook his head. "She called you."

Will's mouth was twisted in an angry scowl. "You're damn right she did. Why didn't you?"

He rolled his eyes and stepped away from the door. There was no doubt the honorable Will Hendricks would feel compelled to come inside. He stood back as Will shut the door behind him. They were standing five feet apart, and sizing each other up. He glared into Will's scrutinizing face. Will's eyes narrowed onto his missing arm, just as everyone else's did. But Will didn't look away, or blush like most observers, he only scowled deeper. "How?"

Tony shrugged. Will, unlike most people, didn't need a lot of details to understand. "Bomber took out a section of the camp. Me and some guys were tossing a football around near it. Next thing I knew, I was lying on a bed and my arm was gone. Shrapnel embedded in it."

"What area?"

"Kandahar Province."

Will nodded. "Tough place."

"Yeah."

"How long ago?"

Tony's jaw worked back and forth. It was odd for him to be so easily understood. "Two years, one month, and fourteen days."

Will shut his eyes and breathed in deeply, then blinked suddenly. Tony stepped back. Tears were brimming over Will's eyelids. "You should have called me. Why didn't you? Because of some stupid, juvenile fight? You decided not to call me about *this* because of that? Come off it, Tony… why? I just don't get why you couldn't call me."

He turned around and wandered into the kitchen. "I don't need this shit, Will. I didn't call you because we aren't friends anymore. Why should I call you?"

Will came after him. "How the fuck do you figure we aren't friends anymore? We've been best friends since we were five years old. So we had a fight. It doesn't change anything. It just put us out of touch for awhile."

"Go home, Will. Go back to your pretty wife. I didn't need you then, and I don't need you now."

Will sucked in a sharp breath. "Are you for real? You think I'm just going to leave here as if nothing happened to you?"

"Yeah, I want you to leave as if nothing happened to me."

Will straightened his back and raised his eyebrows, using his superior muscle to influence him. Tony merely stood up straighter. Damn, if the only thing he had on Will Hendricks was a few inches. He wasn't as muscle-bound as Will. Tony had a long, lean build that eclipsed Will's by just a few inches. "Go home, I don't want you here."

"I don't believe you," Will finally said after they stared each other down with hard, mean glares.

He shrugged. "I don't really care if you believe me. I'm not eating my heart out, longing for you to come talk to me again. Jesus, we're not thirteen-year-old girls."

Tony finally rolled his eyes before sprawling out in his dad's recliner. He clicked the TV on and stared at it.

After three minutes of silence, Will asked, "Do you have PTSD?"

"Well, shit, I must. I don't want to talk to you."

Will grunted and finally came around the couch, where he sat down, uninvited. "Well, you certainly turned into a dickhead. I meant, maybe…"

Tony interrupted him, "I know what you meant. It's what everyone means. No, I don't have PTSD. I just… lost my fuckin' arm and it turned my attitude to shit. I've talked about it. I've grieved for it. I've shed a bucket load of pain over it, okay? I just don't really feel like rehashing it."

Will tapped his hand on the armrest and flicked his fingers at the TV. "This the kind of crap you get into when you hide inside your parents' house? What kind of shit are you watching?"

Tony glanced up at the TV and cursed when he saw a soap opera was on. He cringed and quickly switched the channel. Okay, maybe he was too annoyed by Will's appearance to be aware of the daytime programming.

"I'm not hiding," he grumbled. "I got disability checks coming in. I'm disabled now."

Will shot him a glare, then he sighed. "Sure, Tony. Yeah, you're disabled now. I guess you really are, huh?"

"What? You want to say something?"

"I don't think burying yourself here is the answer."

"No, it's just not what the great Will Hendricks would do. You'd probably go invent yourself a new bionic arm. I'm not you. I just want to be left alone."

"Well, aren't there prosthetics you can wear? Aren't there plastic arms that use micro-computers and move with your nerves or something? Isn't there something you can do, which is more than nothing?"

"The kind I need, upper-limb prosthetics are the hardest to find with all the fancy shit." Tony shrugged and glanced at the TV. "I tried a few in the beginning. They were uncomfortable and hard to wear. They require all kinds of therapy and retraining. I didn't like looking and feeling like a damn robot. It's easier for me to just do without."

"Do without. Without, however, isn't doing anything. You don't seem to be accomplishing anything like this."

"I don't want to change the world. I tried doing that and lost my arm. I'm tired, okay? I don't want to get up and face dealing with the latest electronics and special therapies. I just want to live the rest of my life as it is now."

"But it seems like you're not.

"Why? Because you've seen me all of twenty minutes, and therefore, you know what my life is like now?"

"No... but—"

"But Gretchen told you I wasn't real polite; and that must mean I'm somehow depressed and sad and suffering. So what, Will? What are you going to do about it? Swoop in here and motivate me to go seek out all my options? Believe it or not, I'm not stupid or incompetent. I know my options, and I know what I choose to do and why I chose it."

Will frowned. "When did you decide I was the designated asshole?"

"Just—"

He stopped talking when the door swung open and his mother rushed in, carrying an armful of groceries. Will shot up and sped over to grab them from her before setting them gallantly on the counter.

Leila Lindstrom gasped. "Will Hendricks, is that really you? Oh dear boy, I haven't seen you in years."

Tears filled his mother's eyes and she touched a hand to his cheek. Tony bit his tongue to keep his laughter inside. Holy shit, his mother was sentimental. So what if she half raised Will during most of his boyhood? So what if Will lived there or at Gretchen's more than he ever did at home with his no-good mother? So what? Leila pulled Will in for a long, heartfelt hug.

Will patted her back. "Hey, Mrs. Lindstrom, how are you?"

Ever proper. Ever the gentleman. Ever the gallant Will. Tony rolled his eyes heavenward and threw the recliner back for his feet to rest on. He scratched his chest and yawned as his mother fawned all over Will.

Leila eyed Tony with a frown, then turned back to smile with glee at Will. "I'm fine. Just fine. I'm really thrilled to see you. It's been far too long."

Will nodded. "It's been way too long. I agree. I should have come home sooner, ma'am."

"I know you divorced Gretchen, but I always hoped you'd settle back here. This visit is long overdue."

He smiled. "I have a new home now. But we are visiting here for a few days."

"We?"

"Yes, my wife and child."

Tony grumbled, "You brought them all just to check out my amputation?"

Will stiffened and cast an angry glance his way. His mother's face dropped in horror that he said such a thing. "My wife and Gretchen are close, for reasons that aren't any of your business. Jessie's sister is even Gretchen's best friend. And we brought my baby because I thought you might possibly want to meet her."

Tony snickered. "Wait. Your ex-wife is your current sister-in-law's best friend?"

"Yeah, and my wife too, actually."

Will's tone was very polite in contrast to Tony's rude one. "How do you do that? How do you completely shit on Gretchen and end up having her make nice with your new wife?"

Leila gasped. "For God's sake, Tony!"

Will ignored him and said smoothly, "Let me help you with the rest of your groceries, Mrs. Lindstrom."

Leila smiled and patted his arm. "You were always such a polite boy. Thank you."

Tony nearly choked at all the ass-kissing. Finally, Will brought in the last load and his mother clucked softly, putting everything away, and talking in more depth to Will. She wanted to know all about Will's new civilian job, the town he lived in, and of course, his wife and child.

Tony retreated downstairs to piss. When he came back up, Will was holding his mother's hand saying, "Until then."

"Until then, what?" he asked while approaching them.

"Until dinner tomorrow night. We're all coming. My family."

"And Gretchen? That's fucked up."

"Well, great, we'll see you then." Will smiled at Leila as if Tony never spoke. He shoved his shoulder into Tony's, which should have been a friendly pat, but almost knocked him over. He got the message.

Tony turned on his mother. "You invited all of them to dinner?"

"Yes, Donny did. I was already planning on Gretchen. I'm so excited. I loved having you and your friends in the house. I miss those days."

"Mom…"

She whipped around from stacking canned goods in the cabinet. "Don't, Tony. Don't say a word. No more than you already have. I know why you do it. So did Will. But it's damn tiring to live with. So please, no more today, Tony."

He stiffened and stared at his mother's back. Her shoulders were slumped as she leaned against the counter. Her breathing was ragged. He embarrassed her and hurt her. He finally touched her arm. "I just didn't expect to see him."

She didn't turn his way, but grabbed his hand and clutched it in hers. "None of us expected any of this. But… I thank God, every single day for bringing you back to me. Despite missing your left arm. Why can't you ever, even just once, be glad for that, too?"

He backed up. "Because you're not the one who lost your left arm. You don't know what it's like to look where something is supposed to be, and remember it's gone. Completely gone. Yet, it hurts so much, and I can *feel* everything as if it's still there sometimes. But the cruel joke is, when I look and see they're not there anymore. No arm. No wrist. No hand. No fingers."

"But your heart is still here. And your mind. And both of your legs. I just want some of your former personality that went off to war to return." Leila shook her head, "I have to get dinner started."

Tony turned and jogged down the stairs. He leaned against the door and breathed deeply. The agitation had his head spinning and his chest aching. He failed her. He failed his father, his brother, and now he could add Will and company to the mix. He failed everyone. But he couldn't find the resolve to go back to the man he was before going to war. And that was something no one understood.

****

"You got Will to come up here?"

Gretchen smiled when Donny started talking before she even said hello on her cell phone. It was her lunch hour at the local middle school. She had a consultation with a student and her parents. The seventh grader was

40

having trouble in the classroom and the guidance counselor suggested the family meet with Gretchen and see about obtaining private help. Gretchen's private practice treated a bevy of childhood disorders and emotional conditions ranging from behavioral and neurological problems, to emotional traumas stemming from death, divorce, or abuse.

"Yes. With one phone call. I take it you'll be at dinner tonight."

"Hell, yeah. I wouldn't miss this for anything. Besides, I hope it really does Tony some good. Something has to crack his shell."

"Will said his meeting with Tony didn't go so well."

Donny snorted. "Of course, it didn't. I can imagine. I guess I'm pretty much immune to it by now, but I'm sure it must come as a shock to everyone else. Like you and Will. Be prepared, okay? He's nearly impossible to please or understand. Just... maybe you could take a few minutes and try to connect to him. Maybe even push the idea of seeing him again."

She clutched the phone as her palms grew sweaty. The thought of being one-on-one with Tony's unbridled fury was daunting and unpleasant. Something she couldn't imagine volunteering for; but again, she was not a horrible person and knew she had to do something.

"Okay, Donny. I'll try. But no guarantees."

"I know it's not your problem. I just... I'm at my wit's end here. It's killing my mother. And I can't keep letting it go. I just need somebody to reach Tony. Maybe having yours and Will's involvement could achieve that."

"You really think it will matter to him?"

"I think it could change his entire life. But only if you can get past his bitterness bullshit."

Daunting task. "Speaking of difficult, do you remember my little sister, Vickie?"

"Uh, vaguely. She was several years younger than me in school, so I didn't pay much attention to her."

"Yes, well we had plans tonight. Do you mind if she comes along too?"

"Nah. Not at all. The more, the merrier. See you both then."

"Bye, Donny."

Slipping her phone into her pocket, Gretchen's stomach was already jumping with nerves in anticipation of tonight.

****

Gretchen followed Vickie to the front door of a house she hadn't entered for nearly a decade. How could she let things slide so long? After she divorced Will, she and Tony managed to see each other a few times whenever he was home on leave. Later, however, they seemed to lose each other until there was no contact at all. She spent half her life at his house in her teens. She used to walk inside the house without ever knocking. Leila and she were once very close. Leila was like her second mother as a teen, and yet, despite living in the same town, Gretchen had not visited her in many years.

Leila answered the door. She resembled Tony so much, it nearly took Gretchen a step back in surprise. She had the same shade of brown hair, and ironically, now wore it at the same length as he. She was as tall as Gretchen's own five-foot-nine, so when she pulled Gretchen inside for a long hug, they stood shoulder-to-shoulder.

With a smile, Gretchen patted Leila's back. "Hi Leila."

Leila shook her head and beamed brightly at her. "It's been way too many years." She pushed Gretchen away and surveyed her from head to toe. "My God, you merely grew even more breathtaking. You were a lovely young girl, and now you've grown into a stunning woman. Although, I always knew you would."

She blushed. "You're a tad prejudiced."

"And you are still clueless to your loveliness, which is, perhaps, the best part of you. Now come in, come in. I can't believe you are all here again."

Vickie was quickly introduced before they were inside the family home Gretchen remembered so vividly, and which she found barely changed. They were the type of parents who kept things neat as a pin, but never so much as moved a single candlestick, or restacked the myriad books on their shelves. Continuity was valued here. Leila was the only one in the kitchen besides Will and Jessie. It was a bit disconcerting to walk in and find Will standing with one hip against the counter. Almost a déjà vu. How many times, probably hundreds, had she found Will in this same kitchen, leaning casually against that very counter?

But this time, however, his wife stood beside him and he had a toddler huddled against his legs, wobbling precariously. Gretchen's heart swelled for the briefest moment before it passed, and Jessie burst into a great big smile of warm greetings. She even stepped in front of Will.

Gripping Gretchen's arms, Jessie hugged her fiercely. "Gretchen. It's so good to see you. It's been way too long."

She clasped Jessie in a sincere, heartfelt hug. Oddly enough, Gretchen felt a rush of protective instinct towards Jessie. Jessie was only twenty when she first met her. That was when she was the most tragic, lost, broken person Gretchen ever knew. Despising her for marrying her ex was at the bottom of the list of things

Gretchen could have felt about Jessie. Gretchen had seen the ragged scars from when Jessie cut herself in order to deal with the abuse she had to endure daily. Gretchen oversaw Jessie's long, slow, laborious journey and when she returned to the first semblance of health. Something even Will did not share with Jessie. He never saw how Jessie struggled to learn how to channel her overwhelming grief and emotions in a positive way, and without slicing her own skin. He didn't see her using rubber bands or ice, instead of razor blades, to substitute for what she really craved to do. Gretchen and Jessie's sister, Lindsey, took her to an inpatient treatment facility to start. Later, she went to a new home to live and work, but all the while, continued her intense therapy. As far as Gretchen knew, she was still going to therapy. There was simply no room for catty jealousy or envy between Jessie and Gretchen.

Additionally, Gretchen gave Jessie's beloved sister, Lindsey, a place to recover when she was on the run from her abusive husband. Jessie almost revered Gretchen for all of her generosity in a way that was sometimes nearly embarrassing to Gretchen. Jessie saw Gretchen, who was a full eight years older than she, as a mother figure in some ways. Nevertheless, Gretchen knew Jessie's needs were not her fault, so there was just no way to blame her or even dislike her.

As they were hugging, Tony suddenly appeared at the top of the stairs that led up from the basement. He stopped at the entrance and met Gretchen's eyes, which immediately became locked in a profoundly heated exchange. He was glaring at her. *Why?* She couldn't begin to comprehend this new Tony. His gaze finally shifted from her eyes to land on Jessie.

Jessie leaned back finally, but still clasped Gretchen's hands. Quietly, she said, "I know this is weird. Me being here. Our daughter…"

Gretchen smiled easily. "I came to visit you and Lindsey last time, remember? So stop. Now, it's time you met my sister. Vickie? Come here and meet Jessie, Will's wife."

Gretchen turned and nodded to Vickie to step closer, but Vickie stood back, staring daggers at them during the entire conversation. "Will-fucking-Hendricks," Vickie murmured as she came closer.

"Vickie." Gretchen admonished her sister. Will stiffened behind Jessie and put a hand on her shoulder. He knew how Vickie felt about him. Before they finally divorced, when things were sliding downhill, Vickie more than once expressed her utter disdain for Will.

Jessie merely broke into a huge grin. "Not a fan, I take it. I think this must be the first time that ever happened."

Gretchen felt the tug of a grin at Jessie's unoffended reaction to her sister's insults. Vickie eyed her up. "Hmm, well you might not be so bad. I'm Vickie."

Jessie laughed out loud. "Hi Vickie, it's nice to meet you."

"It's weird you're here, you know that, right?"

"Vickie! Let it go," Gretchen enunciated slowly.

"Well, too-nice Gretchen never sticks up for herself," Vickie said as she rolled her eyes.

Jessie merely nodded. "So weird… but your sister saved me and my sister's lives, despite me marrying her ex. So for me, she's about the most wonderful, kind, amazing woman alive. We're agreed on that. Anyway, that's why I'm here."

Will groaned out loud. Gretchen's blush started in her neck and covered her face instantly. "You two, please just say hello to each other."

Jessie glanced around with a grin. "Why not? It's true. That's what Vickie's so worried about. Why should the second wife be here? I have to agree. But I love Gretchen, so I wanted to come and see her again too."

Tony finally shuffled forward, alerting the others to his presence. The group turned towards him and a thick silence finally fell between all of them. Leila suddenly came around the counter, smiling nervously as she stood between them.

Gretchen's heart seemed to stick in her chest. *Oh God!* It was so startling to see him. Shocking. His hair was clumsily pulled back into a low ponytail. The errant strands of it were tucked haphazardly behind his ears, and it was well past his shoulders. He wore sweats again. Not even a pair of jeans for the company he expected tonight. A t-shirt and a sweatshirt rounded out his casual attire. His empty sleeve was pinned against the side as usual. Gretchen's emotions churned in her gut like a knife twisting inside her. His empty sleeve was all her eyes could see. And she had the wrong reaction. The typical reaction. The every-other-asshole kind of reaction. It was not supposed to be *her* reaction, but she found it so hard not to be that way.

Tony's beard was also distracting and truly changed his entire look. She licked her lips and forced a smile as she swiped her hands on the slacks she wore. She was more nervous than she could remember being in years, an odd reaction to having dinner with the closest friends she grew up with. She had attended important meetings during her career with colleagues, school board members, patients, parents of patients, and any number of situations that put the spotlight on her, and for which she was in charge. But this occasion, here, right now, greeting the one-armed Tony Lindstrom, had her stomach in knots. *Why?* Why was her reaction to seeing him so swift, so brutal, and so wrong? She was behaving completely wrong around Tony. He deserved having her step forward to hug him and chat. Or act even remotely normal. But her tongue seemed to swell in her mouth and her mind went completely blank. She could not figure out how to respond to him.

She had no clue how to act normal with a one-armed Tony.

Jessie stepped forward. "It's been a long time, Tony."

She held out her hand, and Tony stared down at it before looking up into her eyes. Jessie met his without flinching. He reluctantly gave her his hand. *His only hand.* "Yeah, hey."

She smiled. "You know, you helped save my life once."

He pulled his head back in surprise. "How the shit did I do that?"

Leila cleared her throat as a warning, and Jessie smiled. "You sent Will my letters. You can't know what that meant to me. I'm sure he never explained why we asked you to do it… I just wanted to thank you *for* doing it."

He shrugged. It mattered very little to him, or so it seemed. Gretchen had to bite her tongue. Did he have any idea about the magnitude of grief Jessie poured into those letters? Gretchen never read them, but could easily imagine. They used Tony as a go-between in order to evade Jessie's controlling, abusive father.

Will put his hand out next, and Tony had to grasp it in return or look like a complete jerk. Then he stared at

Gretchen. She swallowed and stepped closer. Straightening her back and bracing herself, she tried her best to quit reacting so completely inappropriately toward him. She was freaked out by the obvious changes; but for the first time in her life, couldn't seem to get over it. The thing was: she didn't know why she got so upset by what happened to Tony. She licked her lips, and forced out another smile before stretching her hand out to touch his, which hung loosely at his side. He nearly flinched with surprise before his eyes narrowed and he glared into her face. She gulped down her anxious nerves. *Steady.* She had to be steady and normal when she spoke.

"Hello Tony. It's so nice to see you again."

There. Her voice didn't tremble. It sounded like her usual tone. She sounded almost like she was the thirty-five-year-old adult she was supposed to be.

He discreetly jerked his hand from hers and nodded, "Gretchen." Then he turned away from her as if she were no more than a passing stranger. Her utter surprise at his slight was swift. He really disdained her. *Why?* He didn't know about the inner conflict she was having just to face him; so why did he act so weird with her?

Will and he started speaking, although Tony's tone sounded half as polite or interested as Will's. Leila pulled the women into the kitchen and initiated a conversation, bouncing between all of them. She wanted to first catch up on Gretchen's life and learn how she knew Jessie. Soon, Tony's father, who was even taller than Tony, came in with his distinguished, quiet way that Gretchen fondly remembered. He embraced her warmly.

Donny burst inside in a rush. He was carrying a box, which contained the dessert. He carefully balanced it on his hand as he hugged everyone, pausing briefly when Gretchen introduced him properly to her sister. Vickie went strangely silent at his unannounced entrance, something Gretchen felt pretty sure she'd never seen Vickie do.

Dinner was a casual, easy-going affair served at the table. It consisted of pork chops, salads, beans, and rolls. Leila was an expert cook; and the meal, as well as her table setting, were as inviting as Gretchen remembered from her youth. The conversation was lively and mostly centered on catching up with everyone's lives, and going back at least a decade. Anecdotes and stories were rehashed with humor and sentimentality. Except for anything about Tony.

The excruciatingly oppressive elephant in the room was back. It was hard for Gretchen to not try and sneak glances and peeks at Tony. He could not cut his own meat, so his mother leaned over and silently did it for him. He never lifted his eyes from the utensils she used. It was awkward for anyone to pass the various dishes to him. The heavy bowl of salad made his forearm tremble under its weight, although he still managed to pass it along. Gretchen felt waves of dizziness overcoming her as she repeatedly spotted the empty armhole.

Donny was a lifesaver. His easy-going charm and stories kept the conversation light and effortless, going from topic to topic. He eagerly encouraged everyone to participate, except Tony. Tony didn't say more than three words, if Gretchen counted correctly. Vickie, too, was strangely quiet. That was unheard of. She almost reached over and checked Vickie's pulse.

After they all pushed away from the table, Leila, Jessie and even Vickie were in the kitchen, cleaning up the dishes. Gretchen was still tidying up the table when she heard Will speaking directly to Tony.

"So what the hell are you doing now?"

Tony ran his hand over his beard. Donny froze. He was about to pour ice water from the pitcher into his glass. Tony's father, Lewis, stiffened as Tony shrugged carelessly. "What the hell? What am I doing? Living with this."

He gestured by lifting the affected shoulder up.

Will cleared his throat. "Yes, I know that. But what do you do all day?"

Tony's fierce gaze could have stopped a missile. "Do you think anything about my life is easy to do after this? It tends to keep me pretty busy just doing everything you take for granted."

"So… you don't work?"

Tony's scowl deepened the lines around his eyes. "I told you: I'm on disability."

"Nothing? Nada? You don't get up in the morning and have anything at all to do?"

"Will," Gretchen's tone was low and her warning not very subtle.

Tony glanced at her, and his eyes appeared blank. She had no idea what he was thinking but saw the twitching muscles around his mouth. Everyone else was quiet too and observing the conversation. It felt like the group was collectively holding their breaths in anticipation. Tony's jaw worked back and forth, but he finally muttered, "No."

"Why?"

"What do you mean 'why'?"

"Why don't you do something? How good can it be to do nothing? Or not to be accountable for anything? Or anyone?"

Donny slid his chair out, leaning back as he crossed his arms over chest. "Will has a point. It's doing you no good."

Gretchen stepped back away from the table, horrified they were having this conversation *now* and in front of her.

Lewis swiveled his head between his sons, and nodded finally too. "Well, now, guys, you just don't know what it's like. You don't have to live with it. We do. Leave him alone."

That was a shock. Lewis still ran his plumbing company. After forty years in the profession, he showed no signs of slowing down. It surprised Gretchen he couldn't see any need for Tony to do something too.

"That's exactly the problem. We left him alone for so long, he thinks he's entitled to do nothing. Or even act courteous anymore."

Tony's gaze shot up and pinned her. She stepped back again before freezing. She felt like she was caught in a sniper's sights. She didn't know what she should have done or said, much less, why he was glaring at her when she hadn't said anything. He finally stood up slowly, pushing his chair back.

"I don't need your shit, Will. Nobody asked you to come here."

Will stood up. "Gretchen asked me to come. And Donny asked her to come. So that's a load of shit. You need us. You need everyone here. You need to do something."

He clenched his one fist. Gretchen couldn't keep her mind focused. Every time he moved, she concentrated on staring at his one good arm and hand movements. His gaze again swung her way, nearly incinerating her with its heat. "Yeah? Well, no one asked *her* to do that."

"Don't take it out on Gretchen. You brought this on yourself with your lousy attitude. All anyone has ever tried to do is help you. Or be caring and sensitive to you.

Just look at what all that has *managed not to do* for you," Donny said as he stood angrily up too.

Lewis shook his head. "Stop it, son. It's not your place."

"Why? Why shouldn't I point out the damn obvious? You and Mom aren't helping him. You're completely hindering his recovery. There isn't any recovery for him. He's just hiding from the world."

Tony kicked the chair behind him against the wall, which dented the plaster. "There is no recovery, you clueless, little shit. There is no getting better. There is nothing left to get better. You and Will come in here, thinking I need to do more so I can feel better? Well, what the hell do you know about any of it? Does your mother have to cut up your fucking dinner? No? Well, then don't come to me with any of your good intentions and shit. None of it. If you don't like it, get the fuck away from me."

Donny stepped forward. "I can't. You live in my parents' basement. They are my family too, you big, dumb asshole. I can't simply stop coming around just because you're too sensitive to handle it."

Everyone was now standing at the entrance to the dining room, after having run out when the chair smashed into the wall. Donny and Tony stood there, breathing heavily, an arm's length away from each other and, no doubt, seconds away from one of them swinging at the other.

Chapter Four

"STOP IT! BOYS! STOP IT!" Leila came swiftly forward and stood directly between them. They eyed each other maliciously over her head. "This is still my house, regardless of who lives here or not. And I'll throw both of your miserable, ungrateful asses out."

Their gazes swung down to her in obvious surprise. "Now, sit down, after you politely pick up that chair, Tony Lindstrom. I had better never see you damage one of my walls or furniture again in one of your tantrums, do you get me?"

His mouth dropped open in stunned shock. Apparently, Leila didn't often yell, swear, or say "do you get me?" Will coughed behind his hand and she glanced up. He was trying to restrain a laugh. So did Lewis, and then Donny. Tony came around after he righted the chair. Finally, he slowly lifted the side of his mouth.

Leila sputtered. "Why are you four smiling now? You were just about coming to blows in my dining room."

"Because you're a pretty effective tool in successful negotiations, Mrs. Lindstrom," Will said, fully grinning. He stood there with his hands on his hips and addressed Tony again. "Look, I was being an asshole for how I worded things. It's just that... you kind of deserved it. You've been nothing but an ass to me since you heard I was quitting the Army. I wasn't doing it to abandon you. I was needed more elsewhere."

Tony sat down with his legs sprawled before him, and his arm hanging off to the side. He snorted. When he spoke again, his tone was calmer, but still laced with the belligerent sarcasm that seemed to be his new status quo. "I wasn't an ass because I felt abandoned. I was an ass because you quit the Army for your second wife."

Will frowned, looking puzzled. He glanced around. "Well, yeah. I did. She needed me to."

"Yeah, well, so did your first one, and you never once considered that. Not even for moment."

Gretchen's entire body stiffened. Tony was staring directly at Will without a glance her way to acknowledge her, or her ability to hear him. *He ended his friendship with Will because of her?* She dropped the platter she was holding. All eyes turned her way. Guiltily, she grabbed a dishtowel to wipe up the splattered sauce, but not before she noticed the shock in Will's eyes. They flashed something like regret her way. No doubt, he must have never considered that angle. Gretchen was in tears when she heard he quit the Army to be with Jessie. It was hard to accept rejection from the man she loved for almost two decades, who didn't love her enough to do such a thing, but did so for another woman.

"That's why you hated me?"

"Yeah. You never put her first. I thought it was just how you were. You know, super soldier Will Hendricks. But then... you did it. And it wasn't for Gretchen, who loyally stood by you for more than a decade."

Will blew out a breath and sat back down. "I never considered it from that angle." He glanced up at

Gretchen and pinned her with his gaze. She was speechless just standing there, but feeling completely floored at where the evening was going. Everyone in the room was looking at her now, including Will's new wife.

"Yeah, you never once put her first. It was a shitty thing to do."

Will's eyes moved over her face. "I'm sorry, Gretchen, for doing that. I never considered…"

Gretchen felt the heat climbing into her face once more. Jessie suddenly stepped forward and touched Will's arm. "Oh my God. Stop. You're completely embarrassing her. If you have something to say, do it in private, both of you."

Tony's eyebrows shot up and he muttered something incomprehensible. She cleared her throat. "Yes, well, can we please move onto something else? Something that did not occur a decade ago?"

Vickie suddenly stepped forward and asked Jessie, "How is it you're so awesome?"

Jessie grinned. "Because sometimes, men are just clueless. Now, no more talk that upsets anyone. Got it?"

They all shuffled and glanced around at each other, but finally, nodded their consent.

Soon, the tension in the room settled down while the women finished the dishes and the men had a round of drinks. Jessie quickly took her aside. "Is that true? What Tony said?"

She hesitated. *Did it even matter now?* "Yes. I asked him to quit after I miscarried. He wouldn't even talk about it. He never loved me like he loves you."

Jessie bit her lip. "Why are you the better person and don't hate me? I would hate me if I were you. Thus, illustrating why I was never the better choice."

She shook her head. "It's water under the bridge for me. It's been a really long time. I look at Will and remember a younger, very different version than the Will you know. So, just leave it, okay?"

"Okay. Thanks for not hating me."

"It's impossible to hate you."

Donny and Vickie were soon flirting in subdued tones. Vickie was usually bold and unmistakable in her attractions. The talk turned to a new local club that just opened up in downtown Calliston. It was the first nightclub ever in the area.

"We should all go," Vickie said, smiling directly at Donny.

His eyes sparked with interest as they ran the length of Vickie's legs, which she seductively crossed, thereby allowing her skirt to ride up higher than it needed to be.

"Go?" Gretchen asked, having tuned out the conversation.

"Yeah, to Essence. It's awesome. Well, for Calliston, that is." Vickie actually licked her lips as she stared into Donny's eager eyes. Gretchen nearly groaned out loud. Donny didn't show much interest in her to start... now he was? She wasn't anxious to watch sweet Donny go through the tornado that would become her sister, and surely twist him up, and spit him out in her wake. That was just Vickie's modus operandi.

"We should all go there," Donny said, glancing around with a smile. "Even you, Tony. Maybe you could meet someone and get laid. Might cut through some of your bullshit and crap."

Thank God their parents had left the room. Gretchen really wished she wasn't present for this.

"We're game, if we can get a sitter."

Donny grinned and yelled after his parents, "Hey Ma? Will you watch Christina while we all go out this weekend?"

Leila appeared in the doorway, her hands almost clapping in glee. "Yes, of course. Go. All of you. Have some fun."

Jessie grinned. "Well, then it's a date."

Gretchen kept the wince of displeasure to herself. She didn't really agree to it. Tony and Will both glanced at her with the same frown and she turned away.

It was so much more confusing for them to reunite after all these years than she could have ever dreamed. Back together, the three of them suddenly had a whole lot more baggage between them, and the people now involved with them.

For Gretchen knew she was not a good friend anymore. She used to be one to Tony; and yet, she couldn't figure out how to be so now, today. Why the hell couldn't she just act natural?

They stayed well past midnight. The tension eventually dissipated and they bantered and talked in a more relaxed atmosphere. The Lindstroms fairly basked in all the conversation. Gretchen felt terrible for the long lapse in seeing them. They were undeniably delighted to see her, as well as having Will there with Donny and Tony. They were all becoming masters in ignoring Tony's surly presence. He was not much fun, and rarely smiled. He didn't engage with anyone and seldom commented. Although Tony never talked *to* Gretchen, he talked strangely *about* her. Almost in a clinical way. It was so freaking odd. He disappeared downstairs about an hour before everyone else left.

She was disgruntled when Vickie whispered that she was catching a ride with Donny. She clutched her sister's hand. "Please don't, Vickie. This family means a lot to me."

"Don't what? You act like I'm going to eat him up or something. Lighten up, sis." She kissed Gretchen's cheek as she ran towards Donny, smiling.

Gretchen was already in her car when she realized with annoyance that she left her purse inside. She ran back to the house, but found no one there. She knocked, but no one answered. The door was still unlocked, and she slipped in after a moment's consideration. Where did Leila take the coats? She thought she saw her take them downstairs.

Biting her lip, did she dare go down there? Or just yell out for Leila? But then… something told her to go down to the basement. She paused on the first step and felt like she was entering a dragon's lair, but quietly descended until she was on the dimly lit stair landing. She glanced around. Holy crap, it was exactly the same. She saw the same couch they used to watch movies on. The couch where she made out with Will while Tony was off doing God only knows what. She'd never been demonstrative with her affection in public. She'd always been discreet. Except around Tony. She and Will were a lot more casual and loving around him.

She called softly, "Tony?"

Maybe he was in the bathroom. But no. The door was open and the light was out. She stepped further inside the room and walked over to the couch where she stopped dead. Tony was lying down before her, on the floor, doing one-armed push-ups. Ear buds filled both of his ears, which were obviously why he didn't answer her.

His shirt was off, and he moved up and down with the agility of one strolling. It was incredible. She simply stood there, staring at him, her mouth hanging open in awe. How? How could he possibly lift all of his weight up and down on one arm like that? And holy mother of God, *his chest!* Her mouth nearly salivated. His unappealing attire masked the sheer Adonis body it concealed underneath. His stomach was rippled in hard abs that were almost freaky in their perfection. Smooth as plastic. Hair lightly peppering his chest. Her gaze ended with the arm. It was neatly removed, of course. The shoulder simply dropped off to a nearly perfect incision. It threw her off, momentarily. But her eyes darted straight back to the rippling muscles she saw there. *Holy Christ.*

She jerked to attention when he suddenly stopped and rocked back onto his knees. He yanked the ear buds out.

"What the fuck are you doing?"

She raised her eyes to his face. He was sitting on his heels, his chest glistening in sweat. She swallowed, still mute.

"Gretchen!?"

She jerked back into the moment. "I'm sorry... I was looking for my purse. I thought your mom put it down here. And then I..."

He jumped to his feet with the ease and agility of an eighteen-year-old. Gretchen lost most of her ease and agility about four years ago. He turned from her, grabbing a shirt off his bed that he left unmade behind him. He shrugged into it, pulling it to cover his scar.

"And you decided to gawk?"

"What?" she raised her eyes to his finally. She was still staring at the line his open shirt made. The abs flexed as he moved. "No. Not to gawk. I was startled..."

"By me? Obviously."

59

Her mouth dropped open in shock. "No. No. I was startled by that." She stared down at her feet as she waved her hand his way.

"Yeah, my amputation."

"Not your amputation. Your... chest. Okay? I'm sorry it's hard to look at your amputation with those out."

"Those?"

She felt the deep heat of a blush filling her cheeks. "Your abs. I mean, my God, are you kidding me?"

When she finally glanced up, he was scowling at her. Wasn't that his normal expression of late? "My abs? What are you talking about?"

"Uh, well, yeah. It's just been awhile since I've seen any so... well conditioned." *Hot. Sweaty. Streaming in sweat.* She had to stifle the urge to touch them, and lick them...

She realized then why he was so pissed. *Duh.* He thought she was staring at his empty arm socket in repulsion, and not speechless from the weird twisting in her gut that occurred whenever she observed all the muscles bunching over his torso.

"I wasn't looking at your amputation. I was just looking at your sculpted chest, okay? I was a bit stunned is all. I didn't know you looked like that still. I didn't know you ever looked like that, to be honest."

He didn't answer, so she kept her gaze glued to the seam of his shirt, while still sneaking a peek of his muscles. She continued, despite her better judgment. "I couldn't hold myself off the ground like that with my knees on the ground, let alone, one-handedly. It wasn't stunned shock at your missing arm, Tony. I was stunned and in shock to see you *doing that.*"

He was silent for a moment, then two. She swallowed and tapped her finger against her leg. Holy crap, he made her feel so unsettled, and he used to be her dear, sweet friend. Finally, he said softly, "I'd like to see that."

"What? Me floundering like a beached whale trying to do a push-up? For that's what I would, no doubt, look like. You know, I've never had an ounce of strength, agility or proper conditioning."

"No, you haven't. You were always the worst one in gym class. I used to pick you strictly out of pity. What I meant was, I'd like to see you on all fours before me."

Her gaze shot up to his. Did he just say that? No. No way. And was that a damn grin now lurking in the corners of his mouth? She cleared her throat, but decided to ignore that.

"So, do you know where my purse is?"

He finally turned his gaze away from her face. Throwing some stuff off the couch, he soon raised it up in his hand. She stepped forward to take it, but he didn't let go. Surprised, she looked up, frowning.

"Why did you come here tonight?" he asked.

"We all care what happens to you."

"We? Who Donny? Will? That's why you came? For Will Hendricks?"

"No. Because I care that this happened to you." She took in a slow breath. "Look, I handled this wrong from the first moment I saw you. I'm really sorry I acted like I never met you before. And I'm very sorry to learn this happened to you. I'm sorry you lost your arm. I should have said that right off when I saw you at the grocery store. Instead, I chatted on, like an airhead, who never met you. Anyone can see you had your arm amputated. I should have respected that and simply said so. Instead, it got all weird between us, when we've never been weird together. We were always such good friends. So... I'm sorry."

His face remained glacial, but one eyebrow rose again. She swallowed and cleared her throat, trying to calm her nerves, and recapture the comfortable, friend-vibe they always shared.

But nothing. No response. Okay, this wasn't the way to reach him. He still had her purse and she still held onto the other end of it. He tugged on it, drawing her toward him. He stared into her eyes, lowering his eyes to her mouth. What was going on? Where was this coming from? No. No way. They never experienced such an awkward moment between them. Why was he staring at her so strangely?

"I don't want to be your friend, Gretchen." His tone was quiet and intense. She felt like he became a magnet that was inexplicably attracting her towards him.

She licked her lips. "Wh-why not? Why don't you even remotely want to be friends?"

"You've always mistaken my friendship and what I wanted to be."

Her eyes widened and she took a step back. *No. No. No.* Donny was not right. He never had a thing for her. He—couldn't mean this. He acted as if he didn't even like her now.

He suddenly shoved the purse back at her, releasing the tension that was drawing her his way, and making her stumble backwards. "Go home."

She regained her equilibrium, clutching her purse, as she smiled in forced politeness. It took all her courage to meet his gaze and pull it off, as if they were just bidding each other a pleasant, courteous goodbye. "I'll see you this weekend then."

He turned abruptly with his good arm towards her. "I highly doubt that."

Then he walked into the bathroom and slammed the door.

She stared after him, feeling shocked. Turning on her heel, she fled from what suddenly became the most difficult person she ever had to deal with.

Chapter Five

GRETCHEN GOT HOME FROM work and stared in bewilderment at her closet. What the hell would she wear to a dance club, of all things? She hadn't been out to one in years. Her wardrobe was full of conservative, dressy outfits. She had some casual jeans and shirts for weekends, but nothing that would have been suitable for a dance club. She sighed and pushed her garments around. Finally, she found some dressy black pants, which she paired with a red blouse. As she was shoving her feet into her black, three-inch heels, she heard the door.

She quickly let Vickie in before inserting hoops through her earlobes. Her sister followed her inside. "What are you wearing?"

She glanced up at her little sister. "What do you mean, what am I wearing?"

"Well, you look like you're on your way to work."

She lowered her hands from her ears and took in Vickie's outfit. Okay, so Vickie won the best club outfit, hands down. She had on jeans with rips at the knees and sparkles on her firm, little ass. Her neon-colored bra showed through the cuts in her black top, and seemed like someone had taken tape and wrapped it around her.

"I couldn't wear something like that and you know it." A few years after her divorce, Gretchen had gone out quite a bit and there were lots of dates and a few casual sex partners. But she quit all that when she got closer to thirty and her career started to take off. It ate up all her spare time, and by the weekends, she was tired and looking forward to curling up with a glass of wine and a good book or a movie rather than a night out of getting drunk in a crowd.

"No. You can't. But you can't wear *that*. Don't you have jeans or something that doesn't broadcast you as a CEO?"

She sighed, following Vickie back into her room as Vickie started searching through her selection of pants. Finally, she held up a pair. "These will do. Put them on. Geez, and please let me take you shopping this weekend."

"I don't want to go shopping. I like the way I dress. I don't want to change."

Vickie snickered. "You don't want to get laid either. But some of us do."

Gretchen rolled her eyes as she kicked her heels off, then stripped down and pulled the jeans on. "Please don't do it with Donny. Unless… you already did?"

Vickie sat on her bed and watched Gretchen changing pants. "No. He drove me home and walked me to the front door. It was so sweet, even chivalrous. He leaned in like he *wanted* to kiss me. Oh my God! Gretchen, this is *something*. I'm telling you, tonight is going to be epic. The start of something huge for me. I have this strange feeling."

Gretchen nearly choked, keeping the laugh confined to her throat. Something huge always seemed to be starting for Vickie. Brushing her teeth in the morning evoked nearly the same response from her, so Gretchen didn't put too much stock in her announcement. She glanced at her ass in the mirror, now wearing jeans. Not great. But not terrible. She wasn't as slender as Vickie, but had long legs to help carry it off. She was more of an average weight, and worked to keep it that way. Vickie ate nothing but crap all day, yet never gained an ounce. Vickie was one of those strangely blessed people who did nothing the way she should have, and yet, almost everything she needed came easily to her in some way or another.

Gretchen flipped her blond hair back. The curls were now shoulder-length. After twenty years of having it long, and falling past her shoulder blades, she decided to cut it off above her ears shortly after the divorce. Now, she wore it in a stylish, reverse bob that ended at her shoulders. Dark streaks of brown contrasted in the bottom layer, creating a peek-a-boo effect of light and dark shades. It was Vickie's idea and the only thing that Vickie considered remotely "cool" about Gretchen.

But it was good enough for meeting old friends from a previous life. From her youth. *For meeting Tony Lindstrom.* The odd tingling in her fingertips began again at the thought of Tony. Would he show up? It could go either way. Did she want him to? He was so rude. Gruff. Negative. But hot. Well, so what? Being hot, and even one-armed, did not give any person the right to be so terrible to those around him who were just trying to help. It didn't excuse him or his behavior.

Still, Gretchen knew this tinge of excitement, in anticipation of tonight, wasn't from just seeing Will, or Jessie, or Donny, or Vickie. She grabbed her purse and followed her sister outside.

****

Tony watched Gretchen walk into the club, completely oblivious to the effect she had on the people around her as she made her way through the crowd. All the men's eyes trailed after her. And certainly not because of her ample display of skin. That was never Gretchen's way, and not what captivated most of the guys around her. Quite simply, she attracted them, using her personality, her looks, and the rest of her persona. She was a tall, elegant woman, who kept her posture straight and erect. She walked with a unique confidence in her carriage, keeping her shoulders drawn back, and her hips aligned with them. Her rigid posture reflected her entire life. She had always been that kind of girl. The good one. The kind one. The responsible one. She never once skipped a class in high school, or missed an assignment. Meanwhile, Tony had always been a shit-ass student. Gretchen even tried to tutor him more than once. She sat at his parents' kitchen table, trying to explain his assignments, but he never cared much about schoolwork. Back then, he liked to have her tutoring him, not for the stupid grade improvement, but so he could try and peek down her shirt. That was never an easy feat as she usually dressed modestly. She was always very prim and extra sweet, which went right along with her good grades and perfect attendance. She seemed like complete goodness and kindness to anyone and everyone she ever met. She became an extremely popular girl simply because there was no way for anyone to hate to her. She was nice to everyone. Always. Even those who didn't deserve it.

Kind of like how she was still. With him. And he sure as shit didn't deserve it. He tried not to deserve it.

Tony tapped his finger against the table. Donny sat next to Tony, and Will and Jessie were across from them. They were all talking over the loud music. Taking a gulp of beer for courage, Tony knew he should not have come. Despite Donny's pressure to include him, that wasn't why he chose to. He knew that. It was because he wanted to see *her* again, no matter how stupid the urge was. She felt sorry for him. She was only there because of him losing his fucking arm. If he had been whole and fine, she would have just smiled and kissed his cheek in the grocery store, carrying on with her life as she had for the last eight years. She would have never felt any kind of obligation to see him, or his family again. As always, she retained a kind, warm, generous friend thing for him.

And fuck. Did he detest that about her. She was always that way towards him. He was the nice friend and Will's sidekick. The puppy dog she could pat as she passed by. He was never the one she looked at, or was attracted to. So, he damn well knew it was merely her pity over his empty sleeve that brought Gretchen Moore there. *Hendricks. Gretchen Hendricks.* Even after all these years with his best friend's last name, his brain refused to accept that she was truly Gretchen Hendricks.

Vickie and Gretchen came over to the table and smiled and greeted everyone. Vickie slid in next to his brother, leaving Gretchen standing there, shifting her weight from one foot to the other. The only spot was beside Tony. He slid the chair out with his foot and a careless nod. She darted a glance at him before slowly and elegantly lowering her ass into the chair and scooting it closer to the table.

She was seated on the side of his amputated arm. He should have anticipated that and sat on the other side. She peeked at him from corners of her eyes and smiled slightly, just a small, sweet tilt of her lips. "Hello Tony. I'm glad you came."

He shifted and leaned forward. "Oh yeah? So you can keep trying to nurse me back to health and happiness again?"

She tugged on her lower lip with her front teeth. He utterly puzzled and intimidated her. She was too fucking nice to tell him to go to hell like she wanted to, which was what he certainly deserved.

The waitress was passing by and he flagged her down to intercept Gretchen's, no doubt, angry retort to his surly response and demeanor. "Hey, can my friends here get some drinks?"

She smiled at him and returned to take down Gretchen and Vickie's orders. Gretchen faced forward so she could talk to the rest of the table and avoid Tony's eyes. He leaned back and barely listened. She was discussing something about what she did for work. He stared around, feeling bored. The dance floor was surprisingly packed. The crowd was not just for the young. There were middle-aged couples on dates that were dancing. That was primarily because there was simply no other place to go in Calliston. Tony should never have settled back there. But then again, anywhere else and he'd be doing his own damn laundry and having to pay his own bills.

He observed the conversation as if he were far away from there. When Gretchen's drink came, she took several quick nips, as if fortifying herself. He was pretty sure it was a natural reaction to how uncomfortable he made her. She fiddled with the glass and poked the straw up and down as she talked to Will about her clients. Something about schools and special consultations, and some other rather impressive shit. She never ceased to impress him. Her talents and intelligence were obvious from the time she ran for freshman class president. Not a surprise to him that she remained so remarkable. She was articulate, well spoken, and kept her voice well modulated.

He was never remarkable to anyone. Not in school. Not even, particularly, in the military. Sure as fuck not now, living at home while his mommy washed his clothes and cut his food for him. His only hope for escaping tedious mediocrity was his fucking amputated arm.

Jessie rose, pulling Will's arm, before heading to the dance floor to join the thrashing bodies and the loud, fun music and bouncing lights. Donny stood up and invited Vickie to dance. She nearly jumped out of her black, heeled boots in her eagerness to do so.

Leaving them alone, Tony couldn't even cross his arms over his chest to show his discomfort. He missed doing that. He missed how comfy it used to feel when he held his arms over his chest. One arm across his chest looked stupid, but he sometimes got tired of letting it just hang next to him. Instead, he leaned further into the table and clutched his drink. After several long, tense moments, he nodded towards Will and Jessie.

"So… how did he do it? How did he manage to make you, his ex, and his new wife become friends?"

Gretchen finished swallowing and lowered her drink before dabbing the corners of her mouth with her tongue. The dart of her pink tongue made his dick twitch, like a Pavlovian response. Grimacing, he turned away. He felt like a horny sixteen-year-old with her. He always had. He invariably reacted the same way to her although she never felt the same toward him. Not once. Not even one errant thought or spontaneous attraction could draw her closer to him. In all the years he'd been in and out of Gretchen's life, she never harbored anything except sisterly, platonic love towards him.

She turned her body, so she was closer and could hear him better. "Do you know how he and Jessie met?"

He frowned. *Who cares?* "Yeah, that twisted Mexico shit. The stuff that made Will Hendricks the latest poster-boy for Army courage, integrity and honorability."

"Yes, but do you know how he actually first found her?"

He shrugged. "Nah. Not the specifics."

"She was tied up and being gang raped." Tony's eyes instantly sought out Jessie, whom he found now smiling up at Will. She threw her head back to laugh before wrapping her arms around his neck and squeezing closer to him. *No.* He didn't know that. His stomach fairly knotted at hearing the simple sentence that contained so much horror.

"So, you see, there was never any reason for me to hate Jessie."

"Yes, but he didn't have to make you help him by doing whatever you did for her."

"Perhaps. He called me because I'm a licensed therapist, Tony. I do this for living. He helped finance my degrees while I was married to him. And he called me in a panic, because at the time, he was desperate to save her. He was afraid she would end up hurting herself again. I helped him because of our history, and also because he paid for the airline ticket to get me there, he was so desperate. After I met her, and really, right from the start, my help had little to do with Will, and everything to do with humanity. Any human being with an ounce of compassion would have wanted to help her. You think you know pain? I'm sorry, but yours isn't like Jessie's. No one's pain can hold a candle to her experience."

He cleared his throat. "Oh… I guess I thought you did it purely out of your never ending devotion to him."

She shook her head. "That was a decade ago. I moved on a long time ago, Tony. I'm really not so pathetic that I'd pine after him still. I resumed my life. And Will resumed his. Tell me, Tony, why haven't you? Why do you care what Will and I are like together now?

If Jessie doesn't care, and trusts us being together, knowing that there'll never be anything less than a true friendship between us, why should you care?"

He focused on the gyrating bodies to ignore her green eyes boring into him. "Because he never treated you right. I guess, I thought he was still doing it, that's all."

"Never treated me right? What are you talking about? Will was always good to me."

"Will never once put you first or before whatever he preferred to do. From the start. From the first time you asked him to go to a dance, and he couldn't because there was a football team party he didn't want to miss. It was always about what Will wanted with you guys."

Her body recoiled as if he tried to touch her. She shook her head. "That's… not true."

He felt the urge to cross his arms again; only this time, the feeling was so strong, he had to glance down to remind himself why he couldn't. "It was true. And it's still true. I'm sorry about Jessie. But he should have been there at least a dozen times for you like he always is for her."

"No, Will loved me. We just grew apart as we matured. I never knew exactly why it went wrong…"

"It went wrong because he never loved you like he should have. He should have never married you. But after he did, he should have put you first, and above everything else."

He snuck a glance her way. She was biting her lip and her eyebrows were scrunched, showing obvious distress over what he was saying.

"Did he tell you that?"

He shifted and leaned his one elbow on his knee. "No, of course not. He probably thought he *was* putting you first. He just never once treated you as well as you

72

deserved. I never understood why you put up with it either. Sports. Friends. Army. Take your pick; they were always more important than you. Maybe because he knew you would always be there for him."

"Are you saying he just assumed I would always be there, and consequently, did what he wanted? You think I was some kind of clinging, pathetic doormat?"

He twisted his heel on the floor and stared at it to avoid looking into her beautiful face. "No, you weren't pathetic or clinging. His devotion to everything that came before you was."

She was silent for a long moment. He felt her hand touching the top of his shoulder a few inches above the amputation. He flinched and jerked away from her fingers, then finally glanced up at her.

"I had no idea you thought that about us."

"You never had any idea what I ever thought... period."

"Why is that, Tony? Why did I never know what you thought?"

Heat was spiraling in his guts and warming his face. He never meant to have this kind of conversation with her. However, her continued politeness and courtesy toward Will was hard to swallow after all the years that Will so carelessly neglected her, not to mention how little he respected the gift of her love, which it truly was.

He focused his gaze back on Will. "Because you never wanted to know. Not really."

She was silent again. He must have revealed too much. He turned and grabbed his drink, downing it in a quick shot.

When she spoke again, her tone was softer. "Part of it was my fault. I pressured him to marry me. He wasn't ready. I knew that, even then. I was desperate to keep him. All the time he was gone and traveling on his missions… well, I feared our relationship couldn't handle it. In order to keep him, I thought if we got married, we'd be insulated against the strains of hectic military life. The thing was: I was a lousy Army wife. I wasn't committed, understanding or tolerant. If it comforts you at all, I used to chew his ass out regularly for being gone, leaving me alone, and being emotionally unavailable."

Tony flagged the waitress and pointed at his empty drink; she nodded and headed towards the bar. "Well, I guess he wasn't much of a husband."

"It was mutual. A lot of it anyway. I was focused on school, and nothing came before that. There was a lot more I could have done to be a better Army wife. I didn't want to be one, so I made sure I was a crappy one. And I made sure Will knew how much I detested the role. I wasn't all that nice for him to live with. We were just… so young. And not ready for the marriage we tried to survive. No offense, but maybe you shouldn't judge him so harshly. You didn't try to get married in your early twenties and make a name for yourself in the Army. It wasn't an easy task. And I'd appreciate very much if you tried to quit hating Will, on my behalf. If you feel the need to keep venting your hate for him, do it on your own time. You act like I was a weak, sad, little doormat, getting trampled on by Will. I was not. I am not. I was merely distracted. Busy. And into my own career. There was plenty of blame to go around; and we came to terms with it. So you really don't need to weigh in. You weren't there when we were alone, and therefore, you don't know everything."

He tipped the waitress as she set his drink on the table, having been properly chastised. Glaring into his drink, he mumbled, "Fine. Whatever. Will's wonderful, and you got exactly what you deserved."

She tapped her pink, polished nail on the table. He didn't look into her face, but kept his eyes fastened on her tapping finger. She was annoyed. But that felt better than receiving pity.

"Why? Why are you like this? I didn't do anything to you to deserve this," she said waving her hand towards him. Sighing, she shook her head, "I don't even know who you are anymore. This rude, latest version of you. I liked the old Tony a lot better."

He shook his glass until he found an ice cube, whereupon he tilted the glass until it slid into his mouth. Chewing it noisily, he contemplated the crowd before him. Finally, he shrugged. "Truthfully, you never much liked the old version either, Gretchen. So just try to consider it an extension for the entire twenty years I've known you. Pretend I'm part of the wall again. You always did."

He didn't look at her, but heard the rustle of her clothes as she twitched around in obvious anger at him. "I didn't ignore you! We were friends. *Always.* And good friends. Until now. Until you lost your arm, and along with it every ounce of the sweet, caring, fun person who I used to know and love."

He lifted his eyes in surprise, since she rarely went on the offensive. He couldn't think of one time he'd ever witnessed Gretchen being snarky, rude, or impudent with anyone. Even if the person deserved it. Like he did.

She suddenly slapped her hand over her mouth as her eyes widened in horror, and started shaking her head. "I didn't mean that. I shouldn't have said that."

"Don't apologize. I prefer honesty to your feeble, polite bullshit."

"It's not bullshit. I am polite. And I always mean it. You act like I purposely try to sound trite. It's not like that. And it's not fake."

No, it wasn't. And of course, he knew that. It was part of why he always felt the need to protect her. She was too nice to everyone around her, even those who didn't deserve it. When they were young, she was often asked to do much more than her fair share of any work, or pegged to do the chores or jobs no one else wanted, simply because she was too nice to refuse. Too genuinely kind to even stick up for herself. She never once realized how patronizing Will was to her; or how often everything else took higher priority over her. It was always about him getting his shit together, rather than doing this or that for Gretchen. She, however, never realized that Tony always had her back.

She suddenly stood up and shoved her chair behind her. "If you'll excuse me now, I'm going to the restroom."

She marched off into the crowd and he sighed deeply as he watched her go.

Chapter Six

WILL JOINED TONY AS Gretchen, Jessie and Vickie started dancing together with a group of smiling, happy girls. They stared at the girls for a while, nursing their drinks. Finally, Will nodded towards Gretchen and said, "Do I have to say it?"

"Say what?"

"What I should have said a decade ago. We're over. Done. There's nothing between us. There hasn't been in a long time."

His mouth went dry. "Why should I care?"

"Because you do. You always did. We both know that. We just ignored it for too long. I'm not sure what your strategy is here, being a dickhead and all isn't the usual means to get a woman to notice you; but hell, I guess she's here, so maybe it's working. But whatever you're doing, it has nothing to do with me anymore. Look, I should have said this right after she divorced me, but maybe I wasn't ready for it. Whatever. I'm saying it now. Ask her out. You've wanted to for more than twenty years. You're free and clear to do so now."

"Screw off, Will. I wasn't waiting for your permission. Believe it or not, the no arm-thing works in my favor. Many young, sweet girls, filled with pity, nearly fall to their knees in sympathy for me. Sympathy, which they easily confuse with sex. Watch the waitress. She hasn't quit eyeing my sleeve since she first spotted me. She'll invite me home tonight."

Will fastened his glaring eyes on him. "You just won't stop, will you? I wasn't talking about just anyone. I don't care what you pretend, or how you play it, you want much more than that. You want far more than to just get laid by the waitress, and we both know it. I don't get your insistence on being such an ass, but fine, I'll deal with it. Just know this, we are now friends, and it doesn't matter how long you choose to punish me for Gretchen. Both for how I screwed up with her, and because you always wanted her. I suppose it's easier to hate me in a way. I tossed away, carelessly what you most wanted. But in my defense, I was a stupid, idiotic jock, who really didn't know any better. I never had a real relationship before Gretchen. And Gretchen never needed me. Not really. She didn't demand very much from me. The only thing that changed my outlook was witnessing what Jessie went through. So, hell, can't you forgive me?"

"I don't want Gretchen."

"You never said it out loud, but it never changed; it was always there between us."

He stretched out his legs before him. "Okay, fine. We're friends. Just shut the crap up with all your moaning and groaning about relationships and feelings. Did you start attending therapy with your wife? Or were you always so sensitive?"

Will laughed, and slapped his back. "You have undeniably become a complete and total jerk-off."

Tony's mouth finally tilted up on one side.

The girls returned to the table and it became very apparent that the drinks had worked their magic on Vickie. She was nearly falling over as she walked.

Gretchen's smile seemed less forced, but she could still walk steadily enough. She sat down with the smooth elegance that so defined who she was. Will was a fool for losing her. A fool, perhaps, that he should forgive. Maybe seeing Will more often wouldn't be so bad. That was a contributing part to his confusion. As a friend, there was no one better than Will. No one more loyal. Or reliable. Or who always had your back. That was Will. Yet, he never proved that to Gretchen, and Tony failed to understand why.

Still, it was time to let it go. Before anyone else except Will figured out what he really felt for Gretchen all these years.

The waitress came back and delivered another drink. She stayed chatting for a while. When she left, Tony nudged Will and handed him the napkin with the girl's phone number on it. A number he never asked for.

"No shit?" Will said, his eyes widening in surprise.

"What?" Gretchen asked, peeking across the table to see what Will was frowning over.

Will slid it back to Tony. "He managed to get her phone number without even asking."

Tony smirked at Will's surprised grimace. "Told you. It works wonders."

"What does? What did you do? I didn't see you even glancing up at her."

"The arm. Or lack thereof. Some like it for the freak factor, while others are so sorry for poor me, they don't care about anything else."

Gretchen's mouth dropped open. "You pick up woman because you're—"

"An amputee? Yeah."

"That's… awful. That's an awful thing to do. And an awful thing to use a woman for."

79

He leaned back and grinned. "No, it's really a beautiful thing. And just about the only damn good thing about it."

Will finally laughed along with him as Gretchen sniffed in disdain. "I can't believe you're encouraging that, Will Hendricks. It's an awful, deceptive thing to do. All of it. Let alone, to seek out a woman who wouldn't even get how life-changing it is."

Tony's smile faded. "I don't want them to see how life-changing it is. I just want to get laid."

Donny joined in. "He's right. Sometimes you don't want a girl to get you; you just want her to want you. Hell, you gotta use whatever you can."

Gretchen's lips pursed in disapproval. What else was new? Tony either disappointed, disturbed, or downright pissed people off nowadays. He flicked a few coins of change on the table as a tip before the conversation swung towards more generic things. Jobs, daily routines, the trivialities that kept them all so busy, and meant even less, at least, in Tony's estimation. He leaned back and said very little with his hand tucked into his jeans pocket. *Shit.* He had nothing to add. No job. No mortgage. No car. No friends. No chores. No daily events. Nada. Nothing. He soon grew bored, especially after Will and Jessie departed early, saying they were worried about being out too late for Christina. Another thing he'd never have: kids. Who needed such burdens?

"Let's hit it, Donny. I'm tired."

Donny jerked back in surprise, and his face flushed. "Oh, uh, I was going to take Vickie home. Do you mind hitching a ride with Gretchen?"

"What?" Gretchen spoke before Tony could protest. The horror on her face was obvious. Vickie leaned over and whispered something into Gretchen's ear and she again, pursed her lips. At least, Tony wasn't

the only fountain of fault and disappointment; so was little sis, it seemed. She nodded and glanced up at Tony as Vickie rose to take Donny's arm, which he offered to steady her.

Gretchen swallowed and said, "So, I guess we got ditched. I didn't see that coming."

Tony wished he could have hit his brother. Instead, he merely nodded. "You didn't deduce that they were both working up to getting laid?"

She blushed even though she was thirty-five years old. Didn't she see what Donny and Vickie were doing? Rubbing up on each other as they pretended to dance? Vickie's conveniently torn shirt left little to the imagination. Donny was probably in for a hell of a night. Gretchen seemed put out by it. Even annoyed.

Gretchen stood up and Tony followed after slipping the waitress's napkin into his pocket. She smiled and winked, keeping a watchful eye on him. He realized it, and trying not to hurt her feelings, pretended the number was important to him. Too bad, it wasn't. Not much was anymore. Sex included. He did it sometimes. But not as often as he could. Or should. Or used to. He just couldn't muster enough damn energy to find it worth pursuing or bothering with.

He followed Gretchen out front, not failing to notice her ass swinging in the jeans she wore. Her long thighs twitched as she walked. He could imagine himself, however, bothering with Gretchen.

She stopped beside her sedan. "Do you want to drive? I'm fine, but I wouldn't mind just riding."

He shook his head and leaned his arm on the hood as he replied, "Can't. Don't have a license."

"You what?" Her voice rose higher.

"No license. I never bothered to renew it after I got back. There are restrictions on driving with a disability. I never felt like dealing with it. So I quit driving."

"Oh." She bit her lip again. Obviously, now she regretted asking. Like most people, the thought about any restrictions he now had to observe never even crossed her mind. He could drive, probably; it just seemed more of a pain than not.

Without another word, she got in and sat down. He followed suit. Clicking his seat belt as she started the car and backed out, he stared out the passenger window.

After several minutes of silence, she put her turn signal on and switched lanes. The passing headlights swept over her profile. "Just so you know… my sister, most likely, will cause trouble for Donny. I hate to say it. But it's true."

"What kind of trouble?"

"She's… kind of known for being melodramatic. And causing trouble."

"Donny's smart. He doesn't do dumb or melodramatic. He'll probably just sleep with her, and that'll be that. She *is* hot."

Gretchen's mouth tightened. "She is. But she's much more than that."

"They were going home together to have sex. You knew that, right? I mean, I'm not saying anything that isn't true."

"Yes. I realize that. You don't have a single sentimental bone left inside you, do you? Sometimes it is more than that, you know."

"I guess. But you were watching the same bumping and grinding that I saw. Do you really think they're verging on the start of a sweet romance?"

She stifled a groan. "No. But, the thing is, men get really into Vickie. I'm not sure why. She has an effect over her boyfriends that's hard to explain. She ends up using them sometimes. For money. Or attention. Or gifts. Just warn Donny, okay? He's a nice guy, and probably won't see her coming."

"I'm surprised you'd bad-mouth your own sister."

"I don't mean to. She's been married three times and had passels of boyfriends. She doesn't mean to be so... so needy, for lack of a better word. She just is. And I just wanted to let you know what she's like, so you could let Donny know. I love Vickie, but I would never want to date her. I was hoping Donny might see right through her. But he seemed as taken with her as all the other men."

Tony shook his head. "I wasn't. I could see her game from ten feet off. Donny, however, was more than a little star-struck by all the attention she was batting his way. I'd warn him, but he wouldn't listen to me. Besides, he's a little angry with me right now."

She scoffed. "I wonder why that is? You purposely try to antagonize everyone around you. He's obviously been doing a lot for you in the past two years. As much as your parents. So, be nice to them. I mean, it seems the least you could do."

"Yeah, Donny's been good to me."

"Then quit blaming him and everyone else for what happened to you. They didn't do it. *Obviously*. And Will didn't do it. No offense, but you enlisted with the United States Army, and you had to know there was some risk in that. You didn't sign up for a job manufacturing canned soup; you signed up to be an infantry soldier."

Tony let out a long, slow whistle through his teeth. "Jesus, pull the gloves off Gretchen Hendricks, and look who she becomes."

Gretchen gritted her teeth. "I see what you do. You deflect everyone like a mirror in the sun. Well, I decided after our last fun, little scuffle, that you aren't going to do it to me anymore. Answer me one question: why do act this way to people who have done nothing wrong, but offering you their love and support?"

He twisted around and glared out the passenger window, surprised Gretchen called him out. Fisting his hand and releasing it, over and over, was something he learned in therapy to ease his rage, which now threatened to explode from his throat.

"Tony?" she pressed. "Please, won't you answer me?"

"Because I can't stand their pity. Like I can't stand yours."

"Pity, sorrow, sympathy. Those are not unnatural reactions or responses to what happened to you. You have them for yourself too. You're drowning in unhealthy amounts of sarcasm and bitterness. It's to be expected for awhile. But you can't keep treating everyone as you do. Donny is so fed up, he's going to quit coming around, Tony. Even your parents are exasperated. I know it seems impossible, but you *can* kill love. Even unconditional love."

"Oh yeah? How much do I owe you for this impromptu session aimed at recovering my mental health, Dr. Hendricks?"

She inhaled sharply. "I don't deserve that. I wasn't psychoanalyzing you. I was pointing out that you're such a jerk to your own family, if you don't stop, everyone will quit trying, and eventually leave you all alone to stew in your own festering cesspool."

"You got all this from one dinner? No offense, but you don't know shit about my life."

"No offense? I *do* take offense. I take offense for how you talk to me and everyone else around you. I take offense to your crude, rude phrases that don't advance conversations and accomplish nothing beyond making the other person feel small and bad." She turned slightly and met his gaze before she eyed the traffic in front of them. "People only want to reconnect with you. People like me. But I won't bother if you continue to act like this."

He blew air out of his lips. "You only want to be around me for how sad it makes you feel. My arm is gone and yours is not. It's guilt, Gretchen. Guilt is what everyone feels when they encounter me."

She shook her head as the shadows passed over her face. "No. It's not. I thought about what you said earlier. About me not noticing you as anything but part of the wall. And you know what? You're right; but that doesn't make me a bad person. I was involved with someone for over a decade. I was *in* a relationship. I wasn't supposed to notice other guys. Or boys. Or men. Age doesn't matter. I was committed to Will. Since I stayed committed and didn't look around, it could be considered a positive aspect of my personality. Not a rude flaw as you try to spin it. I refuse to apologize for being trustworthy. Or monogamous. Or loyal. I will not be punished for being a good girlfriend."

Silence thickened the dark between them. He kept his fist clenched and his eyes pinned out the window. Finally, she said softly, "The thing is, you're also right about something else. It was seeing your missing arm that prompted me to do more than say hello and just pass you in the grocery store, never to see you again. I think you called that right. If not for your amputation, I would have thought it was nice to run into you again and just moved on. I would not have been invited to dinner by Donny, or have any interest in going."

The car swung into his parents' driveway. She stopped and turned her body so she was facing him.

"The thing is, your amputation was so horrifyingly sad and unfair, that I wanted to do something for you. Anything. Whatever I could do to help you. So, yeah, you're right; it is pity. I'm sorry if you don't like that. But the primary reason I came to dinner was because I felt sorry about what happened to you."

Right on his lips, he wanted to snarl *fuck you* to her. Instead, he clenched his jaw and kept his gaze focused outside. His entire body froze when he felt something on his leg. Glancing down at her hand, he saw her slender, white, long fingers and painted nails, resting on his knee. "Tony?"

He finally lifted his eyes to hers.

She licked her lips and his focus narrowed onto her tongue. She suddenly lifted her hand off him and smiled as she threw her shoulders back, saying, "The thing is: I don't feel pity for you now. It's hard for me to pity you. You won't even allow me to sympathize. So that's fine. You don't have my sympathy. You don't get my apologies, or my help or my pity. You simply have my attention. Congratulations, Tony, I now give a fuck what happens to you. And unlike your brother or your parents, I don't think I care about how nice I am anymore."

No one but Donny ever called Tony out on his bullshit. And not once had he ever heard Gretchen use the F-word. Never. She rarely swore. His eyes found hers, and she suddenly smiled sweetly, but tilted her head, indicating that he should go.

He opened the door handle and got out, almost stumbling from leaving too quickly and not catching his balance. He stared after her car. What the hell did she mean? He had her attention? What was she up to? He didn't know what to do or think. He shook his head, not believing for five minutes that Gretchen would bother with him past looking at him in her rearview mirror. She never had before. Why would she start now? A missing arm only had so much power when people were busy.

Chapter Seven

THE PHONE RANG FIRST thing Saturday morning. Gretchen was barely out of bed, and cutting up a cantaloupe to eat. She answered while still chewing on the juicy fruit.

"Gretchen, I'm in love."

Vickie. Gretchen grabbed her forehead to relieve the headache suddenly brewing that her sister's screeching voice and upcoming melodrama would do nothing but exacerbate.

"It's been less than twelve hours." Vickie rarely caught the dry, sarcastic edge to Gretchen's tone.

"Time isn't relevant. We haven't even gone to sleep yet. We were up all night. Talking... and oh my, the sex. So good, it's unheard of. All of it is. I've never felt like this before."

Yes, she had. Or at least she proclaimed the same statement on six different occasions that Gretchen could think of offhand. However, they weren't usually the very next morning. It was normally a few weeks, or more. She sighed, anticipating a sudden, giant blow-up and then the crash. Poor Donny. But what could she do? Warning him to avoid her was going against her sister. And besides, as Gretchen knew from past experience, Donny wouldn't believe her. He'd think she was simply exaggerating Vickie's sordid history, or just jealous.

Having become so drawn to her sister's brilliance, like a moth to a flame, he'd simply refuse to see what was right there in front of him.

"Vickie, maybe you need to slow down a bit. There's no hurry, is there? Just start dating and see what happens..."

Vickie didn't hear one word she said. She was off and running for longer than half an hour, giving Gretchen a detailed recap of nearly everything she and Donny had done over the last twelve hours. Gretchen held the phone away from her ear to avoid hearing some of it. Lord! Did Vickie never learn? And in no time, there she'd be, cleaning up her little sister's mess again. Her headache expanded into her temples.

She soon hung up, frustrated and a little despondent over the never-changing cycle of her baby sister. She fielded other phone calls then, from both Tracy and her mom, who also received similar glowing reports from Vickie, and were as worried and exhausted of the cycle as Gretchen was. It might have been time to simply cut Vickie off. Here she was, criticizing Tony's brother and his parents for enabling his outrageous behavior to continue, while ironically, she and her family did the same thing with Vickie. Enabling her. Maybe it was time for Gretchen to take her own damn advice. But then... her mother begged her to check in again and make sure Vickie was okay. And so, the cycle continued, because Gretchen couldn't stand to disappoint anyone in her family.

****

Tony accepted Will's insistence on hanging around him for another week until they were scheduled to fly back to Washington State, Will's new home. And Tony almost grudgingly had to admit it was kind of... *nice,* to hang out with Will again. Jessie wasn't so bad either.

She was kind of funny; especially when she put Will in his place in such a way that Tony could appreciate. She was also extremely kind to him without appearing uncomfortable, as most people were.

They were leaving on Saturday, and his mother invited them over for brunch, along with Donny, Vickie and Gretchen. Tony sucked in a sigh at hearing the news. He'd done more socializing in the last ten days than he had for the last two years, combined. He wasn't fond of it either. He looked forward to Sunday, when everyone would return to their homes, their work, as well as their lives, and forget all about him.

Gretchen trailed her sister. She ducked her head in a shy smile when her gaze caught Tony's. He felt her presence and her smile, which thrilled him right down to the tingling of his toes. What was it about her? Why did she still cause such a physical reaction inside of him just by being in the room? He had reacted to her the same way ever since he was thirteen years old. It was ridiculous. And all it did now was illustrate what a schmuck he had become.

Donny and Vickie cuddled while speaking in hushed tones between themselves. Donny's eyes were glazed over with something Tony had never seen in his usually smart, savvy brother. He was so snowed by Vickie Moore, he couldn't even raise his head to join the conversation. She was, apparently, the most scintillating woman in existence. Tony could hear their giggling, and rolled his eyes at their cow-eyed interactions.

Gretchen and he exchanged a look across the table. Maybe she did call it right, and he should have tried to at least warn Donny. But, looking at him now, he feared he was already too late. Donny and Vickie had his mother's attention. She was watching them with an expression that almost looked like glee on her face. She soon made a huge effort to draw Vickie into the conversation. Tony knew how she longed for both of her sons to get married and start families.

This time, at the meal, there was no near brawl. The conversation was light, easy and casual. They soon finished and dispersed into the living room or the kitchen to start cleaning up.

Alone now, Tony stretched his legs out and glanced down to find Christina crawling toward him. She tried to climb over his legs, but couldn't and nearly toppled over. He moved his leg gently and leaned down to steady her so she could grab onto his sweatpants to pull herself up. Patting her head, he offered her his finger to grab onto. She looked up at him, drool running over her chin before her gummy mouth smiled with delight. She used his leg like a handrail and walked nearly all the way to his chair before she stopped and laughed. Why was she smiling so joyfully? He had no clue. She gurgled and shrieked, so he chuckled and put a hand on her head to pat her. She gurgled all the more, then grabbed his hand, and guided his finger into her wet, gooey mouth where she proceeded to chew on his finger. He cringed, but patiently allowed her to drool all over him. *Ick.* What else could he do? Pull his hand back? She wouldn't understand his reason and it might have even made her cry. So he let her gummy jaws chew on his finger.

"Look at that. You can smile."

He glanced up to find Jessie smirking at him, with one eyebrow raised in surprise. He made sure to scowl again. "Yeah, I can smile."

"I wouldn't have guessed you like babies."

"I like babies just fine. They can't be blamed if they say or do anything stupid."

Jessie laughed. "God, you even got me beat on being the super cynic. That's something I didn't think was possible."

He eyed her. "I'll admit it surprised me that Will's ceaseless optimism hasn't completely brainwashed you yet. He's pretty good at that."

She sat in the chair near him and put her arms out for Christina to hold as she started to waddle her way. Christina reached for her mother's arms with a squeal. "He can't help being so good. You know that. Don't hold it against him."

Tony shook his head in near amusement. "You're really not anything like what I pictured as his wife."

She pushed her dark hair behind her ear. "No. I always come as a surprise to people. But then again, so are you, as his friend."

Tony inclined his head. She had him there. "I'm sure you don't think too highly of me."

"You were nice to my baby when no one was watching. That's enough character reference for me. Besides, Will thinks the world of you; and that means something."

"Will's been a good friend. I guess I forgot that for awhile."

"Maybe you could remember it and try to forgive him for all the things you think he did wrong."

He nodded. "You're good, Will's wife. Yeah. I could do that."

She smiled and sighed as Christina was now racing away on all fours. "Well, we're off again."

Tony watched Will move quickly to block Christina before she could reach the stairs. She giggled and plopped down on her butt. Grinning down at her, Will lifted her up so she was over his head. She reached for his face and giggled with laughter. Her drool ran down in strings onto Will's face, but he didn't flinch, or rub it away. He grinned right back at his daughter and tickled her softly to maximize her already infectious laughter. *Ick.* Tony shuddered a bit at the drool. But Will manned up and didn't even wince or cringe. It was a rare sight for him: seeing his muscle-bound, former warrior friend cooing in strange, nonsensical words, and using a baby-like voice as he smiled and baby drool clung to his face. Huh. It appeared that many more things had pulled a one-eighty from Will's former life.

Gretchen came in and smiled as she patted Christina's back. Did it hurt her to see the baby? Did she picture the baby she might have had with Will? Or Will as the father he could have been to *her* baby? Again, the crux of why their relationship on his end had always been so complicated for him: *Gretchen.* Yet, Gretchen never came between them in Will's mind. Only his.

The Hendrickses soon collected their belongings and little Christina. They both hugged Tony and wished him well, while promising to visit again soon. They made the rounds with the rest of the group and soon left. Tony actually felt a little ping near his heart. *What?* Almost a tinge of sadness at seeing them go. It was a new sensation. He was usually glad when visitors left.

As their car pulled out of the driveway, he glanced up to find Gretchen's gaze still fastened on him. She said few words to him, and he avoided looking at or speaking to her. He didn't know why. He didn't know what she meant the other night. And he, sure as hell, was good and ready for everyone to not know any more about him and leave him the hell alone.

He claimed to be fatigued before loping down the stairs, anxious to get away. The sight of his happy brother, and the train wreck girl, now wrapping him around her finger, irked him. Mostly, however, he yearned to get away from the only person in two years who could make his heart beat faster just by her mere presence.

****

"Gretchen? What are you doing here? Tony's still sleeping. He rarely gets this early."

Gretchen smiled at Leila, and nodded at Lewis before Leila swept her arm, indicating for her to come in. Gretchen showed up there at nine a.m. Leila led her into the kitchen and waved for her to sit down as she quickly poured her some coffee. Gretchen added some creamer while contemplating how to approach this. They might not accept or appreciate her input; but, after witnessing Tony's behavior, she didn't care. She did care, however, about what happened *to* Tony and *for* Tony. Be it based on their history, or losing his arm, or because she suddenly noticed him as something more than just Will's best friend, the reasons really didn't matter; she intended to address Tony's injury and the life he tried to shun and avoid living.

"That's fine. I wanted to talk to you both anyway."

Leila leaned across the counter and refilled the coffee in her cup. "Sure. I'm glad to have you here. Always was. I hope you know that. It means a lot, your returning to Tony's life."

She smiled. That's what they thought now; just wait until they heard the next thing out of her mouth. "I think Tony needs help."

Leila's smile wavered slightly. "I know. We know. We try, but he refuses to accept most of it."

Gretchen sipped the hot liquid to hide the look of shock as she thought to herself. *Could they really think Tony wouldn't accept help?* All he did was sit around idly, soaking up pity and swimming in self-loathing, while his mother performed all the activities he couldn't, or wouldn't.

"No offense, but all Tony does is require help. You need to kick him out. He needs to find something significant to do, something for which he must be accountable. He needs a purpose and a reason to motivate him and force him to deal with his amputation. Allowing him to fester, like a boil, idly passing the time by doing nothing in your basement, isn't helping."

Lewis dropped the cup he took out from the cupboard overhead; and Leila choked on the sip of coffee she'd just taken. "What!"

Gretchen cleared her throat and averted her gaze; now she stared out the window. She tapped her finger on the counter and decided it was better to be quick and get straight to the point with them. "You need to stop doing everything for him. That includes his laundry, and buying his choice of groceries and cooking his meals. You need to make *him* do something. Anything that has even a little bit of value. Whether it's a job, or handing out pamphlets at the local hospital. I don't care. Just urge him to find something to do that has a goddamned point to it. And no more coddling him. He does nothing, because you allow him to. He is intentionally rude and abrasive because he feels like shit when he thinks about his lifestyle. I think we all get that. So, if he won't take any initiative and make the first step towards living without his arm in a constructive manner, I think we have to."

Leila shook her head. "You've been around him exactly three times. You had no contact with him for over five years. How dare you come back now and tell us our methods for dealing with this are failing. You don't know. You don't know anything. So don't you dare sit there and suggest that I kick my handicapped, irrevocably injured son out of my house! I WILL NOT! Do you hear me? I would never do such a thing to him. I am so fortunate he came back to me still alive, and I am grateful for that every single day. A dozen steps to one side or the other, and Tony would have died. My son, *not yours*, would be *dead.* You didn't even stay in touch with him. Some fair-weather friend you are. So don't dare sit there and tell me what *I* need to do. I will *never* turn my back on my son who barely came back to me."

Gretchen's mouth dropped halfway through Leila's passionate speech. Leila nearly screamed as she paced the kitchen.

Lewis put a hand on her shoulder, and glanced at Gretchen with a kind smile. "I know what you think you know, but you really don't. You don't know about this. All the counseling schools in the world can't really teach you what this is like. You don't know what it's like for a man like Tony. Or for parents like us. You simply can't be serious about coming here just to tell us to kick our son out. Forget it."

Gretchen slowly closed her mouth. Then, with a hasty nod, she ran her fingers through her hair anxiously. "Okay, perhaps you're right. But can't you see this isn't doing him any good. He's no longer *Tony.* He's not even nice anymore."

"I don't need him nice, I just need for him to survive."

Gretchen pressed her lips together and stifled her reply. Okay, perhaps she failed to assess the extent of grief this catastrophe created not only for Tony, but also his parents. However, there was such a thing as enabling someone. And also tough love. Or making someone more independent.

She tried a different tactic. "You saw, didn't you? When Donny and he nearly came to blows the other night? I didn't imagine that. I didn't make that up. Donny has had it with him up to here," she said as she raised her hands to chin level. "I'm telling you right now: you're about to lose one son if you don't start trying to change the other. You might think that's okay, but I don't. And I still know what you're currently doing isn't in Tony's best interest. You can hate my reasons, and hate how I say this, and hate me for saying it, but you're not doing him any favors."

Leila gripped the counter. Her breathing was audibly accelerated. "Do you know what the suicide rate is for Afghanistan vets? Do you, Gretchen the Doctor? Do you know how often it happens? Do you know what it's like to check a room each morning, and get flooded with relief at finding the person inside it hasn't taken a gun to his head overnight?"

"*Leila*," Lewis warned softly.

Gretchen gasped at the vivid, gut-twisting image. "No. I don't."

"Thirty percent, Gretchen. Thirty percent of veterans from Iraq and Afghanistan have contemplated or attempted suicide. You see how unhappy Tony is. Can you begin to see my greatest fear?"

She closed her eyes and breathed in deeply. *No.* Her thoughts had never gone there. She never even considered how much Leila feared Tony would kill himself. He seemed unhappy, lazy, unmotivated, but not suicidal. Then again, Leila was right, and she did lose complete contact with him; and was only around him again for a handful of times. She had—

"I'm not going to kill myself."

Gretchen whipped around on her stool when Tony's quiet, deep voice sounded from behind her. He stood at the top of the stairs, completely still, wearing sweats and a t-shirt. It was short-sleeved and he let the left sleeve flop loosely. His hair was down, falling well past his shoulders, and ratty. His beard descended right down into his neck, as she was sure he hadn't shaved or trimmed it in days.

"Tony!" Leila screeched, standing up more erect. "We were…"

"I know what you were doing." He stepped forward and she waited for the inevitable, explosive litany of curses at finding Gretchen there, discussing *him*, with his parents, behind his back, like he was a naughty teen in need of proper disciplining. Instead, he said nothing, but passed by Gretchen with only a quick, vacant glance before heading toward his mother, whom he wrapped in an one-armed embrace. Leila wilted into him, her head only coming as high as his collarbone, and tears filled her eyes when she clutched his shirt. "I'm sorry. We shouldn't have been talking about you. I was trying to explain something to Gretchen. Please don't be mad, Tony."

He patted her back. "I'm not mad, Mom. It's okay." He glared at Gretchen over his mother's head and his brown eyes sparked in anger. But his jaw was clamped shut.

Gretchen lowered her gaze as shame filled her for upsetting Leila so. It was obvious Tony had plenty to say about what she'd just put his mother through. Gretchen was a little bit humbled by the first display of affection and genuine concern she'd seen him show towards Leila. To be honest, it warmed her heart, since she was pretty convinced he felt nothing, for anyone. But he did care for his mother.

He mumbled to Leila, "It's okay. Gretchen was just being *a friend*. I'll talk to her. You don't have anything to worry about. Neither of you do. I promise."

His gaze was still pinned on her as he said "friend." Lewis patted his shoulder and Leila finally wiped her eyes and nodded. "We'll let you two be alone."

Leaving the kitchen, his parents went into the den down the hall. Tony watched them and his gaze lingered until the door clicked shut. Then he turned towards her, and the quiet, controlled demeanor vanished with the clicking of the door. His gaze unexpectedly burned into her. Blazing. Trying to incinerate her. She gulped down the intimidating lump of fear now lodged in her throat, realizing she not only provoked the tiger, but probably lit it's tail on fire.

"What the fuck were you doing?" His tone remained low and quiet so his parents couldn't hear him; but the nasty retort sounded deep and bitter. "How could you go into that with her? Do you know how much she's been through?"

Gretchen stood up slowly, sliding off the stool. Okay, she obviously miscalculated how well Leila was doing with Tony. She should not have approached her with this. But... Fine. She'd approach him instead.

"I'm sorry. I didn't know she'd take it that hard. I had no idea, to be honest. Or that you'd care so much about how she feels. I'm glad to see you still have *some* feelings left inside you."

"I woke up to my mother screaming about me dying. Do you think I enjoyed that? What were you doing? What did you say to her?"

Gretchen stared into Tony's furious eyes. *Leila was his Achilles heel.* He cared more about Leila than he did his missing arm. No, that's not true... both of his parents mattered to him, and he still cared about both of them.

So far, it was the only thing that gave her a glimpse of the old Tony. Now, Gretchen understood why his parents let things stand the way they were. They were right, too. She didn't take it as far as she should have. She did not fully consider the fear they still lived with every day. The nightmare that nearly took their son from them was far from over. She licked her lips, stiffened her spine, and nodded. She got it now; and knew where they were coming from, as well as why they couldn't force Tony to do anything or accept any help.

But she could. Yes. She could do that. He might, end up hating her for it; but she could deal with that. Tony thought she was so nice. Well, he was in for a big surprise now. In the name of healing and therapy, Tony never dealt with likes of her. He should have asked Jessie about what Gretchen did for her. How unkind she could be.

It was what she would now do for him.

"I told her she had to kick you out."

His jaw tightened and she waited for the explosive reply. Instead, he scooted back until his butt hit the counter, which he leaned against, while assessing her. He lifted his eyebrow and inquired, "And you expected my parents to do that simply because you asked?"

She furrowed her brow. Stated that way, it was completely unreasonable that she'd come here expecting to do that simply because she suggested it. She should have begun her suggestions for Tony as something smaller, and way more easily accomplished. Something way more saner, and a lot less overwhelming. Like perhaps, Tony could try washing his own shirts. Coming here demanding Leila and Lewis kick him out... okay, a huge colossal mistake. "Well, no... I guess they wouldn't do that just because I suggested it."

He shook his head, and his expression seemed puzzled. "Why? Why did you come over here first thing just to tell them that?"

"I told you before. I'm going to help you. You're just probably not going to like my methods of helping."

He turned and rummaged around the cabinet, emerging with a box of toaster pastries. He popped them into the toaster and contemplated them. "I don't need help. There is nothing to help me with. This just is what it is. Besides, what exactly would you do?"

He didn't turn around towards her, so she contemplated his back. It was long and narrow, tapering down to his slim waist. The gray sweats, his standard uniform of late, barely hung onto his hips. The t-shirt stretched across his wide shoulders and hugged his lean lower back. Perfect, except... he was lopsided. His right arm looked strong and well developed on one side, and the other had nothing. It still managed to shock and surprise her. Even though she knew it was gone and expected it, the absence still startled her. He rarely let her look at him without frowning back in negative, rude glares. So she tried to sneak in all of her peeks when he didn't know. Her heart twisted at the loose armhole every single time she saw it.

She'd gone about this all wrong. She never took into account how upset and worried his parents still were for him. She had a lapse of judgment and let her emotions rule her mind, instead of remaining objective and relying on her clinical training. She temporarily forgot the psychologist that she was.

She needed to start with manageable steps. She nearly smacked her head against the table. How could she not have approached the Lindstroms with a more normal, sane approach? With a program in mind in which Tony could accomplish little things before she

101

demanded grand, sweeping gestures, like moving out and living alone. She cringed at her lack of foresight. She screwed up. But since she was still there, she wanted to tackle it. Despite whether the Lindstroms—any of them—wanted her to or not.

The toaster beeped and the pastries popped up. Tony grabbed one and starting eating it. After the fact, he mumbled, "You want one?"

"No. Thank you." She stood and got off the stool. "Tony?"

"What?"

"I'm sorry for how I approached this. I got… I don't know, excited, I guess, to get involved and inadvertently pushed my agenda way too far. Will you forgive me for that? And for upsetting your mother? I promise I won't do it again. Never like that."

He slowly nodded. "No, don't upset her again."

He didn't ask her to leave, so she chewed on her lower lip and pondered that. He should have technically insisted that she go home. He certainly could be rude enough to accomplish that if he wanted to. Somehow, even after bringing his mother to tears, he didn't want Gretchen to leave. He seemed to… what? Like her? Have a crush on her? She didn't think she ever had that effect on any man. No one. Not even Will seemed ever particularly smitten by her beauty or personality. But Tony…. was? Or had been once.

Well, now she was going to use it.

"Will you do something for me?" she kept her tone soft and sweet.

"What?" he grumbled, his back straightening. He knew that tone: he already anticipated that she was about to ask him to do something she knew he wouldn't want to.

"Would you come with me somewhere this week? Say… on Thursday?"

His entire body froze. "Where?"

"My office."

He drew in a breath. "As in your therapist's office? What do you want to do? Make me your newest patient?"

"No. That would be inappropriate. And it would never work, either. I'm not the kind of therapist you need. But I think you need one."

"I've had therapy. And I learned that no amount of talking in the world can regrow a limb."

"You're brimming with unresolved anger. Rage might be a better word."

"*Duh*. I know. I don't deny it." He turned away.

"Tony, there's a doctor in my practice who specializes in this kind of work extensively. He often works with veterans of any conflicts and treats all kinds of things from PTSD to the adjustments required for coming home. Anxiety. Depression. Anything else that happened as a result of being a soldier. Please, will you just meet with him once? What could it hurt?"

"I can't afford it," he mumbled without turning around. He grabbed a glass and a carton of milk from the refrigerator. After pouring it, he put the carton back and moved quickly. His motions were fluid and sure, although one-handed. It must have been very frustrating. Her heart pinged again in compassion. He was such a macho, independent man before. How must it have been to suddenly find yourself so limited and hampered by your own body? A body that for a decade was your main weapon and tool of the work you chose to do. And now… nothing.

"You don't have to pay for it. He already agreed to see you as a favor to me." Gretchen didn't inform him that she was providing free services for the child of one of *his* patients in return. Tit for tat. Tony didn't need to know, however, that it took her all week to make the arrangements. Now she just hoped her first blunder wouldn't make him throw her out the front door.

Taking his glass to the sink after downing it in three large gulps, he turned as she spoke. He leaned his hand on the counter and shifted his weight forward, while his eyes stared out the window at the normal, familiar, neighborhood scene from his childhood. He didn't answer her so she quietly stepped up behind him and finally touched his back. He jerked and withdrew as if she suddenly plunged a knife into him. Shifting away from her, he tucked his arm up against his chest.

"Please? Just once? Won't you do this? If not for me, or for yourself, then do it for Leila. You heard her. She was delirious with grief after one sentence from me. I didn't hammer her. She lost it from one simple suggestion I made. She is really afraid for you. Don't make her live with that fear if you can avoid it. You can't be that selfish. I just can't believe that. You can't want your mother to continually fear finding your dead body downstairs. If you do this one thing, it will signify to her that you do care about your life, and about her, and therefore, you won't simply end it all."

His intake of breath was sharp. "You don't sugar-coat anything, do you?"

"You mean, kind of like you?"

He glanced over his shoulder at her, lifting his lip in a half smile of appreciation. "Yeah, kind of like me. Fine. Whatever. If it'll ease my mom's mind, okay; why not? It won't hurt anything. Or help. But at least, she'll think it does."

Gretchen nodded, resisting the urge to argue or point out that it could help a lot.

"It's scheduled for four o'clock. I'll pick you up at three-thirty."

"Hell, I get a free ride out of the deal too? Great. Wanna take me by the pharmacy? I need to grab some things. Kill two birds, you know?"

There was no end to his antagonism. She smiled, despite her annoyance. "Yes, I'll drive you. Extracurricular errands included. Just as long as you promise to see him."

She turned away and quickly entered the den where she apologized to both Leila and Lewis, before informing them about the counselor. Tears filled Leila's eyes, only this time, they were from joy. "You got him to agree to it?"

"Yes. He's going." She didn't elaborate on all the less positive details or the less than positive attitude Tony responded with, as they didn't need to know any of that.

"Oh, Gretchen. That's so wonderful. Thank you. Just... thank you, for taking a genuine interest in his welfare. For trying. Please, don't give up, no matter how hard he makes it on you."

Gretchen squeezed Leila's hand, touched by the tears she saw shining on her eyelids. "I won't, Leila. I promise you. I won't disappear again."

Chapter Eight

TONY ENTERED THE WAITING room and withheld a groan of dismay. Windows provided a panoramic view of the landscaped grounds surrounding the office building where Gretchen worked. Obviously, counseling people paid off. Her office was just off Front Street in downtown Calliston. It had a new brick-and-cedar shingle exterior, a brick-paved entry, high ceilings, and was imbued with plenty of natural light.

Tony said no more than three words to Gretchen on the way there. He didn't bother to shower for the appointment and wore his favorite sweats, t-shirt, and signature ponytail. What was the point in getting more groomed than that? She wore a tan business suit and low heels. When her hair swung around her face, it was as clean and perfect as the rest of her. She was silent after he snarled his answers to her two inquiries about how his week had been; and wisely ignored him.

Glancing at his sneakers as he followed her inside, he could only think, *Damn he did not want to do this*. He saw a couple across the room, and a single woman to his left, reading. He threw himself into a chair, very much alone, on the other side.

Gretchen spoke in subdued, quiet tones to the receptionist. She smiled and tapped the counter before turning and approaching him. He hated how well modulated Gretchen's tone of voice always was. And how she smiled so kindly to everyone around her. And how her legs seemed to go on forever past the edge of her conservative skirt. He glared down at his feet. He was slouched in the chair, his legs outstretched and his ankles crossed. His scruffy, once-white sneakers, nervously bounced.

"So, you're all checked in. It should be only a short wait. Dr. Hart is running a few minutes late. I don't have any appointments right now, so you can just knock on my office door when you're done."

He didn't raise his eyes or respond. She sighed. Her hips, thighs and feet were the only parts of her in his line of vision. She finally turned and gave up.

He sat there for a long while, glaring angrily at his feet, and only turned when he felt a new presence. A little girl stood there on scabby-kneed legs, wearing jean shorts and a t-shirt, beside him. She smiled sweetly before taking the chair next to him. He frowned and glanced around. There was plenty of other seating. Why would she sit next to him?

After only thirty seconds, she asked, "So, how did that happen?"

He glanced down. She had dark, black hair, that was long and straight and drawn into a scraggly ponytail. Her big, blue eyes were staring right at his left shoulder, wide open and curious.

"War," he mumbled.

Her mouth formed a giant "O." "Really? Like Afghanistan? We were learning about that in social studies."

"Yeah, like Afghanistan."

"So, you're a soldier?"

"I was. Not anymore."

"And… you lost your arm? That sucks."

She smiled and kept staring at his sleeve, which was pinned to his side. He finally sighed. "Yeah, it really sucks."

"Is that why you're here? To talk to Gretchen about it?"

"No. I'm not here to talk to Gretchen about it."

She bit her lip. "Why not? She's really, really nice."

"I take it you're here to talk to her?"

She shook her head, sending her ponytail flopping from one side of her head to the other. "Oh no. Not anymore. I used to. Now, we're just real good friends. I come here after school. I should probably go to her office. I just wondered why you didn't have an arm."

The girl hopped up, then smiled and waved as she walked into the door Gretchen disappeared behind. He stared after her, a little surprised, and the ghost of a smile curled his lips. He wished all people could be that easy, open, interested and at ease with his missing arm.

He scowled once again, however, when he heard his name called by an older man with glasses and short, gray hair.

****

"Arm-guy!"

Tony cringed while standing in the half open door of Gretchen's office. He barely arrived there before the dark-haired, little girl spotted him and made the exclamation. She hopped up from the floor where an explosion of paper surrounded her.

"Olivia. You mustn't talk like that." Gretchen stood up from her desk hastily. She went around her desk with a quick, weary glance his way. "That's not nice."

Olivia's little face fell and she bit her lip. "I didn't mean for it to sound mean."

Gretchen's face softened as she got down on her knees before the girl, while adjusting her skirt so it stayed properly together over her legs. She gently stroked the girl's down turned head. "I know, honey. But you really mustn't talk that way."

Gretchen turned towards him. "I'm sorry, Tony. She didn't mean anything by it."

He stepped into Gretchen's office and his eyes darted around for a quick survey, instantly feeling conspicuous. She was so impressive, and he *so* wasn't. Her office was a large room with windows that faced the courtyard, and allowed the light to flood inside. The carpet was a soothing, light blue, with matching walls and photos of pretty landscapes decorating them. Gretchen's desk was a dark-wooded, massive thing that was neatly organized and sat on one end of the room. The other end looked like a cross between a rec room and a kid's playroom. A wide variety of toys lined the shelves, with plenty of books and a huge array of colorful, educational playthings. A table and chairs took up one side, with a couch and chairs on the other. Beanbag chairs were haphazardly strewn about, as were baskets of more kinds of toys and an assortment of stuffed animals.

"It's okay," he mumbled.

"How did you two meet?"

Olivia jumped up. "I sawed him in the waiting room and asked where his arm went."

Gretchen bit her lip and Tony could tell she was trying to restrain a grin. "Uh, probably not the most polite thing to ask someone either, honey."

"Why? I just wanted to know."

Tony stepped inside, feeling lulled by the earnest question in the little girl's eyes. Gretchen met his gaze briefly before she turned back to the child. Olivia looked up at Gretchen with big, honest eyes.

"Because... it can hurt people's feelings when you say something so forward regarding things that are... different about them."

"But, I just wanted to know. I didn't want to hurt his feelings." She glanced up at him. "I didn't want to make you feel bad about it."

"You know what? Gretchen's right, and usually, you probably shouldn't draw attention to people's differences; but with me? I like it. I'd rather have people ask me about it and be honest. So you don't have to be sorry to me. I appreciate your interest."

She grinned, and the smile exploded up into her eyes. "Do you mean that? Mr. Soldier, I promise I won't ever ask questions about it again."

"You can call me Tony."

Gretchen slowly rose to her full height. "Tony, this is Olivia Carver."

Olivia stuck her hand out. He glanced down with surprise, and raised his hand to shake hers. "Pleased to meet you, Mr. Tony."

"Tony. Just call me Tony. I'm pleased to meet you too."

"Does it hurt?" She nodded her head towards his empty shoulder.

He blinked in surprise, thinking, in a strange way, it was kinda nice to meet her too. It had been a long time since he felt even remotely interested in anyone new. He wondered why she was seeing Gretchen. Olivia was direct and easy to tolerate because there was no wishy-washy discomfort regarding his arm. Just youthful curiosity.

"Uh... well, no. It doesn't really hurt. It just kinda feels weird."

Gretchen's gaze rose to his face. He could feel her eyes on him, searching for something more to clarify his statement.

"How could it feel weird if it's not there?"

"Olivia," Gretchen warned.

"No, it's okay. It feels weird because I sometimes think it is still there. But I know it's not. I get sensations, like I can move my arm. But I really can't. It doesn't make sense."

"Kinda like you know you feel things in your heart, but you can't see them? You just feel those feelings are there, even if they're not?"

He stepped back. The kid was sharp. Intuitive. He never heard it described that way before. "You know what? Yeah, kinda like that."

"Why don't you wear those fake ones? Or a hook? Those are cool! Like Captain Hook! You could look like Captain Hook."

Gretchen's mouth dropped. "Olivia, no. Don't talk like that."

Tony chuckled and dropped to a knee so Olivia and he were eye-to-eye. "Captain Hook is bad-ass, isn't he?"

Olivia was red-faced from Gretchen's rebuke and slowly raised her eyes before a tentative smile rounded her cheeks. "You can't say naughty words like that!"

Tony ruffled his hand in her hair. "I can't wear those. They need more of a stump than I have. You know, if I lost my arm here or here," he said, indicating two lower positions, "it would have been easier to use the fake ones or hooks. I don't like the feel of them anyway, so I just go one-armed."

She nodded her head. "My friend's sister has a retainer for her teeth, but she hates it and won't wear it because it bothers her."

Gretchen bit her lip and Tony could tell she was trying to restrain a grin. A smile slipped over her lips as she said finally, "Yeah, almost the same thing."

He met her gaze over Olivia's head. She pressed her lips together and shrugged as if to say, *sorry, she couldn't resist.* He finally tilted his head in understanding. "And I did wonder why you don't wear a prosthesis. Aren't there some that respond to your nerve endings, or some such thing?"

"There are. Most work better with a larger stump to attach them to. What I have isn't the best for most of them."

Her eyes ran down his face, and over the side of his injury. "I didn't realize that. So, it would have been a lot better to have some kind of…"

"Stump?" he supplied when she glanced away, blushing. "Yes, it would have been a degree better to have lost it a few inches lower."

She licked her lips. "That's not what I meant. I don't mean better…"

"I know what you meant," he interrupted. She pursed her lips together in a frown.

Gretchen cleared her throat finally and said, "Start to clean everything up, Liv. We need to take Tony home."

He finally met her gaze and she stared at him for a long moment before going to her desk and shuffling papers. He followed closer. "You chauffeur all your patients?"

"Olivia's not a patient. Well, she was a patient, years ago. Since then, I became friends with her family, and I help them out sometimes. I babysit her after school most days. She hangs out here. It's not real exciting for her, but she's a good sport about it, especially when I have a patient to see, and she has to wait in the waiting room."

"Oh." He waited for her to ask about his session. He stood with his legs parted, and his hand on his hip, ready to tell her what he thought of her old, prying, annoying doctor-friend. Finally, he asked, "Aren't you going to ask how it went?"

She lifted her eyes and took in his angry demeanor. Starting with his disreputable hair, she glanced over his wrinkled clothes and worn sneakers. "No. I doubt you'd have anything good to say. Nor am I the person you should share it with. I was just hoping you'd keep coming back for a while. Your decision to go brought tears to your mother's eyes."

He stared at her hard, and his eyes squinted. Finally, he snorted. "That's low, using my mother."

She flashed a smile. "It is. It is so low. But whatever works, I'll use."

He turned slightly and waved his hand around the office. "Impressive. This place. You."

She stilled, holding a file in her hand. He felt like a jerk when he saw her green eyes looking deeply into him. "Thank you, Tony. For saying so."

"Can we go, Gretchen?" Olivia called from across the now uncluttered office.

"I'm almost done here."

"Ah, please? Can't we go ride the elevator?"

"I can take her down," Tony interjected.

Gretchen paused, biting her lip and scrunching her face as if in disdain.

"If you trust me, that is," he challenged her.

Very softly, she said, "I trust you. Just, uh, you can't talk how you normally do. She's only eight. You can't say the F-word every other word in front of her."

He didn't say it every other word. Just sometimes. Sure. It was an explicit, forcible way to get his point across. But he wasn't a barbarian. He knew not to say it in front of a little kid. Jesus. He didn't also sustain brain trauma in the Army.

"I don't swear like that in front of little kids. Even *I* know that."

Her shoulders slouched and she smiled. "Good. Here are the keys. I'll be down in a few minutes."

Olivia was full of questions. She talked during the entire elevator ride down to the parking lot and for another ten minutes in the car. She asked every conceivable thing a person could about his arm. How did he lose it? What did it feel like it? How could he brush his teeth? On and on, she asked while becoming fascinated at how he managed to do anything.

Gretchen soon appeared and slid into the car, her skirt riding up her thigh a few inches. Still respectable, but a bit more skin than she ever showed. He glared out the window. Her hair swung around her face as she looked over her shoulder and back up at him. He liked the dark strands of her hair against the lighter blond. It was kind of surprising for conservative Gretchen.

He soon noticed Olivia twitching around strangely in the back, reaching for the floor and across the seat. He glanced back at her. She was keeping her left arm tightly next to her body. Gretchen noticed it too.

"What are you doing back there?" she asked, peeking at Olivia in her rearview mirror as she merged into traffic.

"Trying to get my shoe tied."

"Oh."

Olivia wasn't done. Tony already guessed what she was doing. He pressed his lips to hide the smirk.

"One-armed. It's not easy," Olivia commented.

Gretchen gasped. "Olivia!"

"What?" She met Gretchen's gaze in the mirror, completely confused what she'd done now.

"Don't mimic people. That's rude too."

"I'm not mimicking. I'm doing it. It's really hard. How do you do it, Tony?"

Gretchen slid a horrified, apologetic glance his way.

He twisted forward and untied his shoe before deftly retying it. Olivia half stood and half leaned forward to watch. Even Gretchen wanted to see, glancing between him and the road.

"How did you do that?! Show me! Show me!"

He pulled his foot up. "Cross one lace over the other. Wrap it around from behind to form a knot. Good. I have to put my foot down to show you the rest."

He leaned forward again and redid the process to that point, glancing back at Olivia. "Okay, now pull the inside lace toward your other shoe, and pin it down with that shoe."

"Oh! That's what I couldn't get past. The other shoe."

"Yeah, you have to use whatever you got. Okay, now pull the outside shoelace tight and wiggle your foot outward until the knot is secure. Now, tuck that lace into the tongue of your shoe. Take the first lace and loop it inside your back, and pull it through tightly, using your thumb, index and middle finger." He skillfully finished it.

Looking back at Olivia, he laughed. Olivia was barely able to hold the mess of laces in her small hands. "Just use your other hand."

"No. I want to do it like you."

"Well, maybe I can help you sometime, but not in a car."

He felt Gretchen's gaze on him and glanced up. She nodded towards his feet. "To be honest, I wondered how you did that. I mean, neither Leila nor Lewis were home when I showed up. I didn't know if you could tie it."

The fleeting glance at his shoes when she picked him up, which he thought came from disdain, might have only been curiosity about how he managed to do it. "You can always ask me, you know."

She twisted her mouth in a grimace. "No. See, I didn't know that. I didn't know you would welcome questions. You come off the complete opposite."

Oh. Well, hell, yeah, he did. That was true. Except to Olivia. "Well, you can ask. Quit chiding Olivia for trying to figure out the arm thing. It's confusing for any kid. They are always curious. She's just trying to process it. Let her."

She whipped her head toward him. "I know that! I'm a trained child psychologist. It's you I didn't think would be sensitive enough to tolerate it. I'm… well, really pleasantly surprised you do. So, okay, I'll quit chiding her."

They were at his house. He started to hop out when Olivia called out, "Bye, Tony. Will I see you next Thursday? I'll be at Gretchen's, so are you comin' again, too?"

"Yeah, Tony, are you coming again?" Gretchen asked softly, the challenge clear in her tone.

"You're good. I'll give you that. Like I could refuse with the little ears listening."

She smiled sweetly. "See you next week, Tony."

Chapter Nine

"SO I HEAR YOU have an angry, one-armed soldier who has been in love with you for twenty years. How come I've never heard about him?"

Gretchen bit her lip and smiled into the phone at Lindsey's greeting. "Hello to you too, Lindsey. You spoke to Jessie, I see."

"Oh my, did I. She had a lot to say about Will's friend, Tony Lindstrom. Tell me how come you haven't?"

"I didn't know I should."

"You should. Is he as Jessie described?"

"Depends. How did she describe him?"

"She said he was all scruffy, grungy, with kind of a bad-ass attitude, but hot. She seemed to think he was pretty hot. What do you think? Is she right?"

"Yeah. I guess if you could get past his snarling, glaring, awful attitude."

"So, he has a crush on you, huh? Has for like, twenty years Will said?"

Gretchen sat up straighter in her office chair. "Will said that?"

"Will said that. He said he told Tony to go for it, and finally ask you out."

Gretchen's heart froze. Her palms were instantly sticky. She took in a sharp breath. Did she want that? Was her reaction stemming from fear that he would? Or hope?

"And… what did he say?"

"He apparently snapped out something about not wanting you. He apparently doesn't like being told what to do, or so I'm gathering."

Her heart released. "No, he doesn't like being told what to do."

"Especially by Will Hendricks. Did he really quit speaking to Will because Will quit the Army for Jessie and not for you?"

"I—maybe. I mean, he said something like that the other night at dinner. But I can't believe he'd be that offended in my honor. I mean, by then, we weren't in contact, except randomly, and sometimes going months at a time without any correspondence."

"Well, Gretchen, I think you'd better face the facts: the guy's been after you for two decades."

"I can't believe that's the case."

"Sounds to me like that's the source of half his anger; you never saw him like that. You only saw Will, even after Will more or less neglected your needs. Wow. It's kind of flattering."

"There is nothing in him now that remotely flatters anybody or anything."

"He can't be all bad. Jessie said he was nice to Christina while no one was looking. Come on; a real asshole wouldn't be."

"He's just so angry. At a level I can't imagine taking on."

"Except he's a friend? I mean, you don't think of him in any other way, right?"

Did she? At first, she only bothered to greet him because of their history. The longer she was around him *now,* however, the less she remembered her friend-of-old Tony, or Will's friend Tony. Then suddenly, he *was* the new Tony. Why? Why was he so abrasive? And so hard to tolerate? Was it because there was actually something between them she never noticed before? Suddenly, Will had nothing to do with Tony and her. And neither did their adolescence.

"I don't know. First, he'd have to learn how to speak to me with a civil tongue."

Lindsey audibly sighed over the line. "Just make sure he gets that anger under control."

Gretchen smiled and stared out her office windows. Lindsey survived five years at the hands of her first husband's control and abuse. His unbridled rage resulted in him beating her up with sinister regularity.

"I promise you, no one will hurt me. Will would still be the first person I called. You can imagine in that case, there would be no sign of whoever hurt me. Ex or not. Will's still good for a few things."

"And Noah. Noah would do that for you too. He's just not as adept at it."

She laughed. "And Noah too."

Noah Clark was now Lindsey's boyfriend. He and Gretchen offered Lindsey sanctuary when she ran away from her sadistic and very dangerous ex.

"So what's new with you two? Are you finally going to put the poor guy out of his misery and marry him?"

Lindsey made a strangled sound. "I wish. I just... I can't convince myself to do it. When I think of marriage, all of these horrifying, awful images cloud my brain. When I think of Noah, on the other hand, I think of everything that's good in my life. Why would I want to merge the two? I don't think I could ever do it. He says he understands, and he's just fine with it. Do you think he's just saying that?"

"No. There's no one as committed as Noah Clark. Just make sure your decisions aren't determined by Elliot's ghost, but by your own desires. Don't be scared to get married because of what he did."

"I know. I know. I just don't want to yet."

"I think then, you shouldn't worry about it. Noah isn't going anywhere."

She let out a breath. "Thank you. Speaking of Elliot, that's why I called."

"Elliot? Why would you even mention that name?"

"Everything got cleared up in his will. Since I was still legally his wife, I inherited his company, his fortune, the house, and all his investments. His family waived any claims to his estate. They're not contesting it; although I thought for sure they would... Now, they seem to think I earned it. I don't know, payment for all the misery I endured, I guess. His parents even sent me an apology. They swore they never knew what Elliot did to me."

Gretchen laughed out loud and jerked forward in her chair. "Holy cow! Are you kidding me? You're rich now because of him?"

"I am. It's a lot of money, Gretchen. We're talking like, thirty million dollars."

"Wow. That's a big number to imagine."

"I know what you're going to say. I shouldn't take it. I shouldn't want it. I should donate it or something. It's blood money. It's contaminated. The thing is... I do want it. I didn't think I would until I just heard that I got it. He fucked me over repeatedly throughout life, and finally in death, I can get something from him that he wanted most. I know it's a terrible way to think. I can't help it. I'm glad. I'm so glad he's dead. I'm so glad I got his money. I'm so glad I can smear his name and reputation for the rest of my life."

Gretchen leaned back in her chair with a contented sigh. "No. Just the opposite. I think anger is a good thing. I think you finally stopped letting him rule your life or emotions anymore. And you should do whatever *you* want with that money."

"He used it to cover up his abuse to me. Like when he wanted to get elected governor, even though he did not have one decent asset to promote him. He used the money just as clearly as he used me."

"Look at it this way: now, you can use it to do whatever you want. If you want to run for governor, you can. You can do anything you want to now."

She scoffed. "As if I could run for governor. I was just being dramatic. Except, nothing would make him turn over in his grave faster than if I actually had some power. Or some importance. If I managed to accomplish what he couldn't."

Gretchen considered her statement for a moment, then told her softly, "You forget who you are sometimes. You have quite a platform, simply because of who you are. From Will and Jessie, to everything you endured with Elliot. You are quite known now and respected. And you are also a former soldier, Lindsey. As a veteran, you have your own accomplishments to define you. And now, you're rich. So, whatever you want to do, believe me, you *can* do it. No matter how many times Elliot might've told you that you can't."

She inhaled a breath sharply. "I can't believe you said that."

"What? I think, the longer I reflect on it, the more I believe you should really consider it. Your success would be the ultimate revenge. And you deserve that, Lindsey. More than anyone I've ever met."

"I was being sarcastic."

"I know. But I don't think it's so funny. I think it's truly possible."

She was quiet over the line. Maybe someday, Lindsey would find exactly what she wanted to do. Gretchen changed the subject, "So, any news from the investigators who shot Elliot and Cal?"

Lindsey's chuckle was strange. She was always cagey about that subject. Her ex-husband, then the acting Governor of Virginia, and his chief of staff, were both shot down by a sniper, while they were dodging public scrutiny after Lindsey made a very public accusation to Elliot. The rare sharpshooter attack that killed each man with one bullet right through the forehead, dead center, was freakishly comparable to a military sniper hit. No clues were ever found that could tie it to any suspect, however.

"I don't care who did it. I'm just glad it's done, and no one I love can ever go to jail for it, because they didn't do it. Will didn't do it. I didn't do it. Noah didn't do it. Whoever did me that favor, well, I'll be forever grateful to him or her or them, but the blood's on their hands, and not on ours. So I don't care."

"You know what? I think that's a really healthy attitude."

"Ah, the doctor approves then?"

Gretchen rolled her eyes. "I can't even try to be your doctor. You don't listen to me anyway."

"Hmm, you're right. But tell me, do you play doctor with our one-armed soldier?" Lindsey laughed at her own joke.

"Quit calling him the one-armed soldier. It's mean. And you sound just like Olivia. She was calling him that too."

"Ah, so our little Liv has met him already, huh? And how is he with her?"

"Kind of like Christina. He's nice to her. Patient. Tolerant. Although he's not like that with anyone else, not ever. So it was shocking."

"Well, that just means there's something decent left in him still. You just need to find it and nurture it. Like coaxing a young fledgling from his nest."

Gretchen bit her lip at Lindsey's analogy. Yeah, like Tony would ever be considered so fragile he would need any coaxing. "I'm not trying to nurture anything."

Lindsey laughed. "Oh, somehow, I think you are. You can't help it. Me. Jessie. Olivia. Now one-armed, Tony. You're good at it, Gretchen. I'm not insulting you. I'm serious. If anyone can help him, as Jessie says he needs it, then it's you. I admire that about you. My sister and I can almost, just barely help ourselves and our significant others, while you can help almost anyone you meet who needs it. It's a gift, Gretchen. And a rare and beautiful thing. Just don't let him take advantage of that, okay?"

"No danger of that; I'm barely helping him with anything."

"You will though. Somehow, you always do. So, how is Olivia? And how's Helen doing?"

Gretchen immediately sobered up. "Helen's coping. But it's not good. She's in a lot of pain. Everything is getting much harder for her. I don't know how much longer…"

"And you're ready for that?" Lindsey asked quietly.

Gretchen closed her eyes for a moment as her heart rate increased. Was she ready to become a mother to a little girl who was soon to be grief-stricken? A child who really never had a mother to start with? No. Yes. She didn't know. The reality just was.

There was no extra money in Helen's funds, and she lived on practically nothing. She raised Olivia alone and received no help. Olivia's father died in a construction accident and her mother was never even in the picture.

It wasn't long before Gretchen and Helen became friends outside of therapy. Soon, she transferred Olivia to Janis Hensley, a doctor in her practice, and dedicated the time that she spent with her more as a big sister and a mentor, than as a therapist. Gretchen was there when Helen was first told about her advanced stage terminal cancer. She tried to be there as much as she could for them since that time.

It was hard for Gretchen to imagine and impossible for her to be prepared for; but also the most important, scary, tragic thing she'd ever contemplated. Olivia knew her grandmother was dying; and she knew she was going to live with Gretchen someday. But Olivia didn't know the devastating grief that would soon be hers. It churned Gretchen's stomach to think how she'd deal with it, let alone, Olivia's grief.

But Gretchen wanted to do it. She loved Olivia. And there was little doubt in Gretchen's mind that Olivia could become her daughter, which the state would soon legally order.

She mentioned her plans to Lindsey almost immediately. "I'm ready in that I want to just get on with it. But then again, I don't mean it like that, because that would mean that Helen was dead. Of course, I don't want her to die, or for Olivia to have to deal with that when it happens."

"She chose well in selecting you to mother her daughter."

"Granddaughter."

"Daughter. Just as she'll be your daughter."

The ping of longing and love in her heart felt so strong, it seemed harsh.

"It's selfish to want that, but I know it will come at the cost of Olivia's pain. It's confusing."

"It's okay to be confused. It's okay for it to get messy, because it is a messy, awful situation. But it's also what makes you the best candidate. You already understand all these things, and there is no one who could deal with them better. Just as no one can deal with our one-armed hero better. You're a good person, Gretchen. Use whatever you have. Use it to help those around you who can't always be there, or don't know how to. And it makes you feel better to do so anyway. Don't feel guilty for that. Just go and be wonderful. It comes so easily for you."

She grimaced over the phone. "I am not. You make me sound like a lame, goody-two-shoes nun or something."

"You are kinda. My God, you took on Jessie. Who else could do that?"

"Tony said that too. It was part of why he got so disgusted with Will."

"I could kinda get behind someone who doesn't think your natural tendency for niceness should be taken advantage of quite so easily. Yeah, I think I'll have to get down that way soon for a visit."

She laughed before finally hanging up. Olivia would be there from school in only a few minutes. She came almost every afternoon straight to Gretchen's office. A bus dropped her off near there and Gretchen ran down quickly to meet it. Luckily, most afternoons she was able to schedule her patients around Olivia's visits. Olivia often had to wait for them to finish in the waiting room. She soon became a common fixture to many of Gretchen's patients. Olivia's natural inquisitiveness and curiosity managed to create more than one awkward situation, beyond what happened with Tony.

With Olivia, Gretchen witnessed Tony's change in behavior like never before. He was kind and caring, funny and relaxed, and acted like the missing arm was *nothing* with Olivia; whereas with Gretchen and the rest of the world, he made it *everything.*

She was a great kid, who was appreciative of any time Gretchen spent playing or talking with her. She never complained if Gretchen had an appointment and she had to wait. It squeezed Gretchen's heart how little Olivia needed to make her happy. She was used to being alone, and having to play by herself. Her grandmother worked full time until she got too sick. So there was never a time when Olivia was at home after school, or the center of anyone's day. She had always been taken to work, or worked around. Even with Gretchen.

Her grandmother was getting worse of late. She asked that Gretchen keep Olivia until dinnertime now. She couldn't handle much more than that. So Gretchen now had her every afternoon, as well as any days off school, until she dropped her back home around six. Not once did Olivia complain about it. Not once did she whine if Gretchen had to see clients. Not once did she demand anything more than what she already got. That broke Gretchen's heart too. Olivia's childhood had long ago been put on hold as yet another victim of her grandmother's illness.

Gretchen almost took Tony aside and explained the situation to him. If an eight-year-old could be so accepting of life, no matter how hard and unfair it was, while her only living relative lay dying before her eyes, and being unable to barely care for her, he could at least try to show some kind of resignation in accepting the loss of his arm.

But Tony didn't seem to notice that.

****

Gretchen drove Tony to his appointments every Thursday with Dr. Hart over the next two and a half months. Every Thursday, at three-thirty promptly, Gretchen appeared at Tony's front door. Not once did he wear anything but sweats or variations thereof. At first, she tried to engage him in conversation, but finally, gave up after several monotone conversations that always went exactly the same. He was "fine." His week was "fine." His parents were "fine." And no, he didn't want to go to therapy today, as usual. He never spoke except to say that; and usually turned up the radio to indicate the end of their conversation.

Olivia was usually there too. Gretchen timed it so they could meet her bus. He tolerated Olivia sitting next to him as he waited for Dr. Hart. He was always nice to Olivia, where he failed to show the least bit of courtesy to anyone else. It was the strangest damn thing.

And not once did he thank Gretchen for the rides, or inquire how her week had gone. Or how she was doing. Gretchen was pretty sure they could put away any further supposition that Tony harbored a crush on her still. He seemed to have more interest in talking back to the radio than he did with her conversations.

The only thing that made the rides together more bearable was Olivia's presence, which managed to break up the awful tension and uncomfortable atmosphere on the way home.

Tony changed around Olivia. He laughed at her inquiries, and explained a multitude of ways in which to function one-armed. He demonstrated many of the things Olivia asked to see. He never once grew annoyed, angry, or self-conscious with Olivia. Not like he did with Gretchen. Feeling that she couldn't win, eventually, she chose to say nothing, and was satisfied that he continued to see Dr. Hart. His choice not to be even a slight degree less rude or awful was not lost on her, however.

In that time, Donny and Vickie moved in together. Vickie had been living with two roommates in a house just outside of Calliston. She could only afford the house with her parents' assistance. Gretchen cringed when Vickie showed up spouting the great news that she was moving in with Donny. Wasn't that great!? *Oh, just great.* Where would they find Vickie a place to live once all of that crashed and disintegrated?

Upon hearing Vickie's "great" news, Gretchen began to regret ever reconnecting with Tony and Donny Lindstrom.

****

Tony felt his mood lifting as soon as Olivia came into view. She stepped off the bus and grinned from ear to ear, already waving at him and Gretchen before slipping into the back seat.

"Hi! How are you, Tony? You won't believe what we got to do in school today. They had this guy who deals with creepy critters; his name is Kevin the Creep Tamer. Isn't that hilarious! Anyways, he brought snakes, and lizards, and frogs and bugs. They're all caged up and stuff. But we had a presentation where he showed them all to us, and told us everything about them, and all that. Then…you won't believe this. You just won't believe this, Tony!"

He bit his lip, trying to stifle the urge to smile at her big-eyed exclamations, which wasn't easy. Smiling was something he never felt like doing anymore. Or at least, not in years. She just had that effect.

"What? What did he do?" Tony played along, his tone as genuinely interested as his smile. He could feel Gretchen's gaze on him from the corners of his eyes. He glanced at her, only to find her expression foggy with confusion, and her eyebrows drawn together. She didn't know why he was being so nice to Olivia. She never expected it, even after all their trips together. He almost explained to her once that if not for Olivia, he'd have told her to shove her free counseling straight up her pristine, perfect ass the very first time.

But Olivia was always there, all big-eyed, and asking if he would come back. So he came back. Just for her.

"He pulled the snake out and I touched it. I touched it, Tony! It was three feet long. And all brown and slithery… and I touched it! It wasn't even slimy. It was kind of rough and cold and dry. It surprised me. It was so-o-o cool. Have you ever touched a snake?"

"Yup. I used to collect them as a kid and freak my mother out with them."

Rounded eyes stared up at him as her little jaw dropped open. "Like in the house?"

"Yeah, I tried to sneak in more than one when I was a kid."

Gretchen turned and eyed Olivia. "Which no kid should ever do if she wants to be allowed in my house!"

Olivia rolled her eyes. "You're such a wuss, Gretchen."

"Olivia, you can't talk like that."

She threw her shoulders forward. "But Tony says it. Why can't I?"

He squirmed under Gretchen's suddenly narrow-eyed glare. "Well, *Tony* should never have said that in front of you. It's not appropriate, young lady, especially when referring to me."

Olivia stuck her tongue out at the back of Gretchen's head. Tony had to turn his face away to hide the grin of appreciation. Gretchen shot him a look as if she knew, somehow, they were laughing at her. "Well, it would be so neat to have one as a pet. I should ask my grandma."

"No, you shouldn't. She's got enough to deal with." Gretchen's tone was far harsher than Olivia deserved, and Tony frowned at her. She didn't look his way. Olivia's face fell. They pulled into the parking lot just then, and Tony followed them up the stairs. He was annoyed now, as every week, to be ogling Gretchen's long legs, wrapped in nylons and a skirt, as her calf muscles flexed with each step. He and Olivia sat down together. By now, they no longer needed to check in with the receptionist, who waved at him, no doubt, feeling glad he didn't approach the counter.

"Guess what else, Tony?"

"Besides the amazing snake? What?"

"We're going to have a Veterans Day assembly tomorrow to honor soldiers. Like you. We can bring one too. If we have a parent or a grandparent who is a veteran, we get to bring them. But since I don't, I asked if I could bring you, and my teacher said yes. Can you believe it? Are you busy tomorrow? Could you come? Please? Otherwise, I'll have no one to bring. And Tara Barton has three coming with her."

He felt Gretchen's frown. Standing within a few feet, discussing her schedule with her receptionist, she obviously overheard the conversation. She set the appointment book down and quickly turned. He ignored her obvious desire to speak to him and his stomach churned at the prospect of being classified with other "vets." But Olivia was looking up at him with such innocent delight while considering the prospect that she could bring her own "vet" to the assembly.

And besides, to answer her question: no, he wasn't doing anything. "Well that's not fair of Tara Barton to have three. But are any of hers one-armed?"

"No."

"Then I think yours will outdo all three of hers."

She clapped her hands together. "Oh, Tony, I think you're right! So you'll come?"

"I'll be there."

He met Gretchen's stare and her mouth pursed into a sour scowl. She didn't like hearing that. She spun around and nearly stomped into her office. She didn't trust him. He glanced at Olivia. "I'll be right back, okay? I forgot to tell Gretchen something."

He got up and followed Gretchen. She was just sitting down in her ergonomic, too-fancy office chair when he spoke, "You have a problem with me going to the assembly?"

She jerked her gaze to his. "Oh, Tony. You startled me. No, I was just a little surprised you'd go. She's had a lot of disappointments in her life. Please, don't contribute to them."

"I wasn't planning to."

She raised her brows. "Don't snarl at me. It's not so out of the box for me to worry. You're not exactly accountable to anyone or anything, and you don't want to be. She's fragile and delicate. I don't want her getting hurt."

"I wouldn't hurt a little girl."

"Just a grown woman?"

"What?" He stepped back in shock. What the hell was she talking about?

"You can just blithely, and so merrily hurt me? Sorry, if I didn't understand it fully. I expected that attitude might extend to Olivia."

"How do I hurt you?"

She glanced down at her desk and started rifling through her files as if unconcerned in replying to him. But when she finally did, her tone was soft and hesitant. "Perhaps a better question would be: how don't you?"

His jaw fell open in surprise. She suddenly started shaking her head. "Forget it. Dr. Hart just opened his door. Have a good session."

He backed up and shut her door. *Hurt her? He hurt Gretchen Hendricks?* How? Because he didn't feel like chatting about trivia? Because he so rarely did anything the rest of the week, there was little to say to her inquiries about how he was or if anything happened? Because he couldn't breathe around her? Because, even after all these years, his damn lungs hurt whenever he was in her presence?

She jerked the door open behind him. "Are you really going to the assembly for her?"

He nodded. "I said I would."

"I'll drive you there. It's at three o'clock. I'll pick you up at two-thirty. Be ready," Gretchen finished before she slammed the door in his face.

Chapter Ten

O LIVIA CALLED TONY THAT night from her grandma's and asked if he'd mind saying something at the school assembly. Tara Barton's vet-dad was speaking, so wouldn't he? Please? He felt a fleeting urge to grumble at her as he would have at anyone else, but instead, he agreed and hung up before staring at the computer and trying to think of something to write. What does one say about war? About getting injured critically? About losing your arm in a campaign that few Americans bothered to pay much attention to? He finally started typing. He managed to master the Dvorak keyboard sometime last year, after getting tired of hunting and pecking on the traditional keyboard. He didn't really like speaking his thoughts aloud into voice recognition software. This keyboard, however, allowed him some speed and accuracy. And Gretchen wondered why he was so pissy all the time? He couldn't even type easily. He finally retrained his typing skills in order to use the new system. He was surprisingly decent at it now, too.

Writing a quick speech, he supposed it wouldn't kill him to talk to a bunch of kids under the age of ten. It was the adults he didn't much enjoy anymore. Kids were just naturally curious. Usually, they weren't mean-spirited or judgmental.

Gretchen showed up at precisely two-thirty, and was, as usual, prompt. As a functioning, decent, moral woman, who reliably paid her fair share of taxes and held a respectable job, she was the epitome of the ideal, hardworking, decent American. Funny how losing an arm in the service to protect such values couldn't make up for how he didn't participate in society now. He was looked down on for not being the societal "norm," yet most "normal" people had never spent even an hour with a gun aimed at them.

His mother yelled for him and he took the steps two at a time before bursting through the top, and hurrying towards the kitchen counter to find his wallet. His mother and Gretchen were chatting back and forth. Having become closer over the last few months, almost every week now, they discussed the goings on of each other. His mother's fascination was endless when it came to hearing all about Gretchen's practice. However, his mother did respect his privacy and never asked how it was going or if it accomplished anything. He would've hated to tell her the truth if she had asked, for he wouldn't lie to her. There was no reason for her to know that the most he got accomplished was snatching a peek at Gretchen's ass each week as a reward for time served.

He suddenly noticed the entire house had gone totally silent. He glanced up to find Gretchen and his mother staring open-mouthed at him as he grabbed his wallet.

"What?"

Gretchen visibly swallowed and slowly closed her mouth. "Yo-you look wonderful. My God…"

He glanced down at his Army full dress uniform. His pants were perfectly creased and starched; and his hat poised in perfect alignment. His only Army violation was having a ponytail. It was considered rude and disrespectful of the uniform. Tony, however, didn't see why he should have to cut his hair over one school assembly. Neither could he justify going there without wearing his uniform to the Veterans' Day event. Not only for himself, but in respect for so many others who went before him. His beard was trimmed for the first time in a while, and although not totally regulation, it was not as blatant as the hair.

His mother's eyes misted up. "I haven't seen you dressed like that since you were discharged. Oh, Tony, you look so noble. You make me so proud of you."

Looking noble was not *being* noble. He rolled his eyes and kissed his mother's cheek after she wrapped her arms around him in a heartfelt hug.

"I guess we should go."

Releasing his mother, he turned and followed Gretchen to her familiar blue car. He ducked in more carefully now to avoid bumping his head, being almost too tall for the damn thing. His shoes, shined to perfection, nearly blinded him when they reflected the bright sunlight. He almost had to admit that he might've stood a fraction of an inch taller, in his uniform. It represented his entire life at one time. Now, as he followed Gretchen, he actually felt taller than when clad in dirty, stained, slouchy sweats and loose sweatshirts. He looked ten times the man too.

Good thing he usually didn't give a crap.

Gretchen drove for several minutes towards Olivia's school before she asked, "Is it hard to wear the uniform again?"

He focused his gaze straight ahead, to avoid her prying stare. "Yeah, it's hard to wear it without an arm. I haven't worn it since my discharge."

She drew in a sharp breath. "You look really nice, Tony."

"I look like every other hurt veteran you meet. Come on, I don't even look like a damn soldier anymore."

"Do you miss it? Being on active duty?"

He turned his head, his eyes blind to the blur of scenery passing outside. Trees and buildings meshed together as his breath came in short, sharp pants. "Yeah. I miss it. It was the only thing I ever did that had any significance or mattered a damn."

"And now you think nothing else matters a damn. That's why you don't care if you do anything at all." She didn't say it as a question. She was concentrating on the road in front of her. It was almost like she was working out an enigma in her head.

"Thanks, *Dr. Gretchen*. I always love your breakthroughs with me."

She sniffed, somehow finding it harder to ignore his snider comments. "Tony Lindstrom, you can be such a jerk! I think I finally kind of understand what you must be feeling."

"Asshole is a better term. Jerk doesn't have as much punch as asshole. That's what you intended to do, isn't it? Insult me? You're really not very good at that."

"I don't swear much as a habit. And it's a good thing, you know, not to be especially proficient at insulting people."

"I know," he chuckled finally. "You don't do much that could be considered wrong, much less a vice. You have got to be one of the most well behaved people I've ever known."

"That's not usually considered a negative thing either."

"Not by most, I suppose."

"Oh, but it bothers you, doesn't it? Believe me. I would know."

She swung into a parking spot and her movements became jerky. He pissed her off again. Maybe someday, he could quit acting out. He was like the naughty little boy, straining to pull the little girl's hair in front of him just for attention. He was ashamed to confess he actually wanted her negative attention because he knew he could never interact with her in any other way. Negative reinforcement was better than nothing at all.

Of course, Tony would have much preferred that she felt more inclined to screw around with him, versus wanting to save his soul by talking. Instead, he settled for a glimpse of her tits as they filled the blue blouse she wore today so elegantly. She had a really nice rack, and frowned when she noticed where his eyes were fastened. She turned her body and got out of the car, slamming the door to convey her annoyance at his unabashed ogling.

He didn't even have the decency or grace to blush. What did he care if she caught him? He spent enough time talking and doing what *she wanted* him to do. Besides, she was about the only sexual object that could even remotely get him off. Of course, that would remain something no one ever need know or learn about. He could barely get it up anymore. And even more humiliating, he hardly cared about it anymore either.

That was what convinced his fiancée to finally dump him.

That, and she didn't like taking care of his one-armed, lame ass.

****

Okay, Gretchen was ready to admit she'd been completely wrong about it. She almost felt compelled to call Olivia multiple times and cancel Tony's attendance there today. She was sure he'd either be rude or simply refuse to come at the last minute.

She never expected to see him walking up and looking more familiar, like the man she once knew. The honorable, capable, industrious man she was once so fond of. Unexpectedly, her breath expelled from her lungs almost as if he just knocked a fist into her guts. His army persona nearly blew her mind. He looked amazing. Hot. Handsome. The poster boy for the Army bad-ass.

His hair gave him an unusual edge and was definitely not typical. But even so, he looked amazing. It was drawn back, either slicked with product or water, and somehow, perhaps for the first time, did not tweak around as if he slept funny on it. His hat covered most of his head and gave his ponytail more respectability. His beard was trimmed neatly. Now it flattered his face, instead of making him look like a homeless man with a hangover who lacked regular hygiene.

His brown eyes were steady and very intense, which fit the solemnity of his uniform appropriately. His good arm sported the patches and insignia of his position, and his other was pinned neatly up.

Gretchen's heart started beating irregularly. She could not stop staring at him. And Olivia practically went crazy. Rushing from her class as she entered the gymnasium, she launched herself at him, encircling his waist with her arms and burying her face against his stomach. She looked up at him, grinning goofily. Olivia chattered on about how Tara Barton would, no doubt, be drooling because her three veterans were old and ugly, while Olivia's was one-armed and handsome. Gretchen frowned, feeling unsure what Tara Barton's three vets had do with anything, but Tony gave Olivia a huge smile of appreciation and leaned down to say something into her ear that soon had her laughing.

He was *so* different with Olivia. He was a fun, charming, caring man. He easily slipped into the role of protector, friend, and admirer of Olivia. It sent strange shock waves through Gretchen's system. It was not good for Olivia to revere Tony so highly. It was no secret she never had a father, or even a father figure. There were no men in her brief life. So obviously, she would make Tony so much more than he really should have been to her. But Gretchen didn't know how to stop it.

Neither could Tony stop it. He simply smiled and tolerated her incessant questions. She only asked about a million of them. He allowed her to hug him as often as she liked, and goofed around with her, demonstrating his one-armed abilities. Why, then, couldn't he even say hello to Gretchen without cringing or scowling in an expression filled with fierce anger?

How would Olivia handle it when Tony finally got angry at her about something? Gretchen believed it was only a matter of time, given Tony's personality. Or else, he'd simply disappear from Olivia's life. Gretchen sighed, prematurely dreading the day that would happen. It was inevitable and another responsibility for her: to get Olivia through it.

Tony sat beside Olivia, and Gretchen joined the other spectators in the bleachers opposite the seating for the kids. A small representation of the high school band was also there. They began playing the national anthem and the color guard did a formal ceremony, presenting the flags. They all stood for the Pledge of Allegiance. It was a moving performance. She gasped in shock when Tony's brother and parents suddenly showed up, all bearing smiles as they sat down beside her.

"I called them," Leila explained. "They needed to see Tony dressed this way. And doing this… doing a favor for somebody else. It's been so long since he's done anything, let alone, anything worthwhile. I owe you, Gretchen. Thank you. I'm so glad you didn't listen to me that first day and decided on your own to pursue this. Look at our son now." Leila had tears brimming over her eyelids. She smiled with sheer, unadulterated pride at Tony.

Donny leaned in. "I knew you'd work wonders. Thank you, Gretchen. For today. Not for Tony's sake, but my mother's. I haven't seen her this happy in two years."

"Actually, it was more because of Olivia than because of me. She's a girl I look after, and Tony has developed a strong bond with her."

Donny squeezed her hand. "Nah. It's because of you. You just don't realize it."

There were more musical performances and the principal gave a heart-wrenching speech about our heroic veterans and what an honor it is to exalt their loyalty as well as their sacrifices. Then… Tony stood up and the principal mentioned how such sacrifices could be as extreme as losing body parts, "just like Sergeant Tony Lindstrom, here."

The entire audience erupted into loud clapping, that seemed to resonate in the gym, and the mass of bodies stood up in a collective act of praise. Tony walked up to the podium, holding a piece of paper, which he set down. Never smiling, he stared straight ahead as the auditorium reverberated with the unusually loud applause and cheers to honor him and his sacrifice. The brim of his hat kept his eyes mostly shaded, so he was very hard to read. Did the audience's response touch him? It was a unanimous display of people who did indeed care how much he lost and sacrificed.

But wait... what was this? How could Tony be speaking here? How did this happen? When was it arranged? What could the rude, surly, miserable Tony possibly have to say to a vast group of impressionable kids, none of whom had anything to do with how he lost an arm?

Donny looked at Gretchen curiously; and Leila cried more openly as she whipped out her cell phone to take a video. Meanwhile, Lewis just stared, his eyes stricken with wonder as he slowly lifted his hand and saluted his son. The action, so small and subtle, brought a lump to Gretchen's throat. They loved him so much. She wondered if he realized how much love and pride his family harbored for him. Why couldn't he just gracefully appreciate it?

Then he started speaking in a voice that was deep and articulate. As always, Gretchen thought he missed his calling by not becoming a radio broadcaster instead of a soldier. He spoke so clearly and with such a deep baritone as he prepared to give his speech, it was... shocking to Gretchen. He successfully orated a wonderful perception of duty and sacrifice. He carefully explained the history of the military; and what it normally meant to the common, everyday person (or child). He spoke simply, and in terms any youngster could understand. He had most of the teachers dabbing their eyes, male and female. The entire audience exploded into such a roar of applause when he finished, no one could speak for several minutes after he sat down.

"Holy crap. Where did that come from?" Donny whispered into Gretchen's ear.

"I don't know," she replied, stunned.

The assembly finally ended and the students, the audience and the guests were dismissed. Olivia was beaming and threw herself at Tony before she got back into line to go back to class.

Tony frowned as soon as he saw who else was in attendance. Donny happily acknowledged him with a thump of his fist on Tony's back.

"That was something special, man."

Tony shrugged. "Just pleasing Olivia.

"How did you wind up doing this?"

"She asked me to. And after the principal discovered I was a one-armed, Afghanistan vet, it turned out I was the only one. I came from a war that was a little more recent than most of the other vets. So he asked me to speak and try to make my speech relevant."

"You were absolutely astounding. It was a beautiful speech. I never dreamed…" Gretchen started to say.

"Yeah, yeah, I was great. It was an elementary school assembly. I didn't exactly change the world today." Turning, he ignored her as he accepted his mother's hug. Gretchen sighed. As always, he rarely accepted anything from her.

His parents then insisted on treating Gretchen and their two sons to an early dinner in honor of the day's celebration. Reluctantly, Gretchen agreed even though it was not her usual time to eat. Olivia was going over to a friend's after school, so Gretchen was free. She could tell it was near torture for Tony too. Although he could have ridden with his parents or with Donny, he slipped into her car, without a word. She narrowed her eyes at seeing his profile. If he disdained her so much, why did he choose to ride in the car with her?

Donny must have called Vickie because she showed up at the dinner, scooting in happily beside Donny. They were becoming hard to take. They giggled and goo-goo eyed each other incessantly and used banal terms of endearment in practically every single thing they said. For instance, they often yelled, "Jinx" in unison when they inevitably said the same thing. It was like watching a pair of eighth graders.

Tony's family, however, was the most casual she'd ever observed them. They talked openly and freely. Even Tony was a tad less like the Grim Reaper than usual. When Donny stood up unexpectedly, Vickie stared up at him, beaming, as he raised a water glass theatrically.

"I just feel like this is it. The moment we should do this. We were going to wait and make a more formal announcement... but since we're all here now, and it's been such an usually great day, I want to add some icing on the cake to finish it. I've asked Vickie to marry me and she said yes."

Leila gasped as she jumped up, already crying and hugging Donny, before grabbing Vickie and including her in the next hug. Leila pulled on her hand gently to look at the diamond ring that was, sure as shit, proudly wrapped around her ring finger.

Gretchen took a long drink of water. *Damn.* Not what she wanted to hear. Wasn't Donny any smarter than that? Why would he make such a declaration only three months into their relationship? *Holy crap, no.* She could not watch Vickie do this, yet again. And how could Donny believe that being groom number four wasn't a tad deranged, or probably about to go up in flames very shortly? Why exactly, did he think he would be any different than the other three?

She cringed, dreading what her parents would have to go through. Again. As well as she.

"And Gretchen, you simply have to be my maid of honor."

She closed her eyes and opened them slowly. Of course. It would be the second time for her. Up to now, Tracy and she traded off every other wedding as to who played the role of the maid of honor. Lucky for her, this time, it was her turn.

"And Tony, will you be my best man?"

"Yeah, of course. I'd be honored."

Lifting her eyes to Tony, Gretchen made a fake strangling motion. He glanced around, making sure, no doubt, no one in his family could see them. He copied her and then pretended to hang himself. She giggled out loud, but hastily clapped a hand over her mouth. Since when did she giggle like Vickie? She didn't. And certainly not with Tony Lindstrom. He smiled in response as they continued to share a look. Her smile slowly faded into confusion at the sudden intense heat she could feel sparking between them. She was pulled from it by Vickie, now stuffing her fingers into Gretchen's face to give her a better look at the ring. Ring number four, in case anyone was losing count. Gretchen sure hadn't.

Gretchen decided the Lindstroms must have been desperate for any good news after living with Tony for two years, making even Vickie a positive to them. Still, Lord help her, another bridesmaid dress....

"...Christmas Eve."

Gretchen zoned back in on the tail end of Vickie's chatter. "Christmas Eve, what?"

Vickie was pink-cheeked with excitement. Nothing turned Vickie on more than planning another wedding. "Our wedding date, silly."

"What!? You can't get married on Christmas Eve."

"Why not?"

"Well, first of all, it's not fair to make everyone else change their holiday plans around your wedding. And second, that's only six weeks away. You can't get married so soon."

"We can too. When things are right, they're just right. Aren't they, Donny?"

He nodded with love-puppy eyes at his fiancée. "Yes, sweetie." He shrugged and glanced around. "She always wanted to get married on Christmas Eve by candlelight."

Gretchen bit her tongue to keep from pointing out she'd already had *three weddings*, and maybe we didn't have to recreate every single childhood fantasy she could dream up next.

"Yeah, and it's my wedding day; people should just be happy to come."

"But Tracy's girls don't want to spend Christmas Eve at your wedding."

"Oh, they will too. It's not all about them."

Or Vickie. It should not have been all about Vickie. But Gretchen didn't say it. "But—"

"But whatever you guys want." Tony cut her off. She glanced up sharply, frowning in scorn. How dare he interrupt her? Or say that to her? Agreeing to sacrificing her Christmas celebration to go to another pointless wedding for her spoiled sister. Culminating into an even less pointless marriage. She was nearly sputtering with pent-up frustration. Tony was taking Vickie's side? How dare he? Gretchen turned halfway in her seat so she could not hear anymore or have further eye contact with him. She didn't talk to him for the rest of the frustrating meal. Now, of course, the dinner was not about Tony's near breakthrough, or his exquisite words, but about Vickie's stupid, fourth wedding.

Everyone had to hug and kiss Vickie multiple times just to get away from her, since she was so happy. Gretchen stayed off to the side; she was completely done with her sister. She turned to leave, utterly fed up with the stupid proceedings, and only stopped when she heard Tony's voice calling after her. She was stunned as he strode towards her. Her breath caught in her chest upon seeing the elegant, commanding, respectful figure he cut while crossing the restaurant parking lot. Why was he coming after her?

"Did you forget me?"

"I assumed you'd go home with your parents."

He didn't answer, but went around her and waited by her still locked passenger door. *Huh.* Apparently, he intended to come with her, although she couldn't see why. He didn't seem to like her particularly. The rides were usually silent, long, and nerve-wracking.

She unlocked the door, feeling tired of the drama and being treated like a doormat, or as Vickie's trusty keeper.

She nearly peeled out of the parking spot, she was so pissed off.

She had nothing to say to Tony and was sick of driving him around in silence, which had become almost like a reverence for his sour, foul moods. She resented being Tony's weekly chore. She'd had it with people like Tony and Vickie always being rude or careless toward her. She halted her car with a loud screech of tires in his driveway, before shifting the gear into park and impatiently waiting for him to get out.

"Mad about something?"

"Damn straight." She clenched her teeth to keep from adding more.

"What?"

"That! In the restaurant. It's so stupid. How could Donny be so naive? Or your parents? Or you even? *Oh, whatever you want, Vickie.* Holy crap, I could throw you right out onto the curb.*"

He turned his body and stared at her. "Were you just mimicking *me*?"

"You totally bailed on me with that. I mean, Christmas Eve? Why should they get to ruin my holiday? I love Christmas. We go to my parents' and have a traditional dinner. Tracy's kids get to look for Santa as we rush around, putting out all the presents that are from us. We watch the kids open theirs, and then give to each other. I wait all year for it. And now I get to look forward to the fourth, *do you hear me?* the *fourth* wedding of Vickie's. So how dare you speak up and over me, as I tried to point out, and quite rationally, I should add, exactly why she should not have done that. Someone has to teach her, at some point, she can't just do whatever she wants, whenever she wants." Gretchen felt humiliated when her tears started falling down her cheeks. She sniffed, and pushed against her eye sockets to try and stem the flow. It was just so frustrating. She was so weary of Vickie. For her entire life, Vickie got whatever she wanted, and Gretchen was supposed to go along with it, no matter what. No matter how it affected or influenced her. No matter how unfair it was. No matter how it deprived Gretchen of her own desires and needs.

Tony's mouth dropped open, so Gretchen turned and gripped the steering wheel.

"Uh. I didn't mean to make you cry. I…"

She pushed at her eyeballs. "I'm not crying because of you!"

He slammed his lips together and she sneered. He was so clueless. He could do and say whatever rude things he chose to her, but if she dared to react, just once, to one of his barbs, he's stricken speechless? She suddenly stiffened, before yanking the gear shift and backing out of the driveway, albeit with a screech of tires and the jerking of her car as it switched gears.

"Where are you going? I mean, don't you want to be alone or something?" He seemed uncomfortable in the seat, showing obvious unease over her strangely erratic behavior and ever flowing tears. She couldn't help it now. She'd had enough. Her entire life she'd always done everything exactly right. Every little damn thing was done in accordance to what society, her parents, her sisters, and even what Will wanted or expected from her. Will thought it was her job even now to do something about Tony. He flew in for a few days, and called occasionally... but he didn't have to encounter Tony's rudeness and indifference every day. She wasn't fixing Tony. No, but Will expected her to do that for him, all the while, grinning and bearing Tony's frosty personality.

And now Vickie. Again. Her entire life had also been in service to Vickie's whims and demands. Her parents could never say no to their youngest, beautiful, spoiled brat daughter. Never. Not once. They expected Gretchen to understand because she was the oldest and already had her shit together. Always. She was practically born with her shit together. She was one of those people who never screwed up, never doubted who or what she was, and always knew what she wanted from life.

If everyone else could just manage to get their shit together, she could happily exist and keep hers together. But no one else ever did. And that's not all: they thought it was their right to screw up all the time. People like Vickie who never once felt embarrassed that, *Gee, her fourth wedding?* Maybe she shouldn't have interfered with other people's lives, since it *was* her *fourth.*

And what about Tony Lindstrom? He who thought that because of his own tragic circumstances, he no longer had to participate in life, or show common courtesy, like saying hello to others. Or thank you. Or just being polite. She was sick and tired of being the sole person who acted exactly how she was supposed to. How standard decency insisted that people should act. It wasn't rocket science, but simply, behavior modification.

Wisely, Tony said nothing else. His right hand gripped the handle above his door and he periodically glanced at her, seeming to wonder if perhaps she temporarily lost touch with reality sometime between driving from the restaurant to his house.

She pulled the car to a halt right in front of her condo. He glanced up, then all around. She ducked out of the car, slamming her door and stomping through the lobby entrance toward the elevator. He came up behind her, but she could sense his hesitancy, as if he wasn't sure if he should follow her.

The elevator dinged open and she stomped into it. He leaned against the opposite side. She stared hard at the closed doors as they rode up to the fifth floor. Finally, it dinged and she marched straight to her front door. After deftly unlocking the door, they went inside.

Tony gently shut her front door and turned, but stood barely inside, taking in her condo. The door had its own small entry, and the rest of the condo, all the way to the panoramic windows, was visible.

"This is your place, I take it?'

It galled her suddenly that he'd never once, not in the three months since they reconnected, wondered about her life. Or who she was now. Or where she lived, or the kinds of things she chose for recreation. He never even cared. It was all about him and what he suffered

149

and couldn't do anymore. Why didn't he have any interest in *her?*

"It is. Not that you once ever wondered where I lived or relaxed, or even that I still breathed." Her tone was undeniably tight and snide.

"O-o-o-okay," he said drawing out the word. Stepping into the living room, he stared out the picture windows. "Nice view."

"Yes. It is. It's a nice condo. I bought it with my own money, the same year I divorced Will. I did it with money I earned all on my own, and from my share of the practice. I didn't get help with it from anyone. Not Will. Or my parents. Or some other guy."

He raised one eyebrow, which drove her nuts. His disdain was so clear to her then. "And this has to do with your sister and Donny? How?"

She flipped around on her heel and marched away, slamming her bedroom door shut. After flinging all kinds of crap around in her closet, she found what she sought. She finally came back to Tony, holding the three dresses, the ones that she deplored the most, in her hand.

Throwing two of them on the couch, she held one over her. "This is bridesmaid dress number one, when Vickie married a really nice boy she went to high school with. Someone like you *used* to be. She screwed him over, cheated on him, and he paid her alimony. Do you notice anything about these dresses?"

His focus darted from scanning her body to studying the other two dresses. He finally lifted his shoulders. "Sorry, but most women's fashions are lost on me."

She nearly screamed in frustration. "They're *ugly!* Any idiot could see that. Brown, to this strange shade of puke-green, to freaking teal? I mean, no adult woman wears freaking bows on her waist, or like this one here that folds right over my ass and makes it look twice as big. And she does that on purpose. Vickie picks the ugliest dresses in the most putrid colors she can find so that she looks all the more beautiful. Because God knows, she's the most beautiful, charming girl. I mean, who could resist her? And I paid for all of these. Every single one of these, was my own special purchase. Vickie who has never had more than twenty dollars at a time, chooses the ugliest, least flattering dresses for me to buy, usually in excess of five hundred dollars. And guess what? Now I get to do it all over again."

Tony's mouth twitched and she saw it. He was amused by her outrage. She threw the offensive brown dress on the floor and was ready to nearly stomp on it with her foot. "Don't laugh at me."

"I'm not... laughing out loud, that is." His smile, slow and wide, revealed his white teeth as he slid his hat off and gently set it on the coffee table near his knees. When he straightened back up, he was shamelessly grinning at her. Usually, he barely even managed to grimace, but now he was grinning at her? Not with her. For she felt sure he was laughing at her inside. She fisted her hands, feeling sick to death again of him and his tragic, *poor-me-with-only-one-arm* attitude that allowed him to be so stinking mean to her. She was tired of people who deliberately did everything wrong, and steam-rolled over those who tried to do everything right. She was tired of getting the short end of the stick every time. The dresses were becoming a metaphor for her weary relationships with Vickie and Tony in that moment. And she was fed up with both of them, as well as wearing ugly dresses that she had to buy.

Making her even madder was his stupid grin that knotted up her stomach and caused her heart to skip a beat in her chest. *Damn it!* She was not attracted to Tony

Lindstrom. She never had been. Never. Not once. Years ago, she accidentally walked in on him naked when they were barely eighteen, but she felt nothing. Nada. Zilch. Except for her total embarrassment of seeing his naked butt. She hadn't even shown the slightest curiosity as to what the front offered. She never cared if he had a dick or not because he was no more than her dear friend. Will's friend. That's it. She never even considered him as a man. Not even once.

So why, now, would her stupid heart react in such a way to him especially when he was so mean, crude, rude, and awful? Well, there weren't enough derogatory adjectives to describe Tony nowadays, and this is when she decided she might be attracted to him?

It made the anger already rising in her boil even hotter. *No!* She was simply done with terrible people. Or careless people. She was done being taken for granted and walked over, ignored, yelled at, or evoking no damn reaction. Her invariable response was one of understanding, sympathy and care. Well, no more. If people couldn't behave properly with her anymore, then she no longer would either. She obviously couldn't beat any of them. So why not join them?

"I wish I never bumped into you again. If I hadn't, Donny wouldn't be marrying my sister, and I wouldn't be doing this tired routine all over again. And to cement it all, I get to hang out with your miserable, negative personality for the next... however long this lasts. No more. No more rides. No more dinners. No more. Find your own way to the doctor. Or not. Quit. Like you do everything else. Why should I care what you do? Why have I even been trying to care? You don't care. Vickie doesn't care who she hurts, so why the heck should I?"

She whipped around and leaned her hands on the counter top. Breathing deep and hard, she began counting backwards, trying to calm her anger. Where was all of this coming from? She never did or said things like that. Or acted so impulsively and rashly. She didn't even do that when she lost her baby. Or Will, even after Jessie and Will found the life he couldn't with her. She never acted this way before. So why now? Over her sister's wedding?

"That's the thing about you that separates you from me and Vickie. You do care."

His tone was the same calm, silky, deep baritone, the one he used in his speech today. The speech that managed to make her insides lift with such pride, hope, and well... geez, joy that it was Tony on the stage. She had no idea that he even had it in him. He looked every inch a grown up, mature, accomplished man and retired soldier, standing there at the podium, voicing his opinions about real life. Nothing like his usual, slouchy, I-don't-give-a-damn demeanor.

Her shoulders slumped when the truth of how much she cared about what happened to Tony unexpectedly crashed over her and she felt helpless, as he often made her feel, because he so rejected her. "Well, not anymore. I'm tired of caring. I'm tired of getting walked all over. I'm tired of the whole thing."

She sensed him shuffling around behind her. He had no idea how to respond. She smiled in nasty glee to herself. Served him right for every uncomfortable moment she spent, being hesitant and unsure in her conversations with him.

"Gretchen you—"

The knock at her front door interrupted him. She stiffened and glanced at him with a scowl. Only he could luck out and not have to respond because of some random event. She wasn't expecting anyone.

She jerked open the door and nearly slammed it back shut, tightening her jaw as she demanded, "What are you doing here?"

Donny glanced past her and did a physical double take when he spotted his brother standing there. He cleared his throat. "Can I come in and speak with you?"

"About Vickie?"

"Well, yeah."

"Forget it. I don't feel like talking about her anymore." She turned on her heel and started to head towards her bedroom, intending to lock them both out, but he caught her arm.

"Wait. Please, Gretchen. Let me talk with you."

She threw a glance at Tony, whose expression seemed as unsure of her as his brother's. Gritting her teeth, she veered off into her kitchen and poured a glass of wine. She deliberately didn't offer one to either of them.

"Well, what?"

Donny's mouth dropped open too, and he shook his head at her rude prompt. "Uh, well, I guess I came to see why you weren't very receptive to Vickie and my news. It really upset her. So I decided to find out why you were so rude to her."

Gretchen felt like launching herself across the bar that separated her from Donny and scratching his eyes out. Or howling out loud with frustration. That was exactly what she was always talking about. Gretchen's reaction to her news made Vickie cry. *Poor Vickie.* How could Gretchen be so mean? And now, here stood Donny, asking how Gretchen could hurt the sweet, little Vickie. Usually, that question came from her mother, her father or Tracy on the rare occasions when she hinted to Vickie how she really felt about her flagrant behavior.

Tony nudged his brother. "Uh, not the right time, man."

Donny shook his head. "Well, that doesn't excuse being mean to your sister when she only wanted to announce her engagement."

"Yeah. For the fourth time!" Gretchen's exclamation was unnecessarily loud as she slammed her glass onto the counter. Luckily, it didn't break. "She's engaged for the fourth time in eight years. That's an average of every two years. It's not special, Donny. It's just normal and average. And you two chose to announce it on the day that should have been all about your brother. It was *his* day. He accomplished something great. He was extraordinary and succeeded at something special. And you and Vickie had the gall to spin the entire dinner celebration and make it all about you."

Tony's eyebrows shot up as Donny stepped back. "That's why you're so mad? I don't care if they announced it today. All I did was speak at a dumb assembly."

She shook her head. "It was the first time, since I've been seeing you, that you did something completely out of the ordinary. Something special for an unselfish reason. That wasn't just anything you did today; it was brilliant. And very special, and it fully deserved the big deal that was being made over it. It should not have become an opportunity to announce Vickie's latest fiasco."

Donny bit his lip and looked between Gretchen and Tony, confused. Gretchen pressed a hand to her chest, and found her heart beating so ferociously from an unusual rush of adrenaline that she truly feared she'd have a heart attack.

"Look… maybe we were wrong to do this today. I see that now. I didn't at the moment, though; so why are you so mad? Vickie didn't set out to ruin anything for Tony."

"Vickie never sets out to ruin things, she just invariably does."

"That's really unfair."

"Unfair? You don't yet know the meaning of unfair. But you will. Trust me, you will learn and thoroughly understand the definition of that word. Congratulations, Donny. You sure know how to pick them."

Donny's frown was deep as he blinked, in obvious shock. "That's a terrible way to talk about your own sister. I won't repeat any of this to her. But no more. You cannot talk about her like that again."

"Have you ever once listened to how she talks about me? Did she ever tell you how much money I've given her? Twelve thousand dollars, Donny. That was in order to keep some of her bills paid and prevent her from becoming homeless. Did she ever tell you how many times she moved in with me? Five. Five times. Has she—"

He put his hands up, gesturing for her to stop. "Okay, I get where you're going here. She's made a lot of mistakes in her past. But this is different. This is…"

"The same. It's always the same."

"I love her, Gretchen."

"You don't even know her."

"I know enough. I know she needs you."

Gretchen shut her eyes as her anger slowly seemed to dissipate through her wobbly skeletal system as it deflated her stature. "I know that, Donny. I know how much she needs. Far, far better than you'll ever

156

understand. So please, don't stand there and preach to me about Vickie."

Donny glanced at Tony, who shifted his feet uncomfortably. He sighed deeply and finally sat down on her couch, his shoulders sagging as he stared at his feet. "She's pregnant. That's why we're getting married so quickly. And that's why when I say she needs you, I mean, like really, she *really* needs you."

Gretchen skirted around the counter and moved past Tony. She felt their eyes following her as she walked over to the windows and stared out at the view. Calmer now, she shook her head and her stomach tightened. The dirty names hung on the tip of her tongue and she ached to rail and freak out at him, *how could he have let this happen*? How could he not have been smarter than to get Vickie pregnant?

"No. You know what? She needs you. You did this. You weren't more careful, so you two figure it out. I'm tired. And I'm done. I'm not her whipping post, her mother, or her spouse. I'm just her older sister. And I'm done trying to make her grow up and act her age anymore. So no, Donny, you don't get to come in on a relationship that has sucked me dry for twenty years, and lecture me about how I failed her. Or how much she needs me. All I need is for her to *not* need me. She has to grow up. I can't do this anymore."

Donny's shock was evident in his rounded eyes and clenched jaw. She was sure he probably thought that once he leaked his grand, life-changing news, she would soften and return to her usual self. She just couldn't anymore. Not for Vickie. Not for Will. Not for Lindsey. Not for Tracy. Not for her parents. They would, no doubt, soon be calling her to have the same conversation Donny just exchanged with her. *And not for Tony*. She simply had no more to offer anyone. Not right now. The only thing left in her to share was for Olivia. Perhaps that was the primary reason she no longer felt the urge to give herself to anyone else.

She could feel Tony's gaze zeroing in on her as his head shifted to follow the conversation.

Tony suddenly leaned over and grabbed his hat before touching his brother's shoulder. "She needs a break."

Donny slowly nodded. "I see. I guess I'll go. I mean, we'll go. Why were you here, Tony?"

"She had some dresses she wanted to show me." He glanced back at her after turning towards the front door with a half smile on his face. "Some butt-ugly-ass dresses she should have thrown in the fuckin' garbage. But that's just my opinion, of course."

Slowly releasing the grip on her drink, Gretchen shook her head as a soft laugh escaped her lips. She appreciated, for once, Tony's humor. Despite the foul language. His strange show of support and understanding, while clearly lacking judgment, surprised her actually.

"What?" Donny asked. His mind was utterly blown by witnessing her unusual, no, *unheard of* childish tantrum as well as Tony's reaction.

"Let's go."

Tony glanced back one more time, and his eyes sought hers. "I'll see you Thursday."

"I told you, I'm done. I meant that. It wasn't just a rash statement in the heat of the moment."

He lifted his hands as if in surrender. "Don't worry, I get that. I'll take the bus in. I just figured I'd see you because you're usually there to get Olivia."

She slowly expelled a lungful of air that seemed to take with it the rest of her emotions. Her heart slowed down, and the afterglow of outrage that must have been evident on her face diminished. "Okay, yeah, that's good. Then, you're right, I might see you."

She followed both of them to the front door and slammed it with an unexpected relish. For the first time, she was setting boundaries around herself. No one liked it. No one understood it. Well, maybe Tony did. But no one else did or could. She was finally doing it. It was long past time. And long overdue for her to figure out what she wanted, instead of how to help others attain what they wanted.

Chapter Eleven

TONY MISSED GRETCHEN AND he hated the feeling. After getting used to seeing her on Thursdays to break up his weeks, since not much else broke them up, nothing even half as interesting as Gretchen Hendricks ever happened during the rest of the week. But she, good to her word, never drove him to therapy again. He hit his mother up, who gladly took him to his counseling appointments. Leila became almost giddy over his involvement in anything that was positive and could pry him out of the basement.

He asked his mother to drop him off a little bit early so he could be there when Gretchen walked into the lobby with Olivia. He wanted to see Olivia. She was a kick in the pants, who now revered him even more after his performance at her school assembly. She became a little queen for a few days afterwards. Seeing her enhanced his week, and therefore, his life, because Thursdays were really the only thing he looked forward to or cared about.

Gretchen dutifully nodded a polite hello his way, and that was it. More than once, he intended to go to her office and apologize, or say something, or do something. Somehow, he hoped to find a way to atone for exploiting her kind gestures. But invariably, his throat closed tightly and his mind went blank. In a way, he was kind of glad she lost her cool. She finally succumbed to a stunning display of emotion he was sure Gretchen had never allowed herself to indulge in before, even over Will. He was glad, that she got to that point, finally. Now she knew what it was like to lose control, and how hard it was to always be good and calm and wonderful.

He left her alone, as there still was nothing for him to pursue. Even though her presence sent his pulse skittering into a weird throb, and his stomach churned strangely, he could only stare at her for long moments. It didn't matter what she was doing, or what he could see of her, he stared, and memorized every single detail about her. He'd been doing it since middle school. He looked, then stared, then ogled her every single time he caught even a fleeting glimpse of her. Now, as always.

When they were young, he was fascinated by her, even if she were just eating lunch with him, or crossing the campus with a girlfriend, or sitting in a class. He always noticed her. Apparently, despite losing his arm and enduring the ensuing outrage and resentment, the time-honored tradition to obsessively notice Gretchen was not hindered in the least. Meanwhile, she just casually passed by him without another thought.

The week after the assembly, Tony was shocked when he started getting emails and texts from people he hadn't heard from in years… some, even decades. As it turned out, someone filmed his speech at the assembly and it was soon posted on *YouTube*. He was more than shocked when he clicked on it and saw it had over a thousand views in only one day. Apparently, he was being called a hero, not only for what he said, but also for emerging from the service without one arm. His parents worried that he'd be upset at the posting, but he merely got a kick out of it.

In no time, it started to get more viewers, and the following week, it was featured on a local newsreel, before the state news picked it up. Eventually, by Thanksgiving, the national news featured it, along with his growing throng of disciples. It was really quite strange, like a wildfire spreading out of control that all began with a simple speech he made at an elementary school.

He was asked by three other local schools to come and speak at their assemblies. He was puzzled with the invitations. Wasn't Veterans Day over? No one in America really cared about its vets beyond that one day in November, did they? He accepted all three of them. Why the hell not? He really had nothing better to do. He just tweaked the speech, which wasn't very hard. Neither was throwing the uniform back on and quickly reciting the few words. It wasn't like he was doing anything valiant. For about five minutes, perhaps some kids might think about what it was like to lose an arm; or imagine that somewhere out there, young Americans were fighting in actual combat for a war that really had little to do with them, and remained pretty abstract. Several times, he was questioned by the younger students, who didn't even know the United States was at war.

But Tony didn't mind any of the kids' questions. They were, after all, just curious. It wasn't like they could comprehend such things as wars and bombs, and the injuries they inflicted. They merely verbalized what most of the adults cringed and shied away from; although they, too, wanted *to know*. And their interest was just as genuine. Tony preferred their genuine interest to their fake platitudes. He didn't mind explaining stuff to Olivia, or answering her many questions about how he functioned one-armed to accomplish the simplest daily chores.

Soon, after Tony spoke to those first three local school assemblies, others invited him to speak: high schools, middle schools, and elementary schools. Some were clear across the state, while others were up in Oregon and even Washington. Tony's dad volunteered to take off work and drive him to the longer distanced ones. Tony accepted all of them. Why not? It didn't hamper his lifestyle much, since he didn't really have one.

In early December, he glanced up and spotted Gretchen in the bleachers of one of the middle school presentations he was doing. She left before the students were dismissed and he wondered if he just imagined seeing her there.

Thanksgiving came and went, and Tony still had little to no contact with Gretchen. She politely acknowledged him on Thursdays, and that was about it. Thanksgiving Day, Tony tried not to roll his eyes whenever he saw Donny and Vickie together. All the while, his mother fluttered around them anxiously, nearly giddy with the upcoming wedding plans. She didn't yet know about the baby, which was deliberately being put on the backburner so as not to eclipse Vickie's wedding day. Tony had to bite his tongue to resist saying something sarcastic when Donny told him that with a straight face. He tended to agree with Gretchen: four weddings in eight years was a bit much to make it so "special" for Vickie. But none of that could compensate for how much he now missed the woman whom he rather successfully kept from knowing how much he liked her.

****

"You know how to do websites, right?"

Donny glanced up when Tony strode into his small office, interrupting him while he was tapping furiously on the computer. He had a headset on and loosened it to turn and acknowledge Tony.

Tony rarely came to Donny's work. Located in Calliston, it was a small office space where he and three other people typed away on elaborate computer systems all day long.

"How'd you get here?"

"I took the bus. So, websites?"

Donny scrunched his brows as Tony approached him and sat down. "Yeah, Tony, it's what I do for living. Design them, update them, fix them... I mean, tell me you do know that much about me."

"I know you're into computer language and stuff. I just never really understood what you do."

Donny frowned. "What would you need to know about websites for?"

He shrugged and stared down at his feet. "I, uh, could use your help launching one."

Donny suddenly sat up straight and rolled his desk chair away from the keyboard to face Tony. "Okay, you have my attention. Website for what?"

He scowled. "I don't know, but the whole speech thing seems to interest people. Thought a website might make it easier for people to contact me."

Donny studied him across the office with his mouth open and eyes round. "Holy Christ, are you kidding me? You want to make yourself available to the public? Like advertising and volunteering to do this?"

He shifted around, now feeling uncomfortable at Donny's obvious incredulity and sheer, stunned wonder that he, Tony, could contribute anything of value.

"It's not a big deal. It's not for money or anything. A lot of kids are just curious and stuff. And it's fine. I mean, I don't mind that."

Donny finally nodded. "Okay, wow. I'm stunned. You won't say hello to anyone, but you don't mind a bunch of kids mimicking your handicap and asking offensive questions. I tell you, man, I don't get you."

He shrugged. "There's not much to get."

"And as to not being paid, that isn't the point. It's simply that you're feeling a spark of interest to do anything that matters. This is good, bro. Real good. Yeah, of course, I'll set that up for you. I'll get right on it. Tonight even."

Tony swallowed, now ill at ease with all the attention and interest in his idea. "Look, I haven't been any good to you for the last few years. You, uh, saved me, you know. After all that stuff with Audrey... anyway, thanks."

Donny slowly shifted forward, and released a long breath. "Jesus. You've never once said thanks to me for anything. Not in the last two years, anyway."

Was that true? Tony tilted his head back and shook his head. "I was pretty self-absorbed. I didn't know how much so until... recently. I had no right. I wouldn't have stuck by me like you did. You've been a good brother. Better than I deserve, or I've ever been to you."

"Is this because of what happened with Gretchen?"

Was it? Maybe. Yeah. Definitely. He missed her. He treated her like shit, and unlike most, she stuck with him. Far longer than what he deserved. He couldn't blame her when she ultimately bailed. It was what *he* deserved, and what he drove her to do. But he missed her never the less.

But now, it felt nice to have something to do.

"I guess. I mean, she was right, of course. And I realized it, just watching how Vickie's behavior affected her. Well, I'm Vickie to you: a rotten sibling. I do to you what Vickie does to Gretchen. And I don't think it's real attractive."

Donny choked on a laugh. "You know, you just totally insulted my fiancée while attempting to apologize to me. Kind of defeats the purpose."

Tony frowned, but finally, chuckled. "You know perfectly well what Vickie is like. I know that much about you. You obviously choose to live with it."

Donny pressed his lips together in a grim smile. "Okay, I admit a lot of what Gretchen said is true. But Vickie has a huge heart, and a vast amount of loyalty. I just need to help her grow up in some areas of her life. I think she can and will, with my guidance, of course."

Tony stretched his legs out in front of him. When was the last time Donny and he just sat down and spoke civilly about anything? Especially Donny's life? The burdensome weight of how much he failed his little brother suddenly impacted his chest like Donny just reached over and thumped him hard. He had taken his brother for granted, and in doing so, missed out on having a brother, and a friend.

"You're really having a kid, huh?"

Donny winced. "Really. It's a lot, I know. For how long it's been. But…"

"I would have thought you were smarter than that."

"I usually am. Gretchen is right, there is something about her that makes a guy lose his damn mind."

"Among other things."

Donny shook his head no. "It's more than that. But… it's happening. So I can fight it or embrace it. Seems easier to embrace it and find a new life, based on the facts, and not what could or should be."

Tony held Donny's gaze and finally smiled, slowly stretching his lips. "I see what you did there. And noted, Don. I heard what you're saying."

"Well, about damn time. I can't remember when you listened to anything I had to say."

Tony winced. "Yeah, Gretchen pointed that out a time or two."

Donny smiled a secretive smile. "She's been good for you."

He shrugged. "She's fine."

Donny shook his head with a grin. "You just can't give anything up, can you? You've been crushing on her half your life. But sure, she's 'fine.'"

Tony chose to ignore the comment. "Anyway, speaking of Gretchen, any thawing on that front towards Vickie?"

"No. It's a proverbial ice war. However, I never told Vickie exactly what happened between us, so she doesn't know just how mad Gretchen is. All she knows is that Gretchen isn't thrilled about planning the wedding."

Tony snorted. "Understatement. Will she be there?"

Donny sighed. "I don't know. And I have no clue how to tell Vickie I don't know either. She doesn't doubt Gretchen's coming. How can I tell her that her big sister might not come to her wedding?"

"You do realize, don't you, that it's her fourth, right? I mean Gretchen wasn't being dramatic. That's a lot of weddings for a twenty-eight-year-old woman."

"I know. But it'll work this time. You'll see. I got this, Tony. But do you think you could talk to Gretchen? See if she'll listen to you?"

"She won't listen to me."

"She might. She really might. Come on, you were just trying to apologize for the dickhead treatment I've been receiving for a long time. Do this for me: get Gretchen to the wedding and all is forgotten. We're even."

"Really? You'll forgive everything I did?"

"Yeah. All of it. Unconditionally."

Tony didn't relish how he would manage to persuade Gretchen to forgive her sister. But he did relish seeing her again. And receiving Donny's unconditional forgiveness.

"I'll try."

He nodded. "Thank you. Thank you for doing this. Thank you for finally *doing* something."

Tony stood up and shifted his feet, now uncomfortable with all the good will. He was more used to unease. "I'm not doing much."

"It's a hundred percent more than you were."

****

"Mr. Lindstrom?"

Tony frowned after checking the caller ID again. He still didn't recognize the number. "Yeah, who's this?"

"This is the nurse at Calliston Elementary School. Olivia is feeling sick. I wondered if you could come pick her up?"

"Uh, you better call Gretchen Hendricks."

"Gretchen isn't available. We tried. You are listed as an alternate emergency contact. Olivia says you know her."

"Sure. I know her." He pulled at the back of his neck with his hand. "What's wrong with her?"

The nurse dropped her voice. "She has a stomach ache."

Instantly, he did too. *Olivia was sick? No.* He didn't like her being sick or hurt. "Okay, I'll figure out something."

He found his mother busily hemming his dad's slacks. "Can you drive me somewhere?"

She took her half-moon spectacles off. "Sure. Where?"

"To pick up Olivia."

Her eyebrows shot up almost to her hairline. "Pardon me? Why would you do that?"

He shrugged. "She's a nice enough kid. I just found out I'm listed as an alternate emergency contact. She's sick or something, and her school nurse called."

Leila's body went still, but Tony wasn't sure what the significance was. "Of course, I'll take you there."

He entered the school office exactly twenty minutes later. "Excuse me, I'm looking for Olivia Carver."

The secretary nodded to a door on the left. Entering it, he found Olivia lying on her back on a green-colored couch. She perked up when she spotted him. "Hey."

"Tony! I knew you'd come for me."

He glanced at the nurse, who smiled. "She might be feeling a smidgeon better."

"Am not!" Olivia said almost angrily.

The nurse motioned him outside. "I think it's probably just a reaction to her circumstances. But sometimes, kids just need a break; and it never hurt anyone."

Circumstances? What circumstances? "Sure. I'll just take her home to rest."

Olivia slipped her hand into his until they reached his mother's car. "Mom, this is Olivia. Liv, my mother, Leila."

Olivia hopped in the backseat. Tony suspected the nurse was right; whatever was wrong with Olivia wasn't totally physical. "Hi Mrs. Lindstrom."

Leila turned her head with a kind smile. "Please call me Leila, Olivia. Nice to meet you. I'm sorry you're not feeling well. Perhaps a glass of milk and some cookies would help your stomach?"

She giggled. "You're supposed to give me chicken soup when I'm sick, not cookies!"

As Leila backed up the car, she shook her head. "Nope. Those people all heard it wrong... it's cookies when you have a stomach ache."

Olivia came home with them, and soon ran all over the house. She spent an hour checking out Tony's basement, asking questions about everything, even though none of it was very interesting. Leila gave her the promised cookies and milk; and low and behold. She was feeling much better in no time at all.

"Will you play hoops with me? Please? I saw your hoop out front," she asked Tony, her eyes growing big and eager, as she finished her last bite of cookie, and the crumbs fell from her mouth as she spoke. He smiled at her guile, and at the cookie dust clinging to her chin and the excitement in her eyes. He hadn't shot hoops for years. He and Donny used to play one-on-one almost every night when they were younger. Will and he nearly killed themselves at times, trying to figure out who was better. Drenched in sweat, they were as wet as if they'd just showered. Tony's only advantage was being taller than Will, and basketball was the only sport where he managed to give Will a run for his money.

"Sure. I suppose we could do that, since you're feeling better and all."

She grinned and wiped her mouth on her sleeve as she hopped up. "Thank you! I love to shoot hoops! We have one at our apartment complex, but Grandma can't do it, and she won't let me go there alone... so I don't get to very often."

It seemed like there were a lot of things Olivia couldn't do. Often in their conversations, she would mention the things she would like to do. She rarely complained, however, and it was just a fact she chose to tell him. She was a remarkably positive kid, although it was quite apparent she was lonely. She spent a lot of time alone in Gretchen's office and her waiting room. There weren't many other little kids to play with. Perhaps that's why she found Tony so exciting. He had to admit it was a little bit flattering, as no one of late found him exciting anymore. Most people considered him unpleasant, awkward to be around, and downright negative. But Olivia genuinely liked him and chose to be near him. And yes, he suspected she was triply intrigued with him, not entirely because of the missing arm, but because he was a man, about her father's age, and as near as he could tell, Olivia had no one else in her life that came close to that description. She might have been transferring some of her natural longing for a father figure to him.

That was okay. What could it hurt? It's not like he saw her anymore than the one Thursday every week. Her girlish fantasies about him were okay because there would never be any reality to them. He could be nice to her, and let her know what being around a grown man was like, without making it into a big deal. Now, if he sought her out for more than that, of course, it would be wrong. It would be leading her on and developing a relationship with her that he could never sustain or fulfill. But once in awhile, just to hang out with him seemed okay enough.

He bounced the basketball and tossed it to her in a soft arc so as not to hurt her. He was shocked when she grabbed it before dribbling and running, then stopping under the hoop to shoot and making it. She fisted her hand and pumped it in the air. He ran and grabbed the ball, holding it, he grinned, "You tried to tell me you're good at this, didn't you? I don't have to go easy, huh?"

She grinned right back. "Well, maybe a little easy at first."

He mirrored her smile and they started shooting back and forth. She was surprisingly coordinated and dunked quite a few baskets for her short stature. Tony was mildly shocked when he realized that over two hours had gone by. They might have been the most pleasant and fun two hours he'd passed in two years. She was funny and quick, zipping all around the court with endless energy. He had no chance to just stand there, and think or feel awkward while imagining how much easier it would be if he had another arm. Olivia didn't give a damn that he was one-armed and acted completely natural around him. He totally appreciated that about her.

He stopped the ball when Gretchen's car pulled into the driveway. It was close to five o'clock. She got out of her car, wearing dressy pants, low heels and a sweater. Her hair swung around her face and shone, a rich honey blond in the sunlight. She shoved her sunglasses up onto her head, feathering her hair back.

Olivia ran towards her and gave her a hug. "Gretchen! Wanna play?"

She patted Olivia's head, and her gaze locked onto Tony. "Sorry, hon, not the right shoes. Why don't you run inside to get your backpack? I promised your grandma I'd have you home by five-thirty."

Olivia obediently ran inside.

Gretchen straightened up and eyed Tony. "So, I guess Helen must've called the school after the assembly and added your name to the contact information in Olivia's file. I had no idea she'd done so.

I didn't get the voicemail from the school until late. I was with patients all afternoon."

Well, sure, she had a job and real responsibilities. "It's fine. She had stomach ache, which Mom cured in about five minutes with cookies. Thinking she might have been faking a little. Maybe she just needed a personal day."

Gretchen's mouth tightened. "Yes. Sometimes she does. Her grandmother is ill. It takes a toll on her."

He glanced up. "I didn't know that. She never mentioned it."

"She doesn't like to talk about it. Even with me. She pretends everything is fine. Helen tires easily nowadays, and that's why I have Olivia so much. I'm beginning to think Olivia knew your name was added to her contacts, because I told her I'd be busy all day today and unavailable. I'm thinking she got 'sick' just so you'd get called. I think... she has a bit of a crush on you. She talks about you all the time. She even quotes you, for God's sake."

Tony bounced the ball to distract himself from staring into Gretchen's green eyes. "Well that's a first. Not many people do that."

"Do you want me to have your name removed? Tracy is listed, along with my parents, so there is no reason you should be."

He shrugged. "Seems like Olivia thought so. No, it's fine. I'll just make sure to explain to her she can't call me again unless she's really sick. Next time, I won't let her stay home."

Gretchen nodded, her expression appearing satisfied. "Glad you see that," she said, her head tilted in consideration. She was, no doubt, wondering if Tony thought Olivia should do what was expected of her, why didn't he? He ignored her look.

"Tony?"

He had to look up at her tentative tone. She leaned back against her car, folding her arms over her chest. Nothing showed, no tops of her breasts, no midriff, or inches of waist. Yet Tony's heart raced as he gazed at her, looking so cool, professional and put together.

"Yeah?"

"Thank you for doing this today. You probably did her more good in one afternoon than a few sessions of therapy. She sometimes just needs an outlet."

He shrugged, embarrassed by her praise. "Yeah, don't we all? Besides, she's a nice kid. It's no big deal."

"Well, actually it is. You didn't have to. Especially, since you don't usually. But I appreciate it. You mean a lot to her… just don't let her become too much."

"What do you mean?"

"I mean, don't let her get so attached she makes a relationship in her head that you can't sustain. You don't want entanglements; you've been very clear on that. Olivia is a huge entanglement. She's needy and lonely and easily swayed. Especially by a man who likes playing with her, like a father should. You get what I'm saying?"

"Yeah, be nice, but not too nice."

The side of her mouth tilted up. "Yeah, something like that. Again, thank you for today."

He shrugged and shot the ball, which swished in the net without touching the rim. He was aware, way too aware, she was watching him.

"You still do that pretty well. I used to think you and Will would wind up killing one or the other, just from trying to outdo each other."

"That's 'cause it was the only thing I could remotely give Will a run at."

"That's not true. You were the only one who always thought that."

He glanced up at her. What? He gave Will too much credit? Is that what she was getting at?

Olivia came bounding back. "Look at what Tony's mom gave me!" She had a baggie full of homemade cookies. No doubt, Leila was already practicing for Donny and Vickie, in happy anticipation of her first grandchild. He was pretty sure she thought it was going to happen, and soon. Unfortunately, he knew it was. The crisis he saw clearly, the mess Donny was galloping into, which thankfully, his mother didn't.

Olivia ran over to him. "Bye, Tony; thanks for the game." She threw her arms around him and he patted her head. "Yeah, you can come back and try to beat me again… but only after school, when you've stayed all day. No more skipping out, okay?"

She grinned shyly. "Okay, I promise, Tony. But can I come back soon?"

He shrugged with a glance at Gretchen. "Sure, just get Gretchen's permission. But remember; after school only."

She nodded. "After school only. Got it! How about next Tuesday?"

Tony nodded. "Okay, next Tuesday. If Gretchen says it's okay."

Gretchen shuffled off to the side of her car. "Yes. We can plan on it." She mouthed, *thank you*, to Tony with a soft, sweet smile. It made his heart ping in his chest. *Damn.* Why did he let that little bit of encouragement, and friendliness cause him to nearly swoon over her? He became a freakin' girl where she was involved.

As Gretchen and Olivia pulled out, he continued to shoot hoops. He nearly forgot how much he liked to do it. When his dad pulled in and saw him, he got out of his truck and stood there, almost in shock. Then, coming forward, he motioned for Tony to throw him the ball.

The next hour they spent shooting, talking, and giving each other shit over nothing of importance. It was the most normal they felt together since he returned home. Maybe he should have been doing a few more things like he used to enjoy. Wasn't the worst idea in the world. And feeling his dad's warm hand on his shoulder released the most overwhelming sense of pride that Tony felt in a long time.

****

The website was a complete and utter surprise. From the time Donny launched it for Tony, the response almost doubled by the day. A lot of it was stirred by the personal videos that were shot by audience members, who also posted Tony's speeches. Donny managed to collect them all somehow and they stood as testimonials to Tony's effectiveness and integrity.

The next thing he knew, he was getting booked for other things, like luncheons and conferences. Pretty soon, even the VA took notice. He was contacted by them and asked to make a few appearances. He was being hailed as an unsung hero and the Army did all it could to encourage him to continue as such.

What surprised him even more was the outpouring of emails and comments his website got. Some were generic, going on and on about thanking him for his service and major sacrifice. Some came from other veterans, some of whom were hurt, and some who were not. And many asked him for help. So many, he was stunned by the ceaseless requests. Some were like him, either injured or with skills that didn't translate to civilian work. Some didn't have the nice, middle-class parents like he did, who could give them a place to crash. Some were homeless, and some nearly so. Most were as miserable as he. It struck a deep chord in him. But what the hell could he do for them? He could barely help himself. Up until about a month ago, he didn't even want to help himself. Just because he found a reason to get out of bed during the last few weeks didn't mean he was ready to help anyone beyond himself. It was a damn miracle that he might want to do something that could improve his life.

Tony didn't believe, not for a second, that the little bit of public admiration and attention would continue on end. But he managed to engage with it while it went on. And it really did make the days go by faster as well as a hell of a lot more interesting.

Chapter Twelve

"YOU DID ALL THIS for him, Gretchen."

Closing her eyes, Gretchen expelled a deep breath of satisfaction. *Yeah, maybe she'd done something for him after all*. Her heart could have literally burst with pride for him. He had accomplished so much in the few weeks since the Veterans' Day assembly. It should have been no more than a touching, lovely moment for all who attended, and was really never expected to mushroom into anything beyond that assembly. It changed everything, at least for Tony. He was *doing* something. She checked his website daily, sometimes, multiple times a day. Donny had a scroll across the top that asked: *What makes a hero?* It was the title of one of Tony's now famous speeches, of which there were now ten. She clicked on each one of them and nearly had them all memorized by now. They were so shockingly elegant, polite, contrite, funny, sweet, and yes, very heroic. They weren't about him, although his entire personality emerged when he spoke. Or rather, the Tony of old emerged, whom she had not encountered since their reacquaintance.

The website was inundated with comments, and he had a following. In no time, Tony was running a blog. One that Gretchen read religiously. She found him shockingly honest and brutal there. It wasn't directed toward kids. He included pictures he'd either taken or found on line, as well as personal stories about his experiences. He told what it was like being a soldier, then a soldier in combat, and finally, a soldier retired from war, who was trying to live at home again.

Gretchen finally started to understand Tony in a way she couldn't until now. He truly didn't care about all the mundane, ordinary things that she and most people around her cared about. The brooding bitterness that seemed to permeate his entire attitude was due to his entire perception of life and society, which critically changed for him being at war; while most Americans didn't even realize a war was being fought. It humbled and horrified her.

She also, had come to the conclusion that *she was not right*. About any of it. About telling Tony what to do, or how to "heal." She had never considered how hard it was for him to live like any other adult. She never took into account the horrors he experienced, witnessed, and nearly died for. She did not understand it all, or how far off her standards were, for him. He was so much more than a man who just lived in his parents' basement, and it took his own words to finally show her that.

More than once, he made her cry as well as many others too, from what she gathered by their comments. He had thirty thousand-plus people loyally following him in less than a month. It was unheard of, even shocking. But when the news aired his story a week ago, his following as well as his new persona went crazy, practically on fire.

Honestly, to Gretchen, all she could think of was: *he is finally doing something.*

In answer to Will's statement, she scoffed about how little she'd done for Tony. "I only drove him to his counselor a few times. Olivia unlocked this strange, shocking, unexpected talent from the rude, gruff man we knew, and enabled him to write and orate these formal speeches to huge crowds. He articulates his feelings in such beautiful strings of words when he speaks, while to you and me, it's always 'F this or that.' So, really, no. I didn't do any of this."

"You did this." Will's tone was so sure, it was brimming with confidence. She rolled her eyes. Will called her a few times since their visit just to check in on Tony's progress. Now, he simply needed to click on Tony's dazzling website/blog. "He mentioned that very thing to me when I called to congratulate him about all of it."

She froze. "He did? He mentioned me?"

"You did something great here, Gretchen. Please don't continually doubt yourself."

She closed her eyes. "No. The day this started, I lost my freaking mind at him, because of Vickie's engagement to his brother. I refused to ever again drive him or help him. So, no. I really didn't do this. I was awful to him."

Will chuckled. "Yeah, well, he was awful first. Maybe, you should have been awful to a lot more people than just Tony, and starting a long time ago."

"Like to you? No. I didn't like how it made me feel afterwards. Sure, it felt nice to say and do exactly what my inner, nasty child thought, but the real me, once calm, was filled with remorse, and I've had knots in my stomach ever since. I can't be that person."

He let out a sigh. "I have to tell you, I'm glad to hear that. You're one of the few women I've ever met who doesn't want to vent, and therefore, doesn't do it. But once in awhile? You have to embrace the inner, nasty child."

She finally laughed. "Thank you, Will."

He cleared his throat. "Look, we never discussed this... but Tony, he did want you all those years ago. He quit talking to me on your behalf, because I chose Jessie over the Army and not you. He really did always have it bad for you. Really bad. I looked the other way because... well, you know. But it was a real thing. And from what I see now, it isn't gone. Don't let his bullshit fool you. Consider him, Gretchen. He might be changed, but he's a really good guy."

"I know that. I never doubted it. I just don't much like him *now.*" Except now, she seemed to harbor some strange, unending attraction to him, although he treated her much more rudely. Maybe she needed counseling to learn why a guy had to treat her awful before she suddenly noticed him sexually.

No, not sexually. Just noticed him. She just noticed him now.

But now, this whole Tony-doing-something-great-and-important, was throwing a wrench into what she had decided was the "new," but so not improved Tony. Now, he was deep and articulate and his writing was beautiful. His words and descriptions about his life, and living it now, almost made some of his behavior seem excusable. Almost understandable. Almost something she could release. She was finding it harder and harder, however, not to admire him.

She finally ended the conversation with her ex-husband about dating his best friend with a quick, "Tell Jessie hello and kiss Christina for me."

He scoffed. "As if Jessie isn't about to rip the phone from me to talk to you herself. But I will kiss my daughter for you. And Gretchen... just consider Tony."

She barely heard a word Jessie said. All she could think about was Will's parting words... *consider Tony.*

Consider Tony. Consider him for what? What good would come of considering Tony for anything? Now she wasn't even sure she could call him her damn friend.

****

He knocked on her office door before he entered. She leaned back into her chair, setting down the pen she was using to write some notes about a frustrating patient she couldn't make much headway with. Brainstorming her ideas on paper sometimes helped her figure out where to next take a session.

Tony stepped into her office. He wore the usual and his hair was as usual. His entire look was more like a bum on the street than a former heroic soldier. Still, her pulse reacted by bumping up a notch. Yeah, maybe she really needed to investigate the reasons why nice, normal, attractive men couldn't arouse much of a physical reaction in her; but rude, crude, annoyingly uncouth men could.

"Yes?" she finally prompted when he didn't immediately speak. It was Thursday. He was there for Dr. Hart, not for her. Olivia came past him suddenly, skipping over to Gretchen, and giving her a kiss on the cheek. She rounded the desk to steal a granola bar from the bottom drawer. Gretchen kept an array of healthy snacks in there for Olivia.

She took it over to the kids' area and started playing, oblivious to Tony standing there, uneasily shuffling his feet. She tilted her head. Did he seem somehow nervous with her?

"I, uh, wondered if you happened to catch some of the crap going on about me? From the assembly."

His head was down and his eyes darted around to Olivia, then to the window, and finally, to her cabinets. He was asking her if she knew? As if she somehow missed it? Right. But didn't it mean something he cared if she knew about it or not? She could deny it, and play coy. Or play like she had no idea how amazing he and his speeches were. Yet, how polar opposite she found her experiences with him. But lying and playing games was never her way. She was not going to be disingenuous now.

"I know all about it. I read everything you post. Every comment you've written, and I've watched every video of you. So, yes, I know all about it."

"Oh. I was unaware of that."

"And?"

His gaze shot up and he scrunched his eyebrows, as if confused by her question. She sighed and shook her head. "And so what? Why were you asking me, Tony? Do you want my opinion? Do you want my commentary? Do you actually want to have a conversation with me? Because I spent three months trying to have one with you and got nothing in return. So if this is you making an attempt to have a conversation with me, you're going to have to spell it out."

He shuffled around. Then, "Yes, I guess I wanted to know what you thought."

She leaned forward, crossing her arms on top of her desk. "Fine. Then, what you've done in the last month is nothing short of miraculous. I am not only impressed, amazed, stunned even, but mostly extremely humbled by what you managed to do. I really hoped you'd do something. Anything. I was thinking of you bagging groceries at the local grocery store. I never dreamed you'd do something like this. It's important work. And it's helped more than one person. From where I sit, you are worthy again of wearing the uniform that took your arm."

"I don't get paid. It's not like a real job or anything," he mumbled finally.

"It's better than a paid job. It has meaning. And true worth. And it means something to you. I can tell by the careful choice of words you use. I wanted that for you, to feel a sense of worth, which is much more valuable than a paycheck."

His hand cupped the back of his neck as he pulled on it. She well knew from past encounters, any kind of personal talk made him twitch around weirdly. But he came to her for this and she really wasn't in the mood to argue with him or try to make him do it.

Finally he nodded. "Thanks."

She smiled slowly, trying to hide her disbelief. What utter gall he has to be so short, and act nearly put out by her compliment. "Anything else?"

"Yeah, uh, Donny mentioned things aren't too good with you and them. I wondered if you were going to the wedding."

"The wedding? Yes. Do I have a choice? My parents already made sure I was. After all, Vickie *is* expecting a baby. I did get downgraded, however, from maid of honor to bride's maid. And don't worry, the dress she picked out is the ugliest, and the most expensive, to date. So, it's all right on track. And, oh yeah, she is ruining my Christmas. We're celebrating it the weekend before, so poor Vickie won't miss it, since they leave for their honeymoon in Florida on Christmas Day. So, I get to be freaking alone on Christmas. Tracy goes to her husband's family, and Mom and Dad are going to be celebrated out. You can rest assured; Vickie's day is going to be just as wonderful as the other three wedding days. I'll behave as I always do. Besides, she never even knew how upset I was, now did she? Donny never told her. I know he didn't."

Tony smiled. "No, he didn't. He asked me to make sure you would come."

"You? Why ever would he choose you?"

"I owed him."

"For?"

"You know how I've treated you these last months? Well, I was like that to Donny for two years."

"And what? You don't act like that now?"

He shrugged. "Not so far as that. But I'm trying not to."

She nodded and slowly rose. "Really?"

He smiled slowly and she blinked, feeling intrigued. He was a different man when he did so. "Really."

"Well, I hope it continues. Dr. Hart's standing in his doorway behind you."

His eyes traveled over her. "All right. I'll see you. Bye, Olivia. See you next week."

She bounced to her feet and ran to throw her arms around his waist as she smiled up into his eyes. "Promise?"

He met Gretchen's gaze, "If I make a promise, I mean it. I never break a promise."

****

Vickie started through her door the second she opened it. "Oh my God! Did you know about the ex-fiancée?"

Gretchen stepped back before Vickie almost mowed her over. Vickie thrust a garment bag at her and Gretchen caught it against her chest. Apparently, Vickie's gossip must've outweighed her excitement in bringing Gretchen her freshly altered, pressed, and hideous, gold-colored bride's maid dress.

"What ex-fiancée?"

"Tony's!"

Vickie was in the living room now, almost jumping up and down. Gretchen placed the dress on the back of the recliner. "What? What are you talking about?"

Vickie's eyes glowed in excitement. "I knew you didn't know either, so I had to come and tell you. I know you're a little bit ticked about the wedding date and all, but I knew you'd want to know this."

"I'm just worried it's happening too fast." Gretchen hedged, unsure she wanted to get into that, especially when it would go mostly misunderstood by Vickie anyway. "But what do you mean 'Tony's ex-fiancée'?"

"Sit, sit. This is good. Donny and I were talking about the wedding, and somehow, we got into a little disagreement about how much a decent wedding cake costs. I explained he's never planned a wedding before, so he wouldn't know anything about it. Not like I do. So he interrupts me by saying how he planned half of Tony's wedding before it was called off. Well, that ended our argument. I demanded to know everything, and I mean *everything* he knew, knowing you'd want to know everything too."

Gretchen's eyes twitched. She did want to know. And she wanted to know everything as dramatically as Vickie suggested. She was anxious and couldn't wait for Vickie to say it. That was weird, considering Vickie shouldn't have known she'd want to know. Shocking, when her sister sometimes did catch onto things. "So?"

"So, he was engaged for two years to a girl named Audrey Vang. Two years! I mean who could ever picture, that rude, gruff, scrungy hobo Tony is now, being engaged? They were planning their wedding when he was deployed for the third time. They lived together in Calliston, in a little apartment over the bookstore. Then... after the whole one-armed thing happened, and he returned home, she dumped him and called off the wedding. Can you believe that? I mean, the guy loses his arm, and she dumps him? Even *I* would *never* do such a heartless, selfish thing. Oh my God! I really can't believe any woman could do that and live with herself. So after it happened, Tony moved back into the basement of his parents' house and Donny says his attitude went from broken and upset, to the guy we both see now."

Gretchen merely sat there, unable to move or think or speak or blink. *Tony was engaged?* She had no idea. And she couldn't have, for it happened after he quit speaking to Will. And the girl dumped him over his missing arm? Everything became sharply apparent to Gretchen in that moment. He didn't come home to his parents. He came home to his fiancée, broken and hurt, and without an arm. Vickie's right, even she wouldn't have left a man in that condition.

"I don't even know what to say."

"I know. I mean, it's even more tragic than it was before. Spurned by the woman who was supposed to love him no matter what? Of course, he's so broken and angry. Of course, he lives with his parents. How is he supposed to trust anyone after that? And of course, he needs to live with someone, I mean, I saw him trying to plug in an extension cord so he could vacuum out his mother's car. He couldn't do it. He couldn't get the extension cord plug to hold still long enough for him to squeeze in the electrical plug. I ended up doing it for him. He was nice enough about it, but I imagine, being a guy and all, it must be shattering to his ego. So considering that, of course, he can't be alone."

Gretchen shut her eyes when she realized Vickie managed to figure all this out, and not she. Vickie was right, about all of it, and yet Gretchen, the trained therapist, did nothing but judge Tony. She was even disdainful of him. And she had no right.

"I can't believe this. Donny didn't tell me. I wish he'd told me that."

"Tony swore him to silence. Donny said Tony specifically instructed him not to tell you. He does not want you to know. So, of course, I had to tell you."

A ghost of a smile hovered over Gretchen's lips. Vickie was solemn and earnest. She only came there to tell Gretchen because she thought Gretchen would want to know. She ignored Donny's warning as well as Tony's privacy because she wanted Gretchen to know about it. In some ways, she could make up for a lot of the things she did wrong. Gretchen suddenly threw her arms around her little sister. She was, yet again, confused about why she was totally done with her sister before Vickie managed to redeem herself.

"Are you done being mad at me then? I hate it when you're mad at me. More than anyone. You know, I just don't think sometimes. I found out I was pregnant, and Donny's solution was to get married. I was so relieved, I jumped on it, because I was afraid he might not want me or the baby. So I should have told you in a better way."

"I'm not mad. Just… worried. You guys don't have a shared history to base a marriage on."

Vickie smiled. "But we will have this baby. Please, say you forgive me."

Gretchen sighed. "I might have overacted. I'm sorry too."

Vickie waved her hand around as if to say, "Who cares?" "So, what are you going to do now? About this? About Tony?"

Gretchen shook her head. She had no freaking idea what to do, but knew she had to do something about this. For Tony.

****

"Why didn't you tell me about Audrey?"

Donny sighed into the phone as Gretchen spoke without any preamble, even though he was at work. She didn't care what or whom she was interrupting.

"Vickie told you?"

"She ran directly to me with the information. As you surely knew she would," Gretchen flipped her chair around so she was staring out her office window. "Thank you, by the way. It wasn't lost on me you knew she'd tell me. I needed that information, and it explains a lot."

Donny was silent. Then he said in a softer tone, "What does it change for you, Gretchen? What? Are you helping him, as his friend? Or is there something more that you feel about Tony?"

She shuddered at the thought of feeling something more towards Tony. He was impossible for her to imagine caring deeply about. He would more than likely run her over with a car, than ever lovingly return her affection. But no other label could fit for how she felt; and the truth was, this most recent knowledge about him did change something inside of her. She did feel an odd rush to do something about it, or with it. "I don't know. I just know it matters. Can you tell me about it?"

He sighed. "I said too much already. He will not forgive me for saying a word about it, and we've just barely gotten to a decent place for the first time in years. Just… maybe, ask him about it. Tell him Vickie told you. I can defend telling Vickie, but not you."

She bit her lip. Donny had a point. "Thank you. I'll think about it."

189

Donny cleared his throat. "So are you and Vickie good again?"

"I don't think she ever knew we weren't. You never told her what I said, did you?"

"No. Not really. Just that you were worried about the length of time we'd spent together."

"I guess it's good. I don't really want to lose her as a sister."

"So you'll be at the wedding?"

"Yes. I was never *that* mad. Just… are you sure about this? You're assuming a lot of responsibility after a very short amount of time."

"I know. I'm all in on this. I mean it. I love her. I want to do this. I want to get married, and I'm even okay with the baby. Yeah, it's all too soon. But I think we can manage it. I know your concerns and I know why you have them. But she's different with me. She will be different."

No, she really wouldn't. But maybe, just maybe, Donny loved her enough to let it be. But then again, he was careless enough to get her pregnant, so he had to deal with the consequences. No matter what Gretchen thought, Donny was better off going into this thing with his optimistic attitude. Maybe it would make him survive better than Vickie's other grooms.

****

It wasn't hard to find the listing for one Audrey Vang. It was a very unusual name, and she was the only one listed in the area. She moved about fifty miles away and ran her own insurance agency. Gretchen sat on the information for a week. Why did she procure it? What did she plan to do with it? Talk to Audrey? Behind Tony's back? That would be weird. And wrong. And well, why would she do that?

190

So she didn't. She just stored the information on her phone and remained confused over what she was planning to do with it.

Meanwhile, Christmas was fast approaching. She got recruited to finish the last of the details for Vickie's wedding, as Vickie began panicking about everything and had no clue how to really tie up all the loose ends. Gretchen's mother was on her to help her sister, so albeit, unwillingly, she finally did.

Olivia became more and more a part of Gretchen's daily life as her grandmother became sicker and could barely manage to take care of her any longer. She had her every afternoon now, and at least one night or another on the weekend. She hated to remove Olivia from spending more time with her grandmother, but Helen could no longer take care of her very well. Gretchen couldn't stand the idea of expecting Olivia to quit being a kid just so she could take care of her sick grandmother. She was becoming increasingly affected by it. Olivia was often quiet and withdrawn. She even got in trouble twice at school, enough so that Gretchen had to go and speak with her teacher. Although they were aware of Olivia's circumstances, they couldn't allow her behavior to go undisciplined either.

Gretchen's stomach fluttered every time she thought about the day when Olivia would not go home. Her arms ached to hug and hold Olivia as she observed her rising confusion and grief, not to mention fear over her grandmother's declining condition. Gretchen tried to hang back a bit, just to let Helen be her mother still, and primary caretaker, guardian and the first love of Olivia's life. So it was a strange, precipitous road on which she trod now. At some future date, Gretchen would legally adopt Olivia as her daughter. Gretchen hoped she was starting the process already by making her emotionally aware of Gretchen's love and support. But for now, she remained her loyal babysitter and friend whenever she was needed.

Gretchen still saw Tony every Thursday, and purposely left her office door open whenever he was there. She might have even blocked out that time slot, not scheduling any patients for that particular hour. It was fascinating to listen and watch him with Olivia. He smiled and joked with her. He verbally engaged her, while his voice was a flat monotone with any other person. And Olivia loved him. She often talked about what Tony said or did, or how he accomplished this or that, using only one arm.

Still, Gretchen didn't know what to do with her latest bit of information about Tony. Did it reveal something about him? Did it explain why he was the way he was now? Or was this all a direct link to his bitterness?

During some moments, Gretchen was pretty sure she deserved his recrimination and reproach. Only now was she starting to understand the enormity of what Tony had to endure. She sometimes, but only when no one else was around, and in the privacy of her own home, attempted to do things one-handedly. It was, she found, extremely hard to do things she would have never dreamed would become a problem. Even trying to twist the toothpaste cap on or off was tough. And forget about working the average can opener. When it came to preparing dinner; she all but gave up. She lasted less than a minute trying to cut up vegetables before abandoning that. Grabbing the end of one carrot, she gave it a satisfying "thunk!" as she sliced through it with a knife.

It was a bitter and humbling pill to swallow; she couldn't handle being one armed for even a day. She had completely underestimated how hard it was. She could not comprehend how hard a disability like losing an arm was to live with, especially day in and day out, as Tony had to now. She even erroneously thought she understood until she tried to spend an entire day by using only her right hand. It proved to be impossible for her to commit to. So how, then, did Tony? A pang of guilt churned her stomach as she realized she couldn't handle it for a single day. Yet Tony was relegated to it for the rest of his life.

How dare she be so judgmental of him?

She remembered him telling Will how he spent all day just trying to do the things that everyone else took for granted. Maybe... Tony wasn't being so unreasonable. He really was disabled. But for her, it was hard to contemplate or comprehend Tony Lindstrom as being that way. He wasn't the first face to pop into your head when you thought of people with handicaps and disabilities.

Even stranger, ever since she got angry with Tony, and lost her temper right to his face, he started behaving much better towards her. His life in general seemed to improve. She didn't get it. None of it. Except that Tony was one of the hardest people she had ever dealt with. And she didn't know why that was, because she had no label to describe what or who he was to *her*.

Chapter Thirteen

"SO, HOW WAS IT?" Gretchen asked as she opened the door for Tracy.

Tracy rolled her eyes. "As you'd imagine. Just like the other three." Gretchen did not attend Vickie's fourth bachelorette party. She simply could not do another one. It was the same girls, all of Vickie's friends, whom she collected from her menagerie of jobs and living situations. Gretchen, luckily, had Olivia over, who gave her the perfect excuse.

Tracy and Gretchen were doing the centerpieces for the reception tables. They were candles adorned with candy canes and holly all around them, in line with the season. And they also landed the job of putting it all together, as Vickie had last minute fittings and appointments. Their mother shamed them into it with guilt, so here they were, a few days before Christmas putting the centerpieces together.

"Do you think there is any hope for *this* wedding?" Gretchen asked her sister.

Tracy bit her lip and her smile finally stretched around her teeth. "I think Donny is a really nice, stable man; and I just have to wonder, when was that ever Vickie's taste? I think she got pregnant and is now reaping the unforeseen rewards."

"Do you think she meant to?"

"She claims not to have, but I think so. I think she loves falling in love. I think it scares her to be alone, which is why she falls in love. I don't know if she's ever actually been there though. It's sad, really. And unlike most girls who shuffle through men like Vickie does, she invariably chooses the nice guys, and never the bad boys. I think she inevitably leaves them because they're not the kind of man she wants, or the kind she can relate to. Ultimately, I think she leaves them before they wind up leaving her. As we both know, she is impossible to live with, day in and day out. They all eventually discover that... which must be why she always does something horrible and leaves them behind, before she gets left behind."

Gretchen set down the candy cane she was positioning in the fake poinsettia arrangement. With her mouth open, she stared at Tracy in obvious surprise. "Wow, since when did you become the psychologist? You know what? You're right. About this. And about Vickie. About what inevitably happens."

Tracy nodded as she popped one of the candy cane bites into her mouth. She had long, straight, red hair and unusual, gray-hued eyes. Her coloring was a stark contrast to Gretchen and Vickie, who appeared strikingly similar. "I have too much time on my hands to think about it. Micah's been working a lot lately."

"As always." Gretchen corrected her. Micah McKinley perpetually worked long hours. He had eighty-hour work weeks sometimes, and was employed at an investment firm. Being smart and focused, he always managed to provide Tracy and their two daughters with an upscale, solid lifestyle.

Tracy grimaced. "Yes, okay, as always. The weekends, especially. So when Vickie called me to do this or that for the wedding, I agreed."

"Can you imagine how she'll handle a baby? Then again, maybe it will finally make her accountable to someone else, and she'll *have* to do something."

"I hope so, sis, I really hope so. I just don't think Donny has a clue what he's in for. But the idiot walked straight into it with both eyes open, didn't he? Micah always says Vickie's husbands shouldn't be such stupid imbeciles who only think with what's inside their pants."

Gretchen laughed. "I knew I always liked Micah."

Tracy smiled in agreement. "I know you always have. So do I. I just wish I saw him a little more."

Gretchen looked closer at her sister, "You sure everything's okay? You look more tired than usual."

She waved her hand around. "I'm fine. Just a case of the winter blahs."

"You can talk to me; you know that, right? If it's ever anything more."

She shook her head and her hair fell over her shoulder. "I know, my crazy-successful, psychiatrist sister. I know who to talk to, and it's certainly not Vickie."

Gretchen went back to the centerpieces. After finishing three more, she stared at her hands as she tried to ask in a casual voice, "So, what does Micah think of Tony?"

Tracy's eyebrows shot up. "You mean the Tony who looks at you as if he's undressing you and picturing all kinds of nasty in his head?"

Gretchen dropped the arrangement. "Tracy!" Her married, long settled, well behaved sister never spoke like that.

Tracy smiled and laughed with glee as she stretched back and lay down flat on the floor, pushing all the crap around her away. "Oh, my prissy sister, he totally does that. And you're not asking for Micah's opinion, which, I have to say, is surprisingly good. He likes both of them. But you're asking right now because you're thinking that maybe you should know what nasty things Tony thinks about doing with you."

Gretchen abandoned the crafts too, lying beside her sister and staring at the ceiling. "You see what a colossally bad idea that would be, right?"

Tracy shrugged and turned her head to meet Gretchen's gaze. "You and I never did anything but the smart thing, for which there was always a reason. Vickie got to experience what is was like to have all the irrational, crazy, bad ideas. So maybe, just this once, you should try that."

"Do you regret it? Not acting more like Vickie?"

Tracy shook her head. "Not really. I love my kids and Micah. It's just… we were always responsible and smart and centered. Just as Vickie never was. Maybe, after doing everything right, you should try something a little crazy."

"With an angry, one-armed Army veteran who isn't even all that nice or fun? That doesn't sound like fun-crazy, it sounds stupid and ill conceived."

"Maybe… it just might turn out to be everything you ever wanted. You are the nicest woman I know, maybe you shouldn't be with the nicest men we know. Maybe you should try being a little more like Vickie."

Gretchen shuddered. "God, I didn't think you'd ever give me such terrible advice."

Tracy rolled onto her side, and put her hands under her head. "I think you deserve to have a little crazy."

Gretchen studied her sister's face, which now seemed more serious and intent. "You really think Tony Lindstrom is someone I should sleep with?"

"Yeah. I do. There hasn't been any man whom you talk about like you do him. It's complicated and rough and not so nice. Every other man you've been with is usually nice and uncomplicated. Maybe it's time to try something different."

"I wasn't thinking about it even. Besides, you know why I can't. Not right now. This stuff with Olivia is going to do nothing but get more intense, and more time-consuming. It's going to be my entire life in a matter of weeks or months. I owe it to her to give her my complete attention."

"Yes, and you will. Just as I do with my kids. But, Gretchen, the first thing you need to understand about parenthood, is that you have a life too. You don't give it all up. Not like you're thinking, or you'll burn out in the first few months. It's exhausting enough without being super-human. You can love Olivia, and take care of her, and still have a sexual side to your life. You deserve to have a relationship. I don't think Helen meant for you to give up your entire life. Olivia is going to be a critical part of the bigger whole, just like my kids are in my life."

"I don't know. I just don't think now is the time to do anything different or unusual, because so much will be different for her soon."

"Well, think about it. Or, don't think about it. Let yourself... just be. Stay in the moment. With this man. Just be yourself and let him be him, and see what you might find."

She frowned and studied her sister. It was such simple, but serious, advice. And maybe it was something worth considering. She never perceived Tony as someone whom she could be with. Obviously, she never fantasized about Tony. It seemed like everyone else did, however.

Could she simply just be with someone?

She grabbed Tracy's hand and squeezed it. "Thank you. If only I could get my personal life together like my professional life. I wish I was half as good at it as you."

Tracy smiled and tilted her head up before shutting her eyes with a deep sigh. "Ah, Gretchen, no one ever gets it all right, not all at once. You just try to get it so it's livable."

****

Tony watched Gretchen walking down the aisle towards him. He shifted the weight on his feet. *Damn.* She was gorgeous... but the dress was hideous. It was worse than the three she showed him that day in her condo. It was a strange kind of metallic gold-like material, that brushed the floor and appeared to be a giant bell. It shimmered and twirled whenever she moved, bustling up the back, but pulling tightly across her chest. The only positive feature was the way it purposely squeezed her breasts together and formed a deep, mouth-watering cleavage. It created smooth, white globes that his hand itched to touch, and his tongue salivated to lick. Her sister had the exact same dress on, and her red hair clashed even worse than Gretchen's blond. Except for the spectacular cleavage, Tony felt sorry for them having to wear the gold aberrations.

He stood next to Donny at the altar, and was almost ready to step forward to grab his brother. Donny seemed pale and twitchy; and several times, Tony wondered if he would pass out. Or run at breakneck speed the opposite way from where he was staring now, waiting for his new bride.

Well, hell, Tony couldn't blame him. The last week was extra long in preparation for this night. Vickie was bat-shit crazy, irresponsible, and impossible, just as Gretchen tried to explain to him and Donny. She cried about everything. The caterer was rude; and the color of the champagne glasses was wrong. Tony didn't know how clear glass could be the wrong color... but apparently, it could. She was bloated, she was tired, she didn't like the way the hairdresser cut her bangs... And the list went on. More than once, Tony almost dropped to his knees in relief that it wasn't he who was marrying this difficult, demanding, quasi-crazy, but drop dead-gorgeous girl.

When Gretchen paused a moment before him and Donny, her eyes met his. A small, secretive smile crossed her lips and she tilted her head down and up as subtle acknowledgment of his presence. Even in the most repugnant dress he ever laid eyes on, Gretchen could pull it off, making it understated, elegant and gorgeous. He smiled in kind and discreetly lifted his hand and did a strangling gesture at his neck. She smiled even wider as she put her hand to her mouth, letting him know she got it. She assumed he was motioning he'd rather hang himself than be standing there at the altar. She turned and took her place across from him, and next to her sister. Tracy's eyes were shining too, and she must have seen his slight gesture, but apparently, also appreciated it. Tony always liked Tracy better than the sister his brother chose to marry.

The chords of the wedding march started and the entire congregation rose and turned to look at the back of the church. Except for Tony.

He turned and stared at Gretchen; but weirder still, she turned and stared at him. She smiled again, only this time, it was a big, goofy smile, showing all her teeth as she rolled her eyes and tilted her head towards Donny. Tony nodded his agreement. And then... they just stood there, grinning like Cheshire cats rather stupidly at each other. Tony didn't realize it until Vickie came right between them in her rehearsed march up the aisle. She stopped beside Donny, who accepted her hand, before shaking Vickie's father's hand as a symbol of her father "giving" her away. Tony wondered if her father would offer Donny a bill of sale this time, just to get rid of her once and for all.

Unfortunately, Donny and Vickie blocked Tony's view of Gretchen. He could only catch glimpses of her when they tilted forward or backward. When it happened, she instantly beamed with happiness, and stranger still, so did he. When was the last time anything could manage to make him grin like a total fool?

He had no clue what was said in the ceremony, and tuned out the entire cartoon-like event. To him, it was nothing more than a farce. After having witnessed enough of Vickie during the last week, he knew Gretchen was right about everything she originally tried to tell him and Donny.

Donny's marriage was doomed to cold ashes just like Vickie's previous three. The only sickening part was the baby that would now complicate it all.

Suddenly, his brother completed the ritual, kissing his bride and taking her hand before they turned to be introduced to the adoring crowd as Mr. and Mrs. Donald J. Lindstrom. Donny darted a hesitant, strange glance at Tony right as the minister announced them as "husband and wife." Cringing only slightly, Donny turned back and smiled. Tony blinked as he wondered if he just imagined that.

He waited until his brother and bride walked to the back of the large room before he stepped forward. He took Tracy's elbow in his and began heading to the back of the church. She was several inches shorter than her sister with an impish, and very girlish smile, even though she was the mother of two little girls.

"How long do you give it?" Tracy's lips were plastered in a frozen smile. She whispered it so only Tony could hear.

"You agree with Gretchen, huh?"

"I agree with reality. How about you?"

"Unfortunately, I think she's right too. But Donny's a good guy. He can put up with a lot." Tony didn't add that his statement included Donny having to put up with him. Donny's unflagging loyalty in his attempt to be a good brother, despite how hard Tony made it for him, aptly illustrated his ability to bear the most unbearable people.

"A lot? Well, this will surely test it. You don't know my sister. But you do know my other one, don't you? Tell me, Tony, when are you going to make a move? Isn't twenty years long enough? Even I knew how much you liked her; and I was five years younger than you two."

He almost missed a step as they came to the foyer of the church where they were hidden from the other guests' line of vision. Did Tracy really just say that? No, not mild-mannered Tracy, who never said anything out of line, let alone, that.

"I—"

"You're chicken. The missing arm. Will. Donny and Vickie. Whatever you want to blame it on… I think it's just because you're afraid."

He stiffened. "You're not as sweet as you look."

She smiled wickedly. "No, I'm not. Gretchen's the sweet one. So, when, Tony? When are you going to finally admit it to her?"

"Your husband is looking for you." He nodded towards Micah who was scanning the crowd before he found Tracy and smiled as he came walking up to them. Tony gratefully left them without answering her inquiry.

Afraid? He was not afraid. He, unlike Donny, just accepted reality as it was. He saw reality more sharply, and clearly, and would never spit in the face of what he knew to be true.

He did, however, promise his mother he would be nice, if only for tonight. He promised to socialize, smile and not be like his normal self. She rarely asked anything of him. Strangely, she accepted his reclusive, rude ways, and seldom pressured him to do otherwise. He figured he owed her.

Chapter Fourteen

FINALLY, IT WAS OKAY to leave. Tony let out a long breath as his brother and Vickie disappeared down the street, their limo's brake lights illuminating the dispersing crowd before turning and disappearing. He glanced sidelong at Gretchen. She was staring after the car too. She finally lowered her hand from waving and glanced at him with a smile.

"Well, for better or worse, there goes number four. Lord willing, it will be the last."

He chuckled. It was hard to see Vickie as Gretchen's sister, but then again, most people might think that way of him and Donny. Donny, of course, was the good brother, and he more like Vickie.

They were free to leave at long last, after gushing goodbyes to all and hugs to everyone. Except Tony. Most people skipped hugging him as his demeanor scared most of them off. He was glad of it. Hugging the one-armed man was a bit awkward for most people. He seemed weird to them, and they weren't sure how to act.

"Tony?"

He turned when Gretchen's voice caught his ear. She walked quickly toward him, since her heels were now off and being carried in one hand, while she used the other to hold the skirt of her dress back. He watched the swishing of her legs, revealed by the hiked up skirt.

The old, familiar twitch in his dick simultaneously occurred. It rarely happened anymore, but for some reason with her, it did.

"Are you leaving?"

He shrugged and didn't feel much like explaining that he would wait outside for his parents to drive him home to their house.

"Do you want to come with me?"

Versus catching a ride with his parents? Yeah, not much conflict there. He nodded this time as he followed her and she quickly headed toward her car.

She threw her stuff into the back and settled her skirt temporarily as she started the car and brought her seatbelt around her. The skirt was a pre-formed thing with a sewn-in wire or something to keep it stiff. It stuck up awkwardly when she sat. She pushed at it, frowning as it kept interfering with the steering wheel.

Tony couldn't help but laugh. She slid a glance his way, and finally, she laughed too, opening her legs, and smashing the dress between them before clamping her legs back together. "I need a freaking leash for this thing. Can you believe it?"

His eyes never left her thighs until he raised them to her face, and began to flush as he wondered what it felt like to be clamped between those thighs. Luckily, owing to the passing semi-shadows of the car's interior, she didn't realize how much she affected him.

"Okay, you didn't lie about the dress thing. She does it on purpose. What is that thing?"

"I know! I mean it has a hoop skirt. It's metallic, and oh my God, does the gold wash me out so much, I look sickly. But, as always, she did look beautiful."

"She's half as pretty as you. Even wearing that dress."

She whipped her head towards him, stopping her car before backing up. Her gaze roved over him, studying his eyes and moving down his face, as if looking for the joke. Finally, she smiled softly, "Thank you, Tony. It's not often you say nice things to me... or anyone, really."

He glanced out the window to break the soft look he saw in her eyes. She was probably glad to see how well he was behaving.

He tapped a finger on the armrest and watched the fleeting lights of Calliston passing by. He sat up a little when he realized she wasn't heading for his parents' house.

"Uh, you forgetting to drop me off?"

She slid a quick, hesitant glance toward him. "I wondered if maybe you might like to come over for awhile. It's Christmas Eve. I really can't picture anything more depressing tonight than to go home alone, after attending my sister's *fourth wedding*. I already know your family had no plans either, and I thought we could hang out for a little while. And not be alone on Christmas if we're together. If you don't mind, that is."

"Mind? Would I rather go home and sit in my parents' basement or hang out with a beautiful woman? I think I can skip the basement for a few hours. I didn't lose my mind, just my arm."

She smiled, but didn't look at him. "Was that humor? Are you, Tony Lindstrom, attempting to be funny?'

"It's hard not to feel a little humorous, while sitting next to a gold-plated Scarlett O'Hara."

She laughed out loud and shook her head. "That's it. What to call this dress. I couldn't figure out how to describe it."

She pulled into her parking lot and he followed her up the stairs. The strange skirt swung all around as she moved. A bow on top of a kind of box-like thing bubbled over her butt. It looked like she was dressed up for Halloween, not just home from her sister's wedding.

Once inside, she clicked on her lights, and a Christmas tree lit up along with them. It sat in the corner, opposite the couch, tucked against the windows. It was illuminated entirely in white lights and covered in ornaments and ribbons. It reflected colorful, little spots along the wall beside it. Treasured Santas and snowmen lined her mantel, tables and a bookshelf. Another string of lights came on with the flick of one switch. He turned around, taking it all in.

"So, you getting upset about the Christmas Eve wedding date was about more than just your sister getting married again. You really have a thing for Christmas, huh?"

She was setting her purse down on the counter that separated her small kitchen from the living area. An adjoining dining room lay off to the left. She unclipped a bracelet, and slid it off her wrist before plopping down next to her stuff. He had to avert his eyes to quit staring. It was oddly sexy, and surprisingly intimate for him to watch her removing her jewelry, and becoming less made up. She was undoing an earring then.

"Yes. I really do. I love it. And I resent not being able to celebrate it this year with my family. We usually are at my parents' house tonight, and I stay over with them. Tracy's family comes over too; and then tomorrow, we come here to have Christmas Day dinner." She reached up over her head, digging her long fingers into the pile of hair she swept on top of her head. Then she tugged on it and chunks of hair started to slide down until she scratched her head, shaking it out and sighing, as if contented at last. She threw the hair clips next to her pile of jewelry.

"Make yourself comfortable. I have to take off this aberration. My God, six hundred dollars it cost me. Can you believe it?"

He really couldn't. He slid off his dark suit jacket and vest before loosening the bowtie and slipping it into the pocket of his jacket. He sat down on the end of couch closest to the window and stared at the festive, happy-looking Christmas tree. She really like her lights and decorations. He tapped a finger, and his toes jiggled while his throat seemed parched. *Christ.* He felt like he was sixteen and at a girl's house for the first time. Where were all these nerves and anxiety coming from? He didn't get nervous. But strangely, now he was. He wasn't sure what to say or do when she reappeared.

He glanced up when she stepped back into the room, wearing loose fitting, gray pants that clung to her ass and outlined her legs. Her sweatshirt matched in what was supposed to be a casual, nothing-to-do kind of look. Except, on Gretchen, nothing was casual.

"Do you want some wine?" she asked while opening her fridge door and disappearing behind it.

"Sure." He didn't know what he wanted or why he was there. She was acting more comfortable and casual. It was obvious she had him there in the standard capacity, as her normal, comfortable friend. He turned his head to stare out the dark windows.

She came closer, setting the wine on the table next to his hand, where he could comfortably reach it. As she leaned over to set it there, she glanced up at him, and their eyes met and locked for a second too long. Her eyebrows scrunched, as if confused why she was staring at him. She straightened up suddenly and stepped over his legs before heading back to the kitchen. Retreating?

He had the distinct impression whatever just happened must've made her uncomfortable. He took the glass and drank liberally. He wasn't much of a wine enthusiast, but it was better than nothing.

She came back in and flipped the overhead light off, so the Christmas lights created a cocoon-like glow that was at once both cheerful and intimate. She clicked the TV on, which hung on the wall at the right of the tree. She sat down on the couch, unceremoniously, not choosing the opposite end, but not right next to him either.

Why was he there? That's what he wanted to know. Why did Gretchen, after six weeks of almost no direct, deliberate contact, invite him to her house on Christmas Eve? Sure, they were at the same wedding, and kind of at the same place in life, i.e., watching their siblings marry, but to now find himself on her couch on Christmas Eve, made his head spin and his heart beat erratically. It was not what he expected.

"Do you mind?"

He turned his attention to her. "Mind what?"

She indicated the TV, and he turned and realized what she wanted to know. *White Christmas*, with Bing Crosby and Danny Kaye was just starting. He shrugged. "No, I don't care."

She smiled her appreciation. Moving her butt around, she deftly tucked her feet up under her, before switching all around again. The laugh escaped him before he could stop it. She glanced his way.

"Hard time getting comfortable?"

She finally smiled. "I feel... agitated, for lack of a better word. It's such a weird night. Vickie's fourth wedding. Donny and her having a baby... and everything happening on my favorite night of the year, that is no longer my favorite night of the year."

"And me being here makes you less agitated? Don't I usually make things worse?"

She bit her lip. "Yes. You can make a lot of things worse. But for some reason, tonight, you seemed like the only one who would understand."

"That, and I had no home to go to either? So by default, the perfect candidate."

She grinned, and it reached her eyes. "There is that too."

He leaned back and stretched his legs out. "Wow, listen to you. Being so honest."

She shook her head. "Shh, the movie is starting."

So, he shushed; and watched *White Christmas* on Christmas Eve with Gretchen Hendricks. She got up towards the end of it to refill her glass, and when she sat down again, she was half a width closer to him. He sat up straighter, startled. *Huh.* She couldn't have meant to get closer to him. No one did. No one ever tried to get close to him.

She yawned and tugged on a blanket that was folded up and draped over the back of the couch, holding it around herself. He didn't know why he was there. Or why she was so casually nearly lying beside him. Was he nearly hyperventilating now because the girl he spent twenty years fantasizing about having sex with was finally, for once, near him? And she did it all voluntarily and at her own instigation. This time, his best friend wasn't the reason she was so close to him.

"Should you call your mom?"

He jerked from his reverie, confused by her strange question. *His mother? What?* He frowned and asked, "Why should I call my mother?"

"She might be worried. I just realized she doesn't know where you disappeared after the wedding. What if they're worried about you?"

He sighed and leaned forward, resting his elbow on a knee. "Jesus, Gretchen, I don't have to report in to my mommy."

She was silent for a moment and it surprised him, causing him to jerk up to attention when her hand touched his knee only seconds later. "I wasn't trying to insult you. I meant, because you live in the same household. Not because she's your parent. I meant, like I used to let Will know, or Vickie, when she lived here. I just meant it as a courtesy. And it *is* Christmas. She might be worried."

He let out a breath, feeling annoyed before admitting, "I already texted her while you were changing."

"I knew there was a nice guy hiding behind all your... distractions. You're too nice to your mother," she said softly, her eyes looking up into his. Her face was close, as she leaned over to touch his knee in what, he assumed, was a sisterly pat.

"Distractions?"

Her pink tongue came out and dabbed the top of her lip as her throat visibly swallowed. "Yes, the way you bluster around, so rude and uncaring, when I think... no, I feel sure it's just the opposite. You care about still being alive. You care about your parents. You care about Donny. You care about not knowing what to do with yourself, now that you have only one arm," she said in a near whisper As she gazed down towards his lap, she added, "And... you care about me."

You care about me. Everyone knew it. Everyone had already guessed it. Either twenty years ago, or now, whatever, whenever: they all had guessed. His parents. Donnie. Jessie. Tracy. And Will. Will had always known. The only one who never did was Gretchen. Tony's entire body froze. He kept his expression blank and uncaring, fixing his gaze on one of the Christmas tree ornaments hanging directly before him. He scrutinized it and instructed his lungs to lift and release air through them; but to not, *absolutely not*, even glance towards her and see the pity and compassion in her eyes to discover that the pathetic, one-armed, Tony Lindstrom, her dear, friend of many years, *cared* about her.

What he should have done was simply grab her, and show her exactly how much he cared about her. He was not her nice, dear friend and never claimed to be. He wanted her naked and quivering under him, her thighs squeezing tightly around him, her breasts bare and his hand clasping one between his fingers. He wanted her screaming with delight and having orgasms from the things he would do to her. He wanted her to shut up and stop talking about his feelings or getting better, but to just let him *feel* better, simply by being inside her body.

Maybe if he did any of that, she'd get the idea that he did not, in fact, care about her in the tone in which she implied he did.

But of course, he would never attempt such a move on Gretchen Moore back when he was only a teen, and he certainly wouldn't now with Gretchen Hendricks. Not as a one-armed former soldier who lived in his parents' basement.

"Tony?" Her voice had its familiar soft, sweet quality. He finally tilted his head down so he could see her eyes. She slowly slid closer to him, her eyes fastened on his. She sat then, placing her body alongside his, and tucking her legs beneath her before slowly tilting her head until it made contact with his chest. He drew in a sharp breath at the unexpected touch. She was leaning against his armless side. No one ever touched him there. He never allowed anyone that close to it. His entire body stiffened. What was she doing? And why? Why was she doing that?

Minutes drifted by. Five minutes. Ten minutes. Twenty. He finally blew out a long breath and his muscles relaxed just enough to be more comfortable. *Friend.* Gretchen was merely leaning up against him as a friend. As always. Forever friends. Dear, sweet, long time friends.

Wasn't he just the luckiest bastard ever?

Chapter Fifteen

GRETCHEN'S HEART WAS HAMMERING and her breath hitched. Where was this physical reaction coming from? She had known him for so long, how could touching him right now feel so different than it did a decade ago? But suddenly, strangely, everything shifted and changed in her feelings toward Tony Lindstrom. Somewhere along the way, she became attracted to him. She developed new feelings towards him that were nothing like the friendship they shared so long ago.

She tried to gulp down the lump of nerves lodged in her throat. Why was she so nervous? It wasn't like when she was fourteen and hoping Will would kiss her. She was a thirty-five-year-old woman who'd had plenty of partners and relationships over the years. She dated strangers, friends, and friends of co-workers. She went on blind dates and online dates. She did them all.

But none of them could make her feel like she did now. She felt soft as mud, and so scared to move, it was like concrete suddenly replaced her muscles. She was so nervous, her breath couldn't regulate. And so excited to be finally close to him, she couldn't stop her head from spinning. Except, they'd done nothing. She could hear his heartbeat beneath her ear. It sounded speedier than it should have. He had to feel this chemistry too. The rest of his body, however, was tensed in what almost felt like disdain, but she had to believe was just nerves.

She took in a sharp breath and slowly tucked her legs in closer. She slid her head up higher on his chest and turned more fully into him before resting her face inside the crook of his neck, near his chin. There was no arm there to circle around her. It was odd. And different.

But, it didn't matter.

His breath fluctuated and he seemed to freeze all of a sudden. She slid her hand to the collar of his shirt and tilted her head up enough so she could gaze over the planes of his face. She took in his deep, sensuous lips and mouth, the neatly trimmed beard that covered half his face, and his long, perfect nose. His gaze was still focused straight in front of him. As if it was nothing. If this were truly so casual, he would have glanced down at her. He would have done something besides freezing up as if in shock.

Her fingertips touched the bare skin on his neck. She felt the vocal chords of his throat moving as he swallowed. The skin was soft, and so warm. The line of his beard was only inches from her fingertips. She inched her hand marginally lower, to the hem of his white, crisp, dress shirt. She slowly, and with excruciating thoroughness, undid the button, one-handedly. It wasn't something she had any proficiency in. She tilted her head back and saw his lips part. But still, his gaze was far off, and not looking down at her. She proceeded to the next button. Again, she undid it. Then the next. And the next. It took her several torturous minutes. He didn't move. Not an inch, but kept his arm on the armrest of the sofa, with his hand clenched into a fist on top of it. His feet were firmly planted on the floor and his back was almost perpendicular to the couch. He seemed as immovable as a granite statue. His jaw flexed, but his gaze remained straight ahead, like a rookie in boot camp toward his instructor. He never once looked Gretchen in the eye. She had no idea what he thought. Or felt. But, wouldn't he stop her if he didn't want to?

His heart rate accelerated.

Adjusting her calves and feet beneath her, she sat up and twisted her body to face his. She pushed her hands into his hair, tugging on the rubber band he used to restrain it. She freed it, letting the soft, thick strands drift freely through her fingers. She'd never done that with a man. It was odd, and also erotic.

Her face was only inches from his. His nostrils flared and his breath became erratic and ragged, while his pupils dilated.

She had no idea she was going to do this. She didn't even really realize she *wanted* to do it. But she knew now that she really did. She wanted to touch him. She wanted to see his expression soften with her. And for him to engage her, and experience all of the softness she could offer to replace the harshness he now knew and lived his life in.

When his shirt was completely undone down the front, she moved a hand down his chest. The backs of her knuckles slid along the skin of his chest, and down the rippled muscles of his abdomen. His stomach quivered in response. His breath again hitched when she opened the shirt. His chest was sculpted and hairy. She touched it, allowing her palms to feel him, and the hair, gritty under her hand.

She shifted forward and onto his lap, straddling him, with her legs bent back on either side of his lap.

He finally had to turn his head from the formerly scintillating Christmas tree so he could look into her eyes. Her heart stopped and skipped a beat. His gaze was intense and demanding, but also intimidating. She gulped down her nerves and virtual fear. He was too much.

She could feel him under her bottom, getting hard and reacting to her. Her body suddenly screamed its response. Blood rushed through her, and she felt like her body literally opened up for him. She started to slide his shirt off, when he finally responded.

"Don't." The tone was unnecessarily harsh. And commanding. She lifted her eyes to his, and found his jaw tight and thrust forward in steely determination.

She lifted her hands off his shoulder in surrender. Cupping his face, her hand touched his beard. It was prickly, yet soft and kind of feathery. She lowered her head finally and touched his lips with hers, barely applying any pressure with her lips on his. As she did, her entire body reacted as though he suddenly found her G-spot. Her body responded by swelling and expanding in anticipation of him and their practically nothing kiss. She felt him underneath her as hard and scalding as a hot ember of coal. She ground herself into him. Gasping at the sensations that suddenly rocked from her crotch all the way up into her gut, it became so intense, it was almost uncomfortable for her.

She opened her mouth and stuck her tongue into his. It was not soft or slow. She became aroused, and thought if she wiggled around enough, between his tongue stroking her and his dick hardening under her, she just might come.

He finally engaged and lifted his arm to embrace her back, with his hand cinching at her waist. Squeezing it tightly, as if anchoring her, he shifted his hips up into hers. His tongue met hers in wet, sliding ecstasy as he caressed her mouth and tongue with his.

She nearly shouted out with glee. It was *so* good. It had been awhile, years maybe, since she could get so turned on from simply kissing a man. Her last relationship had been a short-lived, casual affair that only lasted five months with a neighbor's son. It ended quite amicably and with no ill will, since they simply didn't have much of a sexual connection. They had a nice time together, and often hung out just because it was better than being alone. But they only had sex every third or fourth time they were together, simply because it didn't seem to matter to either one if they did or not.

Never did sex feel like this. Hot. Smoldering. Her whole body was engaged, although only their tongues actually touched. She wanted him, and it made her heart feel like singing. It had been a long, monotonous while since she really wanted a man like this.

She moaned out loud as his tongue lapped at her lips, and caressed the inside of her mouth. She ran her hand along his chest, letting her fingertips trail over the bare skin, and down lower, over his stomach. His body tensed and reacted. Her other hand clung to his shoulder, just above his amputation; and she could feel his muscles contracting. He reacted to her. And had since the day in the grocery store. No, long before that, since they were barely teens.

She shut her eyes when his body's warmth filled every one of her nerve endings. As his wet mouth surrounded hers, she groaned at the lightning bolt of sensations now stabbing her nether regions. But she had to be sure about this. To do this with him, and to him, she had to be sure. It wasn't fair otherwise. But, how could it feel so incredible if she wasn't really into him? Maybe she wasn't before, but apparently, sometime during the last few months, she developed a kind of chemistry with him that was, quite literally, shocking to her senses. She really didn't know she felt that way, let alone, so intensely that way. But she did. Her body felt like it was on fire. She felt like she was where she was supposed to be.

Or was she just avoiding loneliness on Christmas?

She drew back suddenly and they found each other, both staring at each other in the warm, cozy lights of the Christmas tree. It was as romantic as candlelight. It was pretty and soft, things that Tony was not. He was harsh and rude. And hot and bothered. Rough and tough. He was also adamantly unwilling to let her see him as anything beyond that. He didn't want her pity, concern, understanding or sympathy. She was pretty sure that's what his attitude was all about from the start.

The thing was, of course he got those things from her. She wasn't a monster. His damn arm was missing. As if she could overlook it and not care. As if she could accept it as being just fine. It wasn't fine. But not in the way Tony thought. It wasn't fine because it was so goddamned awful that it happened to him. It was so unfair. And her heart twisted and contorted with pain to try to understand what it must feel like. How it had to change his life. How it altered his personality.

But that didn't prevent her from seeing him as a valid, fascinating, attractive, hot man. She saw him as all that. Not as the project or charity case that he thought she did. No. There was no room for that in how she felt about Tony. She was clear of that one fact.

Even if he wasn't.

But he refused to let her care about him. He did not want her sympathy and care about him not having an arm. He would not soften his demeanor, or his feelings, not even in the way he spoke to her, just because they engaged in sex. She had to know that before having sex, and to be sure she could handle Tony's reaction to something that was rife and full of emotions. She was already very much engaged with her emotions, and most of them were far more than just a physical reaction to him.

His gaze didn't flicker, and his eyes held hers…. waiting. His brown eyes were dark, deep and emotionless while he anticipated her next move. But his intense look was hard and unforgiving. She drew in a breath that filled her lungs and made her head dizzy. Was she ready for something with Tony?

He was already waiting for her to reject him.

Somehow, she was instantly sure of that. His blank look, and almost bored expression were deceptive. Inside, his heart was jumping. She could feel it against her hand. He wanted her, and he wanted her to want him. And the only way she knew it was from his body's reaction to her touch and presence. He probably thought she stopped because of *the amputation*. But that was about last on her top ten list of concerns. She mainly worried that *he* would hurt *her*. But as sure as she knew her own name, she knew he wouldn't understand that. He would never believe that.

He would believe it, however, if she had sex with him. He had to finally believe she didn't see him as Will's old friend. Or even *her* old friend. She almost longed for the simple days when she did think of him that way. At least then, he wasn't the source of all this confusion, which now boiled in her chest.

She licked her lips and tried to swallow the lump in her throat. Lifting her hands off his chest to toy with the collar of his white shirt, she lowered her gaze and smoothed her hands along the tops of his shoulders. She was brushing out the wrinkles until her hands dipped off his shoulders. On one side, her hand kept sliding down his arm, now encircling her waist. The other dropped off to nothing, but she slid her hand down along that side too. She tilted her eyeballs up under her eyelids just enough to see him shutting his eyes while his face contorted. In horror. He was shocked that she was touching his side. His fingers dug into her waist and he had an amazingly strong grip. Enough that she felt like he could one-handedly squeeze her in half.

"Don't touch me there," he finally said through gritted teeth.

"I'm not. I'm touching your shirt. But I want to touch *you*."

His eyes popped back open before he grimaced. She finally found her voice and her bravado. She needed both to get through this with Tony. This meant having sex with him and then continuing to see him afterwards. If she did it, which she knew now she really wanted to do, then they weren't having sex only once. They were doing it as a means of exploration, with the possibility of a relationship. He just didn't know it yet. Since he probably wouldn't believe it anyway, there was no point in even trying to explain it to him.

She waited a moment before staring into his eyes and raising an eyebrow as if to challenge him. She tipped her head closer to his, so their noses were touching, and their eyes nearly crossed, looking at each other. "Unless you don't want me to touch you. Do you want me to stop, Tony? Is that what you want?" Her tone was soft, but insistent.

His breath hitched and increased, and his nostrils flared. She leaned back finally, and waited, doubtful he would toss her off his lap. He was just as hard as she felt turned on. There was no denying that, no matter how much Tony might have feared it.

And no matter how hard he found it to be vulnerable, he had to be for her. At least for this. Sex.

221

Having always had a physical thing for her, there was no way he intended to turn her down.

"Is it?" she whispered.

He shook his head finally, with his jaw clenched tight. "No, it's not what I want."

"Because you want me?"

He nearly growled at her, "You know I do, and I always have."

"No. I didn't know that. Not until recently. So, no, I didn't know that, Tony."

She tilted her head to the side and touched his lips again, this time soft and gentle. But she nearly inhaled him. Her lips closed as she touched them to his. He gasped and suppressed a groan, which she clearly heard as his fingers closed again around her waist.

She leaned back, still straddling his lap, before releasing him. She slid her hands to the bottom of her shirt and slowly brought it up over her stomach, her chest, and her shoulders until she lifted it overhead and threw it down on the floor.

His eyes widened minimally. Tony never offered much. There were no words of tender love or how much he adored her features. She had to rely on the subtle, small signs and let them do the speaking for him. He still had to convince her he did indeed like her and want her.

Her black bra was strapless to fit under the ridiculous bridesmaid dress. Lace covered it, but her nipples peeked through, now pointed and hard from the cool air, as well as the nearly physical grasp of Tony's gaze on her. He suddenly leaned forward and his mouth fell on her left breast. Hot moistness touched her skin through the lace. The trunk of her body jerked in a shocked response. His tongue touched the tip of her nipple through the material, flicking up and then down.

She rocked herself against him in a near mindless response. His arm around her held her and kept her from nearly falling backwards. She should have wanted to take it slowly, and in their own time. To touch and kiss and lick all the different areas of erotic interest to each other. But she didn't take it slowly at all. She wanted him now. Here. Right this instant. She didn't usually go for quickies. Never. No. She was usually agonizingly slow and prolonged. Preferring the leisurely build-up and anticipation. Half the time, she enjoyed all the foreplay more than the actual sex.

But not this time.

She wanted to do it now. Right now. She wanted him inside her. She thought she might simply come while dry humping him with his mouth only touching her through her bra.

No. She was not twenty anymore, and unable to control her damn self.

She grabbed the edge of her bra and simply tugged it down her waist, shoving it out of the way. Tony drew back an inch with surprise at her heated, nearly angry, struggle with the bra. She laced her fingers into his hair, and pulled him toward her. His lips encircled her, wet and sucking, grasping onto the end of her engorged, hard, nearly pulsating nipple. His tongue touched the end of it again, but this time, it was bare. He twirled his tongue over it, and up and down, until sinking his teeth gently around it and sucking. He sucked until she began furiously pushing down on his erection and nearly becoming frantic and screaming. She physically pushed her other breast toward him, hoping to receive the same mind-numbing, erotic treatment.

Her fingers abandoned his hair and went straight down to the button and zipper on his black tuxedo pants. She was so full of nervous, excited adrenaline, her fingers failed to cooperate. They were trembling and fumbling clumsily with his pants. She nearly screeched her annoyance. Finally, the button gave and she managed to undo his zipper with a raspy sigh. Her gut quivered in response and excitement, exposing him and releasing his pants, *for her*.

His teeth and tongue pulled, tugged, licked and caressed her, until her hands eventually quit moving. Then, every thought, feeling and ounce of awareness inside her simply stopped. She was no longer a thinking, functioning woman. She was simply a mess of hormones and sensations that started deep down in her gut somewhere. She was still being pulled and manipulated by his mouth simply being on her breast. He was barely doing anything else. It was hardly more than making out, but suddenly, she was clutching his head against her, and her hands tangled in his hair as she groaned and came without a conscious thought that she even was.

She came in a surprising rush merely from the feelings he evoked by pulling on her breasts. She leaned her forehead down against his collar as the aftershocks, still surprisingly strong, shot off inside her like fireworks that didn't explode with the main event.

She sucked in a deep breath as the silence of her condo finally cut through her blurry haze. Instantly, a deep sense of modesty and shyness filled her. She could feel the heat of a blush starting in her chest, which quickly rose towards her forehead. She came without doing one thing to make him feel good. She came from barely his touch. What was that? How could she have reacted that way? That much? It was almost ridiculous. He would probably think she hadn't had sex in a decade, and simply needed a quick hand to get it.

But that wasn't the case at all. She never came so easily. It usually took at least a bit of work from her partner. And a bit of time. And some effort. She usually didn't behave like a live wire, simply waiting for a connection. She only came because of specifically doing it with *him*.

She tilted her head so her lips brushed over his neck. She could see all the planes of his face. Burying her face into his neck again, she mumbled. "I don't know what that was. I never do that. I mean, I do that, but just not from... *this*."

He smiled for the first time in about an hour and angled his face so he could see her. "This?"

"Nothing. You did almost nothing and you saw how I reacted to it." She had to turn her face away, she was too embarrassed to see how he, no doubt, would smirk at her revelation.

Instead, his tone was quiet, and nearly soft as he replied, "If it's any consolation, I felt the same way."

She went still and peeked back up at him. "Really?"

"Really," he smiled warmly. It was the first time she'd ever seen him smile like that. It was completely different than usual. It was soft and kind. And specifically for her. It was a secret, sweet, almost flirtatious smile. In a way he hadn't looked at her ever. She was sure of that. It wasn't about his missing arm. Or his history. Or her history. Or anything... except this special moment. That he could make her feel that way. Her reaction to him, and his to her. For once, his missing arm wasn't inhibiting how he naturally reacted to her. His usual guard was down.

She needed for it to start again. There was no way she could end it so soon. She touched her lips on his warm neck and felt his pulse through them. He still sat nearly rigidly erect on the end of her couch. His spine was so straight and perfect, it was almost as if he fused it together to remain so. His arm still encircled her and his hand rested on the side of her waist.

She stood up suddenly, from straddling his knee. Nearly ripping her pants and black panties off, she dropped them to the floor before lifting her feet and kicking them away. She unhooked her bra and let it drop too, until she was totally naked.

His gaze started on her knees and rose inch-by-inch up her body. He wanted to take it all in slowly, drawing it out. She felt the urge to shift her weight from one foot to the other because it was so intense. The way he kept looking at her, with his dark brown eyes flashing like sparks could shoot out of them and burn her bare skin. His gaze was very long, staring at the light hairs of her sex, and over her stomach before they lingered on her breasts.

She had never been particularly shy with her body. She knew her long legs attracted some men, and were her best feature. Her butt was fine, if not a little too flat to be called fashionable. Her stomach wasn't perfectly flat, and she was average in weight. She never claimed to be a model or a specimen of perfection. But she was usually attractive enough to the men she dated. And pleased most of them. There were never any comments about losing weight or suggestions to firm this part or another. But now suddenly, with Tony staring at her as if he intended to assess her fitness, she felt her confidence sinking. He was extremely thorough in his perusal, and there was not an inch of skin he seemed to miss. Starting from the stubborn cellulite that clung to the back of thighs, to her stomach that molded out, not in. She was not considered fat by any means, and wasn't like most women, who assumed they were fat no matter what. She knew she was not overweight. But she also knew she was not as small or thin and trim as say, someone like Vickie. She had a few imperfections that were balanced by a few out of the ordinary features. Together, it made for a pleasant enough package.

She couldn't take his intense, undivided focus on her. She dropped down and nearly crawled across him. This time she spanned his chest, with her head on his good shoulder and his arm under her, holding her.

"You don't have to be quite so... much."

"What?"

She gazed up at him. There was something different about him right then. His face was as intense, but not as harsh as usual. He wasn't automatically frowning, and his eyes were alive and bright. Normally, they were dull or angry or dark.

"Do I pass inspection, Sergeant?"

He stared down at her, but after a long moment, his lips stretched back as a smile, young, boyish, and nearly charming, brightened his usually lined, unhappy face. He turned his head, and once more, his gaze glided over her body until his eyes landed on hers. "Well... I guess you passed."

She tapped his shoulder with her knuckle in a fake, light hit. "You are so not funny. Although, I guess we knew that already. Tell me, until this moment, when was the last time you smiled?"

His dry tone and expression went blank as he countered, "Tell me, when's the last time anyone got you off properly?"

Her mouth dropped open. "Did you just say that?"

"Didn't you just do that?" he countered.

Her eyebrows lowered as she tried to figure out why Tony was acting so weird. So different. So... almost likable. She hesitated and finally asked, "Are you... teasing me?"

He smirked and the laugh shook his chest. "I am. I'm teasing you."

Even his tone was different. It was… well, *tender*, for lack of a better word. He was gazing at her, his eyes bright and kind as he smiled down at her cradled in his arm. The soft, ethereal-like lighting transformed him. She lifted a hand from the back of his neck and touched his beard. Her fingertips stroked his hair, kind of brushing it downward in rhythmic motions. "So all it takes is stripping naked for you to be nicer?"

"Well, it certainly won't make me mad."

"Everything makes you mad," she said softly, her tone more serious than a moment before. "Especially at me."

He lifted one corner of his mouth and shook his head slightly, as if in regret. "I know. It's just hard to face someone like you; particularly when you look the way I do."

"Someone like me? How am I?" She frowned at the odd statement. What was it about her that so set him off?

His eyebrows lowered and he tilted his neck backwards. "Perfect." His tone was crisp and sure, and sounded almost annoyed that he had to say it. As if she should have just known that… when it was truly the last thing she ever knew with him.

Her breath released from her lungs in a shocked, surprised exhale. "You think that of *me*?"

"I don't think. I know."

"Will—"

"I don't want to talk about Will." He was instantly sharp-toned and frowning.

She nearly had to choke on her frustration. "'Will' as in, will you stay the night here? I was going to ask you to stay, not call you my ex-husband while I am lying naked across you. Unless, that was somehow lost on you."

His lips twitched and she could see the start of a dimple indenting his cheek. He was amused by her disdain. "It's not lost. Nor unappreciated."

She kicked her feet and started to sit up, feeling annoyed now. He tightened his hand on her stomach. How the hell he managed to hold her back, one-handedly, while most of his arm was under her, was a mystery. But his damn grip was like a steel trap, clamping its jaws around her middle. "I'll stay."

She lay back, letting his words calm her. "And you'll be nice?"

"If you'll stay naked."

She smiled. "I won't stay naked. So you have to be at all times, even when I'm not naked."

He finally smiled his response. "Why would you put any clothes back on?

"Because I don't intend to spend Christmas buck ass naked."

His face dimmed. "We're spending Christmas together."

She tilted her head and said simply, "I hope so."

He nodded. "Okay."

"Okay, you'll be nice to me even when I'm not naked? Or okay, you'll spend Christmas with me?"

"Both."

"Wow. I'm like a double winner. Who knew nudity was my weapon of choice with you? All the doctors, talking, and therapy in the world can't breach your defenses like a glimpse of naked tits, huh?"

His chest again shook. Twice? She made him laugh twice in one evening.

"Only yours. I've waited a long time to see them."

She tugged on his neck until he leaned his face closer so she could kiss him. She wiggled around, and instantly, his body came alive even more than it was under her. Their conversation was lost as their kissing progressed. Minutes passed. Twenty minutes passed. They made out like teenagers. Their mouths, tongues, and breaths all mingled together in hot, moist air and wet saliva. She could stay right there forever. Right there, sprawled across his body, as his mouth did things to hers she forgot that kissing could do.

She felt those feelings building up again. Things that should not have been swirling in her insides so soon, so easily, and over almost nothing. With so little foreplay. It was ridiculous. She shifted around until she was again straddled over him. She scooted back enough to finish the job she started earlier. He shifted around off the couch to let her move his trousers down before struggling with his boxers; but finally, managed to get them enough out of the way.

She wrapped her hand around him. He groaned and shut his eyes as her fingers made contact. He stopped moving, and his breath came in sharp, ragged gasps. She moved her hand along him, pulling, stroking, and petting. Her skin felt nearly burned by the intense heat radiating off him.

"My wallet," he mumbled suddenly. His head leaned back on the couch and his perfect posture vanished as he seemed lost to her ministrations. The feelings it ignited inside her were too strong and unexpected to ignore.

"What?" she asked, puzzled by his request.

"There's a condom in my wallet."

"Oh." She nearly blushed to the roots of her hair. Like a forgetful, turned-on teen, she'd almost given it no thought. She searched his pants until she found the wallet buried inside them. Quickly flipping through it until she found her prize, she pulled it out.

He watched her with his head tilted up as she started to hand it to him. He shook his head and gestured to indicate she should put it on.

That seemed more intimate than touching him. She leaned over and put her mouth on him first. His entire body stiffened and he nearly jerked off the couch. She sucked the tip of him and his head finally flopped back as she slid him inside her mouth. His hand fisted in her hair, which he spread over his lap. She could not believe what they were doing already. Now. Tonight. She didn't plan any of this, let alone, to be kneeling in front of him, completely naked, with her mouth semi-swallowing his penis. Her breasts kept brushing against his legs as she moved up and down on him. They became so sensitized, she had to groan in response. There was nothing he did that failed to turn her on and nearly set her off.

"For God's sake, put the condom on me, Gretchen." His voice sounded strangled. It barely pierced through her senses. She slid her mouth off him and he nearly sprang out of it, he was so hard and ready. Her fingers shook as she worked the packet open. She couldn't manage to open it and finally had to use her teeth to rip it before quickly sheathing it over him.

She spread her knees and settled herself on either side of his trunk, with her body hovering over him. Grabbing onto his shoulders for balance, he gazed up at her, but she couldn't hold his stare. He seemed so intent on watching her. She shut her eyes, falling into complete bliss as she slowly slid herself onto him with perfect ease. She was there. Finally. Tony was inside her.

They nearly groaned in perfect unison. She started moving on him, using her knees as support to push her hips up and down, slowly at first, but increasing in momentum until she was nearly bouncing on him. Her breasts jiggled right in his face until his mouth caught one and she cried out. He was deep inside her and his mouth was on her hardened nipple. He thrust his hips again anchored her waist over and over, while she floated off into Neverland, and with a final groan, he joined her.

Chapter Sixteen

"TONY?" SHE WHISPERED. HER head was resting on his shoulder, and her body was pressed against the front of him. The house was strangely quiet after the frantic, erotic noise of just a few moments ago. Now, yet again, they were back to weird.

"What?" he barely mumbled back, sounding half asleep.

"Can we go into the bedroom?"

He pulled his head back and dropped his hand from her waist. "Yeah." His tone was husky.

She slowly extracted her limbs from where they were wrapped around him. She really wished she'd thought the whole thing through a bit more. First off, maybe not in her living room with bright, happy lights flickering all around her, and being buck naked while he was half dressed. Perhaps on a bed, in the dark; maybe then, she wouldn't have felt quite so weird.

Rising to her feet, there was nothing else to do, but allow her naked body to be scrutinized by him. His eyes stayed on her and she could feel him watching her when she leaned down as politely as she could to retrieve her shirt and slip it over her head. She turned away to end the excruciating self-consciousness and clicked the tree and mantel Christmas lights off, plunging the room into mostly darkness. A faint glow from far off streetlights made it shadowy as she hurried into her bedroom since her bare ass hung out from under her shirt. She dug around in her dresser for a decent, silky soft, pink negligee. Somehow, the moment didn't call for lingerie. Maybe it was because Tony was the most intense man she ever dealt with intimately, and she was a little unsure about where they stood now. It was so hot between them, they didn't need to ever bother with seductive attire or any other props.

But he was also the one man who kept her completely unsure about what he might say or do, not to mention, feel about her. He was so unpredictable, she couldn't fathom his reaction to their lovemaking.

He followed her into the bedroom a few moments later. She dared to glance his way. His shirt was still undone, but on, and his pants were back on too, where they were supposed to be.

She swallowed her anxious nerves and quickly disappeared into the bathroom to get ready for bed. He was sitting on the edge of her bed when she came out. He still said nothing. *Okay. Silence. Awesome.* It was like they were strangers. His gaze was glued onto her as she clicked the bathroom light off and came around the bed. He finally got up to go into the bathroom. She waited and didn't know what to do. Get into bed? Pretend she was asleep? Ask him why he couldn't be just a teeny, tiny more friendly or open, or just well... nice?

He came out and her breath caught in her chest. It was ridiculous. She felt more nervous with him then, at that moment, than ever before. After they'd already had sex. There was no reason for her to feel so weird.

He hadn't done his pants up. No doubt, it wasn't an easy task to do one-handedly. Was that why he so often wore sweatpants? She originally thought it was an anti-fashion, anti-society statement to go with the rest of his new look since retiring from the Army. But maybe it was more a matter of function than statement. She really did underestimate all the obstacles he lived with. Her neck and cheeks grew warm at her new realization. How could she have been so callous at first? She was a trained therapist, and yet, all she thought Tony needed to "get better" was to move out and do something. She thought if he engaged life again, he would automatically heal his wounds.

She had tried to completely downplay how hard every moment of his daily existence was on a physical level, let alone, the emotional ramifications of his limitations. She had not given enough considered how hard it must be for a man who was once extremely athletic and active, to suddenly be *handicapped.* He kept the shirt on and slid into bed beside her.

It was quiet for a long while and they didn't touch. The air seemed taut with unsaid words, along with their nerves, and how weird the situation was.

"Are you okay?" Tony spoke in a hushed, hesitant tone. She lifted her head off the pillow, completely astounded he would even think to ask her.

"Yes... any reason I wouldn't be?" she asked, puzzled.

"This wasn't part of your plans." *Statement. Not a question.* He felt sure she didn't want this. And probably thought she regretted it. She slid across the space that was separating them. She was lying on the side without his arm. She adjusted her body beside his, letting her arms come around him. It was odd. She could lie her head on his chest, with nothing beneath her to make her uncomfortable. She felt around until she found his hand and clasped it in hers.

"Plans are often overrated," she finally whispered, clutching his hand tightly. "Besides, that was the..." *What word could possibly describe it?* "No one could have ever planned on *that*."

His chest moved as he released a breath fraught with tension. He chuckled finally and she just barely made out his nod in the gloom of her room. "Yeah, *that* was good."

"*Good*? What then do you have to do in order to achieve amazing, fantastic, hot, and orgasmic? I mean, Jesus, what kind of sex do you usually have?" Her tone suggested her dismay at his lack of enthusiasm.

"You. I do you and it's that amazing, fantastic, hot, and orgasmic. Is that even a word?"

"It is. And now I finally know what it means. What the action means," she hesitated before adding, "So, it wasn't just me?"

He swallowed, but after moment, whispered back, "No, it wasn't just you."

She let out the breath she was holding. It would have been humiliating for her to be so turned on, after having just had the best sex in her life, for Tony to say it was good, or fine, or decent, or, you know, regular sex, and it would have certainly crushed her. No... it would have totally ruined her.

But he thought it was something else too. Something different and special. And wonderful. What did that say about them being together?

The thing that amazed her most of all was that it had nothing to do with *the amputation*. Because until now, everything about Tony had something to do with his arm.

She suddenly sat up. "We should do it again. See if it was just an anomaly."

"Anomaly?"

"Yes, you know, a one time, freak thing. And since it felt that good, why shouldn't we?"

"Uh, okay? Did you think I'd say no? You don't have to ask me twice."

She straddled him, pushing her nightgown up. It was a lot easier with him flat under her and using the bed for support. He was ready at once, simply from talking to her. Okay. This just might be orgasmic again as her entire body responded to him. She leaned down to start kissing him.

She could feel his mouth stretch into a smile under her lips as he mumbled, "I had no idea you were quite so much... into it."

"Into what? Sex?" she pulled back, frowning. "Why? Why wouldn't I be into sex?"

He cleared his throat. "I don't know. You're kind of reserved and conservative in your real life. I just didn't expect it. It's a good thing. In fact, it's a great thing."

"Will never told you about us?" she said, scowling in childish annoyance.

He squirmed under her. "I really don't need Will's image in my mind right now. Because it's not as easy for me anymore." He reached his hand up behind her head to pull her back towards him.

She resisted, keeping her mouth inches from his. "What do you mean? Not as easy for you?"

He sighed. "I didn't mean to say that. Ignore it. Back to what you were doing."

"No. What do you mean?"

He groaned his annoyance and his stomach contracted under her as he tried to sit up. He finally slid his hand out from behind her neck and used his elbow to get better leverage. He was able to half recline, by sliding her down his legs a bit. They were almost face-to-face. She wrapped her arms around his neck. "What do you mean, Tony?" she asked again, her tone more serious.

"I mean, I'm an asshole for ruining the mood. Can't you just forget it?"

"No. I want to know. Maybe I need to know. I'd like to know you, Tony. As you are now, not the way you were. I'm more attracted to you as you are now, so I guess we're going to have to go with it. And that means you have to answer me."

His eyeballs averted hers to stare at some point beyond her. "It means since I lost my arm I just haven't felt much like… doing this."

Her entire body jerked in surprise at his words. "Sex? You haven't felt like having sex? What about the thing with the waitress? You said women come onto you because your arm is missing, and not the other way around."

He kept his neck strained back from her, trying, she knew, to establish more distance. His tone was grumpy as he mumbled, "They do. She did. I just never call any of them. I don't take them up on it. I-I actually don't know why I don't."

She expelled a sharp breath and blinked. Holy Christ. He was… complicated, to say the least. Her heart fluttered crazily in her chest at how he affected her. Everything about him. When he was rude to her. When he was nice to her. When he was giving heartbreaking speeches, or smiling kindly to a lonely, little girl.

Gretchen was shocked and touched that he'd been so honest with her.

She leaned her forehead in to touch his. "It ruined everything for you, didn't it?"

He closed his eyes and inhaled sharply. "Yes. It did," he replied simply. His tone was soft and crisp.

She touched his cheek with her index finger and he opened his eyes in response. "It didn't ruin this. I can attest to that. It might have delayed you wanting to do this, but it didn't ruin it. Believe me. That was… you were better than any two-armed man I've ever had sex with. Will included."

His eyes widened. "Did you really just say that? Two-armed man? Gretchen, no one says stuff like that to me."

She smiled. Glad to see his incredulity and half smile of amusement. "I did. And I meant it."

He eyed her. "Will included?"

"I thought I just said that. But yes. Will included. Now that you seem interested in me, can we see if it *was* just an anomaly?"

He finally smiled a full grin that went up into his eyes and sent her heart beating wildly. Holy crap, she liked seeing him look so happy.

And she soon realized it was no anomaly. It seemed to be a fact that they would have to deal with.

****

Tony stared up at Gretchen's ceiling. Why did he do this? Why was he there? And why did she have him here? He could hear her out in the kitchen. It wasn't even eight o'clock on Christmas morning. He should have been at home, alone, in his parents' damn basement. He should have been feeling like shit and sorry for himself that it was Christmas, and he was all alone in his parents' basement at the age of thirty-five years old.

But instead, he was lying in the bed of the woman he fantasized about for two decades. It was surreal. Crazy. Bat-shit impossible that he was there. And all at her insistence.

And it wasn't like she didn't know what she was getting into. She asked him there. Drove him there. Came on to *him*. He would have never come onto Gretchen. No. No way. He never believed she wanted him to. She never wanted him before, but now she did?

He didn't know what to make of it. Or what to do now with it. Or even how to act. He sighed and rolled over. It was easier staying by himself in his parents' basement. There were no awkward situations. No contorted moments with his arm. No sympathy. No sorrow. No feeling like a freak.

He finally got up to piss, locating his underwear and pants, which he struggled into. He hated the buttons on pants. They were always a pain, and the material usually too stiff and tough to manipulate one-handed. He took a few moments to do up his shirt.

At some point, the sleeve that he kept pinned came undone. He hunted around the bed until he found the safety pin and quickly adjusted it all. Fine. Okay. He looked kind of presentable.

Gretchen was at the stove, cooking. Breakfast? For him? He stood in the hallway where he could see her. She didn't yet know he was there. She was barefoot, and still had the silky nightgown on. It ended a few inches above her knees. The color was soft, subtle, feminine and pretty. A lot like how he would have described her. A long, flannel robe covered her shoulders, and should have ruined the effect of the sophisticated, sexy nightgown. The robe was comfortable and warm; but all it did to him was cause his damn, stupid, ever greedy heart for Gretchen to bump strangely in his chest. Her hair was all messed up. She hadn't brushed it yet. He remembered his hand running through it as he grabbed it and held her head still so he could kiss her before she did other things to him... He was fully responsible for thoroughly creating the ratty, puffy mess of her hair this morning. She pushed some of it behind her ears. The darker strands were all mixed up and contrasted with the blond. Barefoot and cooking bacon and pancakes, she was the most desirable sight he'd ever beheld.

He shuffled into her living room and paused at the bar. She glanced up and smiled with a shy, sweet—kind of at odds with the forward, exciting woman he recalled from last night— smile.

Was he to believe that soft, dreamy, happy look she had on her face was just from seeing *him?* He was pretty sure he hadn't made anyone happy in many years. Perhaps once, he might have made Audrey a little bit happy, but that was before he left on his last tour.

"Merry Christmas!"

He winced. She was way too happy about it being Christmas. What adult cared so much about a freaking holiday?

"Merry Christmas," he said with half her enthusiasm.

She looked up from her cooking. "Do you like pancakes? And bacon?"

Being cooked by the woman who had sex with him three times last night? Yeah, he liked that. He liked it a lot. But that sounded weird, so he simply nodded. The festive lights were all back on. Christmas carols played in the background, and the table was set with matching china on Christmas-themed placemats.

"Were you expecting company?"

"Just you. I did that for you.

His heart beat faster at hearing her words. They were soft and sweet. They even sounded truthful. Did he hurt her feelings by asking that? "Uh, well, thanks. You didn't have to go to the trouble."

She flipped the burners off and placed the hot food onto the plates she set there. She scooted around the bar and set them on the table. Her next trip brought orange juice and coffee. She finally looked up at him. "Sit. And try to remember to be polite and grateful, so you don't ruin a nice gesture towards you, okay?"

He pressed his lips together to refrain from smiling. It had been a long time since anyone, other than his mother, did anything nice for him. She started to pass by him, her face set in annoyance. He surprised her and himself when he put his hand on her arm and stopped her. She turned with her eyebrows raised in question. He pulled her forward to him, and her head came to rest directly under his chin. She fit him perfectly. Usually, he had to lean way down with women, but not with Gretchen. She was tall enough to lean into him and stand on her own. He leaned down and touched her lips in a soft, closed mouth kiss that lingered in a languid caress. When he lifted his face from hers, her eyes were still closed and her mouth still puckered. She finally lifted her eyelids and her green eyes looked surprised, as well as soft and dewy.

Finally, she nodded and whispered; "Now you're getting the hang of it."

He nuzzled her neck and mumbled, "What? Being nice?"

She grinned. "Yes. You're rather good at it when you choose to be."

They sat down and ate her breakfast. It wasn't as weird as he thought it could have been. The food was easy to cut, so no stress there. He doubted she considered that when preparing it. He could discreetly pick up the bacon and eat it while tearing apart the pancakes with his fork. It was foods like steak, or corn on the cob, or even hamburgers that could be tricky. If he couldn't cut his food, it caused his mood to inevitably plummet and wither. There was something about being a grown man who was unable to cut his own fucking food that made him feel about an inch tall. And no doubt, all of it contributed to his previous lack of interest in sex.

What woman would sit around considering what she could or could not prepare for a meal? His mind started wandering to all the different situations that could arise in which his damn amputation could become an issue. He really couldn't hang out with her beyond this. It would never work. It was part of why he remained so reclusive. He could not stand the attention his handicap aroused. Much less, the sympathy.

It was part of why he became so difficult at times. He was always on edge, expecting the next obstacle that he'd have to try and overcome with his fumbling inability to do things. When would he next need to have his freaking meal cut up for him?

"Sooo—"

He glanced up at Gretchen's drawn out "so," and raised his eyebrows, waiting for her question.

"So what were you doing today?"

"Nothing until about five o'clock when my mother makes dinner for me and my dad."

"And now?"

"Now what?"

He knew he said something wrong for she pursed her lips up as if in annoyance. "Now... are you going to invite me over to have dinner with you?"

He lowered the glass of orange juice and stared up at her with a frown, perplexed. "Do you want me to ask?"

She rolled her eyes. "Are you going to be this obtuse with everything? Will I have to spell out everything?"

"Everything? As in…"

"Us. See? You were doing it again."

"Us?" he grimaced when her eyebrows lowered into a stormy expression. Okay, he'd done it a third time. He just didn't know when to believe her.

"Us, as in, my God, Tony! Get a clue." She nearly gritted her teeth at him as she stood up, scraping her chair on the hardwood floor before grabbing her plate and nearly shattering it when she tossed it into the sink.

"Uh, Gretchen, will you come to dinner tonight?"

She turned toward him, glaring. "Yes. Obviously. Even though I had to convince you to ask me. Anyway, will you come somewhere with me first?"

"Where?"

"To Olivia's. In fact, I need to get there by ten. That's why breakfast was so early. She and Helen are expecting me for a brunch, and of course, to give her some presents."

"Yeah, I would love to see her. I don't have anything for her, however. I already gave it to her last Thursday."

She paused from scraping food off the pan she was scrubbing. "You bought her a present?"

"Of course."

"What? What did you buy her?"

"I don't know, this fashion-doll-kit-thingy she was chatting about for a few weeks."

For some reason, Gretchen smiled. Throwing down the dish, she dried her hands and came over to him. She put her arms around his neck and kissed him soundly on the lips. "Yes, she has been. You really should quit pretending that you're not such a decent, kind, and wonderful man."

He didn't have a clue why she just said that or kissed him for it. "Well, she's a little kid. A nice kid. Of course, I'm nice to her. And why don't you let me do the dishes, since you cooked breakfast?"

She stepped back and smiled smugly, "See? There you go again. Okay, I'll go get ready."

She started down the hallway and he could have sworn she had a happy bounce to her step. Why? Because he volunteered to do the dishes? Or because he invited her to dinner? Or because he bought Olivia a Christmas present? He really wasn't sure what he'd done to make her suddenly so happy with him. She might not be as hard to please as he used to perceive she was. In fact, maybe she was too easily pleased.

Or maybe, she too easily made him feel happy.

Chapter Seventeen

OLIVIA SQUEALED AND JUMPED up and down when she spotted Gretchen and Tony together. All smiles that were punctuated with piercing shrieks, Olivia spent the first hour showing them her new toys from Santa. Tony hung back at first, trying to hide his shocked disbelief. Olivia lived in a small apartment, and apparently slept on the sofa, while her terminally ill grandmother, Helen, lay, now nearly bedridden, in the only small bedroom.

Gretchen explained to him in detail how sick Helen was; and although he had known Olivia for three months, the little girl never once mentioned that her grandmother was dying. How could someone so young keep that bottled up inside? And how could she find so much happiness in her life still? Gretchen wasn't sure exactly how much Olivia really understood regarding what would soon be happening to her.

Olivia had no other family: no parents and no relatives. All of a sudden, Tony felt nothing but a sense of deep compassion for her as well as being angry with himself for not picking up on the unspoken, tragic circumstances of the sweet, guileless, little girl's history.

Olivia was just happy to have them both there. Tony spotted a small, fake tree in the corner that was adorned with more handmade ornaments than store-bought ones. Gretchen provided the entire meal. Much to his surprise, she froze the whole thing so it could easily be re-heated and ready to serve at the small, four-person table. Helen even came to the table, wearing a smile that was soft and strained, but genuine. Tony instantly realized that missing an arm wasn't a death sentence. He was sitting now close to someone who was very close to that and he found a kinship with Helen that he rarely knew with anyone else. She seemed to know and probably felt the same thing towards him in return.

Gretchen had a slew of presents for both of them. When it was time to leave, Tony questioned whether to take Olivia, but Gretchen explained that Helen wanted all the time she could possibly share with little Olivia; and this would be her last Christmas; of that, there was no doubt.

Shooting about fifty pictures of every single thing that happened over the five hours that they spent there, Gretchen was mainly focused on candid shots of Helen with Olivia.

Gretchen and Helen had a long talk, which left Gretchen on the verge of tears. They finally tore themselves away and headed down the sidewalk to her car. Tony kept quiet, sensing the gravity of something much more there.

"What will happen to her?"

Gretchen glanced up at him and sucked in a slow lungful of air. "Can we talk about it later? It's Christmas. I had a lovely day with them, and I'm having just as lovely a time with you. I'd like that to continue."

He shifted in the seat and stared outside the car. "Yeah, there's always time for reality later, isn't there?"

She eyed him sharply, but didn't comment.

They pulled into Tony's driveway. As they entered his parents' house, Leila looked up from where she was mixing a batter in her countertop mixer. Lewis was in the living room, reading the paper; and they both paused and stared with their mouths nearly wide open when Tony and Gretchen walked in. An odd, uncomfortable silence hung between the four of them. He previously texted his mother, letting her know he wouldn't be coming home, and also, informing her of the guest who was coming to dinner. No doubt, she easily figured out why he didn't come home, and damn, if he didn't almost begin blushing under his parents' attention.

Ms. Manners, however, wouldn't allow him to simply ignore the awkward tension in the room. She walked around him towards his mother, while he shuffled towards the counter, following behind Gretchen.

"Hi Leila, I hope it's okay if I join you."

"So happy to have you, Gretchen…"

He quit listening immediately. Of course, his mother was thrilled that a woman was joining him, let alone, a normal, beautiful, wonderful woman like Gretchen. He excused himself to run downstairs and put clean clothes on. Although he tucked his white shirt in to go to Olivia's, trying to look somewhat respectable, he was now rumpled and wrinkled. He changed his clothes and soon joined his father who was watching college football. After the simple hellos, Tony noticed his dad's secret smile. It was hard not to grin back at his dad's meaning: *Nice going, son. She's hot.* Lewis, however, would never have talked about a woman like that. He had to be relieved to know his son seemed to still have some interest in sex. No doubt, his parents knew he didn't often leave the house, so they had to know he wasn't exactly getting any.

Soon, the meal was ready and they were called to the table. His mother, like Gretchen, also set a formal, festive table. It was something neither he nor Lewis would bother doing. His mother's ham, fresh baked bread, homemade baked beans, and salad was melt-in-your-mouth delicious. She set Tony's plate in front of him, with the ham cut into small bites. He refused to raise his eyes to Gretchen while wondering, did she or his mother cut it up? Not that it mattered. It had to be done although it managed to bring his scowl back. He hated having only one fucking arm and the restrictions it put on his life. Conversation was easy and casual, and he eventually ate enough to cause him some slight discomfort.

Finally, the meal ended as both women rose in unison and started clearing the table. He leaned back and finished the beer his mother handed him, pausing in conversation when Lewis left the room. Gretchen sat quickly next to him.

"Why were you scowling?"

"When?"

"At dinner? You were fine, then, all at once, you weren't."

"Oh. Just wondering who cut up my food."

"I figured as much. Me. I did it. I am well aware of what you can and can't do. I mean, do we have to keep pretending it's not so? Or could we just act like grownups now and deal with it?"

"I don't want to talk about it."

She crossed her arms over her chest. Her breasts poofed up against her arms and his gaze stayed there a little too long. She sighed. "Don't make me do it."

"Do what?"

"Start stripping again. If that's the only time you can be nice, then you'll have a real interesting time explaining to your parents why I'm suddenly standing naked in their living room."

At least, her ultimatum made him smile. He smirked and shook his head. "You wouldn't dare."

"I would too, if it improves your behavior."

"My behavior isn't that bad." He lifted his shoulders in a shrug. "Go ahead, strip away. As if I'd stop that. You'd be rewarding me."

"Until your father started eyeing up my tits. That would probably bother you."

His eyes gleamed in humor and smile filled his face. At least Gretchen could find a way to finally make him smile and not take every single situation, good or bad, so serious. "You'd never do it."

"Try me. It's Christmas, and I don't like your bad mood. So try me." Her hand went to the hem of her shirt and she started to lift it up. His hand shot out and wrestled her wrist until she was still.

"Fine. Fine. I'll smile. See?" He forced his mouth into a fake grin.

"Keep this conversation in mind. You stop being nice. I strip."

He rolled his eyes. "You're ridiculous."

She got up, carrying the used salad bowl, and kissed his cheek as she said, "You love me and you know it."

Turning, she sauntered into the kitchen and started washing dishes with his mother. She didn't notice how he froze in horror at her words. Did she really say *that?* His stomach cramped and he fisted his hand. *Love? No, sex.* They were barely having sex. She just meant it casually, and in a quick way. Not that she thought they were… *No,* he would not think about it anymore.

****

"Leila? Is anything wrong?"

Leila glanced up swiftly at Gretchen. They had just finished dessert and the men were out talking and watching TV. Leila was putting the leftover pie in a container. Gretchen was getting a weird vibe from Leila ever since she came in. Leila didn't meet her gaze or talk directly to her. It was very evident she had her own opinion about the capacity in which Gretchen was there with Tony.

Her mouth tightened. "Are you spending the night?"

"Um, well, I don't know. Maybe? I haven't discussed that with Tony. And I don't assume anything with Tony."

"He doesn't need it, you know."

What? Sex? Leila thought he didn't need sex? It made no sense to Gretchen. It's not like Tony was still sixteen. Why would Leila care about his sex life? Did the idea of it really offend her sentiments that much?

"What do you mean?"

"You! He doesn't need you doing this. What do you think that accomplishes?"

"I wasn't trying to accomplish anything. I like your son. It's not unusual for two adults to end up together after that occurs."

Why were they having this discussion? Where was Leila going with it? And why? Leila had always been so nice to her, and nearly treated her like a surrogate daughter. Now, she wasn't welcome there?

"Oh, because you're going to settle down with him? He doesn't work and still lives with his parents. He—"

"It's a little early to tell anything about us, either way. Just as it would be with any man I just started to see. And I already know every single obstacle involved with him. Why are you interrogating me? You act like

I'm here as some kind of predator who intends to hurt him."

"He can't take anymore hurt. Or anymore rejection. I wish you'd just stop. Go home. Leave him alone. He was fine before you showed up."

Fine? How was Tony fine? Unhappy, rude, and holed up in his parent's basement? He was not fine, as Leila herself suggested at the first dinner she shared with the Lindstroms. And as Donny well hammered home to her. How could she think that? And why was there so much animosity in Leila's heated glare? *What was really going on?* Gretchen usually got a read on most people, but she didn't expect to receive that kind of reaction from Tony's mother. Not in the least.

Leila snapped the lid shut on the container and nearly slammed it into the refrigerator as she whipped around. "He has been through so much, and he's finally reached a decent place. Maybe you don't think it's fine, but it actually is. It's a hundred percent better than he was the first year after *it* happened. The last thing he needs is some stupid woman getting involved now and screwing it up for him. When he's worked so hard just to get this far."

Audrey. This had to revert back to her. There had to be a story there that caused Leila to feel unreasonably fearful of Tony getting involved with anyone again, including her.

Gretchen cleared her throat and asked in a low tone. "Is this about Audrey?"

Leila froze and whipped around. "Audrey? How do you know about her? No one was supposed to tell you. Tony wanted it buried in the past. Did he tell you?"

"No, Vickie told me. Donny told Vickie."

"That idiot. He should have respected his brother's wishes."

"He pretty much did. I don't know too much about it."

"Well, I certainly am not going to enlighten you about Tony's private life."

"But you'll tell me to leave? Isn't that called meddling? I never dreamed you'd have a problem with my being here."

"I had no problem with you being his friend. I just never dreamed you'd do something like this."

"Why, Leila? Why did you never consider I might want to date your son? Because he's missing one arm? You thought I couldn't see past that? Or desire him sexually with that? Maybe you should look at yourself first before you start casting stones at me. Why didn't you think I would? And why aren't you glad I do?"

Leila's gaze was fierce. "Because you won't stay with a one-armed man. You aren't going to stick. And he is fine now, living here. He's safe. He's taken care of. There is no more worry. And don't I deserve that? After everything I've gone through to get him back to a safe place in his life?"

Gretchen's mouth popped open. "You don't want anything to change for him. You want him to stay here, and remain living with you."

"I want him safe so no further harm can come to him. If that means he lives here with me, then so be it."

Gretchen started to argue, but Tony came wandering in from the living room. He glanced between them. "Everything okay?"

Gretchen forced a smile. So did Leila. "Sure, we were just contemplating if we should have seconds or not."

"Just what I was thinking," he said with a smile before turning and rustling around in the fridge to take out the dessert Leila had just put away. His smile was easy going, casual, and happy. Something rare for Tony. How could Leila not want that for him?

"Yes, well, if you'll excuse me, I'll be getting off my feet."

Tony frowned as he watched her leave the room. "What's her problem?"

Gretchen bit her lip. Did she dare tell him? She didn't want to ruin today, but neither did she want to lie to Tony. That was no basis for any good relationship. "She doesn't want me here, not like this, I mean."

"As in…"

"Sleeping with you. I should go. It's late. It's been… a lot for one day. For everyone."

She started to reach for her coat hung on the bar stool and her keys. His voice stopped her dead. "You should stay."

She glanced up. "Stay here? Under the same roof as your disapproving mother?"

He nodded, fastening his gaze on hers, intense and bright. "Actually, I think I'm done." He took the dessert and put it back in the fridge before walking towards the top of the stairs and putting his hand out towards her.

Her heart blipped. His mother could still see him from the sofa, even though she probably couldn't hear them. Lewis didn't even take his eyes from the TV. Should they say something to his parents? Should she apologize to Leila? She felt a strong urge to do so even though she had no reason. Leila had nothing to do with them. It was ridiculous to care. But she couldn't help it. She cared. She had always cared about what parents thought of her. Her own parents as well as her friends, and all the men she dated. Most parents, especially the mothers, liked her; and it was a bit shocking that Tony's mother, of all mothers, didn't. But Gretchen stiffened her spine and pretended to be the grownup she was supposed to be as she reached for Tony's hand.

Chapter Eighteen

THE BASEMENT WAS MUCH as she remembered. It had the hazy, kinda gloomy atmosphere that was typical of a basement. The windows were high, allowing some light in during the day, and a few flashes of car headlights and streetlights outside at night. It was quiet in there, muffled from the outside noises by the thick concrete walls, which also contributed to the chill, which was significantly more than upstairs. They didn't turn the lights on. The walkway led to the bed on their left, after only a few feet, and the living area lay on the right of the room.

He released her hand and she slipped her shoes off. "This reminds me a lot of being here at a very different time in my life."

He glanced around, and turned his body from her as he mumbled, "It hasn't changed much, huh? Too weird? You want to leave?" His tone was instantly guarded. Her heart froze and collapsed in her chest. He was always so ready to get rejected by her. She didn't think Tony did that with most people. He was confident enough in himself that he didn't much care what others thought. Nor did he usually assume they'd reject him. But with her, he usually did.

She stepped forward and wrapped her arms around him, pushing her chest into his back while her hand circled his trunk. Again, yeah, kind of… strange on the one side. But not enough to mean anything. Or change anything. Or discourage her from wanting Tony because of it. She leaned her lips into the back of his neck and kissed the base of his skull. "No, not too weird."

He leaned his head back at her ministrations. His entire body went still as if he were holding his breath. Waiting for what? Her rejection? Or for her to jump on him? What? She didn't understand why he always became so intense around her.

His hand came to rest over hers. "It doesn't bother you?"

His tone was quiet and his eyes were closed, but she knew what he meant. "No, Tony. It doesn't really bother me. I wish it wasn't so, obviously, for your sake, but not for mine."

He shuddered when her hands slipped down to the base of his shirt. She tugged on it, pulling it up and he stepped forward. "No."

His tone was almost panicked as he clutched his shirt and pulled it down again.

She sighed and sat down on the edge of the bed. "You know I've seen it, right? When I caught you doing the amazing, super-hero push-ups."

His mouth lifted a fraction of an inch. "They were the same push-ups that any man could do."

"No. Nope. They weren't. But anyway, I already saw what you look like. I'll accept your shirt staying on. I'll accept whatever you need to do, but I wish you wouldn't. I wish you'd just trust me."

He sat down next to her and his tone was weary. "It's not that easy. I feel… incomplete."

"Yes. I get that. But I don't think you're incomplete. It's a little weird to grab you and not feel your arm. And a little weird that it doesn't get in the way when I lay my head on your shoulder. But that's okay. I mean it just is what it is. But it's not something that hangs me up."

"Most people aren't so open about it. They cringe and try to figure out how to talk about it."

"Is that bad? I mean it's obvious you don't have an arm. So sure, it's a little different. But different doesn't mean anything. Not to me, at least."

His eyebrows lowered in puzzlement. "So, what? You don't care about it?"

"Only in how it affects *you*. I find you attractive. I think I've already proven that. So you can keep your hang-ups, the ones that I've witnessed since coming back into your life… Or we could just skip them and be together. Like a normal couple. Like we can change in front of each other. And have sex without our clothing on. You know… normal."

His lips twitched. "So, I am getting lucky again?"

She smiled. "Yes. But only if you're quiet. I'd shrivel into a mortified ball if I thought your parents could hear us."

"It's weird to worry about parents at our age."

She touched his face. "Oh, Tony, your life has been ripped to shreds and nothing is easy now. I get that. Probably even more now than when I first caught up with you. I was wrong for urging you to do some of things I tried to make you do. But you have nothing to be ashamed about. Not with me. Not about losing your arm. Not about where you live or what you can or can't do."

He averted his eyes, but shrugged. "The counseling isn't so bad. Dr. Hart comes off a little stiff and formal, but he's pretty good at getting to the root of things. And seeing through bullshit."

She nodded. "I'm glad. But it's not a requirement for you to be with me. There is nothing you need to do or be, nothing more than you are right now, here, today. And I hope you feel the same way about me."

He glanced at her and slowly extracted her hand from his face. "Okay."

"Okay? Okay what?"

"Okay, we can be normal."

Her heart swelled and seemed to fill her chest. It was overflowing with new joy and happiness. He was trusting her. To see him naked. He would allow himself to be vulnerable in front of her. And different. His breath stopped when she touched the hem of his shirt. He closed his eyes, but didn't try to stop her from lifting the shirt up as he ducked his head through the neck hole. He let her take it off and drop it behind them. His eyes remained averted.

She set her hand at the base of his neck, on his collarbone and ran her fingertips down his shoulder, first addressing his "normal" one. His body shuddered at her touch. She traced his arm, then went back up and down the front of his chest, to his rippling abs. She outlined them.

"I like these."

His eyes popped open and he stared at her for a moment before finally showing a slow, half smile. "Yeah? Well, I have to do something to counteract the missing arm."

She smiled into his deep, dark eyes, lifting her hand and setting it on his shoulder, two inches from his scar. He tensed and his entire body went rigid. His muscles grew taut under her fingers.

"Can I touch you? There?"

He closed his eyes and his breathing sounded ragged, but he finally nodded. He nearly gasped and drew in a breath as her fingertips brushed gently over the puckering of the incision. He kept his eyes tightly shut.

She couldn't think of one thing to say. She didn't know how to make this any better for him. Or how to make it easier for him to face *with* her. She didn't know what words would make him feel like he could trust her with it. So she simply leaned over and kissed him. Right, smack dab, on the incision. Her lips touched and lingered momentarily as she softly kissed above and below it. Then she ran her hand along it, and down the side of his body where his arm should have been in the way. She got more familiar with it as it was, and not as it should have been.

It didn't bother her, but her heart was shattered *for Tony.* For what he suffered and lost. It had nothing to do with her attraction toward him. How he was now truly had no bearing on how much she wanted to look at him and touch him *everywhere*. She didn't want to gawk over his amputation. She simply wanted to be able to touch and look and kiss him freely… and everywhere.

"I don't think anyone's ever touched it before." His tone was barely a whisper and his jaw was clenched. He didn't like it, but he let her touch it anyway. She slid into his lap, wrapping her arms around his neck.

"Even Audrey?"

His heart seemed to slam louder under her ear as his body tensed and his grip around her waist squeezed tighter.

She touched his hand at her waist. "Easy. How the hell can you have such a vise-like grip?"

He relaxed his fingers instantly. "Donny told you?"

"No, not a thing. He didn't tell me anything. Vickie did. He mentioned it to her. He wouldn't tell me anymore when I specifically asked him. So I guess I want to know what happened. From you."

He pushed her off him and stood up. She watched him, and for once, it felt nice to be able to. His chest was long and sculpted. Far more toned and muscled than she would have ever dared to strive for. There wasn't a trace of muscle definition to be found on Gretchen. His missing arm appeared almost startling from the side profile. He flipped around when he realized it was facing her, then clenched and unclenched his fist.

"I never knew you were engaged."

"It happened after Will left for Washington state, so I never told him. No, there was no reason to know."

"Will you tell me about her? You already know about my failed relationship."

He snorted. "Yeah, I fucking lived through it."

She stood up too. "Don't go back to that. I don't even really like the F-word. Could you not get angry at me just for wanting to talk to you?"

He rolled his neck before sitting back down. "You're too damn logical, you know. You take all the wind out of anyone's sails who is trying to be angry with you by how calm you are. And how you never react. And how freaking right you are."

She smiled. "Freaking's better."

She dropped to her knees before him and grabbed his hand in hers, kissing it before she lay her head in his lap.

He sighed. His hand dropped to her hair and he fingered through it. It caused goose bumps to break out all over her skin. "You don't do or say anything like I ever expect."

"Will you talk to me then? Without getting angry? Tell me about Audrey, and I'll tell you about Olivia."

"Having shirtless sex would be more fun."

"Really? Because you wouldn't have said that an hour ago. Talking solved that problem."

He sighed. "Just one of the pitfalls for dating a trained therapist, huh?"

She sat on the bed, before scooting to the middle where she crossed her legs and waited. He leaned back finally to lie flat on the bed, his gaze glued on the popcorn ceiling.

"What do you want to know?"

"She lived in Calliston?"

"Yes. I met her on leave. We hooked up. I was stationed in North Carolina then, so I didn't think much of it. I saw her when I was home for a few years. Until we decided to make it a little more serious."

"How long was it serious?"

"About two years."

"You asked her to marry you?"

He flopped his hand over his bare stomach. "Yeah. Brilliant move. I got caught up, I think, in all the drama of being here, then leaving. She'd cry every time I left, and we'd count the months until we could see each other again. You know the drill."

"Yes, I suffered through many a military separation."

"Well, it added a lot of drama too. Anyway, the engagement just happened. I got word I was shipping out again and she started planning the wedding. And then… this happened."

He shifted his gaze from the ceiling to her face before descending to the wall.

"What happened after you came home?"

"We lived together after we got engaged. So I came home to her. Like this. It wasn't for very long. About three months later, I moved back here."

"What did she do? I mean, how could she do that to you after what happened? After what you sacrificed."

He sat up and his stomach muscles bunched as he did so without the help of his arms. "It's not like what you think. Or what everyone else thinks. I put her through hell. She didn't just dump me because she didn't want to deal with this. She... tried. I didn't let her do too much. I didn't talk to her. I didn't do a lot. I sat there mostly; and there were days when I didn't get out of bed. I didn't have sex with her. I wouldn't touch her. Or let her touch me. I deserved it, Gretchen. I know what you were thinking, that we could blame Tony's bad attitude on the girl who dumped him after he lost his arm."

She ducked her chin down. Yes, she'd thought exactly that. She thought some flighty bitch just dumped him because his amputation was too much to see. Or too much work. Or made him too imperfect.

"You think I'm not so nice now? I was far worse to Audrey. I wouldn't let her near me. Tell me, what was she supposed to do with that? She was only twenty-five. I sometimes wonder about the extent of what I inflicted upon her. So you see, it wasn't like you thought at all. I didn't love her enough to trust her near me. I was mean and depressed and I took it out on her. I moved home to try and shut myself off from society so I wouldn't do that to anyone else. Yet, I still did it to Donny and my folks. I tried to do it to you. This is kind of it for me."

"Wow. No one can fault your honesty. If you really feel that way, did you ever apologize to her? Or try to tell her you were sorry?"

He shook his head. "I haven't seen her since."

"Maybe you should think about doing it."

He met her gaze. He nodded. "Maybe I should."

"And Tony?"

263

"What?"

"'This' isn't all there is for you."

"What else could there be?"

She held his gaze. "Me? Someone else? I don't know. There's no way to know, but look at what you've done in just the last few months. That website is phenomenal. Your speeches bring tears streaming down my face. You are not the same person you describe yourself as being two years ago."

He blew air into his cheeks before slowly letting it escape through his lips. "Yeah, maybe you're right. So what were you going to say about Olivia?"

"Her grandmother asked me last summer if I'd adopt Olivia when she dies. There is no one else. She'll have to go to foster care. I said yes. And I want to. I love Olivia. There is simply no way I could allow her to be lost in foster care. None. No way. I suspect even if Helen hadn't suggested and started arranging it, I'd have petitioned for custody regardless after she died. I can't allow Olivia to be lost in such a harsh system. She's too young. And too fragile. And too wonderful. And she means too much to me. I can help her, so I intend to."

He jerked to sit up and his eyes widened. "You're going to take care of her? As in being a mother to her?"

She pressed her lips together. "I am. I know it's kind of a shock. But there is really no one else. Look, I didn't plan on this thing with you. I don't even know where we're going. Olivia will be mine sooner than later. You saw yourself how Helen is doing. That's why this day was so important to her."

He ran his hands through his hair. "Jesus, Gretchen. That is not what I expected."

"I know."

"You… you're really doing this?"

She met his gaze and her eyes caressed his face: the beard, the brown eyes, the hair drawn back. He could still surprise her at times. She could picture the old Tony in her mind's eye. Not this new, gruffer, scrubbier Tony. This Tony who set her heart racing and her palms sweating. "I'm really doing this."

"And this with us? A last affair?"

"No. I didn't plan for this."

"You can see I'm not fit to take care of myself, or you, or whatever, and there is *no way* I'm ready to be involved with a child. I mean… *shit.*" He ran his hand through his hair restlessly.

"Let's not worry about it tonight. You know. There're no games. Maybe we should try the shirtless sex. We're already halfway there."

He glanced down and frowned. Had he forgotten he was half naked? She smiled slightly. He had. He even forgot to be self-conscious.

He nodded as she pulled him closer and started to kiss him. He held her face for a second. "You understand then, there is no way I'm going to be… whatever, dating you, or something, with a kid involved."

She put her hand over his. "I know, Tony. It's okay. You're the last person I would expect that of."

Chapter Nineteen

TONY SLEPT UNTIL NINE the next morning. When he rolled over, he found a note on the pillow. He sat up and rubbed his eyes, pushing his tangled hair off his forehead. He grabbed the note and read it; then tossed it aside. He felt disgusted because he didn't have to be anywhere and she did. Gretchen said she was sorry, but had to work, and went home to get ready. She would call him later. He flopped down on his back and stretched out.

Was this for real? Had he just spent two nights in a row with Gretchen Moore? *Hendricks.* God, he couldn't get that to stick. He didn't want it to stick.

He quickly showered and dressed. When he ran upstairs, he found his mother alone in the kitchen. He kissed her cheek as she sat reading a magazine at the bar. They exchanged pleasantries, and eventually, he ran back downstairs, turned the computer on, and started to work.

It was kind of new having something to do, and having someone so interested in what he was doing.

She called the next day.

"Hi." Her voice was soft and breathy over the phone. She could easily have been on one of those phone sites where men pay to hear the women talk dirty to them.

"Hey."

"Tony?"

"What?"

"I missed you."

He slouched down and rested his elbow on his knee. Damn if her words didn't make his blood race… and worse, ring completely true. "I think it's been only a day."

"Tony…"

"Okay, okay I'll stop being obtuse. Yes, I missed you too."

They chatted awhile about their days, his website, and ordinary stuff. It had been a long time since he talked about ordinary things with anyone besides his mother.

"What are you doing for New Year's?"

"Uh, less than I planned on doing for Christmas."

"I have a get-together that I attend every year. It's mostly with other therapists I work with. It won't excite you and you'll probably hate it; but I'd like you to be my date."

His heart seemed to stop and restart. It was such a simple statement. One he never expected would be directed toward him. Gretchen wanted him. As a date. As a normal, *let's go out on New Year's*, kind of date.

He cleared his throat, "Yeah. Sure, I'll come."

Her tone was soft and he swore she must have been smiling. "Good. I'll plan on it. Pick you up, say at six o'clock?"

"Yeah. Sure."

He really needed to do something about wheels. He couldn't have her picking him up like he was a freshman in high school who was lucky enough to be dating an older girl with a car.

Maybe it was time to fix that.

****

Tony didn't seem to hate the dinner. They were at a local French restaurant and about twenty of her colleagues and their spouses/dates showed up. It was dry, she felt sure, for him. Not his kind of crowd, but he was polite, and even charming a few times with the women. All around, he was unusually pleasant for Tony.

When she came to his front door, her mouth again dropped open. It might have been the third time she saw him dressed in anything other than sweats, but it still surprised her how he could clean up so well and look so neatly groomed. His hair was pulled back neatly, and his beard trimmed. His shirt was buttoned up and pin-striped with dark slacks. Everything was all tucked in and he looked very nice.

There were some curious glances at his missing arm. It must be hard to be stared at. Her mouth was set in a grim line as she contemplated him while he ate the noodle dish he ordered, most likely because it was the easiest one to eat single-handedly, and with no help. It wasn't like those who glanced at him were trying to be cruel. It was just human nature to look upon that which is different. And Tony's upper body was different. It was even startling. And it was hard not to look at a little, simply just from the curiosity of how it happened. But it didn't involve cruelty or malicious interest either.

But damn, he must get tired of feeling different, and always being gawked at. Again, the magnitude of what he had to live with crushed Gretchen's chest. The longer she was around him, the more she understood what it was like. Right off, the first time she saw him, she thought she could help him. But he really didn't need help. He just needed some understanding.

And his choice to stay home was so he wouldn't stand out as being so different, and so it wasn't so glaring all the time.

He looked up while grabbing his glass of water, and his eyes held hers. She smiled slowly and he responded in kind. His mouth lifted on one side and he winked at her. Her heart responded with a resounding "thump!" She dropped her spoon onto her plate. Surprised, she glanced down and heat filled her cheeks. She cared. She really cared for him. He might make her feel unsettled and uncomfortable, but he also made her heart shift around in a weird way inside her chest. She desired him physically, and felt something very big and deep whenever his eyes met hers. It was an emotional reaction, that went far beyond their new, and very obvious chemistry.

It might have been hard for him to deal with being out in the world and a part of society, but he could handle it. Look at him tonight. He was a perfectly well groomed, polite, mannerly, and well informed. He held up his side of the conversation with both men and women alike, although he knew none of them but he chatted and smiled easily nonetheless. He could do this.

He could actually be part of her life.

Her chest rose and lowered as her breath increased to almost panting. *Shit.* Where was all of this coming from? It hit her like a Mack truck. She was well trained in emotions, observation, and reading the motives behind people's actions and behaviors; yet with Tony, she was completely broadsided. The man she so quickly, and purposely seduced was also the man she might have been falling in love with.

Gretchen grabbed her drink and downed it in near panic. *No. No. No!* This was not the time in her life to harbor feelings for any man. She had gone several years since having a meaningful relationship. She hadn't been in love since Will… and now she was choosing his best friend, and at the time in her life when there was absolutely no room for a man. Or a relationship. Or a change.

His words filtered through her head. "You understand then, there is no way I'm going to be…whatever, dating you, or something, with a kid involved."

Everything all came back to Olivia. Right now, her whole life was all about preparing for Olivia. It wasn't easy. She didn't get to start with a baby and grow into it. She didn't get to share it with a father and have help. She would be taking in a young girl whose life just had everything meaningful destroyed, which would leave her grief-stricken. It wasn't going to be an easy transition, nor an easy fix. It would, no doubt, consume Gretchen.

Who could deal with that? How could she even ask anyone to? Especially, someone as troubled as Tony. She couldn't see it happening.

Why did life give you everything you ever wanted, but at exactly the wrong time? Or in the wrong order?

She knew the answer, of course; it was because life was not fair. Life was hard and long. Good things happened, and so did bad things. She was trained to help young, innocent kids deal with the errant blows from life, which were all extremely unfair to them.

Now she had to grow up and do the same for herself.

****

"So, Tracy, Vickie, and I were going to take a girls' weekend in January. But now, Vickie isn't, and Tracy says she really can't get away… so do you want to come instead?"

Tony glanced up from Gretchen's laptop. He'd been updating his blog and going through his messages. "For what? A girl's weekend?"

"No, we'll call it a lover's weekend with me."

He squinted his eyes at her. "I had no idea you were such a dork when I wanted to get in your pants all these years. A lover's weekend?"

"Ha. Ha. What would you call it then?"

He grinned, and her heart had a spasm, which was a weird reaction. It was so rare, not to mention, beautiful, to see him grinning and so easy going. He grabbed her arm and spun her towards him as he smiled. "Yeah, I'll go with you on a lover's weekend."

She pretended to try and slip away, only for him to do a super-hero hold on her just to keep her trapped against him. The longing look in his eyes had her pulse skittering. His eyes zeroed in on her mouth. Breathlessly, she mumbled, "What you can do one-armed is a little freaky when you want to."

"There again, stuff you shouldn't say to an injured war veteran. I might have to teach you a lesson about respecting our nation's heroes."

He started lowering her to the floor of her condo and she held onto his neck with happy abandon. "Oh, you might have to. So we're on then? Next weekend?"

"We're on," he mumbled as his mouth found her collarbone before he started sucking on it.

****

Leila glared at Gretchen as she stood there awkwardly waiting for Tony. Gretchen didn't know why she hated her so much. Leila did no more than grunt at her the few times she came to pick Tony up or stay there. She rarely stayed, however. It made much more sense to go to her condo. But the few times she crossed Leila's path, it felt like rockets could have been

271

launched from the heated glares she directed towards Gretchen.

"He doesn't need that."

Gretchen sighed and leaned her elbows on the counter. "What, Leila? What doesn't Tony need? A vacation? Fun? Time with someone he likes to be around? What do you think I'm doing to him?"

"You're going to hurt him eventually, and who do you think will pick up the pieces again?"

Her eyebrows lowered. "Why do you assume I'm going to hurt him? Maybe he'll hurt me. You totally underestimate him. He's still a fully grown, red-blooded, adult male. He could tire of me, or find someone new, or suddenly despise how I tie my shoes. I have no idea, but it's a little soon to predict that *I'm* going to hurt *him.*"

"I think you're getting his hopes up and it isn't fair. You're going to… what, Gretchen? Settle down with a man who still lives with his parents?"

She glared at Leila. "I am not trying to hurt him. I am simply dating him. Something that should make you glad. It's a normal thing for a thirty-five-year-old man to do, with or without both of his arms."

"You shouldn't say things like that about him. I've heard you."

"So has he. He doesn't take me seriously. He knows laughing can often make things a lot less weird and not so awful."

Leila shook her head and turned away. "You don't know what you might do to him."

"I only know I'm not trying to do anything negative to him."

Leila stopped talking when Tony appeared at the top of the stairs, his duffel bag in his hand. He smiled when he made eye contact with Gretchen and her heart sped up in her chest. Still. After nearly a month of sleeping with him, he still did that to her. He patted his mother's shoulder as he passed her. "See you, Mom."

"Yes. Have fun." Leila said all the right words, but her scowling grimace was aimed directly at Gretchen, who thought about sticking her tongue out. Instead, she politely followed Tony and tried to ignore why his mother hated her so much now.

Gretchen got her revenge in the end by having the most fantastic weekend of her life with Leila's son.

****

"I got a strange call today."

"Yeah? From who?"

"From some vet who has to do a speech for his daughter's college graduation. He was invited as a guest speaker. Anyway, he asked me if I'd write it for him; and get this, he says he'd pay me. Says he saw some of mine on *YouTube*, and that's the kind of thing he wants to deliver."

Gretchen froze. It was a sunny, cool March day and she came over to sit near Tony, stretching her legs out over his lap.

"What do you mean?" she asked as she sat up suddenly. "Like hiring you as his speech writer?"

Tony shrugged, keeping his eyes glued on the basketball game he was watching on TV. He forgot to answer her as he swore at the opposing team. He was a huge Lakers fan and nearly got into fights sometimes with the TV over bad calls. At last, he glanced back at her as she waited with her eyebrows raised for his reply.

"Yeah, I guess. I mean nothing official like that. I'll just do it for him. Poor guy didn't know how to string two sentences together on paper. He emailed me what he wrote."

273

She scrunched her eyebrows. "Tony? How do you know how to string two sentences together? Where did you learn to write like that? I should know. I've given enough speeches here and there, but they were nothing like the eloquent, articulate, poetry you write."

He tore his eyes from the game with a surprised expression before he laughed. "Are you kidding me? I don't do that. I write some crap down really quick and just memorize it."

She shook her head. "No. No. You're quite talented at it." She tilted her head, studying his profile. He was barely listening to her, and his eyes were back on the game. He flinched and flexed and cheered and groaned. He actively watched sports as if he were doing them. He was such a physical, active man. It still pained her to imagine what his current limits did to his sense of self. "Tony?"

He finally half turned his face to her, although his eyeballs were still glued the other way. "Hmm?"

"You told me once I never noticed you before. I didn't see you. Right?"

His gaze turned fully and sharpened on her face. "Yeah. So?"

"So, I think the first time I really ever saw you was when I heard you giving that first speech. When I say you're talented, I mean, more like brilliant in how you can string incongruent words together. It's kind of funny, seeing how you don't seem to like much conversation... But you are a contradiction quite often to me. You hate adults asking questions about your arm, but you tolerate anything a kid says, be it cruel or rude even. I think you should write it for the guy, but you should charge him for it."

His hand, which was resting on her knee, started stroking her thigh, sliding inches higher. His eyes held hers as he said softly, "You think so, huh? Because now you've finally noticed me?"

She leaned forward, and her body responded to his tone of voice as well as his touch. "Yes. I really, really notice you now. *Right now.*"

He smiled as his fingers slid higher and the tips of them just barely grazed the skin of her thighs. Up and down, he caressed her until she flopped back and nearly groaned in frustration to simply *touch her.* Where it really mattered. But she knew there was no sense in hurrying him. Not if he didn't want to be.

Usually, he didn't want to be in any hurry. He could drive her crazy, to the point of wanting to scratch her fingernails into the wall to express her frustration. But it was also part of his gift.

****

Things were crazy-good between them. There was no other way Gretchen could describe it. They got along like they'd been together for decades, but the smoldering, hot looks and touches felt brand new every single time. She lost her head just thinking about him. She'd be in middle of typing, or working with a patient, when her daydreams would suddenly intrude. She continually thought about him, and anticipated seeing him like she hadn't done since she was a young girl, waiting for Will to meet her between classes.

She often went to his speaking engagements and listened to him, sometimes closing her eyes so his deep voice could travel inside her, raising goose bumps on her arms every single time. He was that emotional and moving to hear. Her heart kept swelling and frequently felt like it would burst with pride over Tony. She wanted to stand up and announce loudly, "Isn't he wonderful? And he's all mine."

At least, for now.

She didn't ponder that too much. She didn't think far beyond now, or here, or today. She lived primarily to see him, and went about her life as required.

Donny and Vickie went on their honeymoon, and upon hearing the news of Tony and Gretchen, they both cornered her on their own to give her their personal input. Donny hugged her as if she just saved his life. He quietly said thank you and left it at that. Vickie, however, kept asking her multiple times if she was sure a relationship with Tony was a good idea.

It was, of course, a little weird. They were married, and all siblings, and even went to dinner with Leila and Lewis on several occasions.

But not on one of those occasions did Leila have anything nice, kind or casual to say to Gretchen. She was always polite in front of anyone else. But as soon as she got Gretchen alone, she immediately started in on her.

The only reason Gretchen held her tongue was because of the fear she saw lurking in Leila's eyes. She truly feared what could happen to Tony.

Tony was suddenly... very busy. He was writing speeches for other veterans who had speaking engagements. He also prepared many more of his own and delivered them. His blog had taken off and now had more than two hundred thousand followers. His daily messages and emails alone took hours to slog through. Yet he answered them all. Each and every one was painstakingly answered and/or offered some kind of help. He also hooked up more than one soldier with assistance groups or organizations that provided much needed help.

He went to his therapy appointments every Thursday and spoke with Dr. Hart, although he never really told Gretchen much about them. He just smiled and said it was going fine. Somehow, she suspected he talked about her to Dr. Hart; although she didn't know if that was a positive or a negative.

She had an emergency appointment one day with a patient, and had to call Leila, since she was desperate for someone to pick up Olivia. Leila, although rude to her, but nice to Olivia, agreed with no arguments. When she picked up Olivia later that day, she found Tony again shooting hoops with her.

Olivia ran in to get her things while Tony kissed Gretchen, letting his hand linger on her butt. He was far more demonstrative with her than she would have ever guessed. He turned back to bouncing the ball. "I don't see why she can't just come here after school regularly. Sitting in your office isn't very much fun for her. A kid like her needs to be outside playing, or at the very least, eating cookies with my mom."

Was Tony really volunteering to watch a little girl he had no relationship or responsibility to? "You want Olivia to come here after school?" Gretchen repeated it as if she didn't comprehend English.

Tony shrugged as he bounced the ball. "It makes sense. She likes my mom. She likes me. So why not?"

Gretchen could think of about fifty reasons why not. The first was that he made sure to let her know he would not be a fill-in father figure to the little girl she was adopting. Second, he was a surly, rude, one-armed vet who only recently came out of his parents' basement to try to embrace a new life. Third, he liked very few people and interacted with even less… Why would he want this little girl to come there every afternoon now and hang out? Why did Tony even care if Olivia was happy at Gretchen's office or not?

Gretchen's heart crumbled right then and there. Tony just kept sinking the basketball and didn't seem to comprehend the magnitude of what he just proposed. It was not only for Gretchen and Olivia, but also for himself. That was a huge step forward.

She cleared her throat, trying to conceal how choked up she suddenly became. "Uh, yeah. That would be wonderful. I mean it. I know my office isn't the best answer. But Helen and I always agreed that daycare was not for her either. So... you and your mother? Yes. I would be eternally grateful."

The basketball went into the hoop. He turned to kiss her cheek as Olivia ran up and threw her stuff into the car. She yelled goodbye to Tony and he just waved and said, "It's no big deal. We'll just plan on it. Have her take the bus here, instead of going to your office."

Gretchen felt a little dizzy, almost like she just stepped off a roller coaster. "Okay, I'll arrange it for tomorrow forward."

It was about the biggest hurdle for Tony emotionally she could think of. He put someone else's needs before his own. Someone he didn't have to care about or owed anything to. So it was a big deal. But she kept that tidbit to herself... along with her hope of what this crucial step might mean. Maybe someday, Tony could contemplate dating a woman with an adopted kid.

****

"Will you come with me somewhere?"

Gretchen paused from cutting vegetables and set the knife down. "You know I will. But where?"

Tony stared down at his fingers, drumming the countertop. "Uh, I was thinking of going to see Audrey. Dr. Hart thinks it would be good to, I don't know, apologize or something. I mean, you suggested that before. You mental health people seem big on closure. I thought maybe I should do it. You know... get some closure."

Her heart lodged in her throat. He was changing by the day. Hearing him instigate this had her gripping the edge of the counter to avoid catapulting over it and wrapping him up in her arms with unbridled excitement. It was a huge breakthrough. Instead, she merely nodded and picked the knife back up. "Sure. I'll go. When? This weekend? I have Olivia Friday, so it'll have be Saturday afternoon."

"Yeah, that'll work."

He swiveled on the stool, avoiding her gaze. Her heart squeezed as he got up and walked down the hallway.

When Saturday came, she picked him up. He wore jeans and his hair was tidier than usual. He slid into the car, leaning across the console to kiss her. He was much nicer as a boyfriend than she ever pictured him to be. He kissed her hello and goodbye. He touched her only with affection. He thanked her for anything she did for him. He called her. He specifically made plans to see her. He watched her little girl every single afternoon, usually playing basketball with her, or helping her with her homework. He was... entirely *not* the man she thought he'd be.

He was quiet on the ride, but unlike months before, there was no discomfort. He stared out the window, obviously lost in thought. He did that too sometimes. He could be very quiet. Very guarded. But the minute she asked him something, or tried to engage him, he turned towards her and gave her his full attention as he spoke to her.

They pulled into the driveway of the address that Gretchen already admitted she had. He looked at her funny when she explained how long she'd been sitting on Audrey's address and information.

"What possessed you to get that?"

"I don't know. I just… wanted it. I wanted to speak with her. I wanted information about you. I didn't think you'd tell me."

"Why didn't you ever contact her? Most women I know would have."

She shrugged. "I told you, I'm not good at game-playing."

He touched her chin and kissed her. "I really appreciate that about you."

Now, however, they just sat in silence in front of the house of his ex-fiancée. Her stomach jumped with nerves. "Should we go up to the door?"

He nodded. "Yeah."

She hung back and to the side of Tony. The woman who answered the door was quite pretty and wholesome and young. She looked right past Gretchen as soon as she spotted Tony. Her mouth slowly dropped open as she lowered her phone from her ear and hung up. She smoothed her hand down her jeans and her eyes went round with curiosity. "Tony? Wh-what are you doing here?"

Tony cleared his throat and glanced at Gretchen, his discomfort suddenly very evident. She nodded at him for encouragement. "I, uh, wondered if I could buy you a coffee?"

A male voice called out from behind Audrey. She glanced inside and said quickly, "It's an old friend."

Tony shifted around on his feet. "I should have called first, I'm sorry. Uh, maybe you don't want to hear what I have to say. I can leave if you're not comfortable with me being here."

She smiled softly, "I would like to talk to you. That's my boyfriend; just let me go explain where I'm going. Do you want me to drive?"

"Yes, sure."

She stopped from closing the door to finally take a look at Gretchen. "You're Gretchen Hendricks?"

"Uh, yes. How did you know?"

"Will's and your picture hung in my house for two years. I would recognize you anywhere. What are you doing here? What is this anyway?"

Tony stepped closer to Gretchen and put his hand on the small of her back. Audrey's gaze zeroed in on his hand, and Gretchen's back, before resting on his amputation. "I had hoped to apologize to you. Gretchen just brought me here."

She nodded. "I see. Yes, okay."

"I'll wait in the car," Gretchen said hurriedly. Tony frowned and seemed about to protest, but she shook her head and tilted it toward the girl standing behind them. She deserved his undivided attention. Even if it made her a little, tiny bit jealous because the girl was so young, so fresh, and so pretty. And Tony was engaged to her. Gretchen really wasn't as saintly as people tried to make her out to be.

****

Audrey toyed with her coffee cup, which Tony ordered, remembering exactly how she liked it. It was something they did on Saturday mornings together whenever he was home on leave. "So, how are you, Tony? Y-you look good. Better than…"

She shifted around, obviously uncomfortable with what she started to say.

"Better than the last time you saw me? Yes, I am."

She smiled softly, "Because of her? Gretchen? I always suspected you liked her as more than just your best friend's wife."

He picked at the napkin. "I've been getting some counseling lately."

281

"With her? Isn't she a psychiatrist?"

"Not with her. Anyway, the thing I owe you is an apology. I've owed you one for years. I was wrong with what I did to you after I came home. Maybe this isn't something you want to hear. You obviously have moved on, and have your own life… I just felt… bad about what I did to you. You were right. Not me. You handled it all well. I didn't. And for that, I'm sorry."

She blew air into her cheeks to push them out before slowly releasing it. She leaned back in the chair. "Wow, you can't imagine how long I stressed over leaving you. I mean, I know what people thought. I know what your parents thought: the bitch left him after he lost his arm. How could she be so awful? So selfish. I just…"

He leaned forward and touched her hand gently. "You just were right. I was awful. I shut you out. I realize now what I did to you. With my actions. No one could have put up with that. It wasn't because I lost an arm that you left me, it was about how I treated you. I know that now."

Tears filled her eyes and fell over her cheeks. She brushed them away. "I really didn't think you'd ever… be better. Or do this. Apologize. It was never in your personality before."

His heart twisted with bitterness. He realized how much destruction he created in the wake of what befell him. The thing was, at the time, he never noticed it. Not even a little bit. He was so focused on himself, and what he suffered, he allowed it to ruin the better parts of his life. And this young girl who once loved him.

"No. It wasn't. Not so much now, but I am trying."

She smiled. "That's all anyone could ask of you after what happened. I just, wanted you to *try*. And you couldn't yet. I wanted to be stronger than I was to deal with it."

"I should have been stronger to deal with it, not you."

She shut her eyes for a long moment. "Thank you for coming here to say this. I never expected it. And it helps. I had a lot of guilt over what happened. It fucked with my head pretty bad, and you saying this now kind of vindicates me."

"It fucked with my mind pretty bad too. Only, I shouldn't be vindicated because of it. I've been realizing lately that losing an arm doesn't give me a free pass to be how horrible I've been to those around me."

A small smile tilted her lips up. "Somehow, I think it's the stunning blond waiting in the car who gave you that revelation and not your counselor."

A small smile tilted his lips too. "Maybe. Yeah. Tell me, the new boyfriend, is he any good? You're happy?"

She smiled. "I am. We just moved in together."

Tony let her smile release some of the guilt that constricted his chest. He couldn't undo anything, not his treatment of Audrey, or his parents or Donny. Nor could he change what he failed to do over the last few years.

As he couldn't change the fact that his arm was gone. Sometimes he remembered the moments leading up to the bomb going off. He was the furthest from it, and consequently, sustained the least injury. Not so for his comrades. His anger was not only at the injury he sustained, but because he wasn't more grateful to be alive when comparing his loss to the death of his friends, and the worse injuries of two others. One got so addled by the bomb, his brain could barely function normally anymore. Tony escaped that.

He often visualized those moments right before the blast that tore through everything. He wished he sensed something, anything, that could have foreshadowed what was to come.

He hadn't given much thought to how he acted since returning home. Not until recently, when Dr. Hart pointed out a few things, things that Tony himself said without realizing what he was saying. He wasn't big on apologizing and closure and all of that, but maybe that was the least he could do to atone for his past actions.

When he got into Gretchen's car, she smiled and asked how it went.

"It might be the first decent thing I've done in awhile, other than being with you. So it went pretty good."

Chapter Twenty

HELEN WAS SOON BEDRIDDEN, and Gretchen hired twenty-four/seven nursing care for her. She didn't mind the cost, since it allowed Helen to stay home with Olivia, thereby retaining some semblance of her former routine. Gretchen figured Olivia needed as much stability as could be provided to survive this. It was the least Gretchen could do for the lonely woman who tried so hard to stay strong for Olivia. Gretchen didn't know which was more heartbreaking: witnessing Helen's slowly declining strength, or the confused, hurt, little girl who kept trying not to upset her sick grandmother. Gretchen took Olivia home to Helen every evening, and brought dinner with her, although Helen rarely ate now. Gretchen ate with Olivia, and helped her get her homework and reading done before settling down for bed. Gretchen left their apartment most evenings at close to eight o'clock.

It was a grueling schedule, not just for the long hours, but the daily trauma of watching someone die. It was horrific and something Gretchen had never experienced before, not long-term, every day, and with all the arduous details. The incessant pain. The end of one person's existence. She was observing the final days of a woman's life, a woman who wasn't even sixty, and looked ninety, but should not have been dying.

Tony met Gretchen at Helen's on some of the days when he had Olivia. It was a little odd with Leila now involved, for she drove Tony and Olivia to Helen's apartment. Leila slowly started coming inside, and eventually became another caretaker for both Olivia and Helen. She and Helen, who were the same age, struck up a quick rapport. Of course, Leila was a mother and genuinely kind, helpful, and decent to everyone she ever met, except Gretchen.

The fun was seeping out of Gretchen's life. There was no recapturing it, not when faced with the daily encounters of death, misery, pain, and a little girl's heartache. There were countless tears, and Gretchen held Olivia, soothing her through the frequent bouts. Some were provoked by Helen having a bad day, while others were unprovoked and came out of nowhere. Gretchen was called to the school more than once to collect a very distraught Olivia.

Her family helped a lot. Tracy took Olivia sometimes and her parents took her on others. They all started treating Olivia like one of their own. If this experience managed to do anything positive, it was by solidifying them as an emerging family. Gretchen had now taken over all the real care and mothering for Olivia, as Helen could no longer provide any of it.

****

Tony often sat with Helen, and the strange part was: it didn't bother him. Her face was haggard and drawn, the wrinkles deeply etched on what was left of her flesh. It sagged off her once robust frame. The only thing Tony learned from suffering through the awkward sympathy of people who saw him was how to withhold awkward sympathy. He could sit beside Helen quietly for two

286

hours and just allow her to simply stare mutely at the wall in front of her. He usually asked if she wanted him to leave, but always, she said no. Sometimes, she tried to hold his hand. She was lonely, scared, and in very serious pain. Far beyond the pain he ever had to endure.

"What are you going to do?"

Tony turned when Helen's whispered voice interrupted the somber mood. A radio played softly in the background, and the shades were pulled, so it was even gloomier in the soft lighting. He leaned forward. "Do? About what, Helen?"

"Gretchen? You know what's coming."

His heart sank into his stomach. "Yes, I know."

She smiled with a faint stretch of her thin lips. "I like that you simply know and let it stand thusly."

He shrugged. "I used to think I had the corner on pain and reality before I met you and Olivia. After I saw how an eight-year-old could deal with it better than I did, I realized the time had arrived for me to at least become a functioning person again."

"My Olivia, she's a strong girl. She's just like her father. I miss him. That was the real pain of my life. This… my own death now, is hard, and sad. But I can accept it more easily because I believe at the end of it, I'll see him again."

Tony leaned forward. Her voice was so low and whisper-like, he almost couldn't hear her. "Your son, you mean?"

"Yes. Losing him was more than anyone should ever have to bear in a lifetime. My death means nothing now. His, however, ruined me. Even Olivia couldn't make up for it. I'm at peace, Tony. With this. Help them find it, so Gretchen and Olivia can be there too. Okay?"

He shook his head as she continued, "Losing your arm wasn't like dying. When I first met you, you thought it pretty much was. I wanted to take you aside and explain to you that it really wasn't. But I feel like you finally see that now."

He dropped his head down as tears filled his eyes. "Yes, I see that."

"You wonder why your mother and I became so close? So fast? Because she lives with the fear of losing her son. I know the reality. She also understands what it's like, but most people can't. So forgive her behavior with Gretchen. She's just worried about you, and because she can't *stand* the thought of anything bad happening to you again."

His head jerked up. "Gretchen? Why should I forgive her behavior with Gretchen?"

Helen licked her thin, cracked, dry lips. "You don't know? Gretchen really is a damn saint. Leila's pretty awful to her. I used to hate Leila for being like that. Gretchen told me about it when I was feeling better. She doesn't anymore though, probably not to bother me as I'm so sick. You're the only one knows that I don't want to think about dying every moment that I have left. The things from real life are what I want to enjoy still. Anyway, after I got to know Leila, I realized why she was acting that way. You can't fathom a mother's fear or pain for her child. You just can't."

He glanced out of the open bedroom door. Gretchen was moving around the living room, helping Olivia pack up her things for school tomorrow. She leaned down, tucking her hair behind an ear as she flipped through Olivia's folder of work. She smiled at something Olivia said before tucking the folder into the purple backpack. He had no idea his mother was acting so mean to Gretchen. She never said a word to him. Nothing. Not in the four months of being together did Gretchen mention his mother was anything less than how he saw her. Why? Why didn't she tell him?

His heart pinged in something close to... what? Respect? Compassion? Love? *Christ,* love for her? He brushed his hand over his face. Yeah, as if he didn't already know he was in love with Gretchen. Only for the past twenty years. As if any idiot wouldn't guess that after being with her once, she'd either spark out, making the fantasy way better than the reality; or the reality would be far better than he could have ever imagined. And of course, it was the latter. So, duh, yeah, he was in love with her. He loved her in ways he never loved Audrey. He clearly and starkly felt that now. He felt her continued presence, and her essence somewhere deep in his guts. In his heart. In his head. He loved her as much as he loved breathing air.

But... she wasn't really looking for that. She was trying to survive the death of a woman who was giving her an eight-year-old daughter to raise. It was the oddest set of circumstances he could imagine. Well, maybe not as odd as adjusting to having only one arm, but a close second.

And yet, Gretchen couldn't even bitch to him about his mother's behavior. He knew why. The amputation. It still added a different dimension to how he was treated. People still behaved cautiously with him. Kinder. Gentler. And it was something Gretchen did not need to start worrying over with everything else she had to take on. He was just another burden.

"Tony?" Helen said softly. He dipped his ear towards her so she knew he was listening.

"You and I both know you aren't ready for this: a woman like her, and a kid as traumatized as Olivia will soon be. You're a good man; but there is no shame in admitting you're not ready for this."

He jerked back in shock. How could sweet, subdued Helen say such a thing to him? She gently lifted a finger to touch his, but barely had the strength to do so now. "I wish you well. But my first concern is Olivia, and therefore, Gretchen. They will need much more from you than you're willing to give them. You have your own stuff to deal with. I'm not convinced that you want to take on anything extra. If you can't, Tony, please let them go now. Before it all gets even harder. Do the right thing, Tony."

Her words echoed through his head. *Do the right thing.* When was the last time he did the right thing for anyone besides himself? And how could Helen know what the right thing was? How could he? He wasn't trying to hurt Gretchen. But neither did he know if he was truly willing to accept all the responsibility and baggage accompanying her. Helen suddenly started wheezing and coughing. Closing her eyes, she waited as the silent oppression of imminent death returned.

****

The knock at her front door startled Gretchen out of her haze. She was trying to catch up on the patient files from work, having neglected them of late between the prolonged evenings with Helen and looking after Olivia. She saw Tony less and less, although he continued to take Olivia after school more often. His help and simple presence were lifesavers, but she still couldn't get all of her work done.

The crappy part was: she didn't much care. All she could think about were Helen and Olivia.

When she answered the door, she almost fell over. Lindsey smiled, stepping forward to support Gretchen before she nearly toppled over with exhaustion into the other woman's arms. Luckily, Lindsey was only a few inches shorter than she, and had the strength to hold her upright.

After they separated, Lindsey smiled as she squeezed Gretchen's arm, "So, I take it you're a little overwhelmed these days."

She smiled gratefully as they separated before stepping back. "Understatement. I'm... well, I don't even have words to describe what I am. What are you doing here?"

"I could tell by your voice on the phone that this was getting to be too much. I decided you needed me for a change. You saved me not so long ago, and it's finally time for me to repay that."

"Meaning...?"

"If you don't mind, I'll stay with you for a little while, and help out with Olivia, Helen, Tony... whatever you need."

"Thank you, I can't believe you would do that for me."

"Why? You're everyone's best friend, and mine, literally. Why would you be surprised not to find everyone you know rallying around you when you finally needed help? It's not often, Gretchen, that you need it."

She smiled appreciatively. "Not the first time I've heard that. And it's driven more than one man away."

"How about our one-armed hero? Does it intimidate him?"

She tilted her head, pondering Lindsey's take on her personality. "No. Surprisingly, I don't believe it does. And you should probably just call him Tony."

She grinned cheekily. "I cannot wait to meet this man."

"Yeah, well, how is yours? He's okay with you leaving to babysit me?"

Her smiled dimmed. "You know he'd never have an issue about anything I did for you. That is, if you want my help. I don't have to stay."

She stepped back so Lindsey could pass, dragging her suitcase behind her. "I can't tell you how much I could use the help."

"Besides, I love Olivia. It will be a pleasure." Lindsey met Olivia on one of the occasions when she visited.

"She's a different little girl now," Gretchen warned quietly.

Lindsey nodded. "She's too young to have changed already."

"I know."

Lindsey touched her elbow. "It's a good thing, what you're doing."

"I never expected to be so bad at handling it."

"It's not bad to be overwhelmed by a tragic illness while becoming an adoptive mother at the same time. You're human, Gretchen, not a saint. I think you need to remind yourself of that sometimes."

Lindsey's help far exceeded Gretchen's expectations, and Gretchen wasn't sure how to thank her. She helped with all the chores that Gretchen never could quite get done. She picked up the slack and began shuttling Olivia around, thereby freeing Gretchen up to work more.

When Lindsey returned home after a few weeks, Gretchen began to flounder again without her help. Even with Tony, Leila and Tracy assisting in any way they could, it wasn't nearly enough to make up for what Olivia was losing, and therefore, what Gretchen was failing to provide. It also struck Gretchen with startling, scary clarity that she wasn't sure she could manage all of Olivia's care on her own. What if she could not take care of Olivia? Not on her own. How could she have signed up for this? Her stomach ache was a constant thing now that never left.

****

"They're moving Helen into hospice."

Tony froze at his computer when Gretchen came up behind him. His mother must have let her in. Turning, he immediately got up and tried to comfort her. Her face crumpled as she fell into him. He held her against his chest, rubbing her back. She nuzzled her face into her favorite spot, right at the base of his neck and shoulder.

Clutching his shirt, she sputtered out, "She's going to die soon. I need to get over there and help Helen, and take Olivia. It's… not going to be very much longer."

"How is Olivia?"

"Not okay. She is so lost and confused. She watches her grandmother with clear confusion and pain in her eyes. She knows technically what's wrong, but she doesn't really understand it. Or that she won't see her grandmother ever again. And pretty soon, she'll be gone forever. She doesn't really get it."

She leaned back to look up into his eyes. "It won't be long now. Things… will soon be changing."

Tony's heart squeezed. He didn't want anything to change. Especially, not between Gretchen and him. He liked being with her. He liked getting up in the morning for the first time since losing his arm. He looked forward to things, when he didn't for so long.

Now, she was going to be the primary caretaker of a little girl who was about to be devastated by grief. The fun, the sex, and the dating they were now enjoying didn't fit into that picture. He didn't fit into that picture. But Gretchen never seemed to get it, which was one of the reasons, he supposed, he responded so differently to her than he did to anyone else. She expected things of him, despite the missing arm, where other people just excused him.

The thing was: he couldn't be a lame boyfriend without a job, or a car, or a home of his own, much less, the prospects of any of those. She didn't care; but finally, he did.

"Can I do anything?"

"Hold me," she said softly, her breath feeling warm on his neck. Her head was turned and resting on his shoulder.

He wished he could stay there for the rest of her life as easily as it was now.

****

The offer came via an old-fashioned phone call. After Tony hung up, he just sat there as if shell-shocked once more. He didn't move for ten minutes, staring at the shifting screen saver which was moving lazily around the monitor.

He'd been offered a damn job.

He didn't know what the hell to do now. A job. Him. Tony Lindstrom. It had been a long while since he had a real anything. He could never succeed in the civilian world. Or could he? Sometimes, he felt so far removed from the typical, normal, average person, he didn't know if he could ever be what he should be again.

It was from former Air Force Major, John Raymond, who now ran the nonprofit nationally recognized, *Hero!Fund*, which was based out of Washington D.C., raising money, which they then distributed through a plethora of deserving veteran charities and organizations. They did anything from placing veterans in the work force, to research for prosthetics, helping vets with PTSD, and even fund-raising for more unilateral free mental health services for all veterans. There was nothing the *Hero!Fund* would say no to if they deemed it a worthy cause, and one which could improve or enrich veterans' lives. They were recognized by the Department of Veterans Affairs as one of the top earning charitable organizations, and were widely sought out by others. The name was bit cheesy for Tony's taste, but their reputation was the best in the business. They wanted Tony to be their new "face." He would be featured on their website front page: the happy, one-armed, employed veteran. He would be assigned to speaking engagements and handle the PR for the organization. He was, John Raymond said, the best man to represent the Army in years. So naturally, they wanted him to come to their corporate offices and work.

In Washington D.C.

He had recently considered moving into an apartment a mile or so away from his parents in Calliston. He was mustering up the damn gumption to do so. To get a license… and drive a car… and perhaps, amp up the speech-writing stuff that people seemed to like so much. He more than once considered doing all this, but hadn't yet done any of it.

Should he move across the country into a city he'd never even visited? *Huh. No. Wow.* Where was this coming from? How could he manage to garner attention from clear across the country? All of it stemming from one elementary school, spur-of-the-moment, little speech he gave? It just didn't compute in his mind that it could really lead to so much more. A job offer. And a good job offer, an impressive and important job offer, without even applying. It seemed crazy to imagine.

How could he do it?

How could he refuse it?

After all he failed to do for the last few years, and all the opportunities he wasted, and the caring people he hurt while doing nothing and stewing in his anger, how could he ever contemplate *not* doing it? Doing something of value and meaning that actually exploited his injury in a way that was positive, and for the betterment of others? Others who suffered much more than he. He finally reached a place where he could remember he was indeed alive, and he did have another arm, and two legs, which functioned perfectly. He finally started to remember how lucky he was, too.

It solved everything. He would leave and be gone. He would be forced to re-enter the world and come out of hiding. He'd have to actually live in the regular world and with one arm. He'd finally have to make a real life, one that included accepting his handicap, but no longer feeling helpless and unable to do anything.

And it would get him away from Gretchen. The one thing he knew, absolutely *knew* right down to the marrow of his bones, was that he wasn't ready for the kind of life Gretchen was living. He wasn't ready to be a father figure to a traumatized little girl. He wasn't ready to be leaned on by a woman who was facing motherhood for the first time.

He was literally barely months out of even leaving his bed to do anything. He just… couldn't be all those things. Not now, and maybe not ever.

But he finally had something decent to do everyday, something that mattered a damn. There weren't too many people or things that still mattered to him: Gretchen, Olivia, his parents and Donny. Perhaps, Donny's kid. But the rest, the fancy cars and big houses, and the pursuit of the American dream… were now things he just couldn't relate to anymore. He didn't get it. He didn't even like it. He wasn't sure he even wanted the American dream.

However, the concept of maybe trying to help others, those who saw and dreamed and suffered as he did, and continued to, wasn't over yet. That's what most people missed. Just because he was home, and out of the military, everything he saw and endured and experienced, were the very things that made up his personality now. They were not simply over and done just because he no longer wore the uniform.

But in a way, this could give him a semblance of that.

He sighed deeply and sat down to further explore the organization that could finally pry him out of his parents' damn basement, and also away from Gretchen.

Chapter Twenty-One

GRETCHEN LAY ACROSS TONY with her hair fanned out over his chest. She traced a finger up and down his stomach. It still made him smile when she mentioned how well toned his chest was. That she could look at him without seeing the sawed-off limb as her focal point stumped him. She liked studying his many stomach muscles while ignoring his amputation. It was a rare, quiet Sunday morning. Olivia was with Helen and the nurse. Gretchen didn't often leave them alone for long. Olivia was becoming impossible to pry away from Helen, and the toll it took on Gretchen was affecting her physically. She'd lost weight and her eyes were ringed in purplish half moons. She also didn't smile as much.

She didn't much feel like having sex, so Tony didn't press her. He understood. Although he never could have if grief hadn't done the same goddamned thing to him. He finally realized his lack of interest in sex wasn't because he was a freak and embarrassed about his missing arm. No, it was because he still grieved over his former persona, and who he was previously, the lost image of the man he once embodied. The crusty, old, kind of brilliant, Dr. Hart might have been helpful in bringing him to that realization.

So he didn't pressure Gretchen, but simply let her show him what she wanted from him.

Today, it was his physical presence, and silence. She lay against him, practically holding on for dear life. Lifting her chin, she slid her head over his chest until she made eye contact with him.

"This is so much harder than I ever dreamed it would be."

"No one could prepare for it."

"That's true. Maybe I kind of knew it would be like this. I tried to resist Helen when she first approached me; but then, I couldn't really deny her."

"Do you want to? In all honesty, do you really want to do this?"

She sucked in a breath before a small smile curled her lips. "Leave it to you to never be wishy-washy about things. Yes, I want to do this. I really want to have Olivia if Helen can't. I just didn't know it would be such a backbreaking endeavor. I have never been so exhausted in my whole life. Even Vickie stopped asking me for help and began inquiring how I'm doing."

He coughed discreetly. "She replaced you with Donny."

"Did he say that?"

"He mentioned she's becoming quite difficult. He tries to blame it on the pregnancy, but well, we all can see it's not."

She slid her face back down so he couldn't see her expression and he felt her swallow. She waited a long moment before she asked, "What is it? You're holding something back from me. I've sensed it for a while. What do you want to tell me, but don't think I can handle?"

He closed his eyes and exhaled slowly. Everything he ever wanted lay across his body, wanting him, needing him, and he was going to… what? Risk it all?

Jeopardize losing her? Or changing whatever they had? It made no damn sense. But then… it did.

"I was offered a job. With an organization that fundraises for veteran causes and organizations. You've probably heard of it, the *Hero!Fund*."

She jerked up, pulling her legs beneath her. Her face bloomed into such pride and joy over his revelation, it seemed as if he'd done something truly miraculous, so he turned away, feeling slightly embarrassed. She grabbed his hand and sandwiched it between her two. He stared at them. She had perfect hands: long fingers, neatly manicured, and delicate nails painted today in purple with little half moons on them. She had soft veins that shone blue through her translucent skin and capable hands. His hand felt rough and hairy inside hers. His only hand.

He just couldn't believe she truly didn't give a damn about it.

"It's in Washington D.C."

Her face crumpled. "D.C.? A-are you considering it seriously?"

"Yes, I am. Gretchen, you know…"

She lowered her forehead to their joined hands, and rested it on their knuckles. Tears fell on his skin. "I know. You don't want a ready-made family."

"It's more than a ready-made family, Gretchen. You're adopting an eight-year-old, very troubled, little girl."

"One that you like. You've helped her more than almost everyone else! You don't have to move across the country."

"Why not? Because I should move in here and… what? Take care of her while you're at work all day?"

She slowly lifted her face and her tears began to dry as her gaze narrowed in on him. "Well… why not? Why couldn't you? Why couldn't you do just that?"

His mouth dropped in astonishment. He never expected that response from her. Her mouth suddenly flattened. "I mean it. Women tend to children all the time while men work, so why couldn't you? It's a valuable job. It's more valuable than anything else there is. So why the hell couldn't you do that? Why can't you stay here? And be with me? With us?"

She suddenly slid off the bed and got onto her feet, now pacing as she spoke.

He flipped off covers and stood up too so they were staring across the bed at each other. "I can't do that."

"What can't you do? Be with me? You already are. And you've been doing it just fine."

"I can't refuse this job. I can't go back to how I was even a few months ago. I want to be different. And it's taken me a long, tedious time to want that."

She crossed her arms over her chest. "So great! I made you feel so much better, you're going to bail on me."

He smiled slowly and shook his head. "Not exactly how I'd explain it."

"Then how would you explain it? Huh? Why don't you just come out and tell me? How you can't be with me because poor you has only one arm. What does that have to do with the situation? Or being in a relationship with me? Despite Olivia or because of Olivia. Why does her living with me suddenly make or break us? Or am I to believe there is no us?"

"There's definitely an us."

"And we are fantastic together."

"I told you from the start, I'm not in this to become a father figure."

"So don't be. Who asked you to?"

"Olivia does. Every time she's with me."

Gretchen rolled her eyes. "So being needed and wanted by a little girl scares you? Why don't you quit hiding from every damn little thing that tries to enter your life? Why don't you muster up some of that courage that you had while you were a soldier and use it here? Now? With me? I deserve that from you. We deserve that. Olivia and I. My ass, you weren't ever doing this! When I told you on Christmas Day, you could have bailed then. You should have made it clear then. You should *not* have started helping me take care of Olivia, or sitting with Helen, and being, oh, I don't know, like the goddamned father figure in the situation!"

Yanking the bedspread off in frustration, she bunched it up and threw it down before fisting her hands at her side. "You are utterly impossible. I can't even tell you how much. First, you hide in your parents' basement for two years after a failed engagement. Then you won't drive. You won't work. You won't talk to friends. You won't even be nice to the people who are trying to help you. Finally, after you stopped doing all that, and just started to make teeny, tiny steps forward, then you do this. You unilaterally decide not to be with me. After three months of you being angry with me because I didn't notice you for twenty fucking years, or that you wanted to be with me. Twenty! That's a really long time—two decades. Who does that? Who gets exactly what he wants, the woman he claims he always wanted so damn much, and then... pisses it all away because he gets a little bit scared? Who does that?"

Her breathing sounded ragged and her voice was nearly a scream at the end. "What's more... I fixed you. I made you nicer and made you value and appreciate what you still have. I motivated you to do something with your miserable ass. You wanted to impress me, so don't you dare stand there now and deny it. *I* am the reason that this new Tony, which the veteran organization wants so badly, even exists. You would have never pursued anything without my presence in your life. Or my influence. Don't you dare try to deny it… you wanted to sleep with me just to not feel like a miserable, damn failure. So my influence is what indirectly got you this offer. And now you're going to leave me over it?"

He couldn't remember the last time anyone could floor him so much, he couldn't even find the words to answer her. *Gretchen?* Was this really the woman who so kindly cared for Olivia, and him, and everyone else while never admitting if it bothered her or not. Was this calm, responsible, respectful Gretchen the same woman he'd been dating now for enough months that he should have known she was prone to dramatic, unreasonable rants? Never, not even at Vickie's choice for a wedding date, had he seen her so inflamed. Or so emotional. Or so crazy.

"Yeah, yeah, it was because of you. You're right about all that. The thing is: once I started to heal, everything else got better too."

"Well, no shit! Engage people and be nice, and gee… look at that! People might want to be around you more. Having other people's comments and feedback about your one-armed heroism seems a lot better than hiding all alone in your basement. Wow! News flash. You found the mysterious reason that most grownups have jobs, girlfriends… and, you know, lives. The things you completely lacked. Until me, that is."

She whirled around and headed for the door, but he was faster. Slamming the door, he stood in front of it and she nearly screeched at him in fury. "Move! I am done. With you. With this. With poor Tony and his one arm. You know what? It doesn't matter. It never mattered. I loved you with it, or despite it, or maybe because of it, whatever you want to call it. I have loved you unconditionally and now, you intend to leave me because of it."

Tears began streaming down her face. She raised her hands and buried her face in her fists. She shook her head as he grabbed her and drew her against him. Her body convulsed. She fought him, pushing against his chest. He could barely restrain her there.

"Shh…" he murmured softly as she finally ceased fighting him. With her hands around his neck, she stood there beside him as her body shook with tears. He leaned his head down until his lips were in her hair.

She finally sniffed. "Aren't you supposed to say 'it's going to be okay?'"

"I hate being told that. I doubt you want to hear it, so no, I'm not going to say that."

She finally wiped her nose with the edge of her nightgown. "I suppose you want to talk about it now? Like adults?"

He shook his head. "No. I want to make love with you and impress you with my one-armed…what did you call me? Oh yeah… show you I'm *not* a miserable, damn failure."

She dropped her head, shaking it against his chest, and hiding her expression from him. "I might have gotten a little carried away."

"Nah. You didn't. I *was* a miserable failure. I was miserable company and miserable to live with. I did nothing, and preferred it that way. You changed everything for me."

She lifted her head and he was taken by the emerald green of her eyes now glossed over from tears. He touched the pad of his thumb to one eye, and then the other. She shut them as she took in a deep breath. "Do you realize what I just said?"

"Yes, I realize what you just said."

"And?"

"And I don't think it should come as a shock to learn that I love you too. I've always loved you."

She clutched at his neck and took in a shuddering breath. "You have a strange way of showing it."

He didn't answer, but trailed his fingertips over her face, to her chin, and her neck. He touched her collarbone and pushed down the straps of her nightgown. First one shoulder, then the other. The gown dropped to the floor in a puddle of fabric. She was only wearing her sheer, lacy, white panties. Standing there with her eyes closed, she allowed him to stare at her. He touched her nipple, which she loved. He liked making her feel good. Her legs wobbled slightly as his fingers played with it, pulling and elongating it. Her breath sucked in. He dipped his head, and put his mouth over it as his arm encircled her waist. She always felt almost crazy-boneless when he did that. He was ready to support nearly all of her body weight while she clung to him. She leaned her head back, and her hair feathered across his arm. Her long, white throat was exposed to his gaze as he sucked and kissed and licked her just the way she liked. And he liked.

He stepped forward, pushing her backwards, and still sucking on her. She clumsily, but somehow, guided them to the edge of her bed, where he lay her down. She wasn't often on the bottom, for obvious performance issues. He couldn't easily support himself above her.

She was, however, game for anything else they could physically accomplish.

Reaching down, he slid her panties down her legs as she lowered her feet to the floor. Sliding his hand up her thigh, he momentarily wished he had two hands just to feel both of her legs. She never complained that he didn't. Her legs trembled at his touch, in anxious anticipation. She arched her back and leaned herself closer to him. He pushed on her thighs, indicating he wanted her to open them. She complied. Her eyes closed, and her breathing hitched. He looked at her, so open and responsive and ready for him. She wasn't shy. Or embarrassed. And she never tried to stop him from doing anything.

He touched his lips to her right knee first and she sighed. Then he kissed the length of her thigh in a long, slow ritual. Her whole body arched and rose up toward his lips as he came closer. She twisted and moaned in anticipation, always totally open with what she wanted and how much she wanted it.

He dropped to his knees before the bed, and leaned closer, kissing her softly at her opening. She nearly catapulted off the bed. Then she squirmed. When he touched his tongue to her, and into her, licking every part of her, she nearly screamed in response. Her entire body reacted to him as if begging for *more.* Now. She was swollen and slick with wetness. Her hands twisted and tugged at the blankets. She was nearly spread-eagled.

Her incessant cries were erotic, calling his name, along with plenty of ohs and groans that nearly made him come just from listening to her. His tongue twirled and twisted inside her. He licked her just like he did her tits until she came the way only Gretchen could.

Finally extracting his mouth from her, he glanced over her. He loved how she never covered herself. She wasn't modest with him. She allowed herself to completely succumb to him and her ensuing reactions were nothing less than *hot*. He crawled up towards her head, and paused to lick her breasts until he was back at her mouth. She opened it and groaned when she tasted herself on his lips. Her tongue touched his lips, and engaged his tongue.

Placing her hands on his chest, she pushed up his t-shirt and tugged it over his head. He leaned back finally, parting just long enough to discard it. He had, long ago ceased caring about her seeing him naked. Or shirtless. Or one-armed. She sometimes kissed him there, or stroked it absently with her fingertips. It wasn't something she ever avoided, or obsessed over. She often grabbed the capped-off spot where his arm should have been for better leverage when they were making love. At first, it nearly stunned him, but she was so damn open about it. He never expected to be so comfortable with any woman. Or to allow any woman to be so comfortable with him. But long ago, Gretchen managed to make him stop feeling weird about his amputation.

She switched to oral birth control after a few weeks of being together with Tony, so when he shifted and she climbed on top of him, he could easily sink right into her. The moan of ecstasy that came from his lips was the most genuine of his life. He could not get enough of her. He slid into her, as always… perfectly. He watched her come every time. He watched every twitch in her face, and her eyes when they shut in bliss or stared at him intensely with her emotions nearly glaring. Sometimes, he merely observed the jiggle or sway of her breasts, or how she flipped her head back and exposed the long column of her throat. She always looked so free, abandoning all worries and cares, when she was with him. Or when he touched her, or made love to her. And it wasn't something he ever expected to encounter in his lifetime.

Gretchen Hendricks. He turned her on, satisfied her, left her still wanting him, needing him, and nearly squirming with genuine desire despite his broken, amputated, incomplete body. It still didn't compute that this was really happening to him. She trembled and moaned before leaning down and setting her palms on his chest for better leverage. Now lifting her hips higher, she eagerly impaled herself on him, engulfing him fuller, and making him harder, and more aroused. Closing his eyes, he finally relished all of the sensations that almost made up for... everything else. Being with Gretchen nearly compensated for everything else he'd ever lost in his life. He was practically whole again, and a complete man, when he was buried inside her. Rock hard and stiff, her wetness, and slick heat nearly finished him off when she climaxed. Feeling her hot body over him, and around him, he happily succumbed to her.

Chapter Twenty-Two

GRETCHEN WAS SPRAWLED ON top of Tony with her face buried again in his chest. Her breathing was calmer now as the sweat on her body cooled over him. Still naked, she finally shifted to the side and swung her legs off him.

She groaned out loud. "What was that? A last lay? A goodbye? Well, it sucks. It isn't enough."

"No, it isn't enough," he agreed quietly. Using the deep, reserved tone she remembered from his speeches, he asked, "Are you done yelling at me?"

She bit her lip in an effort to refrain from crying. Tears filled her closed eyelids. She could not do this anymore. She could not sit there and discuss his departure. Not now. Not right at the same time as watching a woman die, and enduring the excruciating pain of seeing it, along with the little girl most affected by it. Done yelling? No. She wasn't even close to being done with him.

"I just don't know how you can do this. I should have left you stewing in the basement."

His hand lazily made circles on her bare back. "You probably should have. But for some reason, which remains unbeknownst to me, you didn't. I need to take the job. It's important, and a chance for my life, and my job, to mean something again."

"Like it did while you were a soldier?"

"Yes, I felt sure I mattered then. I knew what I was doing and why. I fought for those who stood right next to me and those who came before me, as well as the younger ones who will come after me. I believed in what I was doing. I haven't believed in anything since then. Nothing mattered to me. Not being back here. Not being alive. I became hollow. Until you showed up. I care about you. But that isn't…"

"Enough? Why? Why can't it be enough?"

He squeezed her arm. "Of course, you're enough for me. Don't make it that simplistic. But it's not enough for me to just sit around doing nothing."

"It was enough for two years. Why change it now?"

"Not anymore. It's not enough anymore."

"Okay, then again, you can move in here. There would be plenty for you to do. Oh, wait, I see… only women get hired to stay at home and take care of Olivia. It would only be *meaningful* if I quit *my* job and did that. But you, a big, macho soldier, of course, it's not *enough*."

His chest shook under her. Surprised, she was confused by his reaction and glanced up to find him laughing. *He was laughing at her*? While dumping her? About… well, hell! How could he laugh now, of all the times in the world?

"Can you let me finish with my spiel before you ream me out? It's why I didn't bring it up to you earlier. I was trying to figure it all out first. I am not dumping you. I meant to ask you if you would consider doing this long distance with me. All three of my adult relationships with women were long distance, as I was usually off on tours and serving. Although I don't love it, it's something I've gotten used to. I know it's asking a lot from you. Probably too much. And it's not fair.

You have a lot going on already. But it was the only solution I could think of."

She jerked upright. "Why the hell didn't you lead with that? Or shut me up? You should have tackled me and muffled me. I said horrible, unforgivable things... why would you let me go on like that?"

"I think because I kind of needed to hear it from you. I needed to hear that you really felt passionately about me. Because the usual Gretchen restrains her emotions. Her real emotions, that is. You always keep a tight lid on them. I didn't know you'd react like that, but in all honesty, I'm freaking glad you did. I needed to hear it."

"You needed to hear me call you mean names?" She rounded her eyes in horror at him.

"No, but I did need to hear you felt that strongly about me. I had to know you needed me enough to ask you to do this."

"How could you not know by now that I need you?"

"I don't know. Things like you not telling me my mother is always rude to you. Helen had to tell me that. It worries me that you still handle me with kid gloves because you don't trust me to take care of things."

She scoffed. "I hope you're kidding me. I didn't tell you about Leila because I didn't want you to get mad at me by thinking I wasn't being nice enough to her. It had nothing to do with if I thought you could handle it or not. I didn't want her to start talking in your ear about me and having some influence. I figured ignoring her was better."

"Well, that's the kind of stuff I keep trying to figure out."

"And? Did you figure it out that I love you enough, and that this isn't fake? This, us, is as real as it gets."

He brushed her hair off her face as he stared into her eyes. "Yeah, I get it's as real as it gets."

"And..."

"And I love you."

She let out a breath. "Was that so hard to say? There again, next time, try leading with the 'I love you and want you,' not 'I'm moving out and leaving you.'"

"I'll talk to my mother before I go. I'm sorry if she made this tougher on you. I really didn't know. I have not made life easy for her. A lot of what you're experiencing is probably directed at me."

"She just won't allow herself to get as mad as she really is. She still treats you like you're injured, and therefore, special because of it. I deduced that, Tony. And it's half of why I let it stand. But I always treat you like I would any other man. I swear to you right now, I won't be nice to you just because of your amputation."

He finally let a small smile brighten his face. "You promise, huh?"

"Yes. Solemnly."

He shook his head. "You, somehow, always make it easier for me."

She leaned her head on him. "You make it easier for me too. Don't forget that key part."

"I know how hard you had it with Will when he was gone. I never thought or dreamed I'd ask this of you, but here we are."

She closed her eyes. She hated it. The thought of Tony being gone. Not there. Not in town. The time, the distance, and all the things that could go so wrong. They could meet other people. Loneliness could make one or both of them give up on what they had, or do something stupid with someone else. They could both get fed up with the frustration and start to not care. So many things could happen. They hadn't been dating long enough for this kind of a trial.

But she loved him. She inhaled sharply. More than everything else, and all the reasons why not, was that. She loved him. And he had to do it. One choice: either accept it or be alone.

"I still vote you move in here with me."

He chuckled softly. "I might someday. I hope things go… okay. But not right now. I need this job. I want it. Please understand that. I lost all the ambition to do anything. I literally didn't care if I lived or died. I didn't care what day, or what time it was. It ceased to embarrass me how I was living and what I failed to do. You're right saying that you motivated me into all of this. Suddenly, I cared. You led me out of the depression that nearly debilitated me. I could not feel anything but anger. And now I don't. Now I want to get up and do something. I guess, I also want to see if I still *can* do it. I've never been all that good at anything, Gretchen. Not like you and Will. You were both always superstars of whatever you chose to do. I was mediocre, the nuts and bolts, always the follower and never the leader. This job, being asked to represent an organization I could be proud of, that represents a cause I gave my damn arm for, is not something I ever expected. I want the respect. I want to help. It's more of a shock to me than perhaps anyone else. But there it is."

Her heart cramped in her chest. How could she not want that for him? She sighed and slipped into his lap, leaning her head against his chest and wrapping arms around his waist. "Okay."

He jerked at her voice. "Okay? As in…"

"Whatever you need to do. I'll stay with you if you want me."

"I want you."

"Then we'll figure it out together."

He squeezed her closer to him. "I'm sorry it's now. You know, with Olivia, and all."

"There would never be a good time. It was never easy with you. Why start today?"

Chapter Twenty-Three

"SO, WILL YOU COME help me move?"

Will paused on his end of the phone line, but Tony could hear him breathing sharply. "Are you for real? You're actually inviting me there? To help you?" Tony just spent the last ten minutes explaining the job offer to him.

"Yeah, if it's not too much trouble. Gretchen can't leave now. Not with all the stuff she has going on and the little girl she's adopting. And Donny has his hands full with Vickie being pregnant. She won't let him go around the block."

Will laughed. "God help the man. Why? Why did he take her on?"

"Best guess? He knocked her up before he knew any better."

"Well, it's definitely not too much trouble. I'll come."

"Thanks. I wish I didn't need the help, but…"

"But it's done. I'm there," he said. He was gone for a second before returning on the line, "Jessie will, no doubt, come with me to be with Gretchen."

After he leaves Gretchen. He physically ached at the thought of their separation. "That would be good. I never dreamed…"

"My wife would have to comfort your girlfriend?" Will inquired, the irony crystal clear in his tone. He finally chuckled. "Life is full of surprises."

He let out a long, deep breath. "Yeah. It is. Hey, thanks, Will… I mean, for everything."

"Are you spending a bit too much time in Gretchen's therapy? Don't go all girlie-ass on me now, dickhead. I wouldn't recognize you."

He laughed and it felt really nice to be laughing and joking with the friend who had been his best since he was five years old. "Yeah, well maybe I'm man enough to finally become so."

"I'll be there." This time, Will wasn't joking.

A week was not long enough, but too long to spend dreading. Not soon enough for when Helen died, but maybe it was better for Tony to leave before that event, rather than afterwards.

Now, he just had to tell his mother.

****

"Mom?" he said quietly to get her attention.

She turned from where she was perusing the local grocery ad for coupons and sales. His heart twisted as she innocently sat there, clipping away and glancing up momentarily, but clearly distracted by her steals and deals. He knew better than anyone how taxing and arduous his injury and the ensuing journey was for her. He put her through an emotional and physical hell during the last few years. She tried to help him in the first few months with the phantom pain that nearly cost him his sanity. She counseled him, grieved with him, worried about him, and did anything for him. She actually enabled him, but also gave him the freedom to accept what happened in whatever way he needed to and allotted him however much time it took. She let him absorb all of her spare time without a complaint simply because of her gratitude and relief he was still alive. She perpetually allowed him the freedom to do and say anything.

The time had finally come for Tony to quit ruining her life as well as his own.

Pulling out a kitchen chair, he sat down next to her. She glanced up again and her eyes ran over his face, taking in the dour, serious expression. She pushed her clippings aside and took his hand.

"What is it? Gretchen? Did she... do something?"

He squeezed her hand. "No. She didn't. Other than deciding not to tell me you don't like her."

Leila's expression soured. "Well, obviously she did."

"No, Helen did."

Leila had the grace to blush. "Okay. Fine. Perhaps I was a little bit unreceptive to her dating you."

"A little bit?"

"Okay, more than a little bit. But she comes here and makes all these demands on you, and suddenly changes everything, as if she knows what's best, when she wasn't even here for the worst of it. She didn't see it, or experience it, or worry if..."

Leila's tears were streaming down her face and Tony pulled her against him. "No. No one worried about me killing myself, but you and Dad. No one stood by and let me lie around, day in and day out, for almost two years. No one else made me get out of bed, when I didn't want to ever again. Just you. That will never change. Everything you did for me. Gretchen's involvement will never diminish what you and Dad did for me."

She pushed against him. "I don't need any damn acknowledgment. I didn't do it for the credit. I did it because I love you. I don't need anything except a guarantee that you're going to be okay."

"And the thing is: I'm finally getting there, to that safe place. Thanks to you. And also thanks to Gretchen. She did things for me that no one else could; but then again, so did you. Don't think I don't realize that. Or value what you did or you. You were the only thing I cared about for a long time. You saved my life, Mom. If I never told you that until now, I'm sorry. But you did."

"So, I should stop being so mean to your girlfriend? Is that the point of this conversation?"

"Did you hear what I said?"

She nodded. "I heard you. I just don't need to hear it. You're my son. You're alive. That's all I ever need to know again."

"How about if your son isn't a bastard anymore?"

She shrugged, and a smile hovered over her lips. "Okay, that might be more enjoyable, but I don't need it."

"I would appreciate if you were nicer to Gretchen. She's a good one, Mom."

"I thought she'd get tired and leave you like Audrey did."

"Audrey didn't do that. I did. I've told you that before."

"No one should leave a man who just had his arm amputated."

"Mom…"

She waved her hand around. "Okay, okay, I'll be nicer to Gretchen. I always liked her, I just didn't like her taking you away from me."

"She's not what's taking me away from you now."

Leila froze, and her eyebrows rose in puzzlement. He continued, "I've been offered a job and I've decided to take it. The thing is: it's in Washington D.C. so I'll have to move there…"

She cut him off by throwing her arms around him. Real tears coursed down her cheeks and choked her up. "You're really and truly better now, aren't you?"

He was flabbergasted by her reaction and patted her back awkwardly. Finally, she leaned back and cupped his chin. "I never dreamed you'd be capable, or ready, or even willing to ever work again. It means that everything we endured finally worked."

"You heard about the moving part?" Wasn't that the reason his mother threw herself at him in tears of unhappiness?

"Yes. Of course, I will miss you. But remember, Tony, I spent a decade with you across the country and the world, and half of that time, you were in extreme danger too. So it's not like it's something I'm not used to already. I just never dreamed you'd ever leave long enough so I *could* miss you. Don't you see what this means?"

He scratched his head. "Uh, no. Gretchen, and the website, and all my speaking engagements, and when I actually left the house... none of those clued you in that I was progressing forward? And this does?"

She nodded vigorously. "Yes. This does. What about Gretchen?"

"We're going to try it long distance."

Leila sat back with a huff. "Well, I guess I can give her a chance then."

He smiled slowly, "Yeah, that would be most appreciated."

"When? When are you doing this?"

"One week."

Leila nodded. "Well, there must be a ton of stuff we have to do. Let's get started. Oh, and tell your dad and Donny. We'll have to plan a going away party. Oh, let me grab a pen and paper..."

319

He stared, open-mouthed, and in shock as she started listing off all the things that needed to happen before the end of the week.

****

"I know this is hard to understand." Tony was finishing up his lame speech to Olivia. They sat on a park bench on the warm April day, engulfed in a riot of flowers that were blooming everywhere. The sun was balmy and the new blossoms softened the harsh edge of the landscaping. She was eating an ice cream cone Tony bought for her, mostly out of guilt, before he even started to explain he would be leaving her in one week.

"You're leaving me too?" she finally asked, after being silent for a full minute, her ice cream cone now forgotten in her hand. It dripped, and the tracks of it ran down her wrist and sleeve.

He leaned over and took the melting cone from her before throwing it in the trash behind her. He got up, traded sides, so his arm was beside her and he could hold her next to him. "It's not like your grandma going away. I'll be okay, and I'll be back."

She stiffened. Her little, skinny body strained and pulled away from him. "But it won't be the same. You won't be here. You won't be there after school anymore then, will you? Where am I supposed to go? What about me?"

"Y-you'll go back to Gretchen's office, just like before."

"Before you, you mean. It was fine then. I didn't know any better. But now, I don't want to sit around waiting for her to talk to sad kids. I want to come here and be with you."

He shut his eyes at the intense pain her simple words instilled in his chest. *I want to be with you.* So simple and so innocent. It seemed so long since anyone wanted to just be with him. But then again, it sounded a lot like what Gretchen said. Pressure lodged in his chest, and a knot of anxiety climbed up his throat. He was not expecting to encounter so much of either. Olivia. Gretchen. Helen. He didn't want to be their savior or answer to anything or anyone. He was barely ready to move out of his parents' house. That was a far damn cry from being a fill-in father to this needy, eight-year-old girl.

Perhaps, she was something he could eventually grow used to. But not yet.

Olivia's big, blue eyes were soggy and sad as she stared up at him. He almost felt as if he stole her favorite toy or destroyed her faith in Santa.

"Olivia, honey, I'll be back. I'll come visit you and Gretchen. It will be different, but I promise, I will be back."

She suddenly hopped onto her feet. "I don't believe you! I think you're lying. I think you're leaving us and won't ever come back. I think you're too afraid to tell me that. I hate you now. I wish I'd never, ever, met you!"

She spun around and ran off towards the playground equipment. He jumped onto his feet and ran after her. "Olivia!" he yelled, his voice sharp with annoyance and anxiety. He didn't like her running off and unattended in the park. He didn't like seeing how angry she was. He didn't like knowing how much he was hurting her.

"Olivia, wait! Now. Stop!" He commanded her and his voice lost any trace of niceness. He yelled like he would have at a soldier before running even faster after her. She ducked behind some trees that separated Gretchen's condo complex from the park.

He stopped dead in his tracks when he got around the trees. There, she sat on her tush with her legs against her small chest, both arms clutching them while she buried her head on top of them. Convulsive sobs made her shoulders jerk up and down. His heart collapsed. He rushed forward and dropped down to his knees beside her, pulling her sobbing, little form against him. Big, wet tears fell off her face and gooey snot ran freely into her mouth before she wiped it all on his shirt.

He patted her back and rubbed her shoulders. "Hey, hey now. It's okay. It's going to be okay, honey. I'm here. Everything's okay."

He paused from patting her as his repetitive chant suddenly registered. He was promising the same banal platitudes that he, himself, hated to hear. How could he sit there now and spout it into her ear?

Of course, he knew the answer. He said it because he felt helpless seeing this little girl's unbearable pain. Pain that went far beyond just being over him. It was as deep as his own once was. He realized now, while holding Olivia, that his pain was no longer like hers. His was… adjusting, and he was finally, marginally better. But that was wholly due to Gretchen and this little girl, now sobbing before him. He couldn't stand seeing her tears. It ripped his heart out and shredded the last of his calm reserve. He could not sit there without trying to comfort her, and calm her, and make her believe it would be better… if only for a moment. He loved her too much not to try.

Leaning closer, he tucked a chunk of her messy, dark hair behind her ear as he patted her head and wiped her wet face. This little girl who never once looked at him oddly, or cared, or even noticed he was missing an arm. She readily shared her daily goings on, as well as her life with him as if he were her best friend. Somehow, having her totally guileless friendship helped heal something in Tony, that perhaps no one else could ever have touched.

"It. Will. Be. Okay." His tone was authoritative. He held her attention when he said it. Her tears receded and she sniffed before finally stopping them, although her lips still trembled, and the occasional sob-like hiccup popped out of her mouth like an aftershock.

"Do you promise?" she asked her small, high voice enough to pierce through steel armor. He clutched her closer to his heart.

"I promise." There was simply nothing left to do but keep his promise to her. No matter what he had to do, or how long it would take.

"My grandma is dying," she whispered into his shirt.

"Yes, Liv, I'm afraid she is. I'm so sorry."

"I don't want her to leave me too." The simplicity of her statement instantly made him feel as helpless as he did the morning he woke up and realized his left arm had been amputated. He never thought anything could make him feel so helpless again. Turns out, he was wrong. This little girl managed to do just that to him.

She lifted her face to look up at him with her blue eyes almost fluid in feelings. "Do you promise to come back?"

"I promise I'll come back. Do you remember what I said about my promises?"

Olivia's blue eyes widened as she nodded in earnestness. "You said you always keep them."

He nodded. "Yeah, I always keep them. You can count on that."

****

Gretchen met them at her front door when they arrived. She clasped Olivia to her tightly after quickly scanning her face. It was obvious Olivia had been crying. She met Tony's eyes over Olivia. He shook his head, but his grave expression told her what she already expected. More heartache. More tears. More devastation. She nearly fell to the floor on her knees. It was too much of a burden. Olivia. Tony. Helen. Death. Leaving. Not more than a year ago, she'd been living relatively isolated, but stable, and her life was pretty predicable. It was a little stale, perhaps, but never anything like this. It didn't feel so broken.

The freaking kicker was: she chose it all. She chose to adopt Olivia. She almost chose to fall in love with Tony, after the first night with him, which was better than anything she'd felt in a decade.

She chose the ensuing heartache because the depth and joy and love it brought into her life was well worth it. Even now, as she wearily wondered if she could continue doing it.

"Should we paint your room today? I bought the shade of purple you wanted. I thought maybe we could do some multi-colored handprints on the walls after we paint. Wouldn't that be cool?"

Olivia nodded her head up and down on Gretchen's chest, and Gretchen's heart swelled. Olivia always tried to respond to her suggestions cheerfully. As if Olivia even cared about her "new" room. It wasn't as much fun to decorate a new room when it meant your beloved grandmother was dead. But distractions were all Gretchen could think of to get her through this.

Tony stepped inside and grabbed Olivia's hand. "Well, why don't you show me what shade of purple you picked? I can only do one-sided handprints though."

Olivia finally cracked her first smile at him. "That's okay. I like having your one better than anyone else's two."

Gretchen's heart heaved and ached. How could an eight-year-old so easily capture Gretchen's love and soul with one simple sentence?

Chapter Twenty-Four

TONY DIDN'T HAVE A huge amount of stuff to pack, just clothes and some personal items. He'd buy whatever he needed after he arrived and got set up. The organization was scouting out an apartment already.

The Lindstrom house remained full all week. This time, however, Will and his family stayed with Leila and Lewis. Donny and Vickie hung out as much as time would allow. Gretchen, of course, was there whenever she wasn't with Helen and Olivia. It was a far different feeling now than the nine months previous. Tony smiled and chatted and joined in all the conversations. He wasn't separate. He wasn't a problem. He was just one of them again.

He eyed Jessie as she was taping up a box for him. It would be flown at the expense of *Hero!Fund*.

After an hour of working together, quietly, with very few comments, Tony cleared his throat, causing Jessie to glance up. "So, I was wondering...uh, you know, that stuff in Mexico..."

She stilled and her face changed. "Yes?" she prompted when he didn't speak.

"Did you, I mean, do you ever get over it?"

She leaned back on her heels and smiled slowly. "Yes. No. Both. I got better. But I'm not like other women when it comes to certain things. I used to cut myself in order to deal with it. I'm better now, but once in awhile, it still… happens."

"What do you do then?"

She shrugged. "Like you, I get up and start over the next day. I lost some invisible parts of myself, and nothing totally can make up for that. I just try to live with what I have and love now. But it's not a perfect process by any means."

He nodded. "That's kind of what I'm getting at. I mean, not that this is anything like what happened to you."

She smiled softly. "Pain is pain, Tony. It may come from different sources, and undergo different coping mechanisms, but it doesn't change what's inside of you."

"Thank you for letting Will go with me."

She finished taping the box. "Recovery is what it is. It often hurts people, but the ones who love you always stick."

"You get this stuff."

"I live it every day. I'll keep living it and with it until the day I die. Just as you do with your one arm, Tony."

He smiled. "It's no wonder you and Gretchen get along so well. Neither of you ever beat around the bush. Thank you. I guess that's what I was asking. I sometimes think, no matter how much *better* I'm doing, there are times when things become too hard for me to deal with. Shouldn't I be more used to it by now? Or over it?"

Jessie smiled and nodded her understanding. "No. I used to think that too before I truly understood that living with what happened to me, *all of it,* is a lifelong ordeal. Sometimes, it's like a prison sentence for me.

Other times, I prevail over it. Sometimes though, I manage to forget it altogether and live right in the here and now, and I almost feel ordinary."

"I didn't know."

She shook her head. "Yes, you did. You're doing the same thing that I did. It's like going through all the stages of grief... Achieving acceptance doesn't mean there aren't days when you're right back to being angry, sad, in denial, and swimming in total self-pity. Just remember, that's just one day and don't allow it to rule your life. Get up the next day and choose to have a different kind of day. That's the only power you have over it, or how much you let it control you."

He studied her for a long moment. "Somehow, I sense that wasn't an easy life lesson for you to learn."

"No, just like yours hasn't been."

"I worry Gretchen will grow tired of dealing with it. Like on the days when I'm not fully at 'acceptance.'"

Jessie shook her head vigorously. "No. Like Will, she'll stick. Some people are healthy enough, and strong enough, and whole enough, that they don't need for us to be perfect. They can deal with the bad days."

"I wish..."

"Yeah, me too. But wishing doesn't let you live your life."

He slowly smiled. "That might be the best advice I've ever gotten."

She smiled right back. "That's me. A bastion of light and hope to the wounded."

He let out a breath. "I hate being one of the wounded."

"Me too, Tony. I detest it. But you have to acknowledge it and live with it; just don't make it your life. Does that make any sense?"

"Yeah. Balancing what is with what I wish it was?"

"Yes."

"Thank you, Jessie."

She shrugged. "Thank Gretchen, she first taught me that."

He sighed. "She taught me that too."

****

Tony left on a Wednesday. Gretchen drove him to the small airport a few hours away where he'd catch a commuter flight to San Francisco and right on out to his final destination. Will and Jessie were driving behind them in a rental car. Tony said his goodbyes to everyone, even his parents, at the house. All the while, Gretchen stood by stoically while they embraced and shared loving comments. Gretchen drove because Tony still didn't drive. It was impossible to imagine how he'd learn to navigate in a new city by himself, without a car, when he had never lived alone with just one arm. The anxiety started to build up in his chest. The desire to simply turn around and rush downstairs, back into the basement, was strong, which was why he enlisted Will. No way could he act like that under Will's observation. Will's presence would force him to proceed.

Gretchen's, however, would have the reverse effect.

The ride was quiet with only a few idle comments, and fewer smiles. The atmosphere was taut with unmet expectations. And grief. And things that should have been said. But how did one say it all?

Will and Jessie hung back after getting checked in with their tickets. They stowed the luggage Tony couldn't carry on. Finally, it was time for him to proceed through the security.

He turned toward Gretchen and she blinked back hot tears from her limpid, green eyes. She dabbed at them with the backs of her hands.

"I swore I would not do this."

He dropped his bags, stepping forward to pull her against him. "I'm sorry."

She shook her head and leaned back to bring her hands up and smooth his collar. She kept her gaze firmly there. "No. Don't be. I'm so proud of you. For getting this job. For everything. I'm just going to miss you so damn much."

"I'll come back when things with Helen…"

She leaned into him. "Yes, I know you will."

He took in a deep, shuddering breath. Her voice sounded weird. It was weak and weary and so unlike Gretchen. For once, he was the strong link between them. It didn't sit well with him, however. Leaving her was as hard as he dreaded. He wanted it to be over. Yet he couldn't stand letting her go. He wanted to change his mind. And go home.

He kissed her and finally slid his hand from around her waist, "I'll call you, and all that, when we land."

She didn't register his conciliatory words. Tears rolled down her face. "I love you," she whispered.

He leaned in and whispered it back to her and would have sworn he could feel her clutching his bicep as if holding herself up. Finally, she let go and turned away from him. Jessie came forward and hugged her as she waved for Tony to go. *Now.* He got her message.

He felt like puking as he glanced back one more time and Gretchen slowly started down the corridor with Jessie guiding her.

Will was quiet for a long while. After they were at their gate, just sitting there, watching the plane jockeying around, Will leaned forward. "It's hard. But it'll get easier."

Tony stared out the window. "It was never that hard to leave Audrey."

Will smiled sadly, "It was never that hard for me to leave Gretchen."

Tony frowned and glanced at Will sharply, "My girlfriend now, you know."

He nodded. "Yeah, but it was that hard for me to leave Jessie. My point is: feelings like this can survive temporary separations. Years even. Mine did. And yours can."

He shook his head and frowned, looking puzzled. "That's oddly… comforting. Even if it makes you a total dickhead about Gretchen."

Will nodded. "It does. But it is what it is."

He stared for a few moments before admitting, "I missed being friends with you."

Will slapped his shoulder. "Yeah? Well, friendships like ours managed to survive all the separations too, now didn't they?"

He nodded and finally smiled. "Yeah, they sure as shit did."

As he boarded the plane, his stomach cramped with indecision. Should he really be doing this? Leaving the damn state? And Gretchen? But Jessie's words rang true in his head. Gretchen showed him how to live with his handicap, and now it was time to prove that he could. In a way, she was exactly right; she was the catalyst for him to finally get better, and now, he was leaving her because of it.

Chapter Twenty-Five

"HELEN?" GRETCHEN LIFTED HER head and clutched at Helen's hand. It felt odd. Gretchen frantically touched her fingertips around Helen's wrist looking for a pulse. Nothing. Gretchen yelled for the nurse. She came in and quickly assessed Helen. She shook her head finally, confirming what Gretchen's cramping stomach already knew: Helen was dead.

Helen died in her sleep on a dreary Monday afternoon in May. The nurse had called Gretchen at work and she had gotten to Helen just in time. Helen had not been conscious for several days. Gretchen lowered her head as tears flowed unchecked down her cheeks. She sobbed against Helen's body, free to finally release her long restrained tears. The nurse left the room, giving her some privacy. There was no Tony. No Olivia. And no one to see her. So she cried and cried, preparing to face Olivia's tears. Olivia's sadness. Olivia's needs. *Olivia.*

Gretchen cried for a half hour over the lost life of Helen, and the little girl she was about to gain.

Olivia was at school, and Gretchen did not pull her out. She picked her up as usual, and drove her to their condo. Then, just like Tony did with her the previous month, she sat her down and destroyed her innocence.

Olivia dropped like an anvil into Gretchen and agonizing tears soon had her convulsing so much that Gretchen feared she'd have to sedate her. There was no way to console her. Or convince her that she would live through this and eventually, find peace. There was nothing Gretchen could do to alleviate her distress.

And now, she had to figure out how to help Olivia say goodbye to the only mother she ever knew.

Drizzle was falling all around them. The cemetery plot had a twenty-by-twenty portable cover above the casket, protecting it as well as a few rows of chairs that were closest. Gretchen was gripping Olivia's hand as they stood near what would have been Helen's feet. Olivia would not sit down, no matter how often Gretchen suggested it, or tried to insist. She simply refused to leave her grandmother's casket. The newly dug hole was only feet away from her tiny, black patent-leather shoes. Dirt was smudged on her white tights. She stared down into the open hole. Gretchen wondered what she was thinking and what was going through her head. Did she understand what happened? The minister was eloquent, speaking in soft, soothing tones that added dignity to the passages he read and the prayers he said. Soon, one of the funeral attendants brought around a bucket of roses for everyone to throw on Helen's casket. Gretchen again brushed her knuckles over her wet eyes. She didn't even wear makeup. There was no point. The tears would have long smeared or wiped it away. She shifted her weight, and her high heels sliced and sunk into the soggy grass. Gretchen squeezed the tissue in her hand to restrain a gulping sob that was lodged in her throat.

Life was so unfair.

Quite a crowd of people showed up. Helen's coworkers, several neighbors, and even some of the hospital personnel. She remained a kind, courteous lady to the end, striving so hard to survive on her granddaughter's behalf. It was hard to not feel love for her if you knew her.

Unfortunately, Tony had a previous speaking engagement and couldn't get out of it. He intended to come tomorrow. That was too late. Gretchen immediately banished the thought, and told herself it was being petty and unfair. His sympathy and sincerity was heartfelt, even over the phone. He talked to Gretchen for over an hour, as well as Olivia. But it still wasn't enough. There was no one who could help her. Or comfort her. There was only a disembodied voice.

Olivia suddenly sank down to her knees, right next to the edge of the casket. A velvet rope, like those used in movie theaters, was strung around it as a kind of makeshift handrail to keep people back, but Olivia crawled under it on her hands and knees.

Gretchen gasped, "Olivia! Honey, stop!"

The entire funeral paused as the crowds' eyes watched Olivia. She scrambled towards the coffin, apparently intending to cross the grassy knoll and go directly onto her grandmother's casket. Gretchen dropped to her knees, and her nylons were instantly soaked on the wet, muddy grass. She reached towards Olivia who still eluded her grasp.

Gretchen started to struggle back up, but her skirt hampered her movements. Her heart was thumping in her throat. Olivia! What if she actually got on top of the casket? Or fell into the opening? It was horrifying to contemplate. It would frighten her. And scar her. And make a terrible, tragic loss so much worse.

Out of nowhere, a hand gripped her bicep nearly lifting her up. She turned her head and her breath whooshed out from her lungs. Tears streamed down her face. *Tony.* He was there. His phenomenal, freaky, one-handed grip literally lifted her off the wet ground from where she fell in pursuit of Olivia.

He wore a dark suit, and his hair was pulled back. "I'll get her."

He turned without another word, and ducked under the rope before sitting down right in the grass beside where Olivia kneeled, dangling his feet over the side of the grave. He almost looked as if he were about to dip his feet into the water beneath a boat dock without a care in the world. The crowd looked on, with shock.

Gretchen scooted closer, so she could hear them. Tony simply sat there for a few long moments. His left side was to Olivia so he couldn't touch her easily. She seemed to realize this and slowly, her shoulders relaxed as she realized he wasn't going to grab her.

"It's hard, huh? Letting her go?"

Olivia waited a moment before finally nodding her head up and down. Tony was quiet for another minute or two. Eventually, Olivia whispered, "I just don't want her to leave me. I don't want her to go down there where I can't see her again."

Tony nodded. "I know it seems that way. But she's not in there anymore. She's not in that coffin. That's just her tired body, which can no longer serve her. Who she is to you, and her love for you has now moved directly into your heart, Olivia. You hold it there and keep it safe."

She glanced down at her small chest and Gretchen's entire body froze. *Tony?* The sweet, innocent sentiment was so unlike what she expected. Kind of like his speech writing.

"Really? Is that really what happens?" Olivia finally asked.

"Sure. You don't need to worry about that casket being in the hole. That's just a place to keep Helen safe forever. And so you'll know where she's at. But her essence, and her love and her soul, and all that made her who she was to you, is now safely buried in your heart."

"This place will keep her safe?"

"Yes, so you'll never lose her."

Olivia's face scrunched up, but finally, she nodded. "I guess that's okay… to know where she's at."

"Yes, it's much better to know. Can I take you out of here now, Olivia? Will you let me pick me you up?"

She nodded towards his body. "How? Your arm is gone."

He smiled slowly and Gretchen's entire body froze and shook at the tender, loving smile he bestowed on Olivia. "I don't need two arms to take care of you."

He got onto his feet, and his butt was stained and wet from the grass. Reaching down, he effortlessly scooped her up to his chest and higher, until her body hugged his trunk. Olivia started crying again as she wrapped her arms around his neck and her legs around his waist. She buried her head into his neck and the wracking sobs that came out of her body sounded like a trapped, wounded animal. Tony shook his head at Gretchen when she tried to reach out for Olivia. He simply stood there and let the little girl sob into his shirt.

The minister finally lowered his head and said a hopeful prayer before everyone slowly got up and dropped a rose on Helen's grave. There was an added solemnity to the atmosphere, however, after Olivia's tragic outburst. Gretchen's family came over to Olivia and engulfed her with their embraces. Gretchen started crying when her own father took her into his arms to comfort her.

How could she manage this? The burden of raising Olivia suddenly crashed down on Gretchen like a bag of concrete in her gut. She was now totally responsible for making sure Olivia's life wasn't ruined by the loss of her primary caregiver, and essentially, the only mother she had ever known. It was too much. She couldn't do it. She'd ruin Olivia as well as herself. She wasn't enough for Olivia.

"Gretchen." The voice was soft and kind, but stern behind her. She slowly withdrew her arms from around her father. He was so soothing to her, just like Tony was with Olivia.

Olivia's face eventually lifted. She was calming down, her sobs were over, and her tears came intermittently with little coughs. She still clung tightly to Tony. Gretchen's father stepped forward to take Olivia from Tony. His arm had to be killing him as there was no relief from her weight on it. Olivia let Gretchen's father take her.

Tony then stepped closer to Gretchen and held her against him.

"I'm sorry I'm a little late," he whispered as he kissed her just above her ear, leaving his lips in her hair.

She clutched his shoulders, and her fingernails nearly dug into his skin. She needed him so much. Her bones felt rubbery and wobbly, like she couldn't hold up her body weight.

She couldn't do this. That's all she knew. Starkly. She could not take care of this little, needy, hurt girl. This child whose entire life was now hers to ruin. She couldn't have talked her away from the casket. Not like Tony just did. Not like she should have known what to do. Holy Christ. She was so out of her realm. Professionally, she often handled the kind of grief and emotions Olivia was experiencing. Yet when it

337

mattered; when it was a child she loved, she couldn't seem to tap into her training or capabilities to properly and effectively handle Olivia. The irony was not lost on Gretchen. She was a child therapist who didn't seem to know how to council her new ward.

"I can't do this," she barely breathed into Tony's ear. His bicep muscle tightened around her in reaction to her words.

"You can. You're the strongest woman I know."

"Not for this." She buried her head much as Olivia did in his chest. "Why are you here? I thought…"

"You need me."

She nodded her head. "I need you."

Her body started trembling from the cold as well as her ragged emotions. Softly, she whispered, "I love you. I need you here. *I can't do this*. Any of this. I can't raise Olivia properly. I can't live with you so far away. I need you to come back home now. I need you to come back to me. Fuck the charity. Fuck being better. Fuck it all. Just come back, please, and be here with me. That's all that matters. I just need *you*, Tony. Not better Tony. Not working full time and being productive Tony. I just need the old Tony. Please, please, just come back to me." She started to cry again and gripped him more tightly around his neck.

He went completely still before his entire body stiffened, and he seemed to grow two inches. "Gretchen… you don't mean that. You're just having a really hard moment."

She pulled back and nailed him with her glare. "I do mean that. I am not a damsel in distress. I know exactly what I mean. I am not confused. Besides, haven't you wanted me for like two decades? Why don't you want me to say this?"

"Because two decades ago, I could do anything and everything I wanted. Now I can't. You know all this. I have limited options. And now, I finally have a decent option, and it's working out for me."

"Well… it's not working for me."

There were people now around them and they had to talk directly to each other in low, hushed tones so no one could hear them. Now, wasn't the moment… but she couldn't help it.

"I don't need you to do anything and everything. I just need for you to do what you just did. You helped Olivia, and you saved both of us."

He shook his head, and his eyes were fierce. "Let's not do this now. Mom said the reception is at her house. I'll meet you there, okay?"

She nodded and her shoulders slumped. He was right, of course. Tony turned and said something quietly to Olivia before Gretchen grabbed her hand and she followed her parents toward their car. They drove her there as she was too distraught. She watched Tony walk across the cemetery. He stopped before a dark-colored sedan and her jaw dropped open. He got into the driver's side. She stared incredulously. *Tony was driving?*

****

She quickly learned that Tony did indeed now drive a car. He also learned how to prepare meals and wash his own clothes. He talked about the gadgets he purchased to make things easier for him. She almost pointed out it was more the *trying* to do things on his own, rather than the gadgets that made the new, improved Tony possible. But she bit her tongue to hold back her nasty sarcasm.

He talked about his job. What he did. How long he worked. And it soon became obvious he was passionate about it. Even excited about it. He was proud of himself

339

and the man this job allowed him to be. She could tell that just by the way he moved about in his parents' house. He was completely different than he was when she ran into him at the grocery store. He even stood taller. He kept his clothes neat as a pin again. His dark suit was pressed, and his hair still too long, but now neatly pulled back in a ponytail. Would he cut that too? Now that he seemed to be back to the steady, hardworking Tony of old?

She gritted her teeth as she watched him from the chair in the corner of the living room she commandeered. She didn't have the strength to socialize, take or give condolences, or discuss Olivia. Tracy's kids took Olivia downstairs in Tony's old place to play. Leila recently put a ping-pong table down there, so convinced was she that Tony was never coming back.

"Gretch? How are you holding up?"

She looked up when Tracy put a hand on her shoulder and started to sit down. She handed Gretchen a glass of wine. Gretchen leaned forward and rubbed her hands together, ignoring the wine. "Not well. Why is that? I always hold up well. I've always been the together one. The calm one. The one who did and said what needed to be said and done. Why can't I get there this time?"

Tracy clasped her hands. "Because this time, it's way too personal. And you have had way too much for one month. Tony leaving. Olivia becoming yours... Cut yourself a break."

Tears started to flow again. Gretchen pushed at her eye sockets too hard. She was tired of crying. It hurt. Her eyes ached. Her cheeks were puffy and her throat was raw. "I'm sad Helen died. It hit me harder than I ever thought it would. I thought I was fully prepared. She was my friend."

"I know. No one's ever fully prepared for death. You should know that."

She sneered and nodded toward Tony who had his one hand on Lewis's back as he leaned closer to listen to his father. He stretched back, smiled slightly, shook his head and started speaking. "Look at him. He's fine. He's just freaking fine."

Tracy's mouth tilted up. "Isn't that what you wanted for him?"

"I didn't want him so fine that he could thrive being away from me. He drives now. Did you see that? He didn't tell me because he wanted to surprise me."

"Well, yes. I could see where he would."

"I don't want him to surprise me. I want him to just be here. Do it here. Or don't. Whatever. Selfish bastard."

"Gretchen, hon..."

"I know. I know. I'm being selfish, unreasonable, and horrible now."

Tracy half laughed, half coughed, "Well, at least you're aware enough to know it."

Gretchen finally smiled. "I know it, all right. I just didn't think it would be this hard. Any of it."

Tracy touched her shoulder. "I'm going to come stay with you for a while when Tony leaves. Just until you get your legs back under you."

Gretchen's shoulders sagged. "I've never been this angry. Or felt this incapable before."

"It's about time."

"What about Micah? The girls?"

The corner of her mouth tilted up. "I'm not leaving them; I'm coming to help you. They'll be fine."

She nodded finally and replied, "Okay."

Tracy hesitated. "I know it seems bad now, but things will get easier. You'll get used to having Olivia and it won't all seem so big or so raw, or quite so intense. It will become more normal, more ordinary, just part of who you are and what you do all day."

The thing was, Gretchen could not do anything. She wandered around the reception, totally useless. She barely even fielded comments and condolences. She was too selfishly distraught. She was too worried about Olivia. So much so, at times, she feared she'd throw up. Could she do this? Be there for her? Be a good mother? The gravity of the situation and her responsibility to Olivia suddenly felt crippling.

Tony unexpectedly appeared next to her. He wrapped his arm around her waist and she turned into his body. "Tracy mentioned you might need me."

"Tracy's right."

"Why don't we take Olivia home now? I think we've had enough for one day, huh? It's not like she won't get up tomorrow and have to face it all over again."

Gretchen nodded as she numbly followed Tony. He was quite adept in taking control. He found Olivia and got her coat and shoes before collecting the dress-up clothes she'd thrown off in favor of her pajamas at some point. He went around the entire room and shook hands with everybody, saying goodbye.

"I'm sorry, Gretchen. I know this is hard for you," Leila said.

She turned towards Leila. "I'm surprised you care that it's hard for me."

Leila's face twisted. "I deserve that. I just thought you'd dump him. Or destroy him. Make him revert to how he was post-Audrey."

Gretchen nodded her head towards Tony whom she saw bent over, helping Olivia get her shoes on. When he stood up, he lifted Olivia and held her against him before turning to say goodbye to Micah with a smile and a nod. "Yeah, he looks so much worse off now. Dressed in a suit. Driving. Working. Living not only alone and out of your basement, but across the country from you, in a well-paying, highly respected, highly visible job. And *Smiling. Tony keeps smiling.* I mean when did Tony start smiling? Never? I just ruined him, didn't I, Leila?"

Leila's mouth dropped open as she listened to Gretchen, who could not find her usual reserve or politeness. Leila's eyes filled with tears. "I'm completely sorry. I thought he would get hurt, not you. I see now... I'm so sorry. His departure from here was, for me, the first sign he was healing; but for you, it was being left behind."

Gretchen didn't expect to, but helplessly started to cry again. Leila yanked her closer for a tight hug. "Please forgive me. I was wrong. You saved him. You really did. We both miss him, Gretchen. Maybe you could bring Olivia over next week for dinner? I'd still like to be involved with her caretaking... and you. I could really use the company. And so can you. I would even like to have her a few weekdays after school. I mean, Gretchen, you *do* work full time. You'll need the help, so please, let me help you."

Gretchen nodded her head against Leila's shoulder. "Okay," she whispered.

Tony came up right then with Olivia wrapped around him. He leaned down so Leila could kiss his cheek. "Take good care of them tonight."

Tony glanced from Leila to Gretchen and saw her wiping away fresh tears. "I will."

He tilted his head towards the door, indicating for Gretchen to go first. A small smile touched his lips. "I'd offer you my hand, but..."

She finally smiled. "But yours is already occupied. I told you before, I don't need your hand; I need *all* of you."

"You already have that," he said quietly, his tone sounding low and deep and completely confident. Her heart stilled before swelling in her chest. Leila smiled behind them. Gretchen might have had him, but she needed him to be there more, rather than having his love so far away from her.

Tony slept in Gretchen's bed and talked quietly and often to Olivia. He sat with her on the couch, watching mindless comedies; and when the grief unexpectedly overtook her, he held her tightly while she cried. He did the same with Gretchen, who had no idea what kind of person she was becoming. She'd never felt so incompetent before. She couldn't get her head around being a mother. She couldn't think of anything to say or do for Olivia. She was off from work for at least a week, and Olivia was off school; but all they could do was sit around the condo and cry together.

And then Tony left.

Gretchen managed to cook Olivia some meals and wash a few loads of clothes. She tried to hold Olivia and reach out to her. But Olivia wasn't the same now as she was with Tony. Crazy enough, Olivia got angry at *her* when Tony left, not at Tony.

Gretchen was, however, furious with Tony.

How dare he do *this* to her? He turned her into a weak, needy, incompetent woman. She had become something she had never, ever been in her entire life. How long could she go on like that? Olivia was miserable. She was miserable. Tracy arrived to take care of them for two weeks because Gretchen couldn't find the gumption or the will to do so. At least twice, Olivia reacted with screaming fits at Gretchen for stupid, minor things that were indicative of the deeper, roiling emotions inside of her.

And Gretchen wanted to do the exact same thing to Tony every single time he called her.

Chapter Twenty-Six

GRETCHEN'S WORK BEGAN TO suffer. She was mentally absent in her sessions. Physically, she was there, but she didn't connect with her patients like she used to, and needed to. Her head was crammed full of too much: *Tony. Olivia. Helen.* The same three names and people that kept twisting all around in her head for so many months now. But it wasn't even a year since she had Tony back in her life. How could his absence affect her so deeply? It was like she could not function on a daily basis anymore.

He, on the other hand, was just fine. At least, that's how he always described himself in their long distance communications. She hated corresponding long distance. She hated it with Will and detested it even more now.

School was out for the summer months, and Tracy was kind enough to let Olivia start hanging out there each day to play with her two kids, Alissa and Kylie, who were ten and nine. Leila also watched her two days a week, and a surprising bond was developing between the two. Gretchen suspected Leila must have reminded Olivia of her grandmother more than anything.

Each evening, Gretchen picked her up. Sometimes they ate take-out, while on others, Gretchen cooked. She wasn't very interested in doing it, however. Olivia lifted her spoon one evening and the runny sauce dripped off it.

"What is this?"

"Cheese sauce."

"Isn't that what we had last night?"

"No, that was Alfredo sauce."

"It looks exactly the same."

Gretchen smiled. Silence descended between them and the entire condo seemed soundless. The faint cries of kids playing in the park below drifted up towards them.

"I miss him."

Gretchen turned swiftly at hearing Olivia's quiet statement. Olivia set her spoon down, and Gretchen set the bowl of noodles down. She slid from her seat and dropped down on one knee beside Olivia and started to hug her, but Olivia pushed her back. "Why don't we just go live with him?"

Gretchen nearly fell over.

"What?" The shock and surprise made her tone come out much too high.

Olivia's gaze sharpened and she nodded. "I think we should just go live with him. If he's gotta do this job so stinkin' badly, why don't we just go and live with him there?"

Gretchen sat back on her heels and her mouth remained open in shock. She didn't even know what to say. It was not what she expected to come out of Olivia.

"Well, because, I work here. And you have school here, and our whole life is located here."

Olivia shrugged matter-of-factly. "So, you can get a job there. Schools are everywhere, and I'd rather be there, with him, than here with everyone else."

"Uh... well, crap! Olivia. You can't just say things like that. You don't understand what a big deal it would be. It would require changing everything. My job isn't easily transferable; I have patients, and a stake in the practice. I can't just leave it all…"

Olivia dropped her gaze and stared at her dinner for a long moment. Finally, she mumbled, "Seems like a bigger deal to have to live without him."

Gretchen's mouth opened and closed twice before her shoulders dropped forward and she shook her head in defeat. "It does. It seems like a much bigger deal to live without him."

"Then… let's go to him."

"We can't just show up there. He might not even want us."

"Can't we go see? We can come back and do all that stuff you said. But can't we just go see?"

"We should talk to him about this first. We have to make some plans. I mean, maybe in a few months…"

"I don't want to wait that long. I miss him now."

"So do I," Gretchen whispered. Never in her life had she needed a man. Not even Will. She never needed anyone to get her through the day. Now, all grown up and successful, she sounded like Olivia in her longing for the one man whom she suddenly needed most of all.

"Can't we just go see?"

It was completely irresponsible, and the wrong thing to do. You don't show up at a man's door, thousands of miles away, with a little girl in tow, and ask him to… what? To let them stay there and live with him? It would mean giving up everything she worked so hard for, and many years of diligent career-building. It would change everything, even though it already seemed like everything was irrevocably changed for her.

It meant she would have to lay it on the line, and surrender her heart and soul. The only person she'd ever done that for was Will, and he reacted by rejecting her and refusing to be there in the way she needed him. It was also wrong to get a little girl's hopes up over it. Or even make Olivia a part of it. But… she simply couldn't help it. It was, for once, how she felt, and it dominated her life now. It completely controlled her and was ruining everything else.

"What if… what if he doesn't feel the same? It could hurt us a lot. Maybe you should stay here."

Olivia's eyes sparked. "Stay here? That would mean you're going to see him. I wanna go too! It was my idea!"

Gretchen leaned forward and Olivia crawled from her chair into Gretchen's lap as they both giggled for the first time since Helen died and Tony left. Hugging and giggling on the floor of the condo, the awful silence was finally broken, the one that practically devoured them for the two months since Tony left.

Chapter Twenty-Seven

TONY WAS SPEAKING BEFORE an audience of five hundred today. It was at a fundraising luncheon that focused on research for prosthetic limbs and other body parts. Since the wars in Iraq and Afghanistan, significant breakthroughs in their technologies had occurred: everything from body-powered/cable-operated limbs to cosmetic devices. It was all expensive, however, between funding the research, and designing the parts, to providing them for those who wanted and needed them. Ironically, Tony was nearly the spokesperson for financing prosthetics, yet he still refused to use them. He had no interest in them for himself, but that didn't mean he wanted anyone else to go without them. He, of course, was a damn walking billboard for the cause. Sometimes, it seemed a little much to trot out the one-armed veteran, but hearing all the applause, and seeing the tears rolling down women's faces said otherwise.

What made this particular fundraiser different from the usual was the attendance of the President of the United States. It almost made Tony nervous and edgy, even though he never got anxious at most of these speaking engagements. After a ridiculous amount of security, he was frisked and vetted as thoroughly as if he were applying for work in the CIA. However, owing to the presence of the Commander-in-Chief, today's proceeds would break *Hero!Fund's* records. While he was speaking, Tony saw a blond head of hair that instantly caught his attention.

Gretchen? Gretchen and Olivia? Gretchen held the little girl's hand as they stood in the rear, resting against the back entrance doors, and fairly close to the Secret Service agents flanking each side of them.

He was so startled, he stumbled over a sentence and had to stop, temporarily forgetting what to say next. Clearing his throat, with his eyes glued to the crowd, he suddenly appeared helpless. Gretchen smiled finally and tilted her head as if to say, "Tony, finish the speech." He swore he could hear her saying it out loud in his ear. At long last, after standing up straighter, he found his train of thought again and proceeded with his oration.

His words could have been gibberish, because he couldn't remember anything he said. He hoped he wasn't offensive or confusing; and the loud roar of applause, which quickly became a standing ovation, said otherwise. Somehow, he managed to finish it, but all his excited brain could keep focusing on was: *how could they be there,* and *how the hell did they get inside?* And why did they arrive so unexpectedly? It must have been a surprise visit.

He quickly exited from the podium as soon as he could, and immediately worked his way through the throngs of donors and well-wishers. He found himself detained in order to be escorted into a meeting with the President. He nearly groaned out loud his annoyance. He did not want to meet the President at all. He wanted to see his girlfriend and Olivia. His eyes were on them and she smiled and waved her hand, seeming to realize what was expected of him.

Upon quickly greeting the President and accepting a handshake, along with his sincere empathy and congratulations, Tony could barely endure it for five minutes. After what seemed like an eternity, he finally disentangled himself, and skirted the myriad bodyguards while avoiding any other distractions.

He stopped five feet from Gretchen. "How did you get in here?"

"I asked John to get us in. To surprise you. *Surprise.*" She shrugged and smiled weakly as she answered him.

Stepping forward, he swept her up and kissed her, leaning her backwards so much, she nearly did a backbend over his arm. With a laugh, her arms encircled his neck. Olivia giggled beside him and he only released Gretchen so he could hug her. He embraced her in as much of a bear hug as he could manage. Olivia wrapped herself around his waist and grinned up at him.

"Did you just meet the President?"

"What? Oh yeah, things like that happen sometimes. The whole 'Wounded Warrior' thing really tugs at people's hearts and purse strings."

Gretchen was gazing at him, placing her hand on his arm while Olivia clung to his legs. He finally leaned down and picked her up.

"I can't believe you're here."

"I can't either." Her voice sounded weird. Olivia turned her head and they exchanged a strange look.

"What? What is it?"

Olivia leaned back and took his face in her hands. "Can we stay, Tony? Forever? Can we stay with you?"

"Olivia! No. I told you to let me ease into this," scolded Gretchen.

Tony nearly dropped Olivia, and looked at Gretchen, who instantly blushed. "Stay here? As in... what? What do you mean?"

"Gretchen quit her job!"

Shutting her eyes, Gretchen shook her head while Tony stared at her in puzzlement. "Well, I was going to, you know, work up to that a little more smoothly. But well, she's right. I quit my job. I still hold stock in the practice, but that can be sold eventually. And the condo can be rented or sold, or whatever, but, well, I guess... Olivia's way of telling you is just as good as mine... We want to stay here, Tony. We'd rather be here closer to you, then in Calliston alone and without you."

He nearly dropped Olivia as Gretchen rushed on, "We don't have to live with you or anything. We'll get our own place, and we can date, just like we did in Calliston. I know you can't handle a ready-made family. Or be a father yet... but we could..."

Olivia interrupted her. "What's the big deal about being with us? I know you're not my father. But Gretchen takes care of me now. I love her. And I love you. What's the big deal? It's just us, Tony. Why can't we all live together?"

He was jostled from behind as people kept milling about. *It's just us?* His heart was beating so fast, he feared a cardiac arrest might ruin his moment of joy. Gretchen suddenly stepped closer and took Olivia from him. "We are interrupting you. I'm sorry. This all came out completely wrong. I called the office and John answered; and when I explained I wanted to surprise you, he insisted that I come see you here. And he was right, you're amazing. I'm so proud of you. But... we'll wait for you at your apartment. We can talk then."

She took Olivia's hand and started to rush away from him. The pink of her face was bright and telltale.

It's just us, Tony. Olivia's little voice echoed inside his head. Just us. Only… there was no *just us* when it came to Gretchen and Olivia. They were… everything. They were the only ones he was trying to prove himself to and make a new life for. They were the ones that motivated and inspired him, and now they were *here.* For him. Suddenly pushing aside the suit in front of him, "Wait!" he yelled after them. The crowd between them turned and stared. Gretchen turned too.

He stopped directly in front of her and touched her cheek where fresh tears began to fall. She smiled up at him, and her heart was in her eyes. Along with hope and joy. Everything was pinned on him. How did he manage to get Gretchen to love him? "You loved your job."

She shrugged and shook her head in denial. "I liked my job. But I *love* you."

"You want to give it all up to be here with me?"

"Yes," she said simply.

"You've worked too hard. You can't give up everything for me."

"I can work just as hard here. There are kids who need help everywhere. But there's only one you."

"It's only been a few months."

"Well, I can't take it anymore. I'm not as strong as I once was."

He shook his head. "What about Olivia? And school?"

"It was her idea. Since Helen died, she doesn't care as much about Calliston. She cares more about being with you. And schools are everywhere. The rest? Just minor details we can work out."

There was a small crowd surrounding them as they entered the lobby of the banquet room. "I never intended for you to give anything up."

"I'm not giving it up. I'm changing it. And gaining... you. Everything. I'm gaining everything I ever wanted by having you and Olivia."

Olivia stood quietly holding Gretchen's hand. He bent down and picked her up, as Gretchen leaned into him. He had no other arm to hold her with, again, the crux of half of his issues. She smiled up at him, and her gaze silently told him, she knew what he was thinking. She wrapped her arm around his waist and seemed to say, *It's okay. I don't need your other arm.*

She needed *all of him*. He finally got that.

"Tony, Gretchen and Olivia," he said quietly. Testing it out. "My apartment is quite small."

"We can get a bigger one. Minor details."

She held his gaze with her eyebrows raised, waiting. Finally, he nodded, "Then, let's go home. It sounds like we have a lot of minor details to sort out."

Olivia and Gretchen both gazed up at him. He smiled slowly. It was such a revelation to him. They wanted *him.* He was the one man they both looked up to, and counted on, and wanted...and didn't mind waiting for. And stranger still, he felt no urge to deny it. Or run away from it. Or try to change it.

He was theirs, and they were his. The rest? Gretchen was right, just minor details to be sorted out.

Epilogue: Ten Years Later

"**H**HOW ARE DONNY AND your sister, Gretchen?"

Gretchen turned towards Lindsey. "Good. They have a family trip planned to Lake Tahoe, but they'll be back next week for Olivia's graduation."

"I can't believe it…"

"Tell me about it. She hasn't yet decided which college to attend. I'm dreading that she'll pick the one which is furthest away."

Lindsey squeezed her hand. "If she does, she'll be fine. She's… you. She's you, only reincarnated. She's a wonderful, lovely, girl ready to take on the world."

"I was until I fell in love."

Lindsey chuckled. "Weren't we all?" she asked, staring at Noah.

"Are you ever going to marry him?" Gretchen inquired, something she did about once a year.

Lindsey's smile dimmed. "Gretchen, we're as married, and as together as anyone else in this room. He just gets that I can't be a wife. But that I am in every other sense of the word… do you know what I mean?"

Gretchen squeezed Lindsey's hand. "I know what you mean."

Lindsey and Noah never had kids. They lived happily together in Ellensburg with Noah running his vet clinic and Lindsey using the money from Elliot to do many different things. She financed Jessie's schooling, and provided the funds for Jessie's three kids' college educations, whom Lindsey considered herself a second mother to. She also spent a substantial amount of time and money renovating the local shelter and creating a new one for battered women. Years later, she ran for mayor of the city and won, which gave her more time to address and improve the policies concerning domestic violence, which were being copied and implemented in many other surrounding cities.

Gretchen and Lindsey both turned when Noah stepped forward. They were at Lindsey and Noah's large home in Ellensburg, Washington to celebrate Jessie's recent graduation from veterinary college. It had been a long journey for her, managed around her three kids and working, while raising her family. The vet school had to be squeezed in wherever she could find the time. After finally moving to Pullman in the last few years so that Jessie could finish, they had to make the agonizing decision to uproot their family. Will took temporary employment while she finished up her classes and obtained her degree. Now, they were back to their own home with their animals, and Jessie bought half of Noah's practice.

Noah cleared his throat. "I can't thank you all for coming today," he said, looking around at his family, along with the many friends from around the community. Tony came over and took Gretchen's hand with a smile that made her pulse skitter like a smitten teenager. "I am extremely honored to welcome Jessie Hendricks as my partner in my veterinary practice. She has been an integral factor in its continued success, and I waited a long time for this moment. Welcome aboard, Dr. Hendricks."

Jessie stepped forward, her face all pink in embarrassment and smiled shyly as she shook Noah's hand.

He cleared his throat. "I also hoped that, as my partner you'd cover for me for awhile…"

The entire room went silent. Gretchen glanced at Lindsey who was smiling and caught in an eye lock with Noah. He took in a breath, "We will be moving soon."

Gretchen's mouth dropped open and she turned to Lindsey. "Where? What?"

Noah continued, "Lindsey's been asked by her party to run for state governor. So I don't believe it's premature to say we will be moving very soon, and when we do, I hoped, that you, Jessie, could take over for me for a little while."

Jessie's deep pride at Noah's request showed in her face. She nodded slowly as Will came forward and shook Noah's hand, slipping his other arm around Jessie.

Lindsey glanced at Gretchen with a small smile beaming on her face, "What do you think? Does a single, former soldier, former victim, have a chance of winning the governor's office?"

Gretchen threw her arms around Lindsey. "You are finally taking my advice."

Lindsey patted her back. "You mean wasting Elliot's money? Yes, I am. I might lose, so we can't be too sure."

Gretchen shook her head and pulled back to smile at Lindsey. "I always said: you are a force to reckon with. You will not lose."

Lindsey's eyes filled with happy tears and she turned to Tony. "Will you write my speeches? I know you're busy, but you're the best in the business… and nepotism and everything…"

Tony grinned as he too hugged her, "I'll do it. Happily."

Tony spent five years with *Heros!Fund.* After the war ended, he still advocated for funds to help the country's veterans in a multitude of levels and needs. He kept his website and blog running, which soon became a well known platform for his scathing editorials and opinion pieces. He worked for no one but himself. He wrote speeches for influential people, but all of whom he chose, and no one that he didn't believe in. Years ago, he wrote a book about his experiences, and followed it up with several more that were all related to the status of veterans in modern society. Their success freed Tony up financially from ever having to work again, although both he and Gretchen did.

Tony wasn't impressed in the least knowing they could own three separate houses free and clear if they chose to.

Tony and Gretchen stayed in D.C. until he was done with *Heros!Fund.* They moved Olivia back to Calliston when she was going into High School. They never had any kids of their own; although they contemplated it, but it never worked out. Olivia could not have been more their daughter if they actually biologically created her. She was formally adopted by both of them and now, at eighteen years old, was Olivia Lindstrom.

Olivia was deciding whether or not to leave next year and start college, so Gretchen was dreading an empty nest in her wake.

She had already started searching for a new hobby and kept trying to convince Tony they needed to go on a second honeymoon. She wanted somewhere tropical and warm, but he wasn't much into beachwear. It still made him uncomfortable because of his one arm. But she was bound and determined to win that argument.

Jessie came over to them after winding her way through the congratulations of the crowd. Lindsey pulled her against her side. "I love you. I hope you know how proud I am of you. How proud Mom would be."

Jessie smiled softly. "A long, long time ago, Will told me I should become a vet, not just an assistant. I scoffed at him and never believed I could do it. But, I did. I don't think it's sunk in yet."

Gretchen nodded as Lindsey's eyes filled with happy tears. "Yes, here we all are, still together, still sisters and friends, and even better… nothing is done or over. We survived and we still have everything ahead of us to do; we can still do or be anything we want…"

"Our life is just starting? Have you noticed how old we are?" Gretchen grimaced.

Lindsey linked her arm through hers, "Well, why the hell shouldn't it? Jessie has a new career, I might actually finally have one too, and you and Tony will soon have all the time to explore the world. Why can't life just be starting?"

###

About the Author

I live in the rainy area of Western, Washington, and spend as much time as I can getting away from the rain by traveling to destinations all across the state where my family and I do tons of camping, boating, fishing, and horseback riding. Many of the locations we camp become the basis for my books. Most of my settings are fictional but are based on real places.

I earned my business degree from Western Washington University. I worked for several years in the construction management field before turning to writing and being home with my kids.

I love to hear from readers! Please contact me at dvsleanne@aol.com or www.leannedavis.net.

Thank you for reading! I hope you enjoyed *The Best Friend.*

69594285R00202

Made in the USA
Lexington, KY
02 November 2017